"I can show you the
face of God.
Are you ready?"

WHERE IN HELL DID IT COME FROM?

"Did your colleague tell you anything, no matter how odd, about what happened in the lab that night? About the explosion? The fire? The fossil?"

Carter debated going into it; all he wanted to do was get away, but at the same time there was something in Ezra's query—in the imploring look in his eyes—that made him pause.

"Okay, he did say one thing that might interest you," Carter said. "Now, you've got to remember that he was delirious and doped up to his eyeballs when he said it—"

"Tell me."

"He said the fossil had come to life."

VIGIL

ROBERT MASELLO

BERKLEY BOOKS, NEW YORK

THE BERKLEY PUBLISHING GROUP
Published by the Penguin Group
Penguin Group (USA) Inc.
375 Hudson Street, New York, New York 10014, USA
Penguin Group (Canada), 10 Alcorn Avenue, Toronto, Ontario M4V 3B2, Canada
(a division of Pearson Penguin Canada Inc.)
Penguin Books Ltd., 80 Strand, London WC2R 0RL, England
Penguin Books Ireland, 25 St. Stephen's Green, Dublin 2, Ireland (a division of Penguin Books Ltd.)
Penguin Group (Australia), 250 Camberwell Road, Camberwell, Victoria 3124, Australia
(a division of Pearson Australia Group Pty. Ltd.)
Penguin Books India Pvt. Ltd., 11 Community Centre, Panchsheel Park, New Delhi—110 017, India
Penguin Group (NZ), Cnr. Airborne and Rosedale Roads, Albany, Auckland 1310, New Zealand
(a division of Pearson New Zealand Ltd.)
Penguin Books (South Africa) (Pty.) Ltd., 24 Sturdee Avenue, Rosebank, Johannesburg 2196,
South Africa

Penguin Books Ltd., Registered Offices: 80 Strand, London WC2R 0RL, England

This is a work of fiction. Names, characters, places, and incidents either are the product of the author's imagination or are used fictitiously, and any resemblance to actual persons, living or dead, business establishments, events, or locales is entirely coincidental.

VIGIL

A Berkley Book / published by arrangement with the author

PRINTING HISTORY
Berkley edition / June 2005

Copyright © 2005 by Robert Masello.
Cover illustration by Steve Stone.
Cover design by Erica Tricarico.

ISBN: 0-425-20350-6

BERKLEY®
Berkley Books are published by The Berkley Publishing Group,
a division of Penguin Group (USA) Inc.,
375 Hudson Street, New York, New York 10014.
BERKLEY is a registered trademark of Penguin Group (USA) Inc.
The "B" design is a trademark belonging to Penguin Group (USA) Inc.

PRINTED IN THE UNITED STATES OF AMERICA

10 9 8 7 6 5 4 3 2 1

I'll make this short, I swear, but I do want to thank my literary agent, Cynthia Manson, for her unflagging encouragement and confidence; my editor, Natalee Rosenstein, for immediately grasping where I was trying to go and helping me to get there; and for my long-suffering wife, Laurie Drake, for allowing me to brood in peace.

The search for intelligibility that characterizes science and the search for meaning that characterizes religion are two necessary intertwined strands of the human enterprise and are not opposed. They are essential to each other, complementary yet distinct and strongly interacting—indeed just like the two helical strands of DNA itself.

—The Rev. Canon Dr. Arthur Peacocke,
on being awarded the 2001 Templeton Prize
for Progress in Religion, March 8, 2001

PROLOGUE
Lago d'Avernus, Italy

The boat bobbed lazily on the water, the waves slap-
ping softly against its sides. Kevin lay on the deck, soaking
up the sun, one hand curled around a can of cold beer, his
feet propped up on the furled sail. This was what he'd been
dreaming of for days, all through the endless rehearsal dinner and the asinine toasts, the elaborate wedding and even
more elaborate reception afterward at the Great Neck Country Club. Even as he'd been standing in that receiving line,
shaking the hands of people he'd never seen before and
would probably never see again, he'd been counting the
hours until he could escape. All he'd been thinking about
was the time when he and Jennifer could finally be alone, in
a place where there'd be no more bands, no more dancing,
no more cakes to be cut or presents to be acknowledged or
strangers to greet.

And now, without a doubt, he was there.

On the flight from Kennedy Airport, he'd slept almost
the entire time, and on the shorter connecting flight from
Rome to Naples, he'd finally started to feel like he was really on his way, the honeymoon had begun. In fact, he and
Jennifer had managed to get two seats on the aisle together,

and under a red Alitalia blanket they'd fooled around for the first time on—or at least *over*—another continent.

"Now we've covered Europe and North America," Jennifer had whispered with a smile. "Just five continents to go."

"I'll call our travel agent as soon as we get back," Kevin replied.

The boat they'd rented, as part of their package, wasn't as nice as the ones Kevin regularly sailed on at the country club, but it had everything they needed—a cooler, a CD player, a cabinet filled with everything from suntan lotion to condoms (the Italians thought of everything). They'd have three days on the lake, to relax and slow down, before going on to Venice. Jennifer's parents, he was glad, were footing the bill.

He heard a splash, and a spray of cold water traced an arc across his feet and legs.

"Come on!" Jennifer called out from the side of the boat. "Don't you want to get some exercise?"

Kevin rolled over and propped himself on one elbow. Jennifer, in a bright red bikini, was paddling in the azure lake, her long brown hair spread out across her shoulders.

"Why don't you come back on board?" he said. "We could get some exercise right here."

"That's not aerobic."

"It is if you're doing it right."

Jennifer laughed, then paddled away from the boat. Kevin watched her as she lazily swam toward the rugged gray cliffs surrounding the cove where they were anchored. Draining the beer can, he tossed it into the cooler, then stood up and stretched. Maybe a swim wouldn't be such a bad idea, after all.

He stepped around the mast, took a second to prepare— he already knew that the water was going to be a jolt to his hot skin—then executed a perfect dive into the lake. The water was even colder than he'd expected, and he came up sputtering, wiping his hair back out of his eyes.

"I'm over here," Jennifer called.

Kevin looked around—all he could make out was the

flash of her red bikini, somewhere off to his right—and he started swimming toward it. The water was so clear he could see his own arms cutting through it.

"And you will not *believe* what I've found."

"Atlantis?" he said.

"Maybe."

As he approached her, he started to grow more accustomed to the water temperature; in another minute or two, it might actually feel refreshing. He could see now that Jennifer was treading water in front of what looked like a small cave in the side of the cliff. Jagged gray rock jutted out above its entrance.

"Look," she said, "you can see inside."

Kevin swam up beside her and took hold of the overhanging rock. She was right—the sunlight, glinting off the water, was reflected into the narrow cave. And there was something inside—a mineral phosphorescence?—that made the interior walls sparkle like a million tiny diamonds.

"Look at how it glows," Jennifer said, slipping forward under the overhang and toward the mouth of the cave.

"That may not be such a good idea," Kevin warned.

But with one wide stroke of her arms, she'd already entered. "Ooh, it's so spooky in here," she said, her voice echoing hollowly off the stone walls. "And air-conditioned."

Well, what can I do now but follow her? Kevin thought. *Even if it does seem like a bad idea.* He ducked his head and paddled into the cave after her. The moment he passed inside, he felt the hot sun sliding off the back of his head, and a cool, ancient air enveloping him instead.

Jennifer, a few yards away, seemed to be standing on something, her hand braced against the low roof of the cave. "There's a ledge here," she said, "so watch where you kick."

A second later, he barked his shin on the underwater outcropping. "Damn."

"Sorry. I stubbed my toe on it, too, if it's any comfort."

"It's not." He gingerly put his feet down on the smooth, slimy rock; something—seaweed, he assumed—brushed around his ankles.

"What if we're the first two people ever to discover this place?" Jennifer whispered.

"I've got to believe somebody's anchored here before and spotted it."

"But didn't they say there's been a drought this year and that the level of the lake is lower than it's ever been?"

"Yeah, they might have said something like that."

"Then what if this cave has never been above the water level before?"

Kevin shrugged; he supposed it was possible. And in the dim, flickering light, washed in on the waves and refracted by the crystalline rock, it certainly seemed as if no human had ever intruded there. The cave felt like . . . like the oldest thing he'd ever seen, older than the steep walls of the Grand Canyon, older than the dinosaur bones he'd seen at the natural history museum, older than anything he could even imagine. He felt a chill run down his spine.

"Come on," he said, "it's cold in here. And the tide could turn any second."

"In that case we'd better work fast," Jennifer said, throwing her arms around his neck. "This will be our secret place, forever." She pressed her body against him and kissed his lips. Kevin wanted to resist—he wanted them to get out of there—but when he felt her breasts rubbing his chest, the thin fabric of the bikini top sliding against his skin, his natural caution evaporated. He put his arms around her waist and pulled her even tighter. He closed his eyes—if this wasn't the perfect honeymoon moment, then what was?—and opened them again only when he suddenly heard her gasp and pull away.

"What is *that?*" she said, staring over his shoulder.

Even if he'd thought she was kidding, the look on her face told him no—this was not a joke. He whipped his head around and saw it, barely.

Embedded in the sparkling rock, as if struggling even now to break free, he could just make out what looked like talons, sharp and extended, long and gnarled. They were clearly defined, yet melded to the stony wall.

"It's a fossil," he said, hardly believing it himself.

"Of what?"

He bent to look closer but the water sloshed around the glistening walls and it was tough to see if the talons—or were they more like claws?—were attached to anything else below the waterline.

"You got me," he said. "I got Cs in science."

"Whatever it is, it gives me the creeps," Jennifer said, an uneasy note in her voice. "Let's get out of here."

Kevin couldn't have agreed more, but he didn't want to give Jennifer any more of a scare than she'd already had. "You go first. But just in case this is worth something," he said, touching two fingers to the petrified talon, "maybe I'll just chisel off a little piece."

"No!" Jennifer cried. "Don't do anything to it. Don't even touch it."

"I was kidding," he said, reassuringly. "I don't even have my chisel on me." He could see this was no time for jokes. "Let's get back to the boat. You go out first and I'll follow you."

She slipped past him, into the dark water, and as he turned to watch her go, a wave swept into the cave and pushed her back. He heard her splutter and take a couple of hurried breaths. He'd been a lifeguard enough summers to know the sound of impending panic.

"Take it easy, Jen," he said. "Go out with the same wave that just came in."

But he couldn't help but notice that the opening of the cave did look markedly smaller already, and the light from outside was less than it had been. Was a sudden storm rolling in?

"Just let the water take you," he said, as calmly as he could, and he saw her head dip down, her arms sweep forward. He glanced again at the glistening rock, with its buried claws. Or . . . *fingers?*

Another wave, bigger than the one before, washed up against him, and he felt himself losing his balance. His feet tried to grip the ledge, but the rock was too slick.

Something loose and stringy licked again at his calf. He fell forward into the water, his shin banging on the underwater outcropping.

But Jennifer's head, he could see, had just cleared the lip of the cave; her feet kicked up a flutter of water as she propelled herself out into the cove.

Thank God for that, Kevin thought. *She'll calm down now.*

When he was sure she was clear, he pushed off after her, but he'd timed it wrong, and another surge, cold and stinging, slapped him in the face. *So much for my own advice,* he thought. He wiped the water from his eyes, and to his surprise another wave—how fast could they come?—hit him again. The water rose up, lifting him, and he suddenly felt the top of his head graze the rough wet roof of the cave.

Relax, he told himself. *Just relax and you'll be out of here in a few seconds.*

He took a deep breath and paddled again toward the opening—there was no sight of Jennifer anymore—but the water in the cave seemed to be eddying and churning now, pulling him sideways, pulling him back. He tried to swim harder, but it was like one of those dreams where you're trying to run but never getting anywhere; he wasn't moving forward at all. *Christ—why did I ever let Jennifer go into this damn sinkhole?*

The light at the mouth of the cave was only a sliver now, and the water was swelling upward again. He started to lift his hand to protect his head, but it was already too late; the water raised him up, harder and faster than before, and the next thing he knew he felt his head crack against the jagged stone. Even in the cold, dark water he could feel the sudden seepage of blood; he knew he'd just cut open his scalp.

"Kevin!"

Had he heard that?

"Where are you?"

I'm here, he thought, dazed. *I'm right here.*

He tried again to swim out, but the water swelled once

more, smashing his head into the same sharp rock, knocking the breath right out of his body.

Something in his legs gave way, and they stopped kicking. His arms, too, stopped swirling in the water.

Go with the flow, he thought, dimly.

But it was as if a black velvet curtain, very thick and very warm, were suddenly descending over him. The top of his skull ached as if he'd been struck with a hammer.

"Kevin!"

He answered, or at least he thought he did. His mouth was filled with icy water. The curtain wrapped itself tighter. He felt himself falling, drifting down, it was actually sort of pleasant, and the last thing he saw in his mind's eye—and it made him want to smile—was himself, in his rented tuxedo, feeding Jennifer a big, unwieldy slice of the white and yellow wedding cake.

PART ONE

. . . and the watchful ones looked down upon the daughters of men. Like the dragon who does not sleep, they kept their vigil . . . and abomination filled their hearts.

—The [Lost] Book of Enoch, 2–3
(translated from the Aramaic), 4QEN f–g

ONE

"Next slide, please."

As one image left the screen and another took its place, Carter Cox wondered just how many of the undergraduates ranged around the darkened lecture hall were actually still awake. From the lighted lectern, it was impossible to see them, but he knew that they were hunkered down in their seats out there, the steady hum of the projector providing just the right amount of white noise to help induce sleep and even camouflage the occasional snore.

"This will be over soon," he said, "stick with me," and he was gratified to hear a little laughter from various quarters. "In fact, this is the last slide of the day. Would anyone here like to tell me what it is?"

There was the sound of a few seats creaking as various students sat up to take better notice.

"Looks like a dinosaur fossil," a girl said, from somewhere toward the back; it sounded like Katie Coyne, one of his better students. "One of the smaller carnivores."

"Okay, good. But what makes you say that?"

"Nothing does. I thought of it all by myself."

There was a wave of laughter, and now he knew it was Katie.

"Let me rephrase, Ms. Coyne," Carter said, trying to regain control. "What makes you think, for instance, that it's a meat eater?"

"From here, it looks like whatever it was had sharp teeth, maybe even serrated—"

"That's good—because it did."

"—and although it's tough to make out, maybe its feet had claws, like one of the raptors. But I can't really tell that for sure."

"So you're looking down at this area," Carter said, touching his pointer to the bottom of the slide; there, the creature's feet were splayed apart and did indeed look clawed. But even in its entirety, the fossil image didn't offer much in the way of clues. It was really no more than an impression of faint gray and black lines—twisted and broken and in some spots doubling back on themselves—set against a blue-gray backdrop of volcanic ash. Katie had done a good job of picking out some of its most salient characteristics. Still, she'd missed the most important.

"But what do you make this out to be?" Carter asked, raising his pointer to the top of the slide, where a bony protuberance twisted upward and ended with a blunt flourish. Even Katie was silent.

"Maybe a tail, with something on the end of it," another student hazarded.

"An armored spike," Katie said, "for warding off other predators?"

"Not exactly. On closer examination, which this slide is probably inadequate to provide, that little clump at the end of the tail—and it is a tail—turned out to be," and he took a second for dramatic effect, "a plume of feathers."

The hum of the projector was all that could be heard. Then Katie said, "So I was wrong? It's not a dinosaur—it's a bird?"

"No, you're right, in a way, on both counts: it's a dinosaur, with feathers, called—and be prepared, I'll expect all of you to spell this on the final—*Protoarchaeopteryx robusta.* It was found in western China, it dates from the Jurassic era, and it's the best proof to date that present-day birds are in fact descendants of the dinosaurs."

"I thought that theory had been discredited," Katie said.

"Not in this class," Carter said. "In here, that theory is alive and kicking."

The bell—more of an annoying buzzer, really—sounded, and the students started gathering their books and papers together. The projectionist turned up the lights in the lecture hall, and the slide instantly paled into obscurity on the screen.

"So that thing you just showed us," Katie said, "whatever it was called, did it fly?"

"Nope, doesn't look like it," Carter replied, as the other students shuffled toward the door. Katie was always the last to go, always had one more question for him before she buttoned up her army surplus jacket and headed out herself. She reminded Carter a little of himself at that age, always trying to tie up one more loose end or get one more piece of the puzzle. Usually he hung around after the class to answer any remaining questions, but not today; today—and he'd put a yellow Post-it on his lecture notes so he wouldn't forget—he had an appointment to get to.

He pulled on his leather jacket, stuffed his notes in his battered briefcase, and left through the side door, just behind Katie.

"So, do you believe that *T. rex* had feathers, too?" she asked over her shoulder.

"It's not inconceivable," he said.

"Guess they're going to have to reshoot *Jurassic Park* then."

"Yeah, I'm sure they'll do that," he said, "and while they're at it, maybe they ought to call it *Cretaceous Park.*"

"How come?"

"Because *T. rex* didn't actually show up till then. See you next Thursday."

Outside, it was crisp and autumnal, the kind of day when New York actually seemed to sparkle, when the store win-

dows gleamed, the falling leaves littered the pavement, and
even the pretzel carts looked tempting. For a second,
Carter thought about stopping at one—all he'd had for
lunch was a microwaved burrito—but then he remembered
the *New York Post* exposé about the vermin in the ware-
house where the carts were kept overnight, and he kept on
walking. At times like this, he was often sorry he'd ever
read that article.

The appointment he had to keep, in just forty minutes,
was in midtown, and right now he was only in Washington
Square. But if he walked briskly, he figured he could still
make it in time. A cab would cost a fortune, and the idea
of descending into the subway on such a beautiful afternoon was too painful. Zipping up his jacket, with his
briefcase bulging at his side, he set off, up Fifth Avenue,
for an appointment that he was, in all honesty, not that eager to get to.

It was another doctor appointment, this time with a
fertility specialist, one that Beth had found through her
friend Abbie. Beth was only thirty-two, and Carter one
year older, but they'd been trying the baby thing for over
a year, and so far nothing was happening. Part of Carter
wanted to know what the problem was—and part of him
didn't—but this afternoon, he was afraid he was going to
find out either way.

They'd been married for six years, and for most of that
time the whole subject of kids had been tabled. No, he
couldn't even say that it had been tabled; it just hadn't
come up at all. For one thing, they were both so wildly pas-
sionate about each other, the idea of actually making love
for some other purpose—to start a family—would have
seemed absurd; sex was just for sex, and why would they
have wanted to confuse the issue with . . . issue? That
wasn't a bad way to put it, he thought. They'd existed, quite
happily, in a kind of little bubble, and there was nothing inside that bubble but each other. And it didn't feel like anything was missing.

The other consideration had been their work—Carter
had always said he didn't even want to think about starting

a family until he knew that he was going to get his career on track—until he knew, for instance, that he was going to get tenure somewhere. His nightmare was to wind up like so many of the other postdocs he knew, a gypsy scholar drifting from one temporary post to another, one year in New Haven, two years in Ann Arbor, with a wife to support and a couple of kids in tow, and nowhere to write, no time to think, no freedom to go where he needed to go in order to get the work done that would make his reputation. But that was not a problem anymore. Eighteen months ago, New York University had given him tenure—along with the newly funded Kingsley Chair of Paleontology and Integrative Biology—so there went that excuse.

At Thirty-first Street he made a right and headed toward the stretch of First Avenue he'd come to think of as Medical World. When he'd once been involved in a cab accident, this was where the ambulance had taken him. When he went to see an orthopedist about a climbing injury to his right leg, this was where he'd come. And when he'd had to undergo some physical therapy afterward, the clinic, too, had been just half a block from the avenue. All things considered, he was entering pretty familiar territory.

But that didn't mean he felt comfortable there.

Dr. Weston's office suite was on the second floor of an undistinguished hospital annex. A pair of polished oak doors bore his name on them in raised gold letters six inches high, and below that the letters *P.C.*—for "private corporation." Since when, Carter wondered, had doctors started to seem more like businessmen? As he was ushered through the elegantly appointed reception area and down the hall—polished wood, with an antique Persian runner on it—to Dr. Weston's inner sanctum, Carter felt more and more like he'd entered an investment banking house and not a medical office—an impression that was only bolstered when he got to the private office with the view of the East River.

Beth was already there, sitting on one of two chairs set up in front of the doctor's ornate, antique desk. As Carter came in, Dr. Weston, wearing not a white lab coat, but a sleekly cut dark suit, stood up to shake his hand; the only thing in the office that even suggested medicine was a light box mounted on one wall, where, presumably, X rays were sometimes viewed.

Carter felt distinctly underdressed.

"Your wife was just telling me a little bit about her work at the gallery," Dr. Weston said, sitting back down in his high-backed, red leather swivel chair. He was a lean man, who looked to Carter like one of those guys he'd see running laps around the reservoir. "I collect art myself, as it happens." He gestured at a huge, and hideous, abstract oil hanging beside the door; Carter knew it was just the kind of thing Beth would detest.

"It's a Bronstein," he added, proudly.

Carter stole a glance at Beth, who had a pleasant, but cryptic, smile on her face. Her black hair was pulled straight back, into a tight ponytail, and the look in her rich brown eyes remained noncommittal. "I'm afraid our gallery specializes in much older pieces," she said. "For us, Renoir is cutting-edge."

"Still, I'd like to see what you've got sometime. You never know what might catch my eye," he said, now returning to some notes he'd been taking. "And Carter, I see here that you're a . . . scientist?"

"Paleontology, chiefly."

Dr. Weston dipped his head, as if in professional acknowledgment. "You teach, then?"

"At NYU."

"Very good. I did my internship at NYU-Bellevue."

Weston kept his head down, glanced at a chart in the open folder on his desk. For a few seconds he was silent as he studied the information. Carter assumed the chart contained their personal stats, ages, medical histories, and so on. He'd already answered some of these questions with a nurse over the phone. Carter reached over and squeezed Beth's hand.

"Was I late?" he murmured.

"Not for you," she said, smiling. "Your lecture go okay?"

"It'd be hard for it to go very wrong—I feel like I've delivered it a hundred times already."

"And you've been trying to conceive for how long now?" Dr. Weston interrupted without looking up.

"About a year," Carter replied.

"Fourteen months and counting," Beth said.

Weston made a correction in the chart. Then kept reading.

"Want to go to Luna's tonight?" Carter asked Beth.

"Can't. We've got a private reception for some clients."

"What time'll it be over?"

Beth shrugged. "If it looks like they're in a buying mood, it could go late. Eight-thirty, nine."

Weston looked up at them now. "During these fourteen months, how often have you had intercourse on a regular basis?"

Even if Carter *was* supposed to be a fellow scientist, the question kind of took him by surprise.

"Four or five times a week," Beth answered.

Was that right? Carter had to think about it.

Weston noted it down.

Yes, that did seem about right, now that Carter thought about it. But was that the usual rate for married couples? You could never really know.

"Okay, then," Dr. Weston said, sitting back in his chair and pulling on his cuff.

Carter couldn't help but notice that he wore gold cufflinks.

"You're both young, so unless we find some difficulty down the line, I believe we have a very high probability of success here."

"But why haven't we succeeded so far?" Beth asked. "I mean, what kind of difficulty do you think we could find, somewhere down that line?"

Dr. Weston brushed it off. "A lot of things can impede conception, from a blocked tube to a low sperm count, but the good news is we have ways of getting around nearly all of the problems now. Here's what I suggest we do."

And for the next ten or fifteen minutes, Dr. Weston outlined a number of steps for them to take, from keeping a record of their sexual intercourse activities to changing the positions they used in order to maximize the possibility of conception; Carter, specifically, was advised to switch to boxer shorts instead of briefs—"they keep the temperature in the scrotal sac lower, which in turn produces more, and more motile, sperm"—and to make an appointment with the office for a count.

"So, you'll want me to come in and . . . leave a sperm sample?" Carter said.

"Yes. We'll want you to refrain from any sexual intercourse—more to the point, from ejaculating—for twenty-four hours before coming in. Mornings are the best time."

Beth was advised to make her own appointment for a complete examination, and suddenly Dr. Weston was standing up and offering his hand across the desk again. "I think we're going to have an extremely successful outcome here," he said.

"I'm not looking for triplets," Beth said. "One will do."

"Fine. Then that's how we'll do it—one at a time."

On the way out, Carter had to leave a credit card imprint with the nurse at the front desk, and then he and Beth were back outside, standing on a windswept corner of First Avenue. He put his briefcase down on the sidewalk between his feet, then began fastening the buttons of Beth's long olive-green slicker.

"So what time does that reception start?" he said.

"Not for a few hours," she said, glancing down as he wrestled with a reluctant button. "How about you? Do you have another class?"

"No, just a few papers to grade. But they can wait." Carter smiled and leaned in so close the ends of their noses touched. "Maybe we should put this time to some good use."

"What did you have in mind?"

"Homework?" he said, suggestively. "I mean, we wouldn't want to let the good doctor down, would we?"

Beth furrowed her brow, as if she were trying to make up her mind about a particularly thorny problem. Then she said, "Maybe you're right. It's never a good idea to put things off, is it?"

TWO

"We'll be on the ground in just a few minutes," the pilot said over the cabin speaker. "Flight attendants, please prepare for arrival."

Ezra Metzger opened his silver pill case and took out another tranquilizer, swallowed it with the last of his Evian water. He'd made it this far, he reminded himself. Now he just needed to stay calm for the next hour or so.

"Please buckle your seat belt," the attendant said, reaching for his empty plastic cup. He gave it to her, then heard her say the same thing to the young woman who'd been sniffling in her seat behind him for the entire flight. Everyone had seemed very solicitous of this girl, and Ezra had wondered what it was all about. Was she some TV actress who'd suffered some public heartbreak? He knew he was pretty out of it when it came to popular culture. It wasn't that he was so old—he'd just turned thirty. But he'd been living at the institute in Jerusalem for the past three years, almost around the clock, and even when he'd been living in New York he'd been more inclined to attend lectures at the Cooper-Hewitt than watch TV or go to the movies.

As the plane descended, he closed his eyes and tried to stay relaxed. He knew that he had to appear perfectly at ease when he passed through the customs desk, that he had to look unruffled by any delay or question or request. He reminded himself to look the customs inspector straight in the eye, not to look away, or touch his nose, or rub his jaw, or do anything else that might betray his nervousness or anxiety. And if indeed he was unlucky enough to have his bags inspected, or to be interrogated at any length, to react with equanimity and unconcern. The secret, he told himself for the hundredth time, was to pretend he had nothing to hide, that he was just another American citizen happy to be home after an extended stay abroad.

Even if nothing could be further from the truth.

Once the plane had touched down and taxied to the gate, the girl behind him—pretty, chestnut brown hair, early twenties—was again given preferential treatment. While Ezra and the other first-class passengers waited, she was whisked off the plane first, and down the ramp. She still didn't look familiar to Ezra, and he asked the well-dressed woman waiting in the aisle next to him who she was.

"I don't know her name, but I saw something about it in the *Herald-Tribune*. A honeymooner, from a nice family. Her husband was killed in a boating accident or something like that, near Naples."

Ezra took it all in, then realized the woman was looking at him, as if expecting him to react. "That's very sad," he said, dutifully. *Focus, Ezra, focus.*

"Yes," she said, "isn't it," before moving as far away as the narrow aisle would permit.

As the people ahead of him shuffled toward the exit, Ezra took his cardboard tube out of the overhead bin and cradled it under one arm. *Act normal.*

"Thank you for flying with Alitalia," the attendant said with a heavy accent, as he made his way off the plane.

Moving slowly, so that he'd gradually be caught up in the bigger crowd of passengers from the coach cabin, he followed the signs to Immigration and Passport Control. A woman in a blue uniform said, "Foreign national?" and touched him on the sleeve to direct him to the line on the far right.

He jerked his arm back at her touch, and she seemed surprised.

"Are you a foreign national, visiting this country?" the woman said, slowly, deliberately.

"No, sorry, I'm not," Ezra said. "I'm an American."

"Oh, then you can go to the lines on the left."

He nodded his thanks and moved toward the lines on the left, but he thought he could feel her eyes on him as he walked away. He had to get hold of himself. But he could see why she'd made the mistake—he was dark and intense, his clothes were of foreign manufacture, even his haircut probably looked wrong somehow. In his travels, he was often mistaken for everything from a Spaniard to a Greek, and when he ran a hand over his jaw, he felt the stubble that had grown in over the long flight. If only he'd thought to shave in the airplane bathroom . . .

The passport inspector was an elderly man with wire-rimmed glasses who studied his passport silently, flipping the pages idly back and forth for a few seconds.

"When were you last in the United States, Mr. Metzger?"

"Approximately three years ago."

"You were working abroad?"

"Yes, in Israel."

"What kind of work would that be?"

"I was a fellow at the Feldstein Institute." This was at least partly true—and Ezra had already decided to stick as close to the truth as possible.

The inspector looked at him intently through the top of his bifocals. He seemed to be waiting for more.

"It's a research institute. They use modern technology in the dating and analysis of archaeological finds."

The inspector nodded. "Must be a lot of those in that part of the world."

"Yes, yes, there are," Ezra readily agreed.

"Is that why you were back and forth so much between"—and he stopped to glance at the passport pages again—"Egypt, Saudi Arabia, Kuwait, Lebanon?"

"Yes, that's why. Sometimes I did field work."

The inspector became silent again, and Ezra feared he'd already said too much. He was trying to leave out the important stuff, but at the same time volunteer as much of the rest of the story as he could. The cardboard tube rested carefully against his leg.

The inspector lifted his stamp and rocked it back and forth on the back page of Ezra's worn passport. Ezra breathed a sigh of relief.

"Welcome back," the inspector said, handing him back the passport. "Baggage claim and customs are straight ahead."

As Ezra walked down the aisle past the desk, thinking *One obstacle hurdled, one more to go,* he heard the inspector call out after him. "Mr. Metzger?"

Ezra stopped and turned, his heart in his mouth.

"If you plan on doing a lot more traveling, you may want to apply for a new, duplicate passport. That one's pretty far gone."

Ezra smiled, tilted the old passport toward him. "I'll do that." Then turned back toward the luggage area.

His bags were some of the first to come off the conveyor belt—one more advantage to flying first class—and as he dragged them toward the customs counters, he tried to make a quick assessment. Which customs officer looked the least alert? Which one had the longest line of people already impatiently waiting to get through?

He chose a stocky inspector who seemed to be more interested in joking around with one of her fellow workers than in inspecting the bags passing before her. When his turn came, he smiled at her and nonchalantly passed her the customs declaration he'd filled out on board.

"Long flight," he said, casually stretching and looking around.

She smiled back, glanced down at his paperwork. "You came in on the Alitalia flight from Rome?"

"Yes."

"Connecting?"

"Pardon?"

"You connected there from somewhere else?"

"Yes. I left from Tel Aviv."

"On what airline?"

"El Al."

Why was she asking all this? Ezra hadn't expected it. When had she suddenly decided to focus on her job? The other inspector, the one she'd been kidding around with, had also settled down.

"Has anyone else been left in charge of your bags?"

"Other than the airline, no."

"Did anyone else pack these bags for you?"

"No, I did it myself."

"Please place them on the counter and open"—she deliberated for a second, as if waiting to see which bag his own eyes might flit to—"this one."

Ezra placed the bag flat on the counter, then unzipped it. My God, he'd picked wrong—he *was* going to be inspected. *Stay calm, stay calm,* he told himself. Even if they found what he was carrying, they wouldn't know what to make of it.

She pulled the flap back and began sifting through the contents of the bag. Black cotton turtlenecks, khaki cargo pants—the very outfit he was wearing now—socks, underwear, a couple of books that he didn't trust to the mails and had decided to carry back with him. The other books— several hundred—he was having shipped.

Then she tapped his leather toiletry kit. "Please open this for me."

He took it out of the bigger bag, opened it, and laid it on the counter for her. She rummaged around among the toothpaste and dental floss, razor, and aspirin bottles, and stopped only when she came to the Desert Mirage Exfoliating Scrub. "You use this?" she said.

"I sometimes worked outdoors, and got very dirty," he said. "Nothing else worked as well."

She unscrewed the lid, and he tried not to look concerned. But he could feel his heart pounding, and his palms growing damp. *Don't wipe them*, he said to himself. *Let them be.*

The jar was filled with a dusty red paste. The inspector sniffed it. "Whew," she said, drawing back. "You put this stuff on your face?"

"Yes. If you scrub it in, it feels great."

She screwed the lid back on. "I'll stick to Noxzema."

She put it back in the toiletry kit, and gestured at the cardboard tube. "What's in there?"

"Some papyrus artwork, souvenirs I bought at the airport shop in Israel." He rummaged in his pocket. "I have the receipt," he said, producing it. "They're nothing of any value."

"Just pop the end off the tube, please."

Ezra did as she asked, and she lifted the cylinder like a telescope and rotated it to look inside. How much could she even make out, he wondered?

"Who's the one with the head of a dog?"

"That's Anubis you're probably looking at," he said. "God of the dead. He has the head of a jackal, actually." Jesus, what was he thinking? *Correcting* her?

She popped the plastic seal back where it belonged, then placed the tube on the counter next to his bag. She stamped the bottom of his declaration.

"Thank you," she said. "Ground transportation is down the corridor on your left."

Ezra gathered up his bags, tucked the tube back under his arm, and made his way out of the customs area. His black turtleneck, he could feel, was stuck to his back with sweat, but it was all he could do not to jump for joy.

As soon as he got to the arrivals area, he saw his Uncle Maury in a blue windbreaker, holding up a handwritten sign that said METZGER.

Ezra, burdened down with the bags, lifted his chin to acknowledge him, and Maury hurried over to help. Putting the bags down, they embraced, then Maury stepped back to look him over. "You've lost weight."

"And so have you." Which was a lie—his uncle was not only as heavy as ever, but looked all of his sixty-five years, maybe even a bit more. "But what's with the sign? You thought I wouldn't know you?"

"I thought I might not know *you*."

Maury started to pick up the bulkiest bag, but Ezra stopped him. "Here," he said, handing him a small carry-on, "you can carry this."

Maury walked slowly, listing from one side to the other, on his way out of the terminal. Even though he was only a year older than his brother, Ezra's dad, he looked much older than that. Life had been hard on Maury, and—as he liked to say—he'd been hard on life. While his brother Sam had excelled at everything, and made a fortune by the time he was thirty, Maury had drifted around from job to job, woman to woman, without ever really settling down or getting serious about anything. Finally, he'd wound up working for Sam and his family, as everything from handyman to babysitter, or, as he was tonight, chauffeur.

The black Lincoln town car was parked in the first spot reserved for VIP parking—an instant reminder to Ezra that he was once again entering his father's sphere of influence—and Maury opened the back door for him.

"You don't want me up front?" Ezra said.

"Come on and get in, I got too much of my stuff up there."

Ezra got in back—he knew that his uncle had always preferred it that way—and waited while Maury lowered himself into the front seat, pushed his *Daily Racing Forms* to one side, and navigated the car out of the airport maze.

On the way into the city, Ezra asked where his father and stepmother, Kimberly, were that night. He was hoping that they might be at their place in Palm Beach.

"They're home. In fact, they're throwing a dinner party."

Ezra's heart sank.

"Who's on the guest list?"

Maury knew this wouldn't go down well. "The mayor," he said, somewhat reluctantly, "and a bunch of other big shots."

"Can we go in the back way?"

Maury glanced at him in the rearview mirror. Even after all this time, he thought, not much had changed. "You can try, but they're expecting to see you."

Ezra had always dreaded this homecoming—which was why he hadn't done it for years. The last words he'd exchanged with his father, in person, had been awfully blunt ones. And now, to make matters worse, there were the peculiar circumstances under which he'd had to leave Israel. He wasn't sure exactly how much his family knew of what had happened there—he hadn't told anyone the full story—but his father, as he had known all his life, had sources everywhere. What he didn't know yet, he would soon find out.

For the rest of the ride, they caught up on more neutral topics—the Mets, city politics, Gertrude the housekeeper, Trina the cook—and when they got to the building, Maury pulled the car into the circular driveway and stopped. "You can leave your bags in the trunk," he said, "I'll send 'em up in the freight elevator."

"Thanks," Ezra said. "Will I see you tomorrow?"

"Just try and keep me away."

He picked up the cardboard tube and carried it inside with him. The doorman, someone new, didn't recognize him, but he did recognize the Lincoln town car and Maury unloading the bags.

"I'm going up to the penthouse, I'm Mr. Metzger's son," Ezra explained anyway, and the doorman said, "Should I buzz?"

"No, no, that's all right, They know I'm coming."

In the elevator, Ezra said hello to the operator—one of the building's long-time employees—then stepped out at the top floor, directly into the wide marble foyer of his family's vast apartment. It was lucky he'd been warned that the mayor was there for dinner, or he'd have been shocked by the sight of a policeman, perched on a French Empire chair and reading a tabloid under the Rodin ballerina.

"Who're you?" the cop asked.

"I live here," Ezra said—then wondered if that was quite true.

"Okay, then, you can go inside."

"Awfully big of you," Ezra said.

Inside, he could hear the sounds of glassware clinking and people chattering, but he thought if he was sufficiently stealthy he could creep down the hallway to his old rooms without being noticed.

"Ezra!"

So much for stealth. Or had the doorman buzzed to alert them, after all?

His stepmother—all ninety-eight pounds of her—came out, in a skintight black and silver sheath, teetering on three-inch heels, with a necklace of diamonds and emeralds (no doubt the latest gift from his besotted father) glittering around her neck.

"Welcome home," she said, placing her hands—as cold as the diamonds—on both of his cheeks, in a perfectly simulated display of affection. "It's been such a long time."

"Yes," he said, "it has," wondering, already, if it had been long enough.

"How was your flight?"

"Fine. It was fine, thanks."

"Your father is dying to see you. You are going to come in and at least say hello, aren't you?"

"Sure, of course. Just as soon as I've washed up."

"Good. You do that. The mayor's here tonight."

Ezra knew that Kimberly had dreamt her whole life of saying things like that—and when she'd snared his father, her dream had come true. Now, even though she was just a few years older than her stepson, she could keep right on doing it—just as long as she was able to keep the old man happy.

Ezra started down the hallway toward his old rooms, the cardboard tube still tucked under his arm.

"Ezra, if you could put on a blazer, and maybe a fresh white shirt, that would be super. You can skip the tie—we're all being very casual tonight."

If this was casual, Ezra thought, he'd hate to see what she wore for a dressy occasion. But he nodded his head without turning around, and kept on going. His own rooms were at the other end of the penthouse, and he let out his

breath again only when he was able to close the door behind him and flip the lock.

Leaning back against the door, with his precious cargo
cradled in his arms, he thought, *Home*. Now his work could
begin, in earnest, again.

THREE

After Beth took a quick shower and left for the party at the art gallery, Carter just lay in the bed, idly watching the local news—an impending bus strike, a Broadway opening, a young honeymooner returning to Long Island from some tragedy in foreign parts. Then he got hungry, and went scavenging.

In the fridge, he found the usual fare—a dozen cellophane bags of fresh fruit and produce, all neatly tied; a stack of Dannon yogurts (in all flavors); a six-pack of bottled Pellegrino. Beth did almost all their food shopping, and nothing passed her lips that wasn't healthy, unadulterated, and organically grown. Carter did his best to get with the program, but whenever Beth wasn't actually there to monitor him, he did some serious backsliding. And she knew it.

Fifteen minutes later, he was scarfing down a burger and fries on Sixth Avenue. There just wasn't anything like grease and protein to rev him up, and with Beth at the gallery reception, there was no particular reason to go back home afterward. The night was cool and clear, and Carter was eager to get back to work on some small fossils that had been donated to the university, then passed along to him for identification. They were waiting for him in the lab he shared with several other members of the department, in the basement of the biology building.

The building itself was open, which didn't surprise him, but he was surprised to see, as he approached the faculty lab, that the lights were on inside; most nights, he could count on having the place all to himself. When he heard Eminem playing on the laboratory boombox, he knew whom to expect.

Carter entered quietly, and for a second or two observed Bill Mitchell, perched on a stool, bent low over a specimen, rapping along under his breath. Mitchell was an assistant professor, and this was the make-or-break year for him; either he got on the tenure track or he didn't. Privately, Carter knew he didn't have much of a chance; his work just wasn't good enough, his papers went unpublished, and he had a tendency to rub people the wrong way. But the guy was working overtime in a last-ditch effort to do something, anything, to make his name and reputation, and Carter couldn't help but feel sorry for him.

"You're working late tonight," Carter said, and Mitchell jumped.

"Man, I didn't hear you come in," he said, pushing his glasses back on his nose. His long black hair, which always looked like it had enough oil in it to lubricate an engine, hung down over his forehead. For some reason, he looked even more nervous than usual. "I thought you taught a seminar on Wednesday nights."

"That was last semester."

"So how come you're not home with your beautiful wife?"

"My beautiful wife is working tonight," Carter said, hanging his leather jacket on the back of the door. "I thought I'd just come in and catch up on some stuff."

Mitchell glanced down, as if unsure what to do, at the materials in front of him.

"What's that you're working on?" Carter asked, but even as he moved closer, he could see for himself—and it didn't make him happy. Mitchell had unsealed one of the glassine envelopes and was busy examining under the tensor lamp one of the fossil specimens that had been donated to the university.

"Couldn't resist," Mitchell said, with a sickly smile. "I thought I might see something that could save you some time."

Carter didn't say anything.

"This one here, for instance," Mitchell said, taking a breath, "looks like a fragment of a jawbone. I'm thinking *Smilodon*, but I'm really not sure. What do you make of it?"

Carter didn't know what to say. This was a pretty big breach of lab etiquette—not to mention professional ethics—and if he wanted to, he could get Mitchell into some fairly serious trouble over it. Mitchell, no doubt, knew that, too, which was why he was sweating bullets now. Carter reached over and punched the Stop button on the boombox.

"Is that the first specimen you've opened?" Carter asked.

"Oh, yeah, definitely. I mean, I was working on some other stuff, but I just kept seeing these bags out of the corner of my eye, and well, you know how it is—if you're a paleontologist, how are you going to keep your hands off material this tempting?"

"Yeah," Carter said, dryly, "I know how that is." He also knew how it was to be this desperate, this hard up for the kind of breakthrough work that would get you tenure somewhere. But that still wasn't any excuse. "I think it'd be best if you let me do all the initial work on these; that's what they pay me for."

"Absolutely," Mitchell confirmed, switching off the tensor lamp.

"And if I need some backup, I'll let you know."

"Cool. No problem," Mitchell said, slipping the specimen back into its envelope and handing it to Carter.

Carter turned and went back to his own corner of the lab. What a foul-up. And although he'd already made up his mind to say nothing of what had happened to anyone inside or outside the department, Mitchell said, "Hey, Carter—"

"Yes?"

"I'm sorry if I crossed a line here. It won't go any further, will it?"

Carter shook his head. "No."

He could almost hear Mitchell's sigh of relief.

"Carter?"

"Yes?"

"One more thing?"

Carter wondered if he'd be able to get any work at all done with Mitchell in the lab.

"You mind if I put the music back on? It helps me concentrate."

"Go ahead," Carter said. At least if the boombox was blaring, he figured, Mitchell wouldn't keep trying to talk to him.

At the Raleigh Gallery on East Fifty-seventh Street, the buyers—a smattering of Europeans (two of them titled), a couple of Asian tycoons, and a handful of assorted plutocrats—were milling around the main salon. But the one that Beth kept her eye on wasn't rich at all in his own right. He was the curator from the Getty Museum in L.A. The others could certainly decide to buy something, you never could tell, but the Getty representative, with a hefty annual budget, was pretty much obliged to spend some of it—and the works on sale at the Raleigh were just the sort of thing that the Getty generally liked to acquire. Although there were a few good oils—a Salvator Rosa, in particular—most of the items were Old Master drawings, including several Titians, and it took a real connoisseur to understand just how exquisite and valuable they were.

"So, what's the deal with this one?" said a youngish guy, nodding toward one of the Titian studies depicting a man's head with eyes closed, shrouded as if for burial. Beth turned to him—he had a full face, innocent of wisdom, and a blond buzz cut. This had to be one of those guys who'd escaped from Silicon Valley with his fortune intact. There still were some around.

"It's a late Titian—"

"He's an Italian, right?"

"Yes, that's right." She could see his eyes glint with pride. "From the region around Venice."

"Is the guy in the picture dead?"

"No, he's in prayer. It's the Emperor Charles V, who commissioned a painting from Titian of the Last Judgment. On his own initiative, Titian included the emperor and his family in the painting. This is a study he did for it."

"It's nice," the buzz cut pronounced. "What's the price for it?"

Although she knew without looking, Beth opened her leather-bound brochure and pretended to look it up. She could feel his eyes looking her over as she ran her finger down the exhibition list. "The asking price is $250,000."

The buzz cut didn't blink.

"The Last Judgment," she continued, "is one of Titian's most famous and moving works. If you would like, I can ask the owner of the gallery to come over and speak to you about it, and about this drawing in particular."

"No," he said, looking back at her. "I'd rather talk to you."

What a surprise.

"My name's Bradley Hoyt," he said, extending his hand.

"Beth Cox," she said, taking it.

"I like it a lot, Beth, but I'd never buy anything without having my own people take a look at it first."

"I understand completely," she said, retrieving her hand. "We can set up a private showing anytime. Or, if you'd prefer, we can arrange to have the piece transported to your own experts."

"Nah, that's okay, I can have them come to you. You here all the time?"

She smiled. "Most of it, I'm afraid."

"Where are you when you're not here?"

Now was the time to nip this in the bud. "Home. With my husband."

"Yeah, I saw the ring. But if you have to see a client about a purchase this big, you can get away for a few hours, to consult—right?"

"We can open the gallery anytime."

"I was thinking more along the lines of lunch at the Stanhope. Or dinner."

"I'm afraid I'm not comfortable taking a piece this valuable out of the gallery on my own."

"You don't need to—I've already seen the piece."

Beth closed her leather book. "You'll have to excuse me, Mr. Hoyt. It's been very nice meeting you, but I'm afraid there's someone else who's also expressed interest in the drawing."

She turned around and went over to the Getty curator, who looked at her over his half-glasses and said, in a low voice, "You can't sell the *Judgment* study to that cretin—it would be a crime."

Beth suppressed a laugh.

"You haven't done that, have you?" he asked.

"No, not yet. Can I sell it to the Getty, instead?"

He took off his glasses and slipped them into the breast pocket of his suit jacket. "Let's talk."

"Yes," she said, with relief, "let's do that—for just as long as you can stand it."

FOUR

The first thing Kimberly thought when she awoke the next morning was that it had been a success. The dinner party for the mayor had been a big success.

The second thought she had was, *Ezra*. He'd come back from Israel, he'd moved his stuff into the rooms he'd grown up in, and now she had no idea how long he planned to stay there. The shorter his stay, the better, but she couldn't afford to be too obvious about her feelings. Even though Ezra's relationship with his dad was strained, and as far as she could tell it had been that way for years, he *was* his only son, and blood was thicker than water. She'd have to tread carefully.

Sam came out of his closet, tightening the knot on his tie—the yellow silk Sulka she'd bought him last week— and, for Sam, he looked good. Bespoke blue suit, gleaming burgundy shoes, neatly folded pocket square to match the tie. She'd done everything she could do with him, but there was still only so far her talents could take him; he was still short, bald, and nearly thirty years older than she was. Every time he touched her, she was reminded that his fingers were short and stubby, too.

"Ezra up yet?" he asked.

"How would I know? I'm not up myself." It came out sharper than she meant it to.

"I'm just asking a question."

Temper, she thought to herself, *temper.* She smiled and threw back the Egyptian cotton sheet. "Don't worry about Ezra. I'll make sure he has everything he needs."

"Whatever that is." Sam stood beside the bed, looking down at her, as she knew he would. Her hair, which Franck kept a perfect auburn color, was spread out on the pillows, and her breasts were barely concealed by the lacy black teddy she slept in.

"What are you doing today?" he asked.

"I haven't made up my mind yet." Though she had. "Maybe I'll have lunch with Janine." They had a twelve-thirty reservation at Le Cirque.

Sam snorted; he didn't like Janine. But then, he didn't like any of her friends that he'd met so far. Lord knows what he'd say, she thought, if he met some of the ones she'd been keeping under wraps. It was time to change the tenor of this exchange. With one hand, she languidly touched the front of his trousers.

"Do you have to leave right this minute?" she purred.

"I've got a site inspection in the Village in forty-five minutes."

But she could tell, just from his tone of voice, that she'd already won. "You're the boss. They can wait."

He stood there as she rolled onto her side and began to unzip him. Her fingers were as adept as a lacemaker's. When she noticed him rock back slightly onto his heels and audibly inhale, she knew she had him—and if she were lucky, she'd be done with the whole ordeal in three minutes flat.

After Sam left, Kimberly called Janine to confirm lunch—Sam was right about one thing, Janine was scatterbrained—then flicked on the TV set in her dressing area and listened to one of the morning news shows while she bathed and put herself together. With Sam gone for the day, she had only Ezra, still in the house, to deal with, somehow. As she sat in her robe doing her makeup, she wondered exactly what the young scion—it was a word she'd just learned and she liked to say it in company, with a kind of knowing wink—was doing back in New York. The whole thing had been shrouded in some mystery—one minute he was safely out of the picture, working at some institute in Israel where his father had pull (where didn't he?), and the next he was bailing out of the Middle East altogether and returning on the next plane. She'd overheard Sam shouting at his secretary on the phone, telling her to get the ambassador on the phone and to book Ezra on the next flight out of Tel Aviv, wherever the hell it was going. He shouted a lot, but not usually at his secretary.

And Kimberly had had such great plans for those two rooms Ezra was once again occupying. They'd have made the perfect nursery suite.

Well, nothing was set in stone, she told herself again. Things could still go her way.

After putting the finishing touches on her face, she picked an outfit from her well-stocked closet—a cream-colored blouse and bone-gray pencil skirt, both from Jean Paul Gaultier—tucked her feet into some modestly high heels (she was already taller than Sam, so she tried to keep her footwear within reason), and left the master suite.

There was no sign of Ezra in the living room, the salon, the library, the den, or even in the dining room, where Gertrude, the elderly housekeeper, was putting the silver candelabra back in its usual spot on the table.

"Have you seen Ezra?" Kimberly asked.

"He's having breakfast. He's lost weight."

Kimberly hadn't ever seen enough of him to say, but she couldn't have cared less, either way. "Thanks." She started to leave the room, then stopped just long enough to say, "Maybe that silver should be polished again before it's put back."

Gertrude paused—for a second, Kimberly thought she was about to say something—then silently took the candelabra back off the table and left the room with it.

That makes two people, Kimberly thought, *that I'd like to get out of here.*

She found Ezra in the breakfast nook, huddled over a bagel and cream cheese, juice, and coffee. It was a sunny day, and the view of the East River, far below, and Queens beyond that, went on forever. It never failed to cross Kimberly's mind that from here she could actually look out and over the tenement she'd first lived in when she came to New York, with her Miss Milwaukee crown still in her duffel bag.

"Morning, Ezra," she said, brightly. "Sleep well?"

"Yes, very well."

He didn't look it. He hadn't shaved, there were bags under his eyes, and for a guy who'd been in the Middle East for years—wasn't it hot and sunny there?—his skin had an unhealthy pallor. To Kimberly, he looked like he'd been living under a rock.

"Mind if I join you?"

"Not at all," he said, but his expression indicated otherwise.

Not that Kimberly wanted to go through this exercise, either. But if she was going to make friends with this . . . scion, and find out just what was going on, this was as good a time as any.

"Did you see your father this morning before he left?"

"For a few minutes. He said we'd talk tonight."

Kimberly sat down at the little glass table, and when Gertrude came back in, she asked her where the cook was.

"The party went so late last night, I told her she could come in at noon."

"Oh, then I guess I'll have to ask you to make me my usual—a small bowl of granola, with fresh fruit, plain yogurt, and black coffee."

"You want something more, Ezra?" Gertrude asked, pointedly. "Maybe some eggs, the way you used to like them, with matzoh crumbled in?"

Kimberly wasn't stupid—she knew this delay was a subtle act of defiance—but she also knew enough to keep her mouth shut for the moment.

"Thanks, Gertrude, but I'm fine," Ezra said, and Gertrude finally turned, her long black skirt swirling around her fat ankles, and went into the adjoining kitchen. Kimberly could still hear her bustling around in there, and even that annoyed her.

"I'm so glad you were able to say hello to the mayor last night. He's such a funny man, when he's able to just relax with friends. But we'll have other dinner parties, and you'll get to know him."

Ezra nodded, noncommittally, and sipped his coffee.

"So," Kimberly said, looking for a way in, "with everyone here last night, we really didn't get a chance to visit. What made you decide to come back to New York now?"

Ezra's eyes shifted toward the window, and for a few seconds he said nothing at all. "My work was done in Israel."

Since Kimberly had no firm idea what that work was, and wasn't really interested anyway, she let that slide. "Are you planning to stay here—I mean, New York—for good now?

"I haven't decided."

"You know you're welcome to stay with us for as long as you want to," she said. "Your father, I know, is very happy to have you back."

Gertrude came in with a lacquered tray on which she'd arranged Kimberly's breakfast. She placed the tray on the table and turned to go back toward the kitchen, but Kimberly stopped her.

"Oh, I don't think we eat off trays in this house," she said. "Could you just put the things on the table, please?"

Gertrude turned around again and took the granola bowl, the yogurt, and the coffee off the tray and set them down on the table. Looking past Kimberly and at Ezra, the old woman said, "I'm going to do some marketing later. Do you still like those Little Schoolboy cookies? I can get some."

"Sure," Ezra said. "I haven't had those in ages."

How long, Kimberly wondered, would she have to put up with these little stunts? She'd made over Sam as best she could, but his household was another thing; all these old family servants—Gertrude, the cook Trina, that chauffeur Uncle Maury—it was like living in some village out of one of those old Frankenstein movies. When she went to her friends' houses—her new friends, that was—they had servants who wore proper uniforms, and knew how to serve, and how to behave. She was not only uncomfortable around this staff, but also, she had to admit, a little bit afraid of them. When they spoke Yiddish, or whatever it was, while she was right there in the room with them, she knew darn well they were talking about her.

Time, she thought, to cut to the chase. "Ezra," she said, smoothing her napkin over her taut lap, "have you ever considered working for your dad?" It was her private nightmare. "Would you like me to talk to him about it for you?" She suspected it was Ezra's worst nightmare, too.

Ezra looked at her, and she knew he could see right through her. But that didn't bother her all that much—their cards had pretty much been on the table from the start. Even as the first Mrs. Metzger was going downhill at Sloan-Kettering, Kimberly had been seeing Sam, and Ezra had found out about it. She could explain a lot of it, how she'd tried to get Sam to wait, how she'd never felt right about it, how the whole thing had just sort of happened (well, maybe she did give it a push now and then, like that time she'd pretended that her boss at the ad agency had demanded that Sam himself okay some layouts, which had allowed her to stop by his apartment, on a night when she just happened to be dressed to kill), but what good would that do now? It was ancient history. And frankly, none of it was any of Ezra's damn business, anyway. It was time he got over it and grew up.

"I don't think that would be a very good idea," Ezra said, and she wondered if he meant working for his dad, or letting her feel out the situation for him. "I've never been very interested in real estate."

"So, what are you interested in, then? What do you want to do now that you're back in America?"

"Continue with my work."

That again. "And what is that, exactly?"

"Research."

"And you can do that research here? You don't need to go back to Israel, or someplace?"

"No."

Kimberly's heart sank. This kid—the exact same age as her brother Wayne, though Wayne could cream him with a single punch—might be planning to hang around the house indefinitely. And that was going to put more than a crimp in her style; if she wasn't careful, it was going to put a major dent.

"Oh, wow," she said, "that's some news."

Ezra gave her a wry smile, and said, "I bet it is."

FIVE

This afternoon, the atmosphere in the lab was more to Carter's liking. No Bill Mitchell, no Eminem on the boombox, no one else hogging the electron microscope. Carter was seldom happier than when he had something new to study, to analyze and classify and figure out what it was. Even when he was a kid, he'd been that way. The day he knew his calling in life was the day his parents built a family room onto the back of the house, and the bulldozer, which had just dug a deep trench as part of the foundation, scooped up a rusty spoon and some bone shards from the earth. You'd have thought it had come up with rubies and pearls. Carter, ten years old at the time, raced to school the next morning to show the specimens to the science teacher, who had been singularly unimpressed. But his classmates had shared in his enthusiasm—especially when he suggested to them that the bones were old enough to be a dinosaur's (never mind where the spoon came from)—and from that day forward, he'd had the nickname "Bones." That's what his friends had started to call him, and he'd actually kind of liked it; even now he knew that his students sometimes referred to him among themselves as Professor Bones.

The specimens that had been sent to him for identification were a hodgepodge—no wonder the university wanted some help—and whoever had donated the collection must have assembled them in a variety of ways. One was indeed a fossilized fragment of jawbone from a *Smilodon*—the aptly named saber-toothed cat of the Ice Age—and most of the others were fragments of saurian tibia and tarsal. Not badly preserved as fossils go, but also nothing to write home about. Another hour or two and Carter could finish the job, complete his report, and move on to more challenging work.

As long as the phone stopped ringing.

It had rung earlier, and kept ringing, but Carter hadn't stopped working to answer it. The only person who knew he was there was the department secretary, and she'd just take a message for him and leave it in his in-box—along with the mail that he just remembered he hadn't picked up for three days.

Now it was ringing again, and although he wanted to let it go—it was probably just Bill Mitchell, checking to see if anyone else was in the lab, moving ahead of him on the tenure track—he knew it would only ring again, ten minutes later, and break his concentration all over again. He got up from the stool, stretched, and walked across the room to the wall phone. He got it on the fifth or sixth ring.

"Lab, Carter speaking."

"Carter Cox?" The connection wasn't great, but he could already guess who was speaking. Dr. Giuseppe— Joe, to his American friends—Russo.

"Russo? Joe Russo?"

"Yes! The secretary, she told me you would be there. I have been calling."

"Where are you calling me from? The line is bad—can I call you back?"

"No, no, my friend. Now that I've got you, I do not want to let you go."

"It must be important for you to pay for the call."

Russo laughed—it had been a running gag on the dig site in Sicily, where they'd met, that Russo had no money in his budget for anything, even food and water.

"I have the job now, at the University of Rome."

"Congratulations! That's great."

"That is why I am calling."

"You want me to come and give a lecture? Beth will be ecstatic. She's always looking for an excuse to go to Italy."

"No. No lecture. I do that myself."

"Okay, I can take no for an answer." But then why was he calling, and so persistently?

"Did you not get my package?" Russo asked. "The material I mailed to you with the Federal Express?"

"No, I haven't."

"I send it to your department office, last week."

Shit. "I haven't picked up my mail for days."

The line crackled, but under it Carter could hear Russo cluck.

"You must get it," Russo said, "and read it. Soon. It is very important."

"I'll pick it up the minute I leave the lab. What's in it?"

Either there was a time delay on the line, or Russo was pondering how to respond. "We have found something here," he finally said. "Actually, to be true, it was two Americans who found it first—and it is a very . . . interesting find. We will need your help, I think."

Russo—a man who'd helped Carter unearth the remains of some of Europe's earliest inhabitants from the "Well of the Bones" in Sicily—was not a man to make empty pronouncements. And Carter knew that if he claimed something was a "very interesting find," it meant that something very big might be in the offing. Carter felt a tingle of anticipation in the back of his neck.

"What do you want me to do? Look over what's in the package and call you tomorrow?"

"Yes! My number is on the package. Call me at six in the evening, Rome time. You will want to, my friend," he said, with a chuckle. "You will not want to wait."

Carter could hardly wait right now—and he silently swore to himself that he would never again let his departmental mail back up. As soon as he'd hung up, he put the donated fossils away—force of habit made him do it by the book—then grabbed his jacket and headed for the door.

Mitchell was just coming in, holding a bag from Burger King. "Whoa, Bones, what's the rush?"

"Forgot to pick up something at the office," Carter said as he squeezed past him.

"Good luck," Mitchell said, "they're probably closed up for the weekend."

That was just what Carter dreaded. "You were right, by the way, about the jaw fragment," he shouted over his shoulder as he turned the corner of the hall. "It is a *Smilodon*."

The departmental office was indeed closed up by the time Carter, all but out of breath, managed to get there. Through the glass door, he could actually see his mailbox, the top slot in the wooden cabinet, jammed to bursting—and he could even make out one of those distinctive FedEx envelopes, with its big block lettering, sitting on top of the stack. He rattled the door handle, hoping against hope, but it was locked.

That's when he heard the janitor, Hank, plunging his mop into a bucket down the hall.

"Hank, that you?" he called out, rounding the corner.

Hank looked up, the mop still in the metal bucket. "What's up, Professor?"

"Could you do me a huge favor? Could you unlock the departmental office for me?"

"You know I'm not supposed to do that."

"Yeah, I do, Hank, and I wouldn't ask you to, but there's something in there that I absolutely have to have tonight."

Hank blew out a gust of air, ran one hand over his bald head, and then rolled the bucket and mop against the wall. "I never did this for you, okay?"

"Never."

Hank trudged to the office door, unlocked it, and waited while Carter grabbed the FedEx envelope, which was thick and heavy, from his mailbox; he checked the return address to make sure it was the right one, and sure enough, it had come from Russo in Rome. "This is what I needed," Carter said, showing it to Hank. "You've saved my life."

Hank nodded, locking up the office again. "That's what I do."

All Carter wanted to do next was rip open the envelope and read its contents right there, but it was now close to seven, and he knew he was supposed to be meeting Beth and their friends Abbie and Ben Hammond at Minetta's Tavern for dinner. Opening the envelope would just have to wait. But at least he'd been able to get his hands on it—if he hadn't, the chances of his getting any sleep that night, or all weekend for that matter, would not have been good.

The restaurant was only a few blocks away, and when he got there he spotted Beth and the Hammonds at a table near the bar, sharing an antipasto platter.

"I'm glad you didn't wait," Carter said, bending down to kiss Beth on the cheek.

"It never even occurred to us," Ben said, spearing an olive.

Carter laughed, pulled out the empty chair, and sat down. There was a half-empty carafe of white wine on the table, and he poured himself a glass. Ben was still in his banker's suit, and Abbie—who worked at an ad agency whose name Carter could never remember—was also in a suit, though hers was red with white piping around the lapels and collar. To Carter, she looked like she was auditioning for the role of Santa's wife.

"What's in the FedEx?" Abbie said. "You're clutching it like it's a winning lottery ticket."

"Oh, just some work I need to get done later tonight."

But Beth, who could read him like a book, tilted her head and gave him a curious smile; there was more to it, she knew, than that.

"What are all these?" Carter asked, hoping to change the subject and gesturing at a bunch of photographs spread out on the table. In one, he could see a winding country road, in another an old farmhouse with a wide front porch.

"They bought a country house," Beth said, with enthusiasm. "Upstate."

"In Hudson," Abbie said, proudly. "With four acres of land and an old apple orchard."

"And don't forget the barn falling down in back," Ben added.

"That's terrific," Carter said, studying the photo of the house, which looked small but well maintained, with a range of low mountains off in the distance behind it. "I've been meaning to get out of the city more, I just never had a place to go." He looked at Ben and Abbie and said, "Thank you so much. I'll bring my own marshmallows."

"Don't forget the graham crackers and Hershey bars," Abbie said.

Beth raised her glass in a toast. "To the landed gentry!"

"*Salud!*" they all said, clinking glasses as the waiter approached with the menus.

After hearing the specials and ordering, the Hammonds went on some more about the house; they'd been looking for a place for months—"we've really needed a place outside the city," Abbie said, "to unwind"—but Carter thought he knew the real, unspoken reason for getting the house. It was meant to serve as a distraction from the problems they were having starting a family—and he could certainly relate to that. In fact, before very long, Beth and Abbie had fallen into their own conversation about Dr. Weston (it was Abbie who had consulted with him first). They lowered their heads toward each other and spoke intensely—and not for the first time Carter found himself admiring the depth of their friendship. As far as he could tell, there was nothing under the sun that Beth and Abbie couldn't talk about with each other—and probably nothing that they hadn't. They'd met as roommates at Barnard, and been best friends ever since. Even when Beth went to England for a year to study art history at the Courtauld Institute, Abbie snagged a Sloan Fellowship at the London School of Art. Her original goal had been to be an artist herself, an abstract expressionist, the next Lee Krasner, but things hadn't worked out that way, and she'd had to settle instead for a lucrative but spiritually less rewarding position as an art director for an ad agency.

Ben and Carter were just the appendages in this relationship, and they both knew it. While their wives laughed and chattered, and continued to confer in lowered tones, Carter and Ben searched amiably for one topic or another to talk about. It wasn't that they didn't like each other—they did—but their backgrounds and professions, even their interests, were pretty dissimilar.

Ben came from Main Line Philadelphia money, prepped at Exeter, graduated at the top of his class from Wharton Business School, and had been rising through the investment banking ranks ever since.

Carter's family was what he'd come to refer to, out of their earshot of course, as "comfortably lower class." His father had driven a delivery truck for a dairy chain in northern Illinois, and his mother had stayed home to raise Carter and his four brothers and sisters. A lot of the time, Carter had been home sick; as a boy, he'd suffered from all the usual ailments—mumps, measles, chicken pox—but he'd also had what seemed to be a kind of asthma. He would always say "seemed to be" because it had mysteriously cleared up by the time he was a teenager. And ever since then, he'd done his best to make up for lost time, by rock climbing, skiing, and traveling all over the world. When he'd won a generous scholarship to Princeton—to everyone's astonishment, including his own—he'd grabbed it and never looked back.

But it was only in the past few years—after he'd made his remarkable finds in Sicily, in fact—that he'd ascended to the top echelons of his own field. The chair that Carter occupied at New York University was a much-coveted prize, in part because Mr. Kingsley, after whom it was named, had also left a large enough endowment to generate a respectable salary for its occupant. Carter had not gone into the bone business for the money—no one in his right mind did—but in the end, he would have to concede, bones had indeed been pretty good to him.

While he and Ben drifted from books and movies to foreign affairs, Carter had more and more trouble staying focused. He did his best to keep up his end of the conversation, but his mind kept going back to the FedEx envelope tucked under his chair. He wished he could run home, rip open the envelope, and find out what Russo was going on about. While Carter had first discovered and excavated the Well of the Bones, Giuseppe Russo—then just a doctoral candidate in paleontology—had been his right hand, literally. Once, when Carter's rope had inexplicably slipped its clip, Russo had reached down at the last second, grabbed the collar of his poncho, and hauled him up out of the ground. Carter could easily recall the feeling of dangling in midair over the narrow tunnel that burrowed more than sixty feet into the earth, above a grisly mound of prehistoric human bones; he knew that if it hadn't been for Russo, he would have wound up joining them.

Fortunately, by the time the dessert cart was brought around, everyone was too full even to think about it. Carter prayed that no one would ask for coffee or an after-dinner drink, and his prayer was answered; Ben actually said he had to get back to the office. Outside they parted ways, and Beth slipped her arm through Carter's as they walked home.

"So," she said, "I've been dying to know all night. What's in the magic envelope?"

"I'll know when we get home," he said, "but it's from Russo."

"The guy who worked with you in Sicily?"

"Yes. He says they've found something, something he thinks is special enough that I'll want to take a look at it."

"Does he want you to go there?" she said, sounding concerned.

"Not as far as I know. But why, you don't think you'd find enough Renaissance art over there to keep you busy for a few weeks?"

"It's not that," she said, as they waited for the walk light at Bleecker. "I can't leave the gallery right now, and if you're gone, how can we . . . ?"

Carter got it. "Oh. I guess I couldn't just leave a few specimens in the fridge for you, huh?"

"You're so romantic. But that's what I wanted to tell

you. Dr. Weston's office called today, and you've got an appointment there next Saturday morning."

To have his virility tested. Carter contemplated it with dismay as they walked the last few blocks toward home. Already he could feel the performance anxiety kicking in.

Their third-floor apartment, in an old red brick building, faced directly onto Washington Square Park, and in the madness that was Manhattan real estate it would ordinarily have fetched several thousand dollars a month. But fortunately the university owned the building and made the apartments available to faculty members at a bargain rate.

Carter unlocked the door and flicked on the lights while Beth hung her coat on the wooden hat rack that stood in the foyer.

"You want the shower first?" she asked.

"No, you go ahead," he said, already pulling at the flap of the FedEx envelope.

"That's what I figured."

Carter went into the living room and plunked himself down in his favorite armchair, a worn leather wingback that he'd had since college, and tore the envelope nearly in two. Some glossies immediately started to slide out of a folder and onto his lap, and he had to grab them before they scattered on the floor. With his foot, he pulled the coffee table closer, and poured everything out onto its mottled surface.

On top was a letter typed on the letterhead of the University of Rome, and he picked that up first. *"Dottore,"* it began, which was the salutation Russo had always used for Carter, "I send to your attention all the materials enclosed. Also my greetings. I will tell you now the story of these things, which I think will greatly interest you, and we will then talk about them after." His English, Carter could see, had improved a lot. It still had that wonderfully stilted quality—Russo never used contractions, for instance—but the document, so far, was perfectly comprehensible. Carter flipped through the rest of the letter—it was six pages, single spaced—before starting again at the beginning.

It began, mysteriously enough, with an account of the

water levels at a place called Lago d'Avernus, which Carter had never heard of. Apparently, they had dropped to a point not seen for perhaps several million years. A cave, which would have been underwater all that time—maybe even hundreds of feet deeper than it was today, having been pushed up slowly by the seismic forces active in that region—had for the first time become accessible, and a young American couple had been the first to happen upon it. In a parenthetical, Russo mentioned that the man had accidentally drowned there.

In that cave, a fossilized creature had been discovered. Russo apologized for the use of the vague word *creature,* but explained that this very uncertainty was why he was contacting his old friend Carter in the first place. "It is not clear, from the parts of the fossil which we see, what at all we are dealing with." There were what looked like distended talons, the letter went on, suggesting this might be a moderately sized raptor of some sort, but the talons also appeared to display an articulated metacarpal and phalanx—features that could only suggest a hominid ancestor. "But a hominid that, in the scheme of evolution, is too old to be possible."

Carter could see already why Russo was so puzzled. But why not do a simple carbon-14 test on the specimen and see what it revealed? That's where Carter would have started.

But so, it seems, had Russo. In the very next paragraph, Carter read, "As you would expect, we have employed the standard radiocarbon-dating techniques. While we do not here have the access to AMS"—accelerated mass spectrometry, which, Carter knew, was seldom available outside the United States—"we have isolated 5 grams of pure carbon from the base material and conducted repeat tests on that sample. The laboratory reports on those tests are enclosed—see Appendix A."

Carter riffled through the materials until he found the appendix. It was the usual readout, a complex graph of elemental composition and isotopic decay, but Carter's finger coursed down the pages until he came to the number he was looking for—the final estimate of date. And that number, it was true, didn't make any sense at all; the method worked, when it did work, because the radiocarbon isotope carbon-14, which was contained in all organic matter—whether it was wood, plant fiber, seashells, or animal bones—decomposed at a steady rate of 50 percent every 5,730 years. If you had an adequate sample of the specimen—and at 5 grams, Russo had had it—you could get a very good idea of the age of even the most prehistoric matter. The famous cave paintings at Lascaux, for example, were estimated to be between 15,000 and 17,000 years old. But there was always a small margin of error, since the production of carbon-14 had not been consistent throughout time, and radiocarbon dates had to be "corrected" or "calibrated" to account for the chronological anomalies. The resulting discrepancy could leave you with a possible range of a few hundred, or in some rare cases a couple of thousand, years.

But even a few thousand years' leeway would not make Russo's calculations compute—especially not if he was still entertaining the notion that this might be a hominid-related find. This fossil from Lago d'Avernus, according to radiocarbon tests, dated from millions of years before mankind's most distant ancestors walked, or even crawled, the earth.

Though he couldn't yet pinpoint where the mistake had been made, the results, Carter decided, had to be so erroneous as to be useless. The only thing to do would be to disregard them utterly.

He flipped back to the letter. There, Russo, too, conceded that he could make no further headway using the customary carbon-based techniques.

But Carter's next stop would have been to do an analysis of the surrounding rock formation, and try to figure out what the fossil was, or could be, based on the age, and mineral composition, of the rock it was embedded in. Apparently, Russo had come to the same conclusion: "Studies of the contiguous rock are contained in Appendix B."

Again, Carter checked Russo's work, and again he could find no obvious error or omission. Russo was doing things by the book. But the results, once more, were absolutely baffling. The rock was igneous, basaltic, heavy on the pyroxene, that much was clear. But judging from its stupendously high silica content, striations, and density, it had been corkscrewed toward the surface of the earth from an almost unimaginable depth and temperature. Inside the rock, as a reminder of its tortuous progress all the way from the asthenosphere through the upper mantle, there remained an inordinately high content of trapped, volatile gases. Carter sat back in his chair and thought about it for a second. What they had here, in effect, was an immensely durable and dense lithic specimen, which could also, if handled incorrectly, explode in your face like a homemade bomb. A powerful homemade bomb.

No wonder Russo was hesitant to proceed without plenty of consultation.

The problem, Carter could see, would be to find a way to remove the fossil in as intact a state as possible from the volatile material to which it might be indissolubly wed, without setting off that bomb.

"In the cardboard folder," Russo wrote, "you will find photographs of the fossil *in situ.*"

This was what Carter had been waiting for. When the photos had first spilled out, he'd purposely put them back; he didn't want to look at them until he'd read over the other materials and seen what was what. Now, knowing what had already been ascertained—or, in this peculiar case, left hanging—he was ready to look at the visual evidence and see for himself. He leaned forward and opened the folder on the table.

The top picture was so beautiful, it could have been something from a travel brochure. In the foreground, there was nothing but blue water, with a slight chop, and in the background a wall of craggy gray cliffs with cypress trees up top, bending in the breeze. At sea level, barely discernible in this shot, was the mouth of a cave, still partially submerged. Carter glanced at the back of the photo, where Russo had dated it and printed "Lago d'Avernus, cave, from approx. 150 meters."

Carter laid the photo facedown on the table and lifted the next one in the stack.

This one was from much closer up—the opening of the cave was rough and jagged, and two divers' heads, wearing goggles and clamping down on snorkels, were off to one side. On the back, it said, "Mouth of cave," which was hardly necessary, but appended to it in parentheses was, "Did you know I could scuba dive?" Carter smiled. No, he hadn't known Russo could scuba dive.

The next few photos were from the interior of the cave and were clearly lighted by a high-intensity, handheld lamp. There was a bright, shadowy glare off of the wet walls and ceiling; the rock glittered like pyrite and diamond. But Carter could see nothing of the fossil.

He picked up the next shot—and this time his breath stopped in his throat. In the harsh, bright light shed by the lamp, which was partly visible in the upper left corner, he could now see the bones embedded in the rock. He'd seen thousands of such photos, of fossils from all over the globe, but never anything quite like this; the first thing he was reminded of, oddly enough, was Michelangelo's *Last Judgment,* painted on the Sistine Chapel. This fossil—its claws, or talons, or *fingers,* gnarled and distended—summoned up the writhing figures from the artist's vision of Hell. It was almost as if this creature—*there,* Carter thought, he'd just used the very word that Russo had resorted to—was *in extremis,* suffering beyond endurance, struggling to break free. A portion of its limb was detectable, or at least the vague outline of it was, but that was really all. And yet Carter still felt the most visceral and overwhelming reaction.

There were several more photos, from varying angles, but they revealed nothing more of the fossil; the rest of it was simply buried in the rock. In the next set of shots, the fossil itself was carefully draped and covered, while workers in wet suits actually demarcated a section of wall, drilled bore holes for pressure release, and with jackhammers, electric drills, and hand picks laboriously cut loose the rock. In the last of the on-site shots, a research vessel with a crane mounted on the rear deck was hauling away the slab of rock, now secured to a platform made from six huge yellow pontoons. Russo and the other diver, their masks off but still in their wet suits, stood on either side of the slab, their legs spread and their hands resting on the rock like big-game hunters being photographed with their trophy kill.

In the last photograph from the folder, the slab was seen in what appeared to be an open courtyard, under a plastic canopy, supported by what looked like half a dozen steel sawhorses. On the back, Russo had written, "Hall of Biological Sciences, University of Rome," and then the specimen statistics. "Fossil block measures 3.5 meters long, 3.5 meters wide, and 2.5 meters deep." Or, in feet, about ten by ten by seven. Its weight, measured in metric tons, was 1.25—or, in Carter's quick mental calculation, roughly 3300 pounds. By any standards a massive, and massively unwieldy, specimen.

Carter put the last photo down and picked up Russo's cover letter again. The final line said, "It is my considerable opinion that the unusual characteristics of this specimen suggest it may be of great, scientific importance."

You could say that again.

Carter leaned back in his chair and glanced at his watch. To his surprise, it was almost midnight already. And then his eye fell once more on the photo taken inside the cave, the one where the creature seemed to be clawing its way out of the very rock. It was an image he knew he'd never be able to shake. He got up, turned off the lamp, and then, before going to bed, found himself stopping to turn the photo over so that it was face down on the table.

Now why, he wondered, vaguely disappointed in himself, had he done that?

SIX

•

"It must be difficult for you, coming back home after years away," Dr. Neumann said, touching her fingers together and studying Ezra with her carefully neutral gaze. "How is that going for you?"

How was it going for him? Fine, Ezra thought, just fine—as long as everyone stayed out of his way and left him alone to do what he had to do. "It's an adjustment," he said, figuring that was a perfectly okay response, neither negative nor positive.

"I'm sure it is." She smiled and stayed silent, but he knew that trick—it was one of her psychotherapeutic smiles, designed to bring you into her confidence, and the silence was supposed to become so awkward that you leaped in to fill it, revealing all sorts of secret stuff in the process. Nope, not much had changed, he reflected; even the abstract prints on her office walls, the low hum of the radiator unit, the positions of the two chairs they were now sitting in. He felt like he'd gone back in time, twenty years, to when he'd first had to see her. Right after the headmaster at the Horace Mann School had informed his parents that Ezra, despite his astronomically high scores on the IQ and standard achievement tests, was not, well, fitting in. Academically or socially.

"How are you getting along with your father? Has that improved any?"

"We keep out of each other's way," Ezra said, "as much as we can." Which was true—his father was either at his offices on Madison Avenue, wheeling and dealing for some small portion of the city that he didn't already own, or off at some society function that Kimberly had dragged him to.

"And you've got a stepmother, too, now, don't you? I think I remember reading in the paper that your father had remarried."

Now, Ezra thought, she was being disingenuous. Of course she knew his dad had remarried. She probably knew more about his comings and goings than he did; in all his time in Israel, Ezra had scrupulously avoided the New York newspapers, and he'd never let on to anyone, unless he had to, that he was Sam Metzger's son.

"Yes, he has got a new wife. Her name's Kimberly," he said, his fingers nervously twisting the top of the plastic bag in his lap. When, he wondered, would be the opportune time to broach the real reason he'd made this appointment?

"What's your relationship with her like?"

Ezra almost couldn't answer at all; he was so weary of all this, he didn't want to have to go through this drill, answer all these pointless questions about his family and his feelings and his future. He'd made this appointment because he was running out of his medications, and unless he could get the prescriptions refilled, he was going to have a very hard time concentrating on his work. Or getting to sleep. Or controlling his mood swings. He just needed some refills.

"She's all right. I don't see much of her, either." Then, because he thought this might go over well with the good doctor, and because he felt he had to show just a little more interest, he added, "It's more like having an older sister in the house. She's just a few years older than I am."

"Is that so?" Dr. Neumann said, nodding her head slowly. "How interesting."

Damn, Ezra thought. *She's interested.* Now he'd inadvertently opened up a whole new can of worms; Neumann would be able to milk that remark for several sessions. And when would he ever get her around to the point of *this* one?

"How do you think that's affected your relationship with your father? If you had to characterize Kimberly's effect on that, would you say that she's provided a bridge, or created a dam, between the two of you?"

"I've never thought of it in either of those terms," Ezra said, trying to keep the disdain out of his voice. He could see no end to this avenue of thought. Neumann could keep on coming up with dumb metaphors and pointless questions indefinitely. He fingered the bag on his lap once more, and this time Neumann deigned to take notice.

"I feel you're distracted, Ezra," she said with some asperity, "that there's something else we need to address and get out of the way. What's in the bag you're holding?"

Ezra tried not to appear too eager as he hastily untied the loop on the plastic bag. "These are the bottles from the medications I've been on while I was living in Israel," he said, taking out the bottles, their labels written in Hebrew on one side and English on the other, and putting them on the little table next to her chair. "All I need, I think, are some refills."

Dr. Neumann took her reading glasses off the table, put them on, then started picking up the prescription bottles. "Your doctor over there was named Stern?"

"Yes, Herschel Stern."

"I'll want to get in touch with him, and see his records."

"That's fine. I can give you his numbers."

"But I can probably refill these for now," she said, glancing at what he recognized was his Xanax bottle, "and we'll make any adjustments that we have to, once we've made some progress with our therapy."

As far as Ezra was concerned, they'd already made all the progress he was interested in. But now was not the time, he knew, to say so. As she reached for her pad and began to scrawl the new prescriptions, his heart soared.

Outside, Uncle Maury was leaning against the parking meter, having a smoke. "How'd it go?" he asked, tossing the cigarette into the gutter. "You finally sane?"

"I will be," Ezra said, brandishing the sheaf of prescriptions.

On the way home, they stopped at the first pharmacy they passed, and while his order was being filled, Ezra roamed around the store picking up all the other things on his list, from surgical gloves and isopropyl alcohol to Q-tips and talcum powder. The rest of the supplies he'd need—a drafting table and computer chair, acetates, X-Acto knives and sable brushes, a magnifying glass—had all been delivered that morning, and had only to be properly arranged and put to use. He could barely wait to begin.

At home, Ezra was delighted to discover that everyone was out; even Gertrude was grocery shopping or something. He hurried down the hall, locked his door behind him, and then immediately got to work rearranging the place. Aside from clearing away some things from the nightstand to make more room for his reading matter, he left the actual bedroom pretty much as it was.

The adjoining chamber, which had once been his playroom, was where he'd decided he'd do his actual work. First he emptied out the bookcase, which still contained most of his books from high school and college, everything from *Catcher in the Rye* to the *Norton Anthology,* and then he dragged the empty bookcase over to the window. When his reference collection arrived from Israel, he'd put it there.

Then, where the bookcase had been, he set up the drafting table; fortunately, it didn't take too much work: attaching the legs, getting the top elevated to just the right angle, clamping the lamp on. The drafting table and chair now stood away from the windows, as far from the natural light as they could be—and that was good. Sunlight could do a

lot of damage to materials as ancient as the ones he would
be working on.

Finally, he'd need something to hold his tools and
things, and his eye alighted on an old wooden chest that
had once contained his toys, next to the closet. He bent
down to open it and wasn't at all surprised to find his old
model planes and comic books and bongos—how he'd
driven his parents crazy with those!—still stuffed inside.
He closed the chest and dragged it over to the side of the
drafting table, put the bags of brushes and rubbing alcohol
and surgical gloves on top of it, and then stood back to assess his handiwork.

Not too bad, he thought. In fact, more than serviceable.

Now there was nothing standing in his way. He could
begin again on his work.

He went into the closet and reached up high on the top
shelf, behind the extra blankets. His fingers found the cardboard tube he'd hidden there and drew it down. Although
what the tube contained weighed very little—measurable
in ounces, not even pounds—that's not how it felt as he
cradled it in his arms. It felt as if he were holding something of unimaginable weight and significance. It felt as if
he had climbed to the very summit of Mount Sinai, and he
was holding in his hands the stone tablets once entrusted to
Moses himself.

For all he knew, he was.

SEVEN

Even though Carter's call wasn't due for another hour, Giuseppe Russo wasn't taking any chances; he was going to wait by the phone. Not that venturing outside right now would have been a very appealing prospect, anyway. It was dusk in Rome, and from the narrow windows of his office, on the top floor of the Hall of Biological Sciences, he could already see a huge bank of billowing clouds, dark and angry, buffeting the olive trees and sweeping over the ancient ruins on the Palatine Hill. The storm front had been blowing west from the Adriatic Sea for days, and now it appeared ready to unleash its fury.

Russo settled himself into the rickety desk chair—not an easy task, given his size and the frailty of the old oak chair—and lighted another Nazionali. God, he was tired. It was all he could do to trudge to his lectures every afternoon, and then back home at night. He couldn't even remember when he'd last had a decent night's sleep. No, that wasn't true. He could remember. It was the night before he'd ever laid eyes on the fossil from the cave. The fossil that now resided in the courtyard downstairs. And even though part of him believed that this find would make his reputation, another part, growing all the time, wished that he had never so much as heard of it.

He blew a cloud of smoke toward the faded velvet curtains; a few preliminary raindrops spattered the window. He couldn't understand it. He had been to dozens of dig sites; he had handled thousands of fossils and bone fragments, many of them human; but he had never felt anything like this. A nagging unease, a palpable sense of dread. Ever since his fingers had touched the wet talons, if that was indeed what they were, in the grotto of the Lago d'Avernus, his mind had been troubled and his spirits had fallen. At night, he tossed and turned in his bed, and his dreams, when they came at all, were nightmares. Several times he had walked in his sleep, something he hadn't done since he was a child—awakening once, curled up like a dog, under a table.

With a kitchen knife clutched in his hand.

He stubbed out the cigarette in the ashtray on his desk and closed his eyes for just a second. He had to consider how he was going to make his case to Carter, how he was going to persuade him to join in this vast but curious endeavor. The mounting wind rattled the windows in their lead casements, and the red velvet curtains rustled in the draft. Like a boat unmoored, his mind began to drift. The radiator in the corner hissed, giving off more noise than heat, but under these sounds he thought he heard something else: a distant, irregular clanging. The sound of metal striking stone. He tried to ignore it, but the sound was so persistent he knew he'd never be able to rest or concentrate until he'd found out what it was and put a stop to it. Where, he wondered, was Augusto, the custodian, and why hadn't he taken care of it?

Weary and annoyed, Russo went to the top of the stairs and listened again. The sound was definitely coming from below. The stairs were worn marble and elegantly curved, a reminder that the building, now a part of the university, had been erected centuries ago as a private palace for a Medici descendant. Right now as darkness fell on a Saturday night, it was deserted and only a few overhead lights were left on;

it would be Russo's job—or Augusto's, if he was even still here—to turn them off before leaving.

Russo hated to stray so far from the phone, but the clanging sound came again, and he had to make sure it was nothing serious. He lumbered down the stairs, one hand on the finely wrought iron railing, and into the large vestibule on the ground floor. There was no sign of Augusto, or anyone, but the great arched doors that led to the courtyard were open and creaking in the wet wind.

The clanging came again—and from within the courtyard.

Russo buttoned his cardigan, noticing he had left some cigarette ash on its front, and pushed one of the heavy doors open wider.

The massive black block of stone brooded in the center of the interior courtyard, resting on half a dozen steel sawhorses. A huge blue plastic canopy hung above it, flapping and whipping in the wind. One of the cable lines holding the canopy in place had come loose and it was blowing wildly, banging its metal clip against the side of the stone.

At least the mystery had been solved.

But Russo knew that he couldn't let the cable remain loose, especially as it could cause some damage to the stone.

He stepped reluctantly into the courtyard, the cold wind scouring his face, and approached the block. As he did, he had the unmistakable sense that he was not alone, that there was someone else in the empty courtyard, and his eyes swept the gloomy colonnades on either side.

"Augusto?" he called out. "Are you there?"

But no one answered.

The cable smacked against the cobblestones so hard it threw off a bright blue spark. He reached to grab it, but the wind picked up and the line flew away from his hand. He'd have to be careful. He waited a few seconds, bending down, then reached out again and this time snagged it. He was reminded of a snake charmer he'd once seen grabbing a hissing cobra by its throat.

"*Rompi . . . la pietra.*" Break the stone.

He froze in place, still bent over, the cable in his hand. His head was just a few inches from the fossil, and the words, he could have sworn, had emanated from inside the stone.

But that was impossible.

He secured the metal clip of the cable line to a bolt in the cobblestoned floor, then pressed his foot down hard on top of the bolt to make sure it was deeply rooted.

The rain had begun to fall, pattering on the plastic canopy and driven sideways by gusts of wind captured in the courtyard. The stone grew damp.

He was about to leave when something made him stop and turn back.

He bent his head closer to the surface of the stone, like a doctor listening to a patient's heartbeat. The rock was cold and wet against his cheek.

"Break the stone."

His head instinctively jerked back, his heart pounding. This time the voice had been unmistakable. In the dim light of the courtyard, he could see the bony talons now, and they were no longer fused to the stone—they flexed—and, as he watched in horror, the crown of something's head— round and wet and smooth—also pressed itself outward, as if it were being born. He tried to step back, but it was too late—his sleeve was caught in the creature's claw, and he was being drawn toward the glistening rock. Toward the head that was now emerging and turning its stony eyes upon him. He groaned in terror and heard, as if from miles away, a ringing sound.

The red velvet curtains stirred.

And the ringing came again.

Rain slashed against the casement windows.

He stared out, his eyes wide, as lightning flashed white above the Palatine Hill.

The phone, on his desk, rang a third time.

He'd been asleep. His hand fumbled for the receiver. *"Pronto."*

"Professor Russo?"

He could still hear that voice—sepulchral, persuasive— from inside the stone.

"Joe? You there?" It was Carter. "Can you hear me?"

"Yes, Bones. I can hear you."

"Well, you might sound a little more enthusiastic about it."

Russo shook himself free of the dream and sat up in the creaking chair.

"Especially since I've just spent half the night going over your lab reports and photos."

"You have?" Russo said. He tried to light another cigarette, but his hands were shaking too much.

"Yes. And it looks like you might really have an amazing find on your hands."

"That is what I think, too."

"But there's a lot I don't understand. For one thing, it looks like you've done everything by the book—all the tests, on the fossil, the rock itself—"

"We have."

"—but none of your results make any sense at all."

In a way, Russo was relieved to hear someone else say it.

"And I don't need to tell you," Carter continued, "there might be a lot of trapped gas inside that specimen. You're going to need a good mineralogist to help you figure out how to get that fossil free."

Break the stone.

"You said in your letter that you're not equipped to do accelerated mass spectrometry there?"

"No, we are not." This was just the opening Russo had been looking for. "But at the New York University, you do have this equipment?"

"Oh yeah."

"And magnetic resonance imaging—in an open environment. You have that, too?"

"It could be arranged."

"And what of lasers? Argon-based?"

Carter paused. "They could be had on loan. Why?"

Russo hesitated, then plunged ahead. "Because, my friend, then I will come to you."

"What do you mean? Without the actual fossil, here in New York—"

"I will come to you *with* the fossil. Just as it is, inside the stone. And we will find a way to free it."

"They'll let you do that?" There was surprise in his voice, and the tiniest hint of excitement. "A discovery of this magnitude?"

"I have explained that you are the only man in the world who can do this work, and who can tell us what we have found."

There was a stunned silence on the other end of the line, and Russo could only imagine all the thoughts swirling through Carter's head. Finally, he said, "Joe, this is unbelievable."

Russo chuckled. "What is it you say—just like the old times?"

"Close enough," Carter replied.

For the next half hour, they discussed logistical matters, scheduling, and lab requirements, and by the time Russo dropped the receiver back into its cradle, it was completely dark outside, and the storm had settled into a steady downpour.

But he had what he wanted.

Now he just wanted to go home, take a hot shower, and have something to eat.

He took his old raincoat from the hook on the back of the door, locked up, and started down the stairs. Odd, how much it felt like he'd just gone down them. But that had been a dream . . . a nightmare. He ought to be used to that by now.

In the vestibule, he stopped to put up his collar and take his umbrella from the stand by the door; it was the only one left there. He could hear the rain gurgling through the gutters of the Via del Corso outside. There was a light on now in the receptionist's office, and a moment later Augusto came out carrying a wastebasket over to a large bin in the hall.

"Oh, there you are," Russo said to the old man. "Did you hear a clanging sound earlier, from the courtyard?"

"Yes, professor. It was one of the cables outside. I put it back in the ground."

How had his dream, Russo wondered, been so accurate? "Good. Thank you. If it happens again—"

"No," Augusto replied, shaking his head. "I am not going out there again."

"But you already did."

"No," he said, dumping the wastebasket and looking away, "I am not going out there again." He set his jaw and went back into the receptionist's office.

This was so unlike Augusto—usually so deferential and polite—but after thinking it over, Russo decided not to question him further. He opened the door to the dark and narrow street outside and unfurled his umbrella. No, it was better just to let it go. The wind caught his umbrella and nearly tore it from his hand. Besides, he thought, he might not want to hear what Augusto had to tell him.

EIGHT

The next week was a hectic one for Carter. Russo, it turned out, was moving forward with uncharacteristic speed, and Carter had to scramble to keep up.

First, Russo had procured a temporary export permit from L'Accademia di Scienza, and then, with this permission in hand, he'd enlisted the help of the Italian military, which was going to use one of its own cargo planes to ferry the fossil from an air force base in Frascati, just southeast of Rome, to New York's Kennedy Airport. In a country where the red tape was legendary, Russo had not only managed to cut right through it, but he'd done it in record time. What, Carter had to wonder, was actually the big hurry? Russo was acting as if he couldn't wait to get this specimen to New York.

On Carter's end, there was still a lot of lobbying and a lot of legwork to do at NYU. First thing Monday morning, Carter sent the photos and the appendices to the department chairman, Dr. Stanley Mackie, and that afternoon, he stopped in at his office. Mackie was as famous for his bushy white eyebrows, which had apparently been growing untended for half a century, as he was for his finds in the Olduvai Gorge in the late 1960s. When Carter briefly outlined Russo's plans to send his specimen to NYU, Mackie's eyebrows soared even higher.

"He wants to share something that he believes might be this remarkable? Why on earth would he want to do that?"

"We've worked together before, in Sicily—"

"Where you discovered the Well of the Bones."

"Yes. And Professor Russo was a great help."

"Still," Mackie said, "in all my years in this profession, I could count on the fingers of one hand the number of times a paleontologist, anthropologist, or archaeologist has ever *voluntarily* shared the credit for anything. In my experience, it's always been a matter of *stealing* credit wherever possible, not dividing it up."

Carter didn't know how to answer that; the chairman was right. Anyone who thought the academic establishment was any less cutthroat than the corporate world was sadly mistaken, as Carter had learned the hard way early on. Twice he'd had to share credit on scientific papers with professors who'd nominally headed up the field missions he'd been on, even though the finds and the conclusions drawn in the papers had been entirely his own.

Dr. Mackie didn't wait for him to reply. "Of course, it's always *possible* that this Russo is simply an honest man and a diligent seeker after truth." He said it as if he were suggesting there might be something, after all, to all this talk of the tooth fairy. "But from what I've read in these lab reports, and what I can see in the photos, he's also quite possibly the victim of a hoax."

A hoax? Is that what Mackie had been getting at? Carter was stunned.

"Giuseppe Russo is one of the most dependable and brilliant scientists I've ever worked with," Carter said.

"Brilliant men have been fooled before."

"And everything in this folder indicates he's proceeded exactly the way he should have."

"But look at his results. You've admitted it yourself, they don't make any sense."

"With the right technological assistance—an AMS analysis, for instance—maybe they will."

"So is that what you're asking for? My okay to do mass spectrometry, laser analysis, the whole works?"

"Yes. Among other things."

Mackie leaned back in his chair. He didn't say yes and he didn't say no, but when he finally said, "And what else are you asking for?" Carter took it as a tacit okay.

"A work space."

"What's wrong with the biological sciences lab? You've got full privileges there."

"Yes, but I need absolute security and privacy to do this work right." For one thing, though he didn't want to say so, he needed to be sure Bill Mitchell wouldn't go poking around in it, the way he'd done with the recently donated samples. "And for another, I'm going to need space—lots of it—for the specimen, and for the machinery I'm going to need to perform the tests on it."

Mackie nodded his head, grudgingly. "Something tells me you've already got somewhere in mind."

"I do. Right now it's a storage area right off the loading dock in the back of the bio building. It's easily accessible and it's on the first floor, so bringing in the slab and the machines will be relatively easy. It's also got double-padlocked steel doors to the street outside."

"I doubt anyone's going to try to make off with a slab of rock that weighs over three thousand pounds."

"This *is* New York."

Even Mackie had to smile. "I don't want to hear that this little hobby of yours has detracted in any way from your teaching duties."

"It won't."

"And I don't want this whole thing to blow up in our faces."

If only he knew what he was saying, Carter thought; the one thing he'd studiously avoided going into was the volatility of the gases trapped in the rock, and Mackie apparently hadn't studied the materials closely enough to figure it out for himself.

"I'm still of the opinion," Mackie concluded, "that this

so-called fossil is not what it seems. If you ask me, we're looking at Italy's answer to the Cardiff giant."

Or, Carter thought, the missing link between the dinosaurs and modern birds. Those talons could turn out to be hugely important.

"And if that's indeed what it turns out to be," Mackie said, "I don't want it to leave any blot on the escutcheon of this university."

"Your escutcheon's safe with me."

Mackie looked at him from under his Olympian brow, and with no trace of levity in his voice said, "It had better be, Professor Cox."

With Dr. Mackie's grudging approval of the project, along with a small grant from the department's discretionary funds at his disposal, Carter was off and running. At the bio building, he went looking for Hank, the head custodian, and found him in his "office"—a converted supply closet in the basement. Hank, his head bent over some close task, looked up when Carter poked his head in.

"What are you working on?" Carter said.

"Making a fishing lure," Hank said. "Going upstate this weekend."

"That's great," Carter said, "but I hope you'll be able to find a little time during the week to do something for me."

"Depends."

"You know that storage area on the first floor, near the loading dock?"

Carter could see from Hank's expression that this was already a no-sale.

"We've got a large specimen coming in, from overseas, and we're going to have to convert that space into a kind of makeshift lab."

Hank didn't say anything, but it was clear he didn't like what he'd heard so far.

"If you could get most of the junk in there cleared out— I don't care where," Carter persevered, "I could get you, say, an extra three hundred bucks."

Now Hank put the fishing lure down, and seemed to be considering it. "How about four?" he said.

Carter was expecting that. "If you can also rig up some extra lighting, I'll make it four. But it's got to be done before you go away."

Hank turned back to the lure. "Okay."

The way he was clearing these hurdles, Carter felt like an Olympic athlete. But in some ways, his next stop was going to be the hardest of them all. With Russo due to arrive in only a matter of days, there wasn't time to put it off. He had to bring Beth up to speed and fill her in on what he considered some of the trickier details.

Since it was only eleven-twenty and his first class wasn't until three, as soon as he left the bio building he hopped the subway uptown. Sitting beside him was a heavyset girl in a hooded sweatshirt studying the horoscope page in the back of a glossy magazine. From the intensity with which she was reading it, you'd have thought her life depended in some way on the predictions printed there. Carter ran into this sort of thing all the time, even among his own students, and it drove him crazy: the fascination with pseudoscience in all its many forms, from the zodiac to the Kabbalah, from feng shui to psychics, pyramid power to past-life regression. He'd actually had one student—of course she was from L.A.—who'd told him she was sure that they'd been lovers in a previous life. Fortunately, she'd dropped the course before trying to relive the past.

But it was a constant battle, trying to suck all this specious junk out of their heads and replace it with the genuine beauties of real science and authentic discoveries. There was so much in the world that was true and amazing and almost unbelievable itself that Carter could never understand the fascination with the obviously spurious and unsubstantiated. In his own life he'd found the mysteries of biology and evolution, of the immensity of geologic time and the rise of humanity (did people comprehend just how easily things could have gone a different way altogether?) as satisfying to his sense of wonder, to the reach and power of his imagination, as anything the mystics and TV mediums, the astrologers and New Age prophets could cook up. And he really feared that unless this mindless flood was stopped somehow, its waters would wash over the real ground that scientific inquiry had labored to claim through centuries of exhaustive work and leave everything one vast, muddy, undifferentiated terrain.

But try telling that, he thought, to the girl sucking up her horoscope in the next seat.

At Fifty-ninth Street he got off and strolled over toward Park Avenue. For late October it was unseasonably warm—Indian summer—and he unzipped his leather jacket as he walked. Uptown, there was a definite change in the look of the people on the street; up here, unlike the Village, they were dressed for business, dressed to impress, dressed to make deals. The men wore suits and carried slim leather attachés and spoke into tiny cell phones; the women wore expensive outfits with glints of discreet but genuine jewelry at their wrists and ears and throats. Whenever Carter came up here to what he thought of as Beth's world, he felt a little out of place, a little too downtown and academic to quite fit in.

The Raleigh Gallery, where she worked, only made things worse. Nestled on the first two floors of an Italianate building on East Fifty-seventh, under a rich red awning that extended halfway across the busy sidewalk, it was the kind of place tycoons and society types came, often with their own experts in tow, to view the Constable that had been lurking for decades in someone's country home, or a Claude Poussin sketch that had mysteriously come to light in a Swiss vault. Living with Beth had afforded Carter a secondhand but very rich education in the history of European art—and an appreciation of its staggering value. A white-gloved attendant held the door for him as he entered, and nodded when he recognized him.

"Your wife's upstairs with a client," he said.

"Thanks."

As Carter walked through the main gallery, he noticed several new paintings hanging in ornate frames on the

walls; the most remarkable was a portrait of a Dutch
burgher in a rich fur-collared cloak.

"That burgher, I'll have you know, was once thought to
be by Rembrandt."

Before turning around, Carter knew who was talking—
Richard Raleigh, né Ricky Radnitz—who'd lost, along
with his name, his Long Island accent; he now sounded
like he'd grown up in the Mayfair district of London.

"Morning," Carter said. "I was in the neighborhood,
and I thought I'd surprise Beth."

"If you ask me," Raleigh said, putting his arm through
Carter's and drawing him back toward the painting, "it
should *still* be attributed to Rembrandt. Look at the
brushwork—closely—look at the details of costume.
What student of his was ever that good?"

Carter, of course, didn't know of any, and he really
didn't care; all he wanted to do was get upstairs, fetch
Beth, and see if she had time for lunch in Central Park—
which he thought would be the perfect setting to tell her
about Russo's imminent arrival.

"It does look awfully good to me," Carter said, "but I'm
more used to judging bones than paintings."

"That's right. You specialize in even older things than I
do," Raleigh said, with a thin smile. He was a small man,
dapper, and Beth had let slip to Carter that the gray in his
temples was actually brushed in there by his hairdresser;
Raleigh thought it made him look more distinguished and
trustworthy.

"The doorman mentioned that Beth is upstairs?" Carter
said, discreetly disengaging his arm.

"You know what the difference is between an unchal-
lenged attribution and a 'school of'?"

"Not offhand."

"Millions, my boy, millions. An oil like this? You're
talking fifteen, twenty million dollars' difference."

"Interesting," Carter said, still trying to move toward
the stairs.

"Beth is with a new client," Raleigh cautioned. "I'll have

to ask you not to disturb her, if she's still consulting with him."

So that was it; Carter had had the distinct impression that Raleigh was trying to delay him, and now he knew why. Beth was Raleigh's star representative, the feather in his cap; Raleigh did a brilliant job of assessing the market and cosseting his wealthy customers, but it was Beth who provided the true expertise and the in-depth knowledge of the works, their creators, and their provenance.

"I'll just pretend to be a customer."

"No one would believe you," Raleigh said over his shoulder as he moved swiftly toward the door where some rich young society type was wafting in. "Mrs. Metzger!" he crooned. "I'm so glad you were able to stop by!"

Hanging onto the brass banister, Carter went up the wide, red-carpeted staircase, past a mezzanine area where the offices were tucked away, and then around the landing to a second set of stairs that led to the upper gallery. He could hear Beth's voice before he saw her, and she was saying something about draftsmanship.

At the entryway to the gallery, he stopped, still concealed in the shadows of the stairwell. Beth had her back to him, and her client stood beside her. She was wearing her usual office attire—a slim black pantsuit with a white silk blouse, a black ribbon tying her hair in a short ponytail behind. She called it her tuxedo, and said she wore it for the same reason men did—to blend into the background. The guy beside her wouldn't have blended in anywhere; he was tall and solid, with short, bristly blond hair, and wore a long trench coat made of some shiny, seemingly metallic fabric.

As Beth pointed out certain things about the drawings that were spread out before them on the oblong table, Carter couldn't help but notice that the man spent much more time studying Beth than he did the artworks. Carter couldn't blame him . . . but that didn't mean he liked it any better. Maybe this was part of the reason Raleigh had arranged for Beth to deal with this particular customer, and in the relative privacy of the upper gallery. Maybe he was counting on a little sexual chemistry to clinch a deal for the gallery today.

"The great virtue of drawings," Beth was saying, "especially when they're studies and sketches, is that you can see the artist's hand moving freely, quickly, improvising, trying things out."

The man reached toward her face, and brushed what Carter assumed was a strand of hair away from her cheek.

Beth stopped, looking momentarily flustered.

"Your hair was keeping me from seeing your eyes," the man said.

"Um, thanks. But maybe we should just focus on the drawings."

Carter took that as his cue—he certainly didn't need to wait for another—and, clearing his throat noisily, entered the gallery. "Hope I'm not interrupting a negotiation," he declared.

"What a surprise," Beth said, relief filling her voice.

Carter put an arm around her and kissed her on the cheek, then turned to the customer with his hand extended. "Carter Cox, Beth's husband."

"Bradley Hoyt," the man said, shaking Carter's hand.

"Mr. Hoyt is starting a collection of Old Master drawings," Beth explained.

"And Beth's making sure I buy only the right stuff."

"You couldn't ask for a better advisor," Carter said, giving her shoulders a squeeze. "But why Old Masters?" Carter said, his eyes now taking in, at closer range, the peculiar gray-green sheen of the trench coat.

"All my friends are buying big stuff, new stuff, but the prices are going sky-high now. I mean, I can certainly afford to play that game too, but I don't like to buy things where the upside's already been exploited. I like to buy stuff where the profit potential is still there."

"And that holds true," Carter said, glancing at the drawings on the table, "for these?"

"So Beth tells me," the man said, with a big smile that revealed perfect, white, Chiclet-sized teeth. "It's a classy kind of investment, too."

Carter suddenly realized what the coat was made of. "Is that some sort of lizard skin?"

"Close. It's crocodile."

"The whole thing?" Carter had seen crocodile belts, wristwatch bands, wallets. But a trench coat that fell nearly to a man's ankles?

"Yep. Sumatran croc."

"I've never seen anything like it," Carter said.

"At what they cost, you probably never will." His eyes flicked over to Beth, presumably to see if this further token of his wealth had properly registered.

But Beth was oblivious; she spent most of every working day with people who had more money than they knew what to do with, and the effect, Carter knew, had long since worn off.

"So, what do you do?" Bradley asked Carter.

"I teach."

"High school?"

"No. Grammar school."

Beth looked puzzled.

"What grade?" Bradley asked.

"First. I think the kids have got so much more upside potential at that age."

Now she'd figured it out, and she wasn't crazy about it. "Mr. Hoyt," she said, butting in, "I think we've pretty much covered everything the gallery has in its collection right now. Perhaps you should think things over"—she handed him a glossy catalog from the table—"and come back again when you've narrowed your choices."

Hoyt took the catalog, rolled it up, and slipped it into the side pocket of his coat.

"It was nice to meet you," Carter said.

"Yeah, you too," Bradley replied.

"I'll just put these things away now," Beth said. "Thank you for coming in, Mr. Hoyt."

Finally getting the message, Hoyt turned and left, his heels clicking across the parquet floor. He had on boots, Carter noticed, as he headed down the stairs. Probably fashioned from some other rare and endangered species.

Beth gathered the drawings together and slipped them back into the proper portfolios. When she was sure they were alone, she turned to Carter and said, "First grade?"

"Disinformation, to fool the enemy."

"He's the enemy?"

"Could be. I saw the way he was looking at you."

"Oh, please," she said, smiling. "If that kind of thing bothers you, you'll be handing out disinformation all day."

He laughed, and put his arms around her.

"You do know that they've got video cameras all over this room?" she said.

"What do I care?" he said, kissing her. When he let it linger too long, Beth got embarrassed and pushed him away.

"I care," she said. "I've got to face these people every day."

"Then let's go to lunch. My treat."

"Rumpelmayer's?"

"Central Park, the lake. It's beautiful outside."

On the way to the park, they stopped at a deli and picked up sandwiches and drinks. But their favorite bench overlooking the little lake on Central Park South was already taken; so were all the other benches, in fact. "I guess I wasn't the only one with this idea," Carter said.

They found a place to sit on a big flat rock, just off the pathway, and spread out their lunch there. While Carter twisted the top off Beth's bottle of Snapple, she said, "So you never did tell me—what were you doing uptown today?"

"Seeing you for lunch." He handed her the open bottle.

"Really?" Beth said, smiling but skeptical. She took a sip from the bottle, then carefully placed it on the rock. "So, walking all the way to the park to have this little picnic . . ."

"Yes?"

"This was all just a spontaneous display of your affection?"

"Absolutely."

She took a bite of her sandwich, chewed it slowly, put the sandwich back down on the wrapper, and said, "Okay, I can't stand the suspense anymore. How bad is it?"

"What?

"The problem you're about to tell me about."

Carter feigned indignation. "A guy can't surprise his wife with a romantic lunch on a beautiful autumn day?"

"Not when it's a guy who thinks he's crossing the Rubicon when he goes above Fourteenth Street. You don't make that trip unless it's for a darn good reason."

Why, Carter thought, did he ever think he could sneak one past her? But no point in dragging it out now. "I did have one piece of good news to share with you," he confessed. "Remember that package I had from Joe Russo?"

"Of course. You told me all about his big discovery."

"Well, in a few days he'll be able to tell you all about it himself. He's coming to New York."

"That's great. I'd love to meet him." Acting as if the danger had passed, she picked up her sandwich again and took a big bite.

Carter plunged ahead. "That should be no problem," he said. "In fact, he needs a place to stay while he's here."

Her jaw stopped moving midchew.

"And I told him it'd be okay to crash at our place."

She swallowed. "Where? In case you haven't noticed, we don't have a guest room."

"He's not particular. The sofa in the living room will do."

"That sofa's not even comfortable to sit on."

"He's slept on worse. In Sicily, we slept on rocks and scorpions."

Beth blew out a sigh, and Carter knew she was already giving in to the idea. "How long will it be for? A week or two?"

"I don't really know," Carter said. "Maybe more. Depends on how long it takes us to finish our work."

"What work?"

"Didn't I mention that? He's bringing the fossil to New York with him. We're going to work on it, here, together."

"He's bringing that massive fossil you told me about—"

"Over three thousand pounds!"

"—all the way to Manhattan? Just so you can work on it together, like old times?"

"That's exactly what he said. Almost."

Carter knew he was asking a lot—Beth liked her privacy, especially lately, while they worked on the baby issue—but he also knew she'd never do anything to stand in the way of his work. One of the thousand and one reasons he loved her so.

"Anything else I should know?" she finally said.

"Well, he's built on kind of a grand scale. He smokes like a chimney—but I'll tell him not to in the apartment—and he never has any money."

"I like him already."

Carter laughed and threw an arm around her shoulders. "And weren't you the one who said you wanted to hear the patter of little feet around the apartment?"

"*Little* feet," she replied. "The operative word was *little.*"

"Oh," Carter said, "sorry. How about if I tell him to tiptoe?"

NINE

All day long he had encountered nothing but resistance, interference, and meddling. Why, Ezra wondered, couldn't they just leave him alone, stay out of his way and let him do the work that he, and he alone, had been destined to do?

It had started at Dr. Neumann's office where, the moment he sat down, he noticed the telltale letterhead of Dr. Herschel Stern, his psychiatrist in Jerusalem, on a batch of papers in her lap. So, she'd been in touch with him, after all. He knew what was coming even before she mentioned the words *Jerusalem syndrome*.

"I'm sure you've heard of it," she said. "In fact, I believe Dr. Stern discussed it with you?"

"He might have."

She pressed on. "It's an affliction that befalls certain people—evangelicals, religious laypeople, scholars like yourself—who come to the Holy Land and become overwhelmed by it. They are so absorbed, so moved, so changed by the experience that they become, to some extent, delusional. In the most extreme cases, they become convinced that they are, for instance, the Messiah."

"Yes, I'm aware of the syndrome," Ezra replied, "and no, I am not suffering from it. Trust me, I know I am not the Messiah, Moses, or the Angel of Death."

"I'm only mentioning it as a preface," Dr. Neumann replied. "There are other kinds of disturbances"—she uttered that last word, Ezra noted, with the same caution with which she'd used *delusional* a moment ago—"that can also crop up there. It's very fertile ground, very potent, and Dr. Stern has written me and told me a little bit about your work in Israel. I must say, it's no wonder you began to feel a certain strain."

"Did the good doctor also inform you of the difficulties I got into? With the authorities?" Ezra had no particular desire to go into it himself, but he felt he might as well find out exactly how much she knew.

Dr. Neumann paused, as if she wasn't sure how much of her hand she should show yet.

"The Dome of the Rock?" Ezra prompted her.

"Yes," she finally admitted.

Ah, so he'd told her that, too.

The Dome of the Rock, the holy Muslim shrine, erected above the ruins of the Second Temple. That was the key. Ezra had read the scrolls, and he knew what they were saying. No one else ever had, no one else had ever put it all together. He knew that if he could burrow, unobstructed, into the foundations below the dome, he could find there the most holy relic in all the universe. In fact, he'd almost succeeded. He'd found the subterranean tunnel; he'd seen the clay tablet sealing the aperture; and he had heard, in the chamber within, the sound of all the winds in the world.

The rumbling groan of a living, breathing God.

The sound of Creation itself.

But it was then, before he could get any closer, that the Israeli security agents had grabbed hold of his ankles and dragged him out.

It was a sound that still sometimes filled his ears.

"I'm concerned that your work here, the work you're doing in New York, is tied to the work you were pursuing there. Some of the things you said at the time of your arrest"—and here she'd stopped to put on her reading glasses and refer to her notes—"are powerful, and troubling. 'I've communed with angels.' 'Creation can be unlocked.' 'I can show you the face of God.' " She took off her glasses and looked at him. "You're a very intelligent man, Ezra, so I need hardly point out to you the nature of these comments—the self-aggrandizement, the epochal content and context, the messianic fervor. What do we do with those thoughts and those emotions? And even more to the point, do you still feel them?"

How was he supposed to answer that? On the one hand, he could lie, and keep Dr. Neumann where he wanted her—acting as his psychiatric parole officer, guaranteeing any authorities who asked after him that his delusional episodes were under control and that he, Ezra, was no longer a threat to anyone, and certainly not to the sovereign state of Israel. Or, on the other hand, he could tell the truth—he could tell her what the stolen scroll was gradually revealing to him—and risk being committed to some institution where the only rolled-up paper he'd ever see again would be the toilet tissue.

It wasn't a tough call.

"The change of scene has done me good," he said. "Here, in my old rooms, in New York City, I feel a lot more relaxed. I don't feel any of that mania I experienced in the Middle East."

She gave him a fishy look. He hadn't sold her.

"And the voices? Of angels?"

"I never claimed that it was angels who actually talked to me. Even at my worst, I never said that."

But she wouldn't let him duck the question. "Whatever you believed the voices were, do you still hear them? You have to tell me, Ezra, if you are still experiencing auditory hallucinations. Otherwise, it's very hard for me to help you."

That, he thought, was worth a laugh. The very idea that Dr. Neumann could offer him any help at all, apart from keeping his prescriptions filled, was a joke.

"No, I'm not having any hallucinations," he said, once

again carefully skirting the truth. "Everything I hear, and see, is real."

From the look on her face, his powers of persuasion still needed work.

As did his patience. Sitting, now, in the dining room of the Sutton Place apartment, it was all he could do not to bolt from his chair. But the price of living here, Ezra reminded himself, was enduring the occasional scene like this.

His father sat at the head of the table, in a silk smoking jacket—since when had he started wearing those?—and Kimberly sat at the other end, with her perfect hair and makeup and outfit. Ezra was stuck in the middle, and in jeans and a Gap sweatshirt he was feeling distinctly underdressed.

Gertrude put the bowl of sautéed potatoes and onions down by Ezra's elbow—"Eat all you want," she said, "but save room for dessert"—then turned back toward the kitchen door.

"That will be all, Gertrude," Kimberly said, quite unnecessarily, as the door had already swung shut behind her.

Ezra took some of the potatoes and onions, then tried to pass them to Kimberly, who held up her hand as if he were trying to pass her a bowl of rancid milk. He handed them instead to his father, who had to pull back on the sleeve of his too-tight smoking jacket in order to reach them.

"I had a chance to talk to somebody in the Israeli embassy today," Sam said, portentously.

Ezra kept his head down and ate his veal and potatoes.

"They're not going to pursue the matter," Sam said.

"What matter?" Kimberly asked, sipping her wine.

"The matter of Ezra's criminal trespass."

Here it came. First Dr. Neumann, and now his father. Was anyone ever going to let it go?

"Criminal trespass? Where?" She looked at Ezra with what might have passed, if he hadn't known better, for maternal concern. "What's this all about?"

"You want to answer that, Ezra?" his father echoed.

"If you spoke to the embassy, then you already know all about it."

"I want to hear it from you."

Ezra took another quick bite—there was no telling how much longer he'd be at the table—then said, "I knew what I was doing."

"Don't you always," Sam replied acidly.

"They've got so many rules and regulations over there about where you can go, what you can do, who you can talk to, that if you observed them all, you'd never get anything done."

"Don't you think that maybe, just maybe, they have all those rules for a reason? That maybe the government of Israel knows more about how to run things than you do?"

"They know how to run a government—and even that's debatable—but they don't know a damn thing about what I do."

"And what is that, Ezra?" Kimberly interjected. "I've never been exactly sure."

Ezra turned toward her; for once, he thought she was actually speaking the truth. She didn't know, and even if he told her, in a million years she would never understand. Still, he had to say something. "I look for answers to the big questions."

"What kind of questions?"

"The biggest. Why are we here? Is there some purpose? Is there a God, and if there is, how can we discover what he wants from us?"

"Those *are* big questions," Kimberly said.

"But you're not going to find the answers," Sam interjected, "skulking around in the middle of the night at highly restricted holy sites. That whole country is a tinderbox, and somebody like you, doing whatever he wants, paying no attention to the authorities, can inadvertently blow the place sky-high. It's a lucky thing you didn't."

"There was never any danger of that."

"That's not what the Israelis think. If I hadn't pulled the strings I did and gotten you out of there, you'd be sitting in a jail cell in Jerusalem right now."

That much, Ezra had to concede, was probably true. The problems he'd had with the directors of the Feldstein Institute paled in comparison with the trouble he'd stepped into at the Dome of the Rock.

"It might interest you to know," Sam went on, "that I'll be making a substantial contribution to the re-election campaign of the mayor of Jerusalem."

"Maybe you can swing a real estate deal there," Ezra said, and regretted it even before his father's fist had hit the table so hard that a lighted candle fell out of its holder.

"You think this is some joke?" Sam shouted, his face turning the crimson of his jacket.

Kimberly grabbed for the hot candle rolling across the tablecloth.

"You think I'm always going to be around to clean up your messes, to bail you out and make things right? What the hell is wrong with you?"

Ezra wiped his mouth, folded his napkin over, and put it on the table.

"Answer me!"

"I assumed that it was a rhetorical question," Ezra replied.

His father looked apoplectic.

"Sam, your heart! Calm down," Kimberly said.

"What do you care?" Ezra said to her. "You waited around for my mother to die, now you've just got one to go."

"You lousy son-of-a—" Sam shouted, jumping up, but Ezra was too fast. He was out of the room and halfway down the hall before his father had unsnagged the sleeve of his jacket from the arm of his chair. He could hear Kimberly trying to settle him down with "Let him go" and "Don't make this worse than it is." For perhaps the first time in his life, and wouldn't you know it was right after he'd insulted her, he was actually grateful for Kimberly's presence.

When he got to his room he locked the door and waited, breathing hard, to hear if he was being followed. How old was he, he thought? Thirty years old, and here he was, acting like some grade school kid running from a spanking. He put his ear to the door, but the apartment was so vast, and the dining room so far away, he couldn't hear a thing. What had just happened? What had he just said? He could hardly believe it himself. He'd been so careful, so far, to mind his manners and stay out of everyone's way, and now, in a couple of minutes, he'd blown the whole thing. Not that he cared all that much about his rapport with Kimberly; that had never been great. And his relationship with his father had been deteriorating for years. But what he did want was a safe haven, a place to do his work unmolested, unhampered—and until a minute ago he'd had it. Had he just chucked all that out the window with a few ill-considered, inflammatory remarks?

At least it appeared the battle was over; no one was banging on his door. But his heart was racing and he could feel the blood pounding in his temples. He had to calm down, especially if he still had any intention of working that night. He went into the bathroom, threw open the medicine chest, and took a couple of the Xanax he had gotten Dr. Neumann to represcribe. He swallowed a couple of the quarter-milligram tablets, went back into the bedroom, and flopped down on the edge of the bed. In fifteen or twenty minutes, he'd start to feel the effects.

He shouldn't have made that remark to Kimberly, about her waiting for Sam to die, too. Until that point the situation had been salvageable. But among the many things he'd never forgiven his father for, Kimberly was at the top of his list. While Ezra's mother had been suffering through years of surgery and chemotherapy, his father had been increasingly remote, even uninterested, and it fell to Ezra—and even his Uncle Maury—to be there for her, to comfort and take care of her. In fact, on the night she died in her private room at Sloan-Kettering, Sam was nowhere to be found; Ezra had called home, had spoken to Sam's secretary at his office, had called the Metropolitan Club, but Sam was missing in action. Later, he learned that his father had been holed up at Kimberly's place, a tidy little maisonette he had purchased for her on Beekman Place. While Ezra's mom was breathing her last, Sam was probably breathing hard over his very accommodating advertising exec.

But as he calmed down and took stock of the situation, Ezra realized that if he kept the lowest profile imaginable, and maybe even found a way to apologize (though how could you ever really claim you hadn't meant to say something so pointed?), he might be able to hang onto his little sinecure. He'd had plenty of blowups as bad as this one over the years with his father, and his stepmother would probably be as anxious as he was to pretend it had never happened; it wouldn't do her any good to be perceived as having come between Sam and his son, no matter how estranged they were. And while Ezra recognized that most sane people in his shoes would be moving out and finding a new place to live, for him it wasn't that easy. It wasn't as if he had money of his own, or even a credit card; everything came from Sam, doled out by one of the drones in his business accounts office, and the last thing Ezra wanted to do was stir things up and have to ask for a new deal. Sam might let him be if he stayed where he was, comfortably under the radar, but if he started asking for more, it could get tricky. His father might even cut him off completely and demand that he get a job.

And as far as Ezra was concerned, he already had a job—the most important one in the world.

As the Xanax took hold, and afforded him this new and more serene perspective, he felt himself relaxing enough to think again about that job—and the work he'd been planning to do that very night. The house was quiet now—for all he knew, his father and Kimberly had gone out somewhere—and nothing was standing in his way. He got up from the bed and walked to the French doors that opened onto the small balcony; he opened them and stepped outside. Far below, the taillights of traffic on the FDR made a bright red ribbon through the night, and across the river in Queens, a silver cross, barely visible, was illuminated high atop the bell tower of a church.

The night air was bracing. He felt ready to get to work. Stepping back inside, he shut the doors, then pulled both sets of curtains closed. He'd asked Gertrude to put up a second set so that no sunlight would penetrate the room; she'd looked at him quizzically, but done it.

In his workroom, he turned on the lamp attached to the drafting table, then knelt down by the toy chest and opened it with the key he'd found taped to its bottom. There, right where he'd concealed it, among the comics and bongos, lay the cardboard tube.

He popped the lid off one end of the tube and removed the cheap papyrus scrolls he'd bought at a gift shop just before leaving the Middle East. The top one was Anubis, the jackal-headed god, weighing the soul of a dead man. The next was Osiris, presiding over the creation of the earth and heavens. But it was the third, in its own cellophane wrapper, coiled around the others, that he was after—and this one he removed as delicately as he could. Tossing the other two scrolls aside, he laid this one reverently on the clean, flat surface of the drafting table; the surface of the table was tilted just a few degrees, to make his work easier.

Not that it would ever be that.

What he had in his hands, smuggled out of the archives of Hebrew University, where they had yet to be assembled, much less understood, were the fragments, the strips and bits, of a scroll undoubtedly more than two thousand years old. Scraps of parchment, some connected, some loose, together they constituted what Ezra was convinced was the most sought-after and elusive prize in all of biblical scholarship. Other scrolls from the Dead Sea that had already been pieced together, translated, and read alluded to this scroll. Indeed, there was an Ethiopic translation of it dating from the fourteenth century. But that version, in the estimation of most scholars, had been heavily edited over the centuries by church copyists; appalled by the relentlessly occult and speculative bent of the original Aramaic text, they had exercised their own judgment and cut out what offended them. No, not until now had anyone ever been in a position to piece back together the original, to decipher and read what had been known for millennia as the Lost Book of Enoch.

But then, no one had ever been looking for it among
the ancient scraps of routine documents—the bills of sale,
the marriage contracts, the business correspondence—
where Ezra had found it. Was it serendipity or something
more? Ezra often wondered. For there, buried in the detritus
that Ezra had first been assigned to catalog, he'd stumbled
upon this incomparable jewel. Had it been overlooked entirely, lost in the jumble of more mundane stuff? (The Cairo
Genizah alone, for instance, contained more than fifteen
thousand documents, many still to be studied, dating from
the eleventh to the thirteenth centuries.) Or—as Ezra had
come to suspect—had it been hidden there by some prede-
cessor, decades before, who for whatever reason had been
unable to complete his crime, or trumpet his discovery?
Scroll scholarship was rife with such skullduggery—which
might have been one reason Ezra felt so at home there.

Putting on a pair of the surgical gloves he'd bought, he
carefully unrolled the largest segment of the scroll that was
still intact, but even this was less than eighteen inches
across, and only an inch or two wide. The pale yellow
parchment, lying flat on the drafting table, was the color
and consistency of an autumn leaf that had been pressed
between the pages of a book long ago. A tissue-thin fila-
ment, it was probably papyrus, as were most of the scrolls,
but Ezra could not be completely sure; some of the earliest
finds had been on animal skins, scraped and pounded and
stretched until they were as smooth and fine as almost any
paper made today. If he hadn't had to leave Israel under
such short notice, fleeing like a thief in the night, he'd have
found a way to use the lab facilities at Hebrew U. or the institute to determine just what this text was written on.

But wasn't that just one more example, he thought, of
petty bureaucracy impeding the progress of human knowledge? Nothing made him angrier.

Still, this was no time to let anger get in his way. All
things considered, he'd done pretty well; he had his prize,
he had a place to work in private (tomorrow, he reminded
himself, he would have to start mending his fences), he had
no other pressing duties to take up his time. If left to his

own devices, he'd piece together and translate the lost scroll that, according to legend, made the Book of Revelation read like a fairy tale.

Carefully lifting another scrap of the parchment between his gloved fingers, he laid it on the table and gently flattened it with his fingertips. It was densely covered, as were all the fragments of the scroll, with the distinctive Aramaic script, which was darker, closer, more square than the more common paleo-Hebrew or Greek uncial. How did this piece of the scroll, ragged at all its edges, fit together with the rest, and what, once it was translated and properly placed in the body of the entire text, would it say? What would it tell us of the War in Heaven, the word of God, the Apocalypse?

As Ezra touched the edge of this small fragment to the longer strip to see if they were meant to connect, something flashed in front of his eyes, like a blue spark, and his fingertips suddenly tingled. He sat back and caught his breath.

Had that just happened?

He blinked and rubbed the tips of his fingers together. It wasn't a painful sensation, by any means, but it wasn't exactly pleasant, either. There was the faintest whiff of cordite in the air, and his fingers felt—and there was no better way to describe it—as if they'd just come into contact with a live electrical source.

TEN

When the alarm clock went off at seven-thirty on Saturday morning, Carter didn't understand it.

It was *Saturday*.

Still half-asleep, he rolled over toward Beth and slipped one arm under the blanket, around her waist. As his hand slid lower, she caught hold of his wrist.

"Aren't you forgetting something?' she mumbled, her eyes still closed.

"What?"

"You have an appointment—remember?"

Now it came to him. Nine o'clock sharp, at Dr. Weston's office. For the much-dreaded sperm test.

He withdrew his hand before things got any harder to undo, and Beth, perhaps to make it even easier, rolled away to the other side of the bed. Carter lay on his back, thinking about the next few hours. First, the test—then a trip out to Kennedy Airport. Russo's flight was due in that afternoon.

He rolled out of bed, padded barefoot across the hall and into the bathroom—Beth had bought him slippers, twice, but he never knew where they went—and flicked on the light. He was wearing only the plaid boxer shorts he slept in. Doctor's orders—only boxers would do.

After a quick shower and even quicker breakfast—coffee and a Pop-Tart—he caught the IRT uptown, arriving at the doctor's offices a few minutes early, which was just as well since there were reams of forms and questionnaires to fill out about his health history, his family's health history, his present medications, his insurance coverage, and so on. When he was done, he turned the paperwork over to the nurse at the reception desk, who glanced over a few of the pages, checked for his signature at the bottom, then said, "And you have not had an ejaculation for at least the previous twenty-four hours?"

Carter was tempted to say it was a close call, but decided against it. "No. I haven't."

She made a notation on his chart, then led him down a narrow corridor—muted lighting, gray carpeting, no sounds at all—lined with white, numbered doors. She opened one, and inside the small cubicle he saw a chair, a wall-mounted TV, and a night table stacked with pornographic magazines.

"The TV has a tape preloaded," she said, "and you just have to press the On button to start it. The magazines are also there for your use."

Carter, who hadn't even thought about what to expect, was nonplussed.

"Please try to capture as much as you can in the receptacle," she said, handing him a plastic cup much like the ones, he thought with horror, that were used for salsa samples at his favorite fast-food Mexican restaurant. "When you're done, bring it back to me."

Carter stepped into the room and the nurse closed the door. He looked around and didn't know where to start. How in the world did you get from here to Eros?

Still, fifteen minutes later, he poked his head out the door, looking for the nurse, but there was no one in sight. Concealing the specimen cup in his hand, he went back to the reception area, where a couple of other patients were now waiting. The nurse who'd shown him to the room was talking to someone on the phone.

Carter caught her eye. Still talking, she held out her free hand.

She really expected him to just hand it to her?

He did. She put it down next to her appointment book, smiled, and waved three fingers good-bye.

Carter felt like he'd just had the most peculiar morning of his life, and it wasn't even ten o'clock yet. At least he'd have plenty of time to get to the airport and meet Russo. It was just too bad he couldn't get home again first; he'd have really liked to see Beth right now.

At the airport, he saw that Russo's flight was due to land right on time, a miracle considering that it was an international flight. And since he was early, he had time to call home. Beth picked up on the second ring.

"You know, I could have used you there this morning," Carter said.

Beth laughed. "I don't think it's allowed."

"Well, it ought to be."

"How'd it go? Was it weird?"

"Kind of."

"I appreciate your going. It means a lot to me."

"Yeah, well, I'm signed on for this project, too, you know."

"I know," she said, softly. "And about this morning? I'll make it up to you when you get home."

"That may be easier said than done. Don't forget I'll have about two hundred and fifty pounds of fine Italian luggage with me."

"You want me to go shopping and get some food? Maybe he'll be tired and just want a quiet dinner at home?"

Although Carter didn't want to say anything, he knew that Beth's idea of a quiet dinner at home was a light meal, heavy on salad and fresh veggies, with maybe one skinless chicken breast per person. Joe Russo would regard all that as an appetizer, and not a particularly enticing one, either.

No, Carter was planning on taking him out, maybe to one of the steak houses like Morton's or The Palm. "Let's see how he feels when he gets here."

"Okay. I should be in and out all day."

Carter heard an announcement over the P.A., something about an Alitalia flight from Rome, so he said goodbye and headed for the arrivals area. After a long wait, he saw a surge of passengers emerging from the customs and baggage claim areas. Like the rest of the people waiting, he had to stand behind a glass wall and scan the crowd for the person he was looking for. But these definitely looked like Italians, a lot of them, in neatly tailored suits, sleek sunglasses, and small, polished leather shoes. A woman in a fur coat was carrying a Gucci bag with a tiny dog poking his head out of the top.

And then Carter spotted his friend, lumbering along with a garment bag slung over one shoulder, a bulging cloth suitcase clutched in one hand, a battered valise tucked under his arm. Carter rapped on the glass as he passed by, and Russo looked over and raised his chin—the only part of him that was unencumbered—in acknowledgment. Carter pointed down the corridor toward the exit, then went to meet him there.

"Mio fratello," Carter shouted, his arms wide, as Russo came out.

"Dottore!"

Russo dropped his suitcase and garment bag, and he and Carter hugged, their hands clapping each other on the back. And even though Carter was over six feet tall and rangy, he felt himself dwarfed in Russo's bearlike embrace. Russo carried that stale smell of the airplane cabin, and his beard—short and black and bristly—scratched the side of Carter's face.

"It's great to see you," Carter said, drawing back. "How was your flight?"

Russo shrugged. "How are they ever? Too long—and not enough room."

Carter picked up his suitcase. "Come on, we'll catch a cab outside."

"Yes. I am dying to have a cigarette."

"You'd better have it before we get a cab. There's no smoking in the taxis here."

Russo rolled his big dark eyes, like a water buffalo stuck in the mud, and stopped. "And they say that New York City is civilized?"

Carter cocked his head and said, "You'd never hear that from me."

Outside, the taxi line was interminable, which gave Russo plenty of time to light up a Nazionali and to tell Carter all about his recent appointment at the University of Rome, his new apartment, the paper he'd just finished on the olfactory bulbs—much larger than had previously been thought—of the *T. rex*. Carter filled him in on some of his work at NYU, but as if by tacit agreement, neither one of them brought up the big issue, the elephant in the room, the reason for Russo's being there in the first place. It was as if it was simply too important to discuss while waiting in line for a cab, or even later, as they crawled through the dense traffic into the city.

When they got to Washington Square, Carter paid the fare while Russo wrestled his bags into the foyer of the building. In the elevator on the way up, Russo said, "The university—it pays for this place to live?"

"No, I do. I pay the rent, but they own it."

"But the university, it gives you the break?"

"Yes," Carter said, "a big break."

Russo nodded, as if in agreement. "I will tell this to the University of Rome. They should know how well American professors are treated."

Carter had the feeling that Russo was going to be making mental notes on all aspects of his American counterpart's lifestyle, in order to make a case for academic improvement back in Italy.

"And your wife, she is at home?" Russo said, as they dragged the bags to the door.

"We'll find out in a second," Carter said, unlocking the door and swinging it open. "Beth, you here?"

But there wasn't any answer. On the foot of the sofa was

a neatly folded sheet and blanket, and a pillow in a fresh case.

"This will be my room?" Russo said, dropping his garment bag by the coffee table. "I like it very much." He glanced at the framed prints over the sofa, two Audubon bird studies, and immediately understood the connection for Carter. "Dinosaur descendants?" he said, plopping his suitcase on the sofa and unzipping it.

"Isn't it obvious?" Carter said, and Russo shook his head ruefully. It was one of the few paleontological points on which they did not fully agree. "If you want to wash up," Carter said, "the bathroom's down the hall."

"I would like to take a shower. The woman next to me, she was carrying a bag of Genoa salamis."

He pulled out of his suitcase a blue nylon toiletry kit, and ambled toward the bathroom. "*Oo fa,* I am so stiff still."

"Take your time. I don't pay for the hot water."

"I love America."

While Russo was in the shower, Carter checked his answering machine—there was only one message, from Hank the custodian, telling him the overhead lights had cost thirty-five bucks over what Carter had allocated. Other than that, it seemed that the lab they'd improvised at the back of the bio building had pretty much come together right on schedule, and roughly on budget. He was eager to show it off to Russo.

But he didn't want to push him too hard, not today; he looked pooped. Maybe it was just the long flight, in a seat that was undoubtedly way too small for a man his size, but Russo didn't look like his old hale and hearty self. His olive skin had a slightly yellow tinge; his eyes had bags under them; his expression, even when smiling, had a kind of haunted cast to it. Something wasn't going well for him.

Carter was just about to run downstairs to check the mail when the door opened, and Beth, her arms full of grocery bags, pushed it open. "Help," she said, an oversized envelope clenched in her teeth. Carter grabbed the biggest bag, the one that was most in danger of spilling, and carried it into the small kitchen. The rest of the mail was stuck in the top of the bag. She followed him in, dropped the other bags on the counter, and let the envelope in her mouth fall on the little breakfast table. "I had to sign for that one," she said.

Carter glanced at the return address; his Italian was still good enough that he could easily make out that it was an Italian military address, a base in Frascati. He opened it up and saw a raft of documents on onionskin, all notarized, stamped, and requiring signatures at places marked with a big red X.

Beth said, "So, where's our guest?" as she opened the fridge.

"In the shower."

She put a bag on the floor and started transferring the items inside into the fridge and freezer. Carter was still studying the papers when Russo appeared behind him in the doorway to the kitchen.

"That feels much better," he said, and Carter turned to see that he was still damp and naked, except for a bath towel that was just barely tied around his waist. A St. Christopher medal on a silver chain dangled down on his hairy chest.

Beth, kneeling and concealed by the open fridge door, stood up and said, "Hi, I'm Beth."

Russo, who had clearly not seen her, grabbed at the knot on the towel. *"Maron,"* he said. "This is not how I have wanted to meet you."

But he put out a big, wet hand anyway, while hanging on to the towel with the other. Beth shook it, and then gave up trying not to laugh. "This is *exactly* how I wanted to meet you," she said, and Russo laughed, too.

"You do not have a robe I could borrow?" he said to Carter. "I forgot my own."

"Yeah, sure. But take a look at these," Carter said, handing him the papers before going to get the robe.

Russo flipped a few of the pages—military paperwork, that was all it was—before saying to Beth, "I would help you with your things, but it could be dangerous," he said, waving the papers at the flimsy towel.

"That's okay," she said, turning back to the grocery bags. "I'm almost done. I didn't know what you like, so I just bought an assortment of things—apples, arugula, tomatoes, some cheese, some bread, some wine."

"That was not necessary, but thank you."

"You had a good trip over?"

"The lady next to him was smuggling Genoa salamis," Carter answered for him, handing Russo a terrycloth robe.

Russo gave him back the papers, then turned around and pulled the robe on over the towel. "These are all just forms and receipts," he said of the paperwork, "but they say you must bring them and sign them tomorrow when we take possession of the fossil." He lashed the belt of the robe. "Otherwise they will not release it to you."

"Did they say what time it would get here? I've got the head custodian on hold all day, to let us into the biology building." Because it was a Sunday, it had cost Carter another hundred dollars.

"It says morning, approximately eleven o'clock. But I do not need to remind you, these are my countrymen."

Carter wondered if it would get there at all the next day. The advantages to a Sunday delivery on campus were that there'd be very little traffic and the loading dock would be free. In addition, he'd made arrangements with the university's cartage contractor to pick it up; normally, this company moved things like heavy machinery, but he had impressed upon them that they should treat this specimen—which might just look like a huge hunk of rock to them—as if it were the most delicate piece of high-technology equipment.

"But let me go now and put on some clothes. I do have them," he said to Beth.

Carter stayed in the kitchen with Beth while she folded up the paper bags and stowed them away. In a low voice, she said, "So, the test this morning, it really went off okay?"

"Yes," Carter said, with a smile, "and so did I."

"That is so gross," she said, not really meaning it. "Giuseppe—"

"Just call him Joe—he prefers it."

"—seems very nice. And very *big*," she said, in an even lower voice. "That robe barely made it around him."

"Believe it or not, I think he's actually lost weight since I last saw him."

"Is he hungry? I also bought a pack of turkey cutlets. Or do you think he wants to go out?"

Carter laughed. "It sounds like you're talking about a dog. Don't worry about it—he'll tell me what he wants to do. One thing about Joe, he's not shy."

"That much I noticed."

After he was dressed, it turned out that Russo wanted nothing more than to stretch his legs; he'd been wedged into airline seats and taxicabs so long, he just wanted a chance to walk again. The three of them went outside and into Washington Square Park. A Frisbee sailed lazily over Russo's head as he stopped to light another Nazionali. Carter glanced over at Beth to remind her silently, *I told you he smokes a lot.*

They walked around the crowded pathways, and Carter pointed out some of the local landmarks, such as the Washington Square Arch, where a steel band was banging away, and the Bobst Library across the street, where a steady stream of NYU students in backpacks and headphones was pouring in and out.

"In Italy too, we have this," Russo said, cupping a hand over his ear as one of the students passed by, nodding to the music.

"Headphones," Carter said, supplying the word.

"*Stupido.* Why can they not talk to each other, instead?" He ground out his cigarette butt underfoot. "If people do not talk, they do not learn anything."

"You should come to some of my classes," Carter said, wondering why he hadn't thought of it sooner. "My students love to talk. You can guest lecture, if you want." He thought of Katie Coyne, in particular—she'd never met a lecturer she didn't like to grill.

"That's a great idea," Beth said. "And if you'd like to see a bit of the art world, Joe"—she said his name as if she were trying it out—"you can come up and visit me at the gallery."

"Yes, I would like that. Carter tells me that you sell the Old Masters."

"We do."

"The Old *Italian* Masters."

Beth smiled. "Is there any other kind?"

For dinner, they went to Sparks, where Carter splurged on porterhouse steaks for himself and Russo; Beth, of course, stuck to the Caesar salad and a baked potato stuffed with sour cream, butter, and chives. "They didn't tell me it would be the size of my head!" she said. And although Beth abstained from the wine, Carter and Russo had no trouble at all knocking off a fine bottle of cabernet sauvignon, and a couple of brandies with dessert.

When they got home, Carter thought Russo looked ready to fall off his feet. He and Beth made up the sofa, tucking the edge of the sheet under the cushions and spreading the blanket. They had hardly finished when Russo came out of the bathroom in Carter's old robe and plopped himself down on their handiwork. "If I do not sleep tonight," Russo said, "then I will never sleep again."

"If you want anything from the fridge, help yourself," Beth said.

"I will never eat again either."

"See you in the morning," Carter said.

"*Buona notte,* Bones," Russo said, and Carter was inevitably reminded of the nights they'd bedded down with the rest of their expedition in the rough hills of Sicily.

While Beth showered, Carter got undressed and cracked open the bedroom window. When she came back into the room, she was wearing a long white nightgown that went from her ankles to the base of her throat. "In deference to our guest," she said.

"Very kind. And let's buy him a robe tomorrow," Carter said, heading across the hall in his boxer shorts and a *Godzilla* T-shirt. When he returned, he closed the bedroom door, which they normally kept open, and slid into the bed.

"I'd be surprised if he woke up before noon tomorrow," Carter said, turning out the light.

"He looks exhausted." She put her head back on the pillow and her dark hair fanned out on either side. "You've had a long day, too."

Carter rolled over toward her. "It ain't over yet," he said, as he fiddled with the buttons on the top of her nightgown. "Did you actually have to button these?"

"I read in *Cosmo* that men like a challenge."

"Not really."

He opened the buttons, then leaned down and nuzzled the bare skin of her neck. It smelled of her favorite sandalwood soap. Beth closed her eyes. Reaching down under the blanket, he lifted the hem of her nightie, and she raised her hips to let the fabric slide more easily up her body.

"Was it awful this morning, at the doctor's?" she whispered.

"Why are you whispering?"

"I don't want to wake Joe."

"A nuclear bomb could go off tonight and Joe wouldn't hear it." He let his hand run gently over her thighs, and then up onto her abdomen. "And yes, it was pretty awful."

"How did you . . . I mean, what did you think about?"

"This," he said, rolling over on top of her and planting his elbows on either side of her shoulders. When he bent down to kiss her, her lips were dry, and he wet them with his own tongue. Beth raised her arms and clasped them around him.

"Did it work?" she mumbled.

"Like a charm."

And then Carter silenced her with another prolonged kiss. Her legs opened beneath him, and he could tell she was already awaiting him. He put all thought of the clinic out of his head. He put all thought of everything out of his head and lost himself in the moment, in the warmth of Beth's embrace, in the smell of her skin and hair, in the taste of her.

So deeply was he immersed that he didn't hear the creaking of the bedroom door, or feel the cool draft that

now blew into the room. But Beth did, and the next thing he
knew her fingers were digging into his skin, she was staring over his shoulder and urging him to "Turn around, turn
around!"

Carter grunted and reluctantly turned his head—and
saw in the open doorway something blocking the light. He
had to break away from Beth and look again before he realized that it was Russo, in the borrowed bathrobe, staring
blankly ahead.

"Joe," Carter said, "are you okay?"

"La pietra," Russo said, in a monotone. *"È all'interno
della pietra."*

The stone? Something inside the stone? Carter had
picked up some rudimentary Italian in Sicily, but even that
was rusty now. But he did know that Russo wasn't actually
answering him; he doubted his friend had even heard him.

Beth yanked the sheet up to her chin. "What's going
on?" she said, fearfully.

"I think he's sleepwalking," Carter whispered, slipping
naked out of the bed. "Don't do anything to scare him."

"Scare *him?*" she said, but softly.

Carter approached Russo slowly, with one hand extended. "Joe, you've got to go back to bed."

"Sta provando ad uscire."

Something was trying to get out? Carter guessed that
Russo was saying something about the fossil—and perhaps
the gases trapped inside it. Was he having a nightmare
about the volatile contents of the fossil exploding?

Carter put his hand gently on Russo's shoulder and said,
"Come on, Joe."

Russo didn't respond.

"Let's go back to bed now."

Carter steered him by his shoulder, and together they
went back toward the living room. Carter guided Russo
down the hall, around the edge of the coffee table and
chairs, and then over to the side of the sofa, where the
sheet and blanket trailed onto the floor. Under Carter's
gentle pressure, Russo subsided onto the sofa, still mumbling something, agitatedly now, about *la pietra.*

Carter thought it was best not to leave him in the midst of this nightmare—if for no other reason than that he might start wandering around the apartment again—but he wasn't sure how to go about waking him.

"Joe," he said again, looking straight into his empty eyes, "you're having a bad dream," and he shook his shoulder several times. "You're just having a bad dream, Joe."

Slowly, he saw a flicker of consciousness return to Russo's gaze.

"That's it," Carter said, "that's my boy. Wake up now, Joe."

Russo's eyes seemed to focus and gradually take in Carter, kneeling directly in front of him. "Bones?"

"That's me."

"What are you doing?"

"Waking you up. You've been sleepwalking."

First, there was comprehension, then surprise, followed almost immediately by embarrassment. "Oh, no, no, no . . ." Russo muttered. "Oh, Bones, did I . . ."

"No harm done," Carter assured him. "You might have taken a few years off my life, but I'll get over it. Wait here."

Carter went back to the bedroom to check on Beth.

"Is he all right?" she said, still huddled in the bed with the light on now.

"Yeah, he'll be okay," he said, grabbing a pair of jeans from a chair and pulling them on. "How about you?"

She shrugged. "Nothing a new lock on the bedroom door won't cure."

Carter went into the kitchen, got a bottle of ginger ale out of the fridge, and brought it into Russo, who now at least looked fully awake.

"Thought you might like this," Carter said, handing him the ginger ale. "Maybe it was all that wining and dining we did."

Russo took the little bottle gratefully, twisted off the cap, and downed nearly the whole thing.

"Feel better?" Carter asked.

Russo nodded his big head, but still looked troubled. "Did I do anything? Did I talk?"

"Not much. You did say something, in Italian, about the rock, and I'm assuming you meant the fossil. You worried about it?"

Russo nodded again. "I have been worried for much time now," he said. He swigged the last of the ginger ale. "Bones, I have not been fair to you."

"You mean not telling me you're a sleepwalker?" Carter said, with a smile. "I'll just tie you to the sofa from now on."

Russo shook his head. "Ever since the day I saw it, and touched it inside that cave, I have not been right, here," he said, tapping a finger against his skull.

"You've been crazy?" Carter said.

"No, not that." Russo searched for the words. "I have not been comfortable in my head. I have had trouble in my thoughts, I have had the bad dreams—like tonight."

"What about, exactly?"

Russo grimaced and turned his face toward the pale glow of the streetlamps coming in through the windows. Carter could see now just how deeply troubled he was.

"I wish, sometimes, that we had not ever found it," he finally said, in a low voice.

"But it could turn out to be a stupendous find," Carter assured him.

Russo appeared unmoved. "I do not want what has happened to me to happen to you. I should not have made you involved."

Carter slapped him playfully on the shoulder and said, "No getting out of it now. The fossil arrives tomorrow, and by next month we'll both be on the front page of the *New York Times*."

Russo looked up at him balefully, as if he could believe that—but not for any reason Carter had in mind.

"Get some rest," Carter said, lifting the blanket back onto the sofa. As he did, he noticed that one of the Audubon bird prints was now off the wall above the sofa and lying on the little table they'd set up by the bed. "We'll talk about it in the morning."

Russo lay back and Carter draped the blanket across him.

"I am sorry, Bones," Russo said, and Carter wasn't entirely sure what he was referring to.

"Don't sweat it—everything's fine." But before he left the room, he glanced up at the wall where the print had been, and saw that Russo had replaced it with something else. It took him a second in the dim light to make it out, and then another second to reconcile it with what he knew of his friend, a man of science if ever there was one. But right above the end of the sofa where he laid his head, Russo had used the nail from the print to hang a gnarled old wooden crucifix.

ELEVEN

The third time Carter called the number on the inter-national transport license, he finally got through. But when he asked if the Italian military plane carrying the specimen had arrived at Kennedy Airport yet, a harried operator said "Hold on," and then left him hanging once again.

"What do they say?" Russo asked nervously as he stood by Carter's chair.

"I don't know; I'm on hold while she's checking on it."

"It should have arrived hours ago," Russo said, tamping another Nazionali out of the nearly empty pack in his pocket. "What is the problem now?"

Carter, of course, had no more idea than Russo did. And though he knew Beth wasn't crazy about Russo sneaking the occasional smoke in the apartment, this didn't seem like a very good time to ask the man to quit.

"The plane has been delayed," the operator said, abruptly coming back on the line. "It's now due in later this afternoon. Around four."

"What delayed it?"

"Weather. Unusually strong head winds, from the east."

"I thought I once heard that head winds usually blew from the west."

"You heard right. But that's why weathermen are always wrong."

When Carter hung up and broke the news to Russo, Joe went to the window and blew out a cloud of smoke. In perfect keeping with his mood, it was shaping up to be a gray and gloomy day outside. And when Joe thought about what had gone on the night before, he wanted to crawl under a rock and die. On his very first night in New York, he had humiliated himself in front of Carter and Beth—how much so, he still wasn't sure. Carter hadn't elaborated on his sleep-walking performance, and Russo had been too embarrassed to ask. He only hoped that Carter hadn't spotted the crucifix above the sofa. He'd intended to take it down in the morning, before anyone saw it, and before he felt like he had to offer some explanation for his sudden conversion to the Holy Roman faith. It was stashed now, in the bottom of his suitcase.

"So what do we do until then?" Russo said.

Carter wondered about that, too. Beth was off with Abbie, helping her pick out curtains and wallpaper for the country place she and Ben had bought upstate; in fact, as Beth had informed him that morning, they were scheduled to go up and see the place for themselves on the coming Halloween weekend. As for today, Carter had planned on using most of the day to get the fossil delivered and installed.

"We could go over to the biology building," he suggested, "and I could give you a preliminary tour of the lab where we'll be working on the fossil."

"Yes, that is a good idea," Russo said, jumping at the chance. "I would like very much to see the lab first."

Before leaving the apartment, Carter gave Russo an umbrella and took another one for himself; it looked like they might need them any moment. Outside, a cold wind was blowing, and the trees in the park, their boughs bending in the wind, were shedding their last gold and orange leaves. Just the regulars were out; the homeless couple who lived on a bench near the Arch, a chess hustler in a Mets jacket who played against himself when nobody else would give him a game, the would-be comedian who stood on a fruit crate braying through a megaphone under the nonfunctioning fountain.

As they approached the biology building, Carter said, "Let me show you the main lab first, where I do the day-to-day stuff."

Inside, the place was deserted and empty, and only one panel of overhead fluorescent lights had been left on in the hallway, for the die-hards who wanted to work even on a Sunday. Carter took Russo downstairs, and to his surprise—though, now that he considered it, why should he be surprised?—he could hear the distant strains of Eminem or some other rapper (he never could tell them apart) issuing from the main faculty lab.

"You're about to meet a guy named Bill Mitchell," Carter confided to Russo, "an associate professor in the department."

The door was ajar and Mitchell was at his usual spot in back, his boombox on the counter, his lank, black hair falling down around his glasses.

"Hey, Bill," Carter said loudly, to be heard over the music.

Mitchell looked up, squinting. He had a brush in one hand and what appeared to be a black rock—though it was probably a coprolite—in the other.

"I'd like you to meet a friend of mine, Giuseppe Russo. He's on the faculty at the University of Rome."

The word *faculty* was enough to get Mitchell to slap off the boombox and bound up from his stool with his hand extended. "I'm Bill Mitchell. Really glad to meet you. You in paleontology?"

Carter could almost hear Mitchell's mind clicking over the questions—*What kind of openings might they have in Italy? How hard would it be to adapt? What's the current exchange rate?*

"Yes, I am," Russo said. "Carter and I worked together years ago in Sicily."

Mitchell was turning it over quickly. "You were part of the team that turned up the Well of the Bones?"

Russo smiled; even scientists were flattered when their reputation preceded them. "Yes, I was."

"That was great work, groundbreaking work," Mitchell enthused. Then he paused and a cloud crossed his face. Carter could guess why. "You just visiting Carter, or are you looking at a position here at NYU?" With one more full professor on the ladder above him, Mitchell's chances of advancement would be that much slimmer.

"No, no. I am here just for a short time, to work on something with my old friend."

Mitchell's ears pricked up, something that Carter was sorry to see.

"Really? What?" Mitchell asked, pushing his glasses back up to the bridge of his nose.

"Just something that needs a little technological analysis," Carter intervened. "Nothing special."

At hearing this, Russo glanced over at him, and instantly understood. "Sometimes, in Italy," he chimed in for Mitchell's benefit, "we do not have the machines we need. That is all."

But Mitchell had picked up the scent of something, and Carter could see that he wasn't about to lose it just yet. "You going to be doing the work in this lab?" Mitchell asked. " 'Cause I'd be glad to help out."

"No, that's okay," Carter said. "We've got a separate area set aside." Carter was sorry he'd ever gotten into this; he wanted the project to remain as private as possible, and he certainly didn't want to be torturing poor Mitchell with the idea that some earthshaking discovery—the kind of discovery that got you tenure overnight—was being done virtually under his nose.

Then he noticed the orange and black envelope taped to his own lab stool.

"What's that?" Carter said, and before he could open it, Mitchell blurted out, "It's a party invite."

Carter slid the invitation, a black cat with its paw extended, out of the envelope. But he didn't need to read the fine print.

"It's for the night before Halloween," Mitchell said. "We figured we'd get more people to come that way."

"I'm afraid Beth and I are going out of town that

weekend." He glanced at Russo, who appeared unperturbed by the news. "Sorry, I meant to tell you."

"Sorry you can't make it," Mitchell said, but then, turning to Russo, he added, "But maybe you can? The more, the scarier!"

Carter handed the invitation to Russo. "Why don't you?" It would actually take a load off his mind if he knew that Russo was having some fun while he was off in the country.

"We live pretty near here," Mitchell went on, "and my wife makes a terrific brownie pie."

"Thank you," Russo said, nodding and sticking the invitation into his shirt pocket. "I will be happy to arrive."

"We'll see you around then," Carter said, ushering Russo toward the door. "Don't let us interrupt your work any longer."

"No problem," Mitchell replied, standing in place like a kid being ditched. "And remember, if you need any help, just say the word."

As Carter and Russo left, Carter closed the door behind him and motioned for Russo to follow him. They moved quietly down the hall and around the corner before Carter said, "The guy's okay, but he's kind of a snoop."

Russo nodded. "Very . . . eager."

"And we're probably better off if he doesn't know what's being done through here." With that, Carter opened a metal door, flicked on the light, and led Russo through a series of cement-floored storage areas lined with boxes, crates, and discarded equipment. At the opposite end was another fireproof door, and to get this one open Carter had to lift a metal arm from the inside and then give the door a good shove with his shoulder, its bottom screeching on the cement.

"Welcome to your home away from home," Carter said, bowing and waving Russo inside.

Although they were already at the basement level, a corrugated metal ramp led another ten feet down. Russo lumbered down it, holding to the iron rail, and Carter followed. At the bottom they were in a large, raw space with a stained concrete floor, walls lined with stacked crates, and a pair of huge, heavily padlocked doors that opened to the loading dock on the street outside. Off at the far corner, Hank the custodian was sitting at an old beaten-up gray desk. He had a newspaper, a phone, and a portable TV on the desk, and he was watching what sounded like a nature show; Carter could hear something about the "swift and clear waters of the running stream." Hank looked up as they came in, and said, "Hey, Dr. Cox. I've been here all day and nobody's showed up with anything."

"I know," Carter said. "In fact, the specimen won't be here until late this afternoon. Probably not before five or six."

Hank shook his head, and turned off the TV. "I can't stay that late."

"I understand that, Hank," Carter said. "Professor Russo's here now—"

Hank and Russo nodded at each other.

"—and we'll take over. All we need is the keys to the loading dock doors."

Hank stood up and took a massive key ring off his belt; flipping through the various keys, he stopped and then detached two big keys. "These'll unlock the padlocks on the loading doors. Once you've got that done, you press that button on the wall over there—"

He pointed to a red button in a red circle, painted on the wall.

"—and the doors'll slide open. Press it again, and they'll slide closed." He handed the keys to Carter. "That's about it."

"Thanks."

Hank glanced up. "You haven't said anything about the lights I rigged."

Carter, who'd been in the lab earlier, had already admired them, but it was true that he hadn't said anything yet to Hank. "They look good—and they're just what we'll need."

Overhead, on two thick, criss-crossing wires, Hank had hung four high-intensity lamps.

"Watch this," Hank said proudly, stepping to the wall and flicking the switch on a jerry-built fuse box. The dim, high-ceilinged room was immediately bathed in a glaring white

light. Carter instinctively shielded his eyes for a second—
was this more wattage than he'd bargained for?—but then
his eyes seemed to adjust. He looked over at Russo, who was
also pointedly not looking up.

"Too much for you fellas?" Hank asked. "You said you
wanted a whole lotta light, Professor."

"No, it's fine," Carter said, reminding himself to bring a
baseball cap with a visor when he came in next.

"Well then, if it's okay by you, I'm gonna take off."
Hank pulled the plug on the TV, started to wrap the cord
around it, then stopped. "You want me to leave the TV? It's
mine, but I can leave it here if you want it."

That suddenly seemed to Carter like a very good idea.
"Could you?"

"Sure. I'll pick it up tomorrow morning." Hank pulled
his parka off the back of the chair and headed up the ramp.
"Hope you don't have to wait too long," he said, leaving by
the door that led to the interior storage rooms.

Carter went to the wall and flicked off the overhead
lights. Instantly, the room went back from glare to gloom.

"I will have to wear suntan lotion while we work,"
Russo said.

"Maybe we can get him to disconnect one or two of the
lamps."

Russo looked around for another chair and spotted one
between two crates. He dragged it over toward the desk.
"Does American TV show football?"

"Not the kind you mean," Carter said, knowing Russo
meant soccer. "But on a Sunday afternoon in October, the
chances of getting an American football game are pretty
damn good." Carter loosened the cord, plugged the set in,
and turned it on. The show that Hank had had on was about
fishing in Minnesota—that figured—but with two turns of
the dial, Carter found a Chicago Bears–New York Jets game.
His hometown versus his adopted home. They might have a
long day ahead, but it wasn't going to be an impossible one.

**Every hour or so, Carter called the transport office at
Kennedy Airport for an update, and after returning from a**

quick food run to the corner deli, he was told the office had called while he was out. "It is on the ground," Russo said, as Carter brushed the rain—it had already started to drizzle—from his jacket. "It will be here in perhaps one hour."

Carter could hardly contain his excitement, but Russo, he noticed, was curiously dispassionate. He unwrapped the roast beef sandwich and Coke that Carter had picked up for him, and kept his eyes glued to the TV screen. Maybe that's what came from living with the fossil for so long already, Carter thought. The thrill had worn off.

That, or nervous exhaustion had taken its toll.

Neither one of them had said much about the goings-on the night before—Carter had purposely downplayed it—but if this was how Russo had been living for the past few weeks, Carter could see why he looked so tired and distracted. And as for that crucifix above the sofa . . . well, Russo wouldn't be the first scientist in Carter's experience to secretly harbor a belief system that harmonized poorly with the empirical nature of his—of *their*—calling.

When the truck did arrive at the bio building, exactly two hours later, Carter heard it backing up in the loading zone outside before the driver had even rung the delivery bell. Like a kid on Christmas morning, Carter leapt up from his chair and fumbled with the keys at the padlocked doors. By the time he'd finally gotten the locks undone, the driver had hit the delivery bell and a loud clanging echoed around the chamber. Russo stuck his fingers in his ears while Carter slapped the red button that triggered the electric release. The loading doors retracted slowly, with a high-pitched whine that added to the cacophony.

Night had fallen, and the loading zone outside was illuminated now by the blazing red taillights of the truck and the baleful yellow glare of the halogen streetlamps. A cold wind was blowing, blowing so hard in fact that the streetlamps were swaying, throwing their light in moving shadows around the wet, black asphalt. A heavy rain was coming down at a slant, drumming hard on the roof of the truck and gurgling down the gutters.

Carter stood in the doorway, getting wet all over again,

but he didn't care. He only wanted to see the fossil. Two workers were already putting down a ramp from the back of the truck to the ground. But so far, all that Carter could see huddled inside the truck was a huge, black block. It appeared to be secured there in sheets of heavy-duty plastic, broad strips of bright yellow tape, and several loops of thick, silver chain. And it looked like it was slightly raised on a platform of some kind.

A small man in a brown military uniform sprinted out of the cab of the truck and ran into the building. He was wearing a cap with an insignia of his rank, and as soon as he was under the roof of the makeshift lab, he whipped the cap off and knocked the rainwater from its gleaming black visor.

"*Professore* Cox?" he said to Carter, with a heavy accent.

"Yes, that's me."

The man's eyes were small and dark as pebbles, and they darted around the room as he spoke. "I am Lieutenant DiPalma. I am in charge of the cargo. I can only release this cargo to you."

"Great. Then we're done. I accept it."

"It is not so simple. I must first see your copy of the international transport papers. You have them with you, yes?"

"Oh, right. I do." Carter turned to get them—but Russo was already bringing them over from the desk. "This is Professor Russo," Carter said, "the man who—"

"I know who the *Professore* is," DiPalma interrupted, taking the papers and starting to look them over. "*Non vedo l'ora di lasciare questi problemi nelle tue mani,*" he rattled off to Russo.

"*Perché?*"

"*Da quando ho preso controllo di questo, è stato un problema dopo l'altro. Un soldato è rimasto gravemente ferito caricandola a Frascati. Abbiamo avuto mal tempo per il viaggio intero. Abbiamo dovuto fermarsi a Halifax per rifornirsi di carburante.*" He flipped another page, hastily initialed it.

Carter, unable to keep up with the rapid-fire Italian, looked over at Russo, who nodded, and muttered to him, "Problems. A bad storm all the way over." He said it as if he had expected no less. "And engine trouble."

"Is that why I thought I heard him mention Halifax?"

"Yes. They had to go there for more fuel."

"I'm glad that's all it was."

"Not all." Russo gave him a level look, then said, "A soldier in Frascati was badly injured. Loading the stone."

Carter was starting to be grateful the fossil had arrived at all. He shook his head. "Didn't you tell me that some guy, on his honeymoon . . ."

"Yes, he died. In the cave."

"Wow," Carter said. "It's as if the thing had a curse on it."

Russo swiftly looked away, as the teamsters working this job attached a couple of heavy chains to the block of stone and its platform; the chains were then hooked to what looked like an electric winch in the truck's rear cargo area—in order, Carter guessed, to control the block's rate of descent down the ramp.

The lieutenant glanced back at the truck, then said, "Make sure that the stone is very secure, gentlemen," he said. "It is very ancient."

The workers kept their heads down, doing what they had to do as quickly and as wordlessly as they could. Even they, it struck Carter, looked like they couldn't be finished with this assignment too soon.

DiPalma ripped the last page of Carter's documents free of the rest, folded it up, and slid it into his pocket. Then he took out another document of his own, written in Italian, with all kinds of official stamps all over it. "You must sign this here, and here," DiPalma said, poking a finger at two spaces on the bottom.

Carter, who couldn't plow through all the Italian officialese fast enough, held it out toward Russo, who looked it over and said, "It is just the receipt for the transfer, and it must go back to the Academia in Rome."

While Carter dutifully signed, DiPalma nervously tapped

his foot on the increasingly damp cement. Rainwater was splashing into the makeshift lab and trickling down the ramp from the back of the truck. When Carter had finished, DiPalma snatched the receipt back just as the winch was turned on; it came to life with a loud grinding groan, and DiPalma jumped to one side, away from the ramp.

"Slowly," he cried to the workers in the truck, "slowly!"

The block was about the size of a couple of refrigerators, and the two workers stood on either side of it as the descent began. Afraid, Carter assumed, of getting injured, they kept their hands well clear of the block. Now Carter was able to see that it was mounted on a steel trolley, with wide steel wheels that rumbled angrily as they met the corrugated metal ramp.

Russo, too, had moved off some distance, and was standing beside the desk. His eyes, though riveted on the stone, were wary. In Carter's view, the lieutenant, Russo, and the workers all looked like a bunch of horses skittishly scenting smoke in the barn. As for himself, he couldn't be more excited. The block was already halfway down the ramp.

And then, so fast that his own reactions were no more than instinctive, it all happened—he heard one of the workers scream, "Watch out!" and he saw a length of the chain holding the trolley flash out of the truck bed like a lashing rattler. He jumped up as the wildly thrashing chain whipped under his feet, then spun toward the desk and Russo—who flattened himself on its surface as the steel links wrapped themselves around the legs of the desk, wrenching the whole thing several feet across the floor.

"*Dio!*" DiPalma cried out.

The block of stone, now unchained, trundled across the room, the wheels of its platform screeching on the cement floor. It turned itself halfway around before its sheer weight brought it to a grinding, suddenly silent halt.

Only seconds had passed. Russo clung to the desk like a shipwrecked sailor to a raft, the lieutenant crossed himself and muttered something else in Italian, and one of the workers in the truck stumbled down the ramp. "The goddamned winch broke," he cursed, cradling his right arm. "I think it broke my wrist!"

Carter took a deep breath, then let it out. *Stay calm,* he told himself. The endless length of loose chain lay on the floor like a spent animal. The block of stone hadn't been damaged in any way; in fact, it had come to rest right about where he'd wanted it, under the center of the lamps that Hank had rigged up.

"God *damn* it," the worker moaned, sitting down on the ramp and bending forward, protectively, over his injured arm. Carter went over to him and said, "There's a hospital just a few blocks away. I'll get a cab and take you over there."

"I know where the hospital is," the worker said in disgust, "and I can get there myself."

"The fossil?" Russo said, timidly approaching. He was thinking, despite himself, of the dream he'd had in Rome.

"It looks okay," Carter said. "Thank God it didn't fall over."

Russo walked in a wide circle around it, making a cautious inspection, remembering his nightmare of the loose cable whipping in the wind, snapping at the stone. Had it been, in actuality, a premonition?

Lieutenant DiPalma bent to free the chain from the desk, and with the help of the uninjured worker tossed it back up into the rear of the truck. It landed with a muffled clank. Coming back to Carter, he declared, "The fossil is now in your possession, *Professore.*" He said it with obvious relief, as if he were making a sworn statement before an unseen court. He adjusted his cap on his head and put out his hand to shake. Carter took it, and as the lieutenant held it tight, he said, "Be careful." His eyes flicked over to the brooding block of stone, then returned to Carter, full of meaning. "Accidents—you see?—can happen."

TWELVE

Dawn was nearly breaking. Only moments before, the sky had been pitch black, and now it was a deep, dark indigo. Ezra walked swiftly, his eyes on the sidewalk, his arms crossed in front of his chest, holding his coat closed.

He didn't know where he was going; he didn't care. He only knew that he had to be out of his rooms, out of that apartment, that he had to keep moving. He needed to be out among people, even the few who were scattered on the street at this ungodly hour, with buses lumbering by and off-duty cabs returning to their garages. He needed the activity, the absolutely mundane, everyday nature of it all, to surround him.

Needed to forget what had happened that night.

He'd been working. What else did he ever do? The scroll was coming together nicely, faster than he'd expected. The pieces were falling into place. He'd been at it for hours, losing track of the time, as always, and the CD player was switching to the next disc—Beethoven's Emperor Concerto. In the temporary silence, as his gloved fingers gently positioned a scrap of scroll between two others, the dense, elaborate script appeared, to his delight, to flow together, to make sense. But as he bent his head lower to examine his work, he heard, as clearly as he heard the ticking of his wristwatch, a voice whispering in his ear. The words were indecipherable, as if from an unknown tongue, but the meaning was somehow plain. It was *yes . . .* it was *go on.*

And it sounded as if the speaker were leaning over his very shoulder.

His head had jerked back and he'd whipped around in his seat. The back of his neck tingled, and his heart was pounding in his chest.

But no one was there. There was no one in the room.

But he had *heard* the voice. And he had felt a breath, a warm exhalation, on his face.

The concerto began, playing softly.

He got up from his chair; his legs felt a little weak. The curtains by the window, the double curtains he'd had Gertrude hang, were stirring—barely perceptibly, but stirring, nonetheless. With faltering steps he went toward them. Took hold of them. Drew them apart.

He felt a slight draft, cool wind from outside blowing through the cracks in the French door frames. But the doors were locked, and the balcony was empty.

He was alone in the room.

He went back to the drafting table, looked down at his work. The surface of the table was half-covered now, with bits and pieces of the scroll that he had painstakingly restored, fitted together . . . and to some extent translated. It was indeed the Book of Angels. Also known to scholars as the Lost Book of Enoch. He'd been right about that. Dead right. It was Enoch's account of his journey to Heaven, and of what he saw there. Of angels, burning bright around the throne of God; of others, fallen from favor. Of a coming war. And pestilence upon the earth. It was a dream, it was a prophecy . . . and it was his. No one had seen it, no one had read it, probably for thousands of years. Sometimes the sheer weight of that revelation felt like a hammer inside his head, threatening to crack open his skull.

And maybe that's what had happened tonight, he thought. Maybe a tiny, tiny fissure in his skull had opened up, just for a split second, and let the sound of that voice escape. Maybe it hadn't come from outside at all; maybe it had come from *inside* his own head. The bicameral mind, once again in operation.

A fire truck, siren wailing, barreled up First Avenue, with several cabs trailing in its wake. A limousine pulled up at the curb and a girl in a glittery party dress, carrying her shoes, got out. A line of pigeons walked in a perfect line across his path—like the Beatles on the cover of *Abbey Road,* he thought.

The sky was dark blue, but the sun was coming up.

Ezra kept going; when he had to stop at a corner to wait for the WALK light, he marched in place. He needed to feel the movement, to expend the energy. He needed to hear his feet pounding on the pavement, the cars whooshing by—anything, so long as it wasn't that voice in his ear.

A man in a flower shop was hosing down the sidewalk, and stopped to let Ezra pass.

Outside a Japanese restaurant, one that Ezra had occasionally gone to, a wooden pallet of fresh fish was waiting on the sidewalk. As he went by, a large fish, its silver scales gleaming, seemed to fix him with its dead eye.

He moved on quickly. The traffic was getting heavier by the minute. The sun was up, the sky clear. A Korean deli owner rolled up the heavy metal grates that covered his windows and door.

Ezra kept walking; the farther he went, the better he felt. The sound of the voice diminished in his ear. It was good to be out, good to feel the morning air and the pulse of life around him. Maybe he should do this on a regular basis, he thought; maybe he should start taking long walks, getting some exercise.

Before he knew it, he was at the corner of Eighty-ninth Street—his Uncle Maury's street. He noticed it when he had to stop outside the old Vienna bakery where his uncle liked to buy his Danish. The bakery door was locked, but there were lights on inside, and he could see a woman sliding a tray of orange Halloween cookies into the display case.

He knocked lightly on the glass in the door. Wouldn't it be a nice surprise to show up at his uncle's with some of his favorite treats?

The woman came around the counter, wiping her hands on her apron.

"You open?" Ezra said through the door. "Can I buy some things?"

She leaned closer, then drew back. "We're closed," she said, turning away.

Closed? She'd looked like she was reaching for the lock, to let him in. What time did they open? He stepped back to see if any business hours were posted. Then he caught his own reflection in the glass. A glassy-eyed man with a thick stubble of beard and messy hair, his overcoat gathered around him. One of his shoes, he now noticed, had even come unlaced.

No wonder. He considered knocking again and trying to persuade her of his sanity, but she'd disappeared into the back—no doubt waiting for him to go away.

He crossed the avenue, and walked past a row of decrepit brownstones. His uncle lived on the third floor, in front, and Ezra knew that he was a bad sleeper and an early riser. He stopped in front of the stoop, where someone had deposited an empty beer bottle, and looked up at his uncle's windows. The lights, sure enough, were on.

In the foyer, Ezra buzzed, but knowing his uncle, he didn't wait for him to respond; instead, he stepped back outside, knowing his uncle would simply stand at the window, looking down at the sidewalk to see who had bothered him.

Ezra waved when he saw the curtain pulled back. His uncle, in a bathrobe, stared down at him, as if processing this unlikely information. Then he simply dropped the curtain, and by the time Ezra got back into the foyer, the door was unlocked and buzzing.

He had his door open when Ezra came around the landing. "What the hell are you doing up here at this hour of the morning?" Then, as if something dire had occurred to him, he said, "Your father? He's okay?"

"For all I know, he's fine. He's still in Palm Beach, with Kimberly."

Ezra came into the kitchen, where the apartment began. It was a railroad flat, with the kitchen in back, then a bedroom, and then the living room—such as it was—in front.

"You want some coffee?" his uncle asked, gesturing at the jar of Folger's Coffee Crystals on the counter. "I was just making some."

"Yeah, that would be great. I stopped at the Vienna bakery to buy you some Danish, but they wouldn't let me in."

Maury chuckled, said, "I can't say as I blame 'em. You look like you just jumped out a window at Bellevue."

In a way, Ezra thought, that's how he felt. That spectral voice—low, insinuating, strangely sinister—echoed again in his head.

Maury took another coffee mug from the dish rack, spooned in some coffee crystals—"You like it strong?" he asked—and when Ezra nodded, spooned in some more. He poured in the boiling water, then led the way into the living room.

His uncle settled himself into his white Naugahyde Barcalounger—with the heat and massage controls—and Ezra sat down on the sofa across from him. Plaster was peeling away from the walls and hanging down in what looked to Ezra like furled scrolls.

"I'm still waiting for an answer," his uncle said. "This isn't the usual time for a visit. What's wrong?"

Ezra took a sip of his coffee. "I couldn't sleep, and just started taking a walk."

"Gertrude tells me you don't sleep at night at all anymore. She says you don't go to bed till dawn and you get up in the afternoon. What are you doing all night, Ezra?"

"Working."

"You can't work during the day, like most people?"

"It's better at night. Quieter. Fewer interruptions." Until, of course, this particular night.

Maury didn't look convinced. "What's your doctor say? That Neumann woman?"

"I haven't discussed it with her."

"Maybe you should. She's got you on some medications, for the mood swings and the rest?"

"Yes," Ezra said, looking down into his cup, wondering at the way the lamplight shone in iridescent circles on the surface of the hot coffee. He hadn't told Neumann about his insomnia; he knew she'd only prescribe some sleeping pills for him, and sleep wasn't what he wanted. Not when he was doing such exciting work, such breakthrough stuff. The only prescriptions he wanted from her were for things that would keep him focused, keep him alert, keep him calm enough to concentrate on the momentous task before him.

Which was why he wouldn't—why he *couldn't*—tell her about the voice he'd heard that night, any more than he could tell his uncle. He knew what that could lead to—endless psychotherapy at best, and an involuntary commitment at worst. The scroll was coming together, bit by bit, but it was a mind-boggling task, the sort of thing that drove one mad; in fact, as Ezra knew better than anyone, it had done just that to many of his predecessors. The first to feel the curse had been Shapira, the man who'd originally discovered some ancient manuscripts from the Dead Sea shores in the late nineteenth century. In his lifetime, his discoveries were considered forgeries—nothing, the scholars of his day concluded, could have survived so long in such an inhospitable climate—and after enduring years of professional disdain and dismissal, Shapira checked into a Rotterdam hotel and put a bullet through his head. Since that time, and with the amazing finds at Qumran in 1947, Shapira had been vindicated—for all the good it did him— and others had picked up where he'd left off, often with equally dire results. Scroll scholars were famous for their descents into madness and despair, for their alcoholism and drug abuse and suicidal tendencies (acted upon at a fairly regular pace). Ezra knew of one such case personally, an Australian woman, the most prominent authority on the theology of the Essenes, who'd worked on the Dead Sea Scrolls housed at the Shrine of the Book in Jerusalem; in less than two years' time, she had been reduced to a babbling fanatic, raving about the Apocalypse to come, and running from an omnipresent specter she called the Shadow Man. At a conference in Haifa, she'd rushed to the podium, and after shouting something about the Sons of Light, she had set fire to herself. Badly burned, but still alive, she'd been sent back home to Melbourne, where, last he'd heard, she lived under heavy medication and constant care in a private sanatorium.

When you studied the Scrolls, Ezra knew, you had to keep a firm grip on yourself.

"Gertrude called me yesterday," his Uncle Maury was saying now. Ezra looked up from his coffee. "She had some news, and she was going to tell it to you today, whenever you woke up."

"What was she going to tell me?"

"Your father and Kimberly are flying back from Palm Beach. They'll be back in New York in a few days."

That *was* news. Right after the fight at the dinner table, they'd packed their bags and fled, without a word, to more hospitable climes.

"Now your father's not an easy guy to get along with," Maury confessed, "and sometimes I don't know how your mother put up with him for all those years. But if you want to stay in that apartment—and Gertrude tells me that you do—you're going to have to work a little harder at it. You've got to make more of an effort, Ezra."

His uncle was right, of course, though Ezra had no idea how that effort should manifest itself. If his mother had been alive, there'd be no problem. She had been proud of everything he did, whether it was drawing a picture of a horse or guessing all the right answers to some TV game show. It was his father who never seemed to think anything he did was good enough. It was his father who never believed he would measure up. Who didn't understand anything Ezra enjoyed or was interested in. All Sam Metzger knew was how to make money, how to put up buildings and parking garages and shopping centers. Everything he touched turned to gold, while everything Ezra touched turned to dust.

But the scroll would change all that. Ezra was going to do something here that would make the world sit up and take notice. And then his father would have to acknowledge him and admit that Ezra had done something—something momentous—that even he, the great Sam Metzger, could not have done himself. When that day came, it was going to be the sweetest in Ezra's life.

And it wasn't far off.

But in the meantime, what was he supposed to do as a peace offering—bake a cake? Leave a letter of apology on their pillows? "I'll try to make it work," he simply said.

"Good. You do that," Maury said, putting his coffee mug on the floor and struggling up out of the Barcalounger. The morning sunlight was now streaming through the dirty windows of the apartment. "Me, I'm ready for some Danish. How about you?"

"I'm buying," Ezra said.

"Better leave that to me," Maury said. "You, they won't even let inside the place."

THIRTEEN

"Is it okay if I ask Professor Russo a question directly?" Katie asked, and Carter, who was sharing the lecture hall stage with him, said, "Be my guest."

Katie stood up and leaned on the back of the seat in front of her. Russo and Carter were on opposite sides of the slide screen, on which an artist's rendering of a pterodactyl in flight was depicted. "Professor Cox believes that birds are the modern-day descendants of dinosaurs," Katie said, "and that some of the dinosaurs, including a fossil of one that we saw in a previous lecture, actually had feathers. I know this is a big debate, but which side of it do you fall on?"

Carter should have known Katie would try to nail him; she was the smartest kid in the class, but she liked to make mischief, and Russo's being there provided her with the perfect opportunity. It was almost as if she'd guessed that this was one of the few paleontological points on which he and Russo did not agree.

Russo stuffed his hands in the pockets of his tweed jacket and looked like he was wondering how to answer that one—truthfully, or to defer to the views of his host?

"Yes, you are right. There is much debate about this point," he said, to buy some time. When he took his hands out of his pockets again, he had a matchbook in one and a crumpled pack of Nazionalis in the other. He tamped out a cigarette and actually started to light it before a couple of the students laughed, and Carter had to say, "Joe, I'm afraid you can't smoke in here."

For a second, Russo looked stumped, as if he were even aware that he was lighting a cigarette at all, then flicked the match out. "Yes, of course."

"I've read that they found some fossils in Madagascar," Katie interjected, "that showed some kind of animal that had feathered forearms, like a bird. But it also had the kind of claws that made it seem more like a dinosaur."

"Yes, and I believe that a mistake has been made. I believe that the excavation there has uncovered pieces of separate creatures. For me," Russo said, glancing apologetically over at Carter, "there are still too many, how do you say . . . gaps. I do not see in birds, for instance, the beginning of a thumb"—he held up his own and wriggled it—"that we can see in dinosaurs. I see that there are similarities, yes, between the birds and one branch of the dinosaur tree—"

"The theropods?" Katie said, showing off.

"Yes. You have been paying attention to your professor," Russo said, with a smile, "but even with these theropods, these meat eaters, I do not yet see the definite link." He shrugged. "But that is what science is all about. Debate, discussion, discovery. I could be wrong, and my friend Carter could turn out to be right. It is possible. But since you are in his class, and not mine, I think that you should agree with his views."

There was scattered laughter around the lecture hall, and Carter was about to step forward to take control again when one of the other students said, "Is there a European consensus about all this, and is it different from the American one? What does the Italian scientific community, for instance, think?"

"You want me to speak for all of Europe, or even Italy?"

Russo said, wide-eyed, and Carter said, "Go for it. Nobody's taping, as far as I know. The stage is yours."

Russo walked more toward the center, and Carter retreated into the shadows toward the rear—which was right where he wanted to be today; he'd had a bad night's sleep, and even now his thoughts kept returning to the events surrounding the delivery of the fossil.

Free at last to start his own investigation, Carter had gone to work with a vengeance. He'd removed the chains that anchored the rock to the platform and stripped away the wide bands of yellow tape that held the plastic sheathing in place. Then he'd carefully cut away the plastic itself, from the top first, so that the pieces fell away from the rock like the petals of a flower opening wide and drooping down. In the end, the plastic sheets lay in a pool around the base of the stone. The rock itself was a miracle—a massive, bumpy, granular block, striated, studded, and sparkling all over with a score of different minerals. Geology had never been Carter's greatest strength, but even with the naked eye he could see—hell, *anyone* could see— that this particular specimen had led a very long and eventful life.

"In Italy, perhaps because we do not have so much access to technology—the government is very stingy with its resources—we like to *think,* to work on *theory,*" Russo was saying. "Then later we try to make the evidence prove it."

The students laughed again, another one asked a question, and Carter was relieved to see that Russo was warming to the task; Carter could tell he was a good lecturer, and guessed he was popular with his own students back in Rome.

But that first night, in the lab, he'd shown a lot less interest and enthusiasm than Carter would have expected— maybe the whole thing was just anticlimactic for him. Russo had stood back, making occasional comments and observations, while Carter had clambered all over the rock, like a kid climbing a tree. At one point, he'd lain flat on the top of it, just trying to imagine what was fossilized inside, which way it lay, what bones were preserved, what they might be able to tell him about evolution and the prehistoric world.

"You should be careful, lying on a ticking bomb like that," Russo had said, referring to the pockets of volatile gas that they both suspected were embedded in the stone.

"Long as I don't puncture the damn thing, I should be safe," Carter had replied, though the time for that, he knew, would come. Eventually, they would have to figure out a way to chisel, sand, hack, blast, or laser away the stone encasing the rest of the fossil within. For now, all that could be seen, all that had ever been seen, were those long, twisted talons that seemed to be struggling to claw their way out of the very rock. Carter, who'd seen countless fossils from all over the globe, had never seen anything like this one; it would have been nearly impossible to put into words, or to convey to someone who hadn't seen it first-hand, but this fossil carried a kind of ineffable *vitality*. There was no other way to say it. When Carter stroked the prehensile claw—and he could not resist doing so—he didn't feel that he was touching some long-dead specimen, some calcified, ossified, petrified thing. He felt that he was touching something . . . dormant. And though he knew this had to be wrong, there was no way it could be true, he felt that the thing was perceptibly, maybe even measurably, warmer than the surrounding stone.

"The pelvic bones, the pubic bones too, are all quite primitive in the Madagascar fossil," Russo was explaining. "For the late Cretaceous, this is unusual."

"Any reason why you think this could have happened?" Katie asked.

"Isolation, possibly. On an island, a species could survive longer than it might be able to do on the mainland. It might be able to evolve in its own way, at its own rate, and in its own . . . niche."

True enough, Carter thought, and it might explain some of the anomalies in the Madagascar find. But their own prize fossil, from Lago D'Avernus? Over the eons, the Italian boot, like every other present-day country and continent in the world, had migrated and changed, but for more than two hundred million years it had remained an integrated part of what was known by earth scientists as the Laurasian land mass. Nor had it ever been made, in any way, impervious to extraterritorial influence or mutation; even the Alpine folding that took place in the Cenozoic era was, geologically speaking, no big deal.

"Can I ask a sort of personal question?" Katie asked, and Carter's ears perked up.

"Ask it, and then we will know," Russo replied good-naturedly.

"Why are you here, in New York? Are you just visiting with your old friend Professor Cox, or are you here doing work of some kind?"

Odd, how on target that kid could be. Even Russo looked nonplussed, and glanced over at Carter just as the class bell went off.

"A little of both," Carter said, over the din. "The good news is, Professor Russo will be at your disposal, on an informal basis. And the bad news is, the work we're doing is—to put it professionally—none of your beeswax. See you all next week; don't forget to leave your term papers in my box at the departmental office." He turned to Russo, as the students made for the exits. "So how do you like teaching in the States?"

Russo wagged his head back and forth. "Not so bad. But it would be better if I could smoke."

"You'd have to apply to the department head for a special dispensation."

"I could do this?"

"Not really."

After lunch in the faculty dining room, where Russo had the dubious pleasure of meeting the departmental chair, Stanley Mackie, Carter spent the rest of the day working in the lab; the argon laser had been delivered, and a techie from the medical sciences department spent several hours walking Carter and Russo through its operating procedures. On the whole Carter figured he knew how to use it, but he wasn't about to try it out until the following week, and even then he'd only test it on the *Smilodon* specimens recently donated to the university. Not only were they unremarkable—they were also free of any dangerous gas pockets.

At six o'clock sharp, while he was still immersed in the laser manual, there was a honking outside, just beyond the metal doors to the lab.

"Carter?" Russo said.

"Huh?" Carter replied, without looking up.

"Your friends, I think, are here?"

Carter couldn't believe it; he glanced at his watch. He'd agreed with Beth that he'd be ready to leave for the country at six, and to make it easier on him, she told him she'd get Ben and Abbie to bring their car around to the very door of the lab.

Carter threw the manual into the duffel bag with his other things, then pulled on his leather jacket. "You going to be okay?" he said to Russo.

"I am a big boy," Russo said. "And tonight, I have a New York party to go to," he said, brandishing the invitation to Bill Mitchell's pre-Halloween bash. "Have a good time."

The car honked again, and Carter slipped out the side door.

Beth was in the backseat, and Carter slid in beside her. "Sorry, hope I didn't keep you all waiting," he said, propping his feet on the duffel bag.

"No problem," Ben said, turning to look out the rear window as he backed up.

"We were planning to stop on the road and have dinner," Abbie said, from the front seat. "There's a great little place, with a moose head over the bar and all that, about an hour and a half away."

"Sounds great," Beth said, squeezing Carter's hand in the backseat. These days, she reflected, the only time they were in the backseat of a car together, it was a taxi, and then they were holding on for dear life. This was a lot more romantic.

"So Beth tells us you're working on something very

exciting," Ben said, as the car crawled westward, through heavy traffic, on Houston Street.

"Can you say what it is," Abbie asked, "or is that information classified?"

Beth wondered what Carter would say; he was normally so secretive about his research—this project especially—and she felt guilty that she'd said anything about it at all.

"It's like nothing I've ever seen before," he said, the wonder in his voice surprising even Beth. "A massive sample of primarily igneous rock, but with what appears to be a perfectly preserved fossil embedded inside it."

"And that's rare?" Ben asked over his shoulder, as he navigated through a crush of cars, all of them no doubt trying to make their way, as he was, to the West Side Highway.

"It's not only rare, it's basically impossible. Especially since from all the empirical evidence so far, the rock is almost as old as the molten core of the planet, as old as the earth itself."

"So how could something that old hold a fossil?" Ben asked. "Even an investment banker knows that life came along a whole lot later."

"That's what makes it so puzzling," Carter said.

When he talked like this, leaning forward in his enthusiasm, he looked to Beth like a little boy.

"We've taken a specimen from the fossil itself—"

"I thought you hadn't used the laser yet?" Beth interjected.

"We haven't—we did it the old-fashioned way, with a chisel, removing just a small fragment from the end of one talon."

"And what do you hope that will prove?" Ben asked.

"We sent it over to the medical sciences lab, and with carbon dating, maybe we'll be able to get a fix on its relative age. The weird thing is, all the tests so far have come back with completely untenable readings."

"What do you mean," Abbie said, "untenable?"

"It means that the fossil predates every form of life that ever existed, anywhere in the world; it predates the dinosaurs, the lowest plankton or moss or amoeba. It existed, if you want to put it that way, before the dawn of time."

There was a momentary silence in the car.

"Sounds like an *X-Files* case to me," Ben finally said.

"Or an extraterrestrial," Abbie added.

Carter leaned back. "It does, doesn't it?" He looked out the window. "I've brought some books and reports to study this weekend," he said, "so maybe I'll crack it, once and for all, at your place."

Beth's heart sank; she'd imagined long walks in the woods, holding hands and sharing intimate thoughts, followed by cozy evenings in front of a crackling fire. But now, suddenly, she saw herself walking in the woods, alone, while Carter hunkered down in the house with his lab reports. That had not been part of the plan. Her plan was for time together, time outdoors . . . and time spent working on that little idea they'd had about starting a family. Still, unless Carter had changed utterly, there was one thing she could count on; the boy in him loved dinosaurs, but the man in him loved Victoria's Secret. And she had picked up a few naughty little surprises there on her lunch break.

The score was going to be lingerie one, dinosaurs nothing.

When they got to the restaurant, it was just as Abbie had advertised it—dark booths, basic fare, and a mournful-looking moose head over the bar. But things between Ben and Abbie were going downhill fast; they'd started bickering in the car, and now, after Ben had thrown down a few too many drinks, they only got worse. Maybe it was the accumulated stress of buying the new house, driving out of the city in crazy weekend traffic, trying to start a family—Beth could understand where it was coming from, but it didn't make it any more comfortable to be there to witness it. After dinner, Abbie insisted on driving the rest of the way, and after a little tussle with Ben over the car keys—which they pretended was playful, but wasn't—she won.

The drive got darker and lonelier the farther they went, and the towns they passed through became more desolate and forlorn. Beth began to wish she'd never agreed to this

plan—would Carter ever forgive her?—but it was too late
to do anything about it now.

After they'd been on a winding, pitch-black, two-lane
road for about fifteen minutes, Ben said, "Slow down—it's
right there!" and Abbie said, "Where? I don't see it!"

"There, there, behind the big oak!"

She slowed the car. "What's an oak? I can't tell an oak
from an elm, even in the daylight."

"It's the big tree you just passed," Ben said. "I told you I
should drive."

Abbie slowed down even more, then turned the car on a
dirt patch; there was a large open trench marked by orange
highway cones running along the side of the road.

"They're replacing all the water mains in the area," Ben
said. "The old ones were put in around the Civil War."

Turning back, they found the driveway, which was partially concealed by the massive old oak and descended
steeply from the main road. They bounced down it for a
few hundred yards, and at the bottom stopped in front of a
small, old-fashioned green and white house with a low-
slung front porch and a high-pitched roof.

Beth got out first. "It's great!" she said, with as much
conviction as she could muster. But her heart wasn't in it. In
the photos she and Carter had seen that night at Minetta's,
the place had looked sunny and kind of cute. But here, at
night, surrounded by barren trees and fields and bathed only
in the cold glow of the moon, it took on a rather sinister
cast. The front door, which even now Ben was struggling to
get open, screeched and stuck.

"You have to turn the key all the way to the left," Abbie
said, and Ben shot back, "I did turn it all the way to the left.
The lock needs to be replaced—that's all I can tell you."

Carter and Beth busied themselves with the bags, and
pretty much kept their heads down. They toured the house—
with only five or six rooms in the whole place, and most
of them still unfurnished, it was quick work—and then went
up the spiral staircase to their own room on the second floor.
The walls had been stripped of their paint and the curtain
rods were barren. When the door was closed behind them,

Beth flopped down on the edge of their bed and mouthed the word *Yikes*. Carter nodded. Then he came and plopped down beside her, slinging one arm around her neck and kissing her on the cheek.

"Ever notice," he said in a low voice, "how another couple's marital difficulties can make you really appreciate what you've got?"

In the master bedroom, which was directly downstairs, they heard a drawer slam, and then the sound of lowered voices. Beth thought she heard Abbie saying something was "so embarrassing" (she could think of several things that might have qualified) and Ben saying, over and over, "Give it a rest."

"Remind me never to buy a country house," Carter said.

"At least not this one," she whispered.

"Kind of spooky here, isn't it?"

Beth smiled. "And kind of freezing," she said, in a voice as low as his.

"Take a hot bath," he said. "I'll unpack."

Beth fished a few things out of her bag, then crossed to the bathroom. The window in there didn't have any curtain or blind either, but it looked out on an endless expanse of black fields, withered trees, and off in the distance, what looked like the hulk of an abandoned barn. She turned the hot water on full and listened as the pipes groaned and gurgled. The water came out brown at first, then cleared up, and felt like heaven when she stepped into the deep old porcelain tub. She put her head back and let the heat soak into her bones. God, she hoped that Abbie and Ben would be getting along better the next day. There was nothing so awful as being marooned in the middle of someone else's marital spat—especially as she had been so looking forward to an intimate and romantic weekend. She and Carter had a good life in the city—a great life, she knew most people would say—but they'd both had to work hard to get it, and they were still working hard to maintain it. It was time they kicked back and enjoyed themselves a little.

When she got out of the tub and opened the door to the

bedroom, Carter was doing exactly what she'd imagined—sitting up in bed, his nose buried in a bunch of papers.

But when he looked up, and saw her modeling her new Victoria's Secret outfit—she might not be Heidi Klum, but she didn't look half bad in it, even if she did say so herself—the papers dropped into his lap and his jaw nearly went with them.

"Don't let me disturb you," she purred.

"Too late for that now."

Nice to know, she thought as she crossed to his beckoning arms, that she could still beat out any fossil on earth.

FOURTEEN

In retrospect, Joe thought, a cruise was probably not the best idea. But he'd already bought the ticket, and he thought the fresh air might do him good.

He'd had too much to drink at the party last night. The minute he'd walked through the door and into the crush of bodies, Bill Mitchell had appeared and pressed a glass of Halloween punch into his hand. He still didn't know what was in it. Then Mitchell had introduced him around as if he were the most noted paleontologist in all of Europe. "He's in New York on some top-secret project," Mitchell had exclaimed, "and if anybody here can find out what it is, please tell me!"

Russo had done his best to downplay the publicity, and he'd had a pretty good time—the party guests were a mix of young faculty members, doctoral candidates, and even some undergrads. He met that student, Katie Coyne, who'd asked him some questions in the lecture hall; she was a very beguiling and opinionated young thing. Even at the party she wanted to know all sorts of stuff about how he got where he was today, what kind of excavations he'd been on, where he thought the next great discoveries were likely to be made. He'd seldom met students her age so focused.

"When you graduate," he'd told her, "come and see me in Rome. I think you are going to do great work one day."

He'd stumbled home after midnight and got up the next morning, late; he didn't even bother to fold up his blankets, as Carter and Beth wouldn't be back till Sunday night. And he was determined to take that Circle Line Cruise; he wanted to do something touristy, and today was the perfect opportunity. But he hadn't counted on still feeling queasy. Nor had he realized just how many people would be crammed onto the boat, or how many of them would be boisterous children, some of them already in their Halloween costumes. He'd tried staying in the inside cabin, but between the heat and the commotion, he'd decided to try his luck outside on the open deck.

Over the loudspeaker, the ship's captain announced the various points of interest as the boat chugged past them— the South Street Seaport, the Brooklyn Bridge, Hell's Gate, Gracie Mansion. Russo took special note when they passed a tiny island in the East River where the city's smallpox hospital had once stood; now it was just a pile of broken bricks and dust. The patients had been ferried there and marooned, as it were, to keep their contagion from infecting the rest of the city. Charles Dickens, the captain said, had once sailed past this place, Blackwell's Island, and the patients—along with the inmates of the neighboring lunatic asylum—had waved their hats and handkerchiefs in salute. In America, Russo was always surprised to find anything, even ruins, that had been there for more than a century.

When the boat docked again, Russo waited for most of the other passengers to disembark, then walked off himself. Even though the cruise had been fairly steady, it still felt good to be back on land, to no longer feel the thrumming of the engines under his feet. It was getting dark fast, but he thought the long walk home might give him some exercise, which would in turn help him get to sleep that night. He still wasn't sleeping well, and even last night, when he'd fallen onto the sofa half-drunk, he'd awakened several times from bad dreams. Tonight, he wanted to try to wear himself out.

The closer he got to the West Village, the wilder the street scene became. Girls dressed as vampires, guys in cowboy gear, and in what he assumed was a tribute to Bergman's *The Seventh Seal,* a whole group of people made up to look like medieval penitents, in brown robes, waving smoking censers, and flagellating themselves. All day long, he hadn't really felt like eating, but now he realized he was getting weak. When he found himself outside some kind of Italian trattoria, he suddenly thought that what he'd really like right now was a hot bowl of pasta fagiolo. In Rome, he lived above a place where the cook made the best he'd ever tasted.

What he got here was barely recognizable; he could have counted the kidney beans in it on the fingers of one hand. He knew Americans were supposed to love Italian food, but if this was what they were getting, what on earth were they so fond of? He paid the check with cash, left what he hoped was the right tip, and went outside again. Things had definitely heated up in the last hour or so. There were more people than ever on the street, dressed in all kinds of weird costumes—three bald men painted blue were walking with a woman dressed as the Statue of Liberty—and the streets were clogged with cars and taxis blaring their horns and struggling to make some progress. As far as Russo could tell, walking—though not easy—was still faster than any other way of getting around.

It was a full moon tonight, no doubt contributing to the craziness, and the city seemed ablaze with light—traffic lights, headlights, neon signs, the flashing red beacons of police cars, glowing green necklaces that dozens of the revelers wore around their throats or foreheads. As Russo made his way through the throng, it felt more and more like Mardi Gras to him, with the noise, the elaborate costumes, the pushing and shoving; the very air seemed to be filled with a sense of excitement and expectation, of suspense and sexual heat, of forced merriment and even, truth be told, of menace.

As a newcomer to the city, it was interesting for him to see, but he could well understand why Carter and Beth had wanted to get out of New York for the weekend.

By the time he got close to Washington Square, the crowds on the sidewalk were so thick he could hardly get anywhere at all; he was forever colliding with people, apologizing (not that they could hear, or cared), getting tripped and jostled and shoved. A guy with a plastic cup of beer banged into him and spilled most of it down the front of his raincoat, then whirled away without a word or even a glance back. Russo brushed off as much of it as he could. Maybe, he thought, if he got off the main streets, he might be able to wend his way back to the apartment a little more easily. When he neared the bio building he took a side street, and decided to go around behind.

He came around the side of the massive old building—yellow brick that had long since turned brown—and the mobs immediately thinned out. There were revelers, but they were bent on making their way back to the action. By the time he turned the corner and was crossing behind the loading area, there were just a few stragglers—and the ever-present transvestite, a tall black man in a red suede coat, leaning into the rear window of an idling limousine. Working even on Halloween night, Russo thought; there was something laudable in that.

His eyes turned inevitably to the loading doors, which were all the way down and locked. And he had almost looked away again when something caught his eye. At first he wasn't even sure what had gotten his attention, but then he realized that under the side door, the one on the loading ramp level, there was a very thin sliver of light.

He stopped. Had he left the lights on when he closed the lab on Friday?

No. He distinctly remembered turning them off, and looking back, just before he closed the door, at the brooding shapes of the laser and the slab.

Could the janitor, Hank, be in there? It certainly didn't seem likely—especially at this hour, almost ten o'clock on a Saturday night.

He wanted to walk away, to just pretend he'd never seen it, but he knew he couldn't do that. He had to see what was going on. He felt in his pocket for the keys, then walked up the concrete steps to the loading ramp. At the door, he looked down again—yes, light was spilling out from the thin crack at its base. He put his ear to the cold metal surface and he could hear, faintly, a radio playing.

Could Carter have come back early, unannounced? Now *that,* he suddenly thought with relief, was a possibility. Russo knew that Carter, down deep, thought this fossil might turn out to prove some kind of connection between the birds and the dinosaurs, and maybe, now that he was so close to finally proving his pet theory, he'd come rushing back. Maybe he'd been bored, even by one day in the country, and couldn't wait to get back to work.

Cheered by the thought, Russo unlocked the door and stepped into the makeshift lab. His first conclusion was that he was right. The radio was blaring rock and roll, all the overhead lights were on, and the plastic sheath he'd thrown over the laser was now lying on the desk.

But to his immense surprise, the laser itself was on— and emitting a steady, high-pitched whine. It had been moved so that its barrel was positioned right up next to a portion of the stone—almost touching it, in fact. Had Carter decided to go ahead and try it on his own? Russo was a bit taken aback; it seemed like the kind of thing they would have done only together. There was so much preparation to go through, so many precautions to take, so many steps to ensure the safety and efficacy of the procedure. He and Carter had agreed, right at the outset, that this was a terribly fragile and volatile specimen that had to be treated with the utmost deliberation. But now, as Russo looked into the lab, he saw Carter come around from the other side of the stone with a pair of heavy green goggles on his eyes and walk confidently to the laser assembly.

Only it wasn't Carter, he suddenly realized.

This guy was too short, and his hair was long and lank, and when the guy looked over and saw Russo he pushed the goggles onto the top of his head and sheepishly said, "Wow—I never expected to see you here tonight."

"Mitchell?" Russo said, in amazement. "What are you doing in here?"

Mitchell looked at a loss for words. But the humming laser answered the question for him without his having to say a thing—and he knew it.

"How did you get in here?" Russo said, striding into the lab.

"Through the storage rooms. I mean, I didn't have to pick any locks or anything."

"This is a private lab. You have no business in here."

Mitchell looked like he was casting around for an answer to that one, too. "Hey, you can't keep a secret this big under wraps for very long." He offered a weasely grin. "A private lab, an overseas delivery, a laser on requisition—hey, I'm no Sherlock Holmes, but this was kind of hard to miss."

"How do you know about any of this?" Russo said, indignantly.

"I know plenty," Mitchell said, his own temper starting to flare. "And in case you've forgotten, I'm an assistant professor here. I think I'm entitled to know what's going on."

"You are not entitled to come in here and . . . mix with our experiments."

"I've got to say, Joe, you've got some nerve." He pulled the goggles off the top of his head and threw his lanky hair back behind his ear. "You're not even on the faculty here, and I am, and you're telling me what I can and can't do in the department? I've been nice to you, I invited you to my party, I've gone out of my way to be friendly. And what have you done for me? Other than not tell me one single thing about why you're here, or what you're doing, or what"—he said, gesturing toward the black slab—"the incredible thing is that's buried inside this rock?"

Russo glanced at the slab—the pinpoint light of the laser was trained on the very spot where the specimen had been taken from the fossilized talon. And there was a very faint but acrid smell in the air.

"How long have you had the laser on?" Russo asked, urgently.

"A few minutes, no more," Mitchell said. "I was just going to see a little of what it could do."

"Turn it off! Now!"

"I don't think you're supposed to do that. Once you turn it on, you have to leave it on for—"

Russo remembered enough from the run-through with the techie to know where the on and off switches were. He went around to the back of the assembly and bent his head over the control panel, but Mitchell intervened.

"It's not going to do any harm to let it run for a while," he said, putting his hands over the controls.

"This rock is very, very dangerous," Russo said. The smell of burning grew stronger. "Get your hands off it!"

"What's so dangerous about it?" Mitchell said, though he did take his hands away.

"Gases! They are trapped inside!" Russo pushed Mitchell roughly out of the way.

Mitchell must have smelled the burning, too. "I thought this was a cold kind of burn. It's argon-based, which means—"

There was a pop, no more than the sound of a pin puncturing a balloon.

Russo was suddenly thrown up into the air and carried across the lab on a deafening blast of searing hot wind and blazing light. He slammed up against the far wall, then slid down to the concrete floor as an ocean of flame surged like a lightning tide across the lab at him. He couldn't move, there wouldn't have been time anyway—the flames engulfed the floor, and then his legs, his body, scouring him, singeing him, washing over his face and crackling in his hair. The lab echoed and shook with the roar of the explosion. The overhead lights burst, the air was filled with a thick rain of broken glass, a swarm of shards and pebbles and stones that ricocheted around the lab like bullets.

Russo couldn't breathe; he could barely see. The flames raced around the room, licking at the walls and doors like wild dogs trying to break free; the air was filled with a fine black mist of pulverized rock.

But the lab was not dark.

Even with his injured eyes, Russo could see a light. A white light, shimmering, in the middle of the lab—right where the slab had been. But the light seemed to move; it seemed to have . . . a shape.

He tried to catch a breath; the smell of his own smoldering clothes and skin filled his nostrils.

The shape rose up, unsteadily.

Mitchell? he thought. No, this wasn't anything he'd ever seen . . .

It seemed to expand, like an eagle stretching its wings.

Was he dead? Was this his . . . shepherd?

The shape glowed, like a column of light, and it moved . . . toward him.

Russo blinked, but nothing seemed to happen; were his eyelids gone? His eyes ached; parts of his body still sizzled like a steak just off the grill. His hands lay useless at his sides.

The shape came closer. Russo struggled to breathe the burning air. Struggled to stay alert. Alive.

He stared up into the black mist.

The shape hovered over him, inspecting him. Sniffing him.

And it was so bright, so burning, Russo could hardly look at it—but he couldn't bear to look away either.

Because it was the most beautiful thing he had ever seen.

A face made of light itself. A human face, but not human. Perfect, beautiful, terrifying. The last thing, he thought, he would ever see.

You are suffering.

They weren't words exactly—it was more like a thought—that Russo heard, somehow, as if it had been implanted inside his head.

The shape reached out—with a hand, not a talon—a hand also made of light, and touched his head. It felt like an icicle grazing his seared skull.

Suffering is a gift from God.

Again, as if through telepathy.

And the shape rose up and began to move away. Russo was terrified it would stay, but at the same time afraid to see it go. Afraid to be left alone in this inferno.

It drifted toward the loading doors, shimmering, constantly rippling and twisting and turning . . . a glowing candle the size of a man.

And then the agony overcame him. As if it had gathered its forces for a final assault, the pain swallowed him up whole, and he toppled over, too burnt even to scream, onto the concrete floor.

PART TWO

PART TWO

FIFTEEN

Ironically, it was only on Sunday afternoon, when it came time to pack up and go back to the grind of the city, that Carter really felt like he was starting to unwind in the country.

He hadn't had a call from Russo all weekend, but then Carter hadn't called him, either. For a couple of hours on Saturday, he'd studied up on the finer points of laser technology, before Beth had finally insisted he put the manual down and come outside for a walk in the woods. Later, Abbie and Ben, who seemed to have ironed out whatever problems they'd been having on the drive out, invited them to go apple picking in a nearby orchard; now they had about two heaping bushels full of fresh apples that Carter wondered what on earth they were going to do with.

Even Russo wouldn't be able to plow through more than a dozen of them.

Driving back to the city, in a car redolent of apples and pumpkin pies (which Abbie and Beth had made that morning), they turned on the radio to hear the traffic report. "Unless I hear otherwise," Ben said, "I'll stick with the Saw Mill River Parkway."

But first they had to suffer through a battery of commercials, a weather report, and then several minutes of idiotic banter from the two wild and wacky radio hosts Gary and Gil. Carter wasn't paying much attention to their observations on Elvira, the amply endowed Mistress of the Dark— "I mean, are those breasts real? They've been right where they are for, like, thirty years!"—but he did start to listen more carefully when Gil said, "And what about that craziness with the New York City bells last night?"

"Is that spooky, or what?" Gary chimed in.

"For anybody who's still too hung over from Halloween parties to remember what happened last night, at exactly ten-sixteen P.M., every church bell in the city of Manhattan—"

"—and we mean every bell, in every church, mosque, temple, you name it," Gary broke in again.

"—started ringing like mad."

"It was like some kind of air-raid warning system," Gary said.

"Incoming! Incoming!" Gil shouted.

"But nothing came, right?"

"I sure hope not!"

"But let me tell you, if that was some kind of Halloween prank—"

"What else *could* it be?" Gil asked.

"—then I've got to say, those guys did an amazing job of coordinating things. How in the world do you get every church bell, from the old-fashioned kind hanging way up there in the belfry, to the electronically controlled chimes in places like St. Patrick's Cathedral, to ring all at once?"

"And why at ten-sixteen P.M.?" Gil wondered aloud. "I'd have waited till midnight myself, if I was planning something like this."

"Well, all I can say is, if the guys behind this Halloween stunt are listening to us now, give us a call at 1-800-GIL-GARY, and tell us just how you managed to pull it off! Very cool stuff."

"Very scary."

Ben turned down the radio. "What do you want to bet

it's that magician, that David Blaine guy, who's behind it? The one who stood in a block of ice in Times Square."

"But if he doesn't take credit for it," Carter asked, "what would be the point?"

"Maybe he just wants to let the mystery build for a while?" Beth said.

"In this town, it'll be old news by Tuesday," Abbie observed. "He'd better move fast."

Even after the traffic report, Ben left the radio on low, and callers from all over the city weighed in on the question of the ringing bells. A couple of them subscribed to the Halloween prank theory, but most of the others, to Carter's dismay, seemed to vote for some supernatural—in other words, *irrational*—cause. One guy claimed it had been done by "the ghost of Houdini, to prove there's an afterlife," but most of the others took a more traditional religious tack. A Jehovah's witness called in to declare it was a sign of the coming Apocalypse. A minister from Harlem called to say it might be a wake-up call to New York, "the Sodom and Gomorrah of our century," to change its evil ways. And a professor in the religion department at Columbia explained that ringing the church bells on Halloween night was an ancient way of warding off witches.

"It was thought," the professor went on, "that if a church bell rang while a witch was in flight overhead, the sound of the bell would knock her out of the air like a Patriot missile."

"So all we have to do now," the radio host Gil interrupted, "is look around the streets to see if we've got any downed witches?"

"Well, yes, I suppose you could do that," the professor replied, "but I wouldn't put too much time into it if I were you."

"I still say it'll turn out to be David Blaine," Ben said. "Anybody mind if I change the station? I can only take so much of Gary and Gil's antics."

No one objected, and Ben punched a couple of buttons until he found NPR again.

The rest of the way into the city, they listened to *All Things Considered*, talked about more sensible matters, and once they'd hit the West Village, navigated through the congested streets until they got to the front of Beth and Carter's apartment building.

"Thank you so much, we had a great time," Beth said, getting out of the car with a delicately balanced pumpkin pie in her hands.

Carter got out the other side and, with Ben's help, unloaded their bags from the trunk, along with a lifetime supply of apples.

"Don't eat those all at once," Ben said.

"Fortunately, we have a hungry houseguest," Carter said. "Thanks for the weekend. It was just what the doctor ordered."

"Come on, Carter!" Beth called from the front steps. "I'm sure Abbie and Ben would like to get home, too, sometime tonight."

"See you," Carter said, hoisting an overnight bag in one hand and a sack of apples in the other.

Upstairs, Carter knocked on the door first, just to give Russo fair warning.

"I don't think he's home," Beth said. "The paper's still on the mat."

She was right; the Sunday *Times,* all twelve pounds of it, was lying in front of their door.

Inside, all the lights were out, and when Carter turned them on, he could see that Joe wasn't there; his bedding, which he normally folded up and stacked under the coffee table, was still spread all over the sofa and hanging onto the floor. And that crucifix, the one he'd seen the night Russo first arrived, was up on the wall again.

Beth dragged the apples into the kitchen.

"Is there a note in there?" Carter asked. "I wonder where he is."

"Nope," she said, "no note in here." She came back out again. "He's not in the bathroom, is he?"

"No," Carter said.

"Though he *used* to fold up his blankets every morning," she grumbled, glancing over at the sofa. "And what is that on the wall?"

As Beth went over to inspect it, Carter tried to put it all together in his mind. Something was off. It wasn't like Russo to leave the sofa a mess like that; it wasn't like him to leave the paper on the mat. He liked reading the paper.

"Carter, have you seen this? It's a crucifix. I didn't know that Joe was so religious."

"Neither did I. He wasn't when I knew him in Europe."

"You know, something's just occurred to me," she said, with a half-smile. "Didn't you say he was going to a party at Bill Mitchell's?"

"Yes. I gave him the invitation."

"Maybe he met somebody there."

"That was Friday night."

"I know—but maybe they spent last night together, here." She looked at the tangled sheets and blankets on the sofa. "You think we should have told him it was okay, with us gone, to use the bedroom?" She gingerly lifted the hem of the sheet and tossed it back onto the sofa. "Maybe he's over at this mystery woman's place right now."

It was certainly possible; Carter had never known Russo to be much of a ladies' man, but that was back when they were on a dig site in Sicily. Here in New York, Russo might have some extra cachet; here, he was an eminent scientist, visiting from Italy yet.

"You want to order in some Chinese food?" Beth said. "I'm too tired to go out again."

"No, I'm not that hungry," he said. "If you don't mind, I think I'm going to go over to the lab and see if Russo's there."

"I don't mind at all. In fact, I'm pooped. Why don't you guys go out and have some fun?"

Fun wasn't really uppermost in Carter's mind as he went back downstairs. He still had sort of an odd feeling. He'd come back expecting to find Russo with his feet up on the coffee table, watching TV. But instead he'd found an unmade bed, the crucifix, the paper still at the door—and none of it added up.

At the corner, Carter waited for the WALK light to flash. Maybe he was being ridiculous, and Beth was right. Maybe

Russo had just gotten lucky with someone at the party and he was out having a good time with her. Maybe he'd dragged her along on that Circle Line Cruise he'd said he wanted to take. If she'd gone along, then they *must* be in love.

Or else he'd be at the lab, wondering what had taken Carter so long to get back to work there.

As Carter approached the front of the bio building, he thought he detected a faintly ashy smell in the air. And as he went around the side to enter through the loading area, the smell only got stronger. The West Village always went a little crazy on Halloween night, and Carter figured somebody must have set a bonfire back there the night before. But as he came around the back of the building, the yellow brick, which was always pretty dirty, started to look a lot worse than usual—black and smudged, sooty. And the smell of smoke got overwhelming.

Then he saw the wet cement, the yellow police tape, the wooden barricades . . . the buckled loading doors. He stopped in his tracks.

What had happened here?

Russo.

He ran toward the loading area and easily skirted two of the wooden barricades. No one was around but a couple of students on the other side of the street, casually taking in the damage. One of the two had taken his freshman seminar.

"You know what happened here?" Carter called out to them.

"I heard there was a fire—that's all I know," his former student said.

"Was anyone hurt?"

The other one said, "Yeah, I think so. But I don't know who it was."

Carter jumped up on the loading ramp that led to the side door. There was a police tape across it, and a posted warning from the Fire Department that said DANGER—NO ADMITTANCE UNTIL FURTHER NOTICE.

Carter pulled the tape away from the door and fumbled

for his key. He unlocked the door, but it was wedged into the frame. Putting his shoulder against it, he forced it back, the bottom screeching on the cement.

"Hey, Professor, I don't think that's safe," his student called out.

But Carter had the door open just enough to slink through.

Apart from the light from the open door, the makeshift lab was dark. Still, there was enough light for Carter to see that the place was a total disaster area. The floor was damp and covered with gray rubble, charred wood, broken glass. The overhead lights, nothing but empty shades now, dangled listlessly from the ceiling. And in the center of the room where the fossil used to rest, the cement itself was gone, and in its place was a depression almost a foot deep and burnt to an even black. It looked like a bomb had gone off there.

Was that what had happened? Had something exploded here? The slab of rock—they'd suspected it had pockets of trapped gas inside it. But the rock was static—the laser hadn't even been tried on it yet.

Or had it?

And where was Russo? Had he been in the lab when this accident, whatever it was, had occurred?

Carter was turning it all over in his mind, trying to make sense of it, when a slant of light hit the floor from the other side of the lab.

"Who's in here?" a voice said. "This area is off limits!"

It was Hank, the custodian.

"It's me, Hank—Carter Cox."

Hank, wielding a big flashlight, came in from the storage rooms. "Oh, I knew I heard somebody in here."

"Hank—what happened? Where's Professor Russo?"

Hank shuffled in, picking his way through the wet rubble. "Who the hell knows what happened? All I can tell you is, it wasn't the lights."

"The what?"

"The fire marshal is claiming it was those lights I rigged up, with the separate fuse box, that set it off. But those lights were fine, I tested 'em myself."

"Was Russo in here when it happened?" Carter reiterated.

Hank took a breath, as if this was the question he didn't want to have to answer. "Him, and that other guy, the young professor."

"What other young professor?"

"Mitchell something."

"Bill Mitchell?" What the hell would he have been doing in here? He wasn't even supposed to know this temporary lab existed.

"Yeah. He's the one who got the worst of it." Hank paused, bit his lip. "He got killed."

Carter was stunned. Speechless.

"Last I heard, the other guy, your friend Russo, is still alive. But not by much. He's over at St. Vincent's."

Hank had hardly finished before Carter had turned to go.

"I don't know what went wrong in here," Hank called after him, "but it wasn't those lights!"

Outside, Carter ran down the loading ramp just as a sedan pulled up and a tall black prostitute in a short white rabbit's fur jacket got out of the passenger seat. The sedan pulled away quickly. It wasn't until Carter was moving past the hooker and she reached out to grab his sleeve that he realized it was a man in women's clothing.

"You work in that building?" the transvestite said.

But Carter was already pulling away. "Let go—I'm in a hurry."

"I *said,* you work in that place? Because if you do, I want to know what goes on in there."

"What are you talking about?"

"I was here—last night—and I saw what came out."

Against his own will, Carter had to stop. "What do you mean? What did you see come out of there?"

"That's what I want to know. I saw a man, only it wasn't a real man. And he was all made of light, glowing."

Now Carter knew this guy was crazy.

"Good for you. I've got to go."

But the man followed him and grabbed his sleeve again.

He was strong enough to stop Carter in his tracks and spin him halfway around. "I gave that man—that *unreal* man— my coat. My best red coat. You want to know why?"

"Why?"

The transvestite looked him in the eye, hard. "Because that man didn't have a thing on."

Carter broke free and turned away. He did not have time for this gibberish.

"And you know the other reason I did it?" the transvestite called after him. "Because I think that man was an angel."

Carter had to stand there, waiting for the light to change; when it did, he hurried across the street.

"I've got my eye on you!" the guy shouted. "Oh yeah! I know when something's up!"

Carter was sure he did. But whatever this guy might or might not have seen, there was no time now to figure that out. All Carter could do was get to the hospital as fast as he could; even stopping to flag down a cab seemed an intolerable delay. He just wanted to keep moving, and did—dodging past the other pedestrians, racing across the streets as soon as the lights changed, making his way the remaining blocks to the hospital.

As long as he was concentrating on that, he could keep from thinking about what might actually have happened to Russo. And what condition he might find him in at St. Vincent's. Alive, or . . . and his mind could not even go there. Not yet. Not yet.

The light changed, and he charged across another avenue.

SIXTEEN

Fire.
Then light.
As before.
So long before.

And then, again, night.

But a night filled with lights, all around.
And sounds. So many sounds.
And voices. So many voices.
So many . . . people.

Was this . . . what had come of it?

Cold.

A cloak.

So many people.
Everywhere, speaking.
Different voices.

Their smells.
Every one of them a different smell.

But was he . . . alone?

The dark.
The cold.
Eternity.

Was he alone?
Was he the last?

And was he, at last . . . free?

SEVENTEEN

Even on a day as bleak as this, Ezra was amused by the inscription. There, chiseled into the wall above the curving steps, across from the massive UN tower itself, were the words of Isaiah 2:4: ". . . and they shall beat their swords into plowshares, and their spears into pruning hooks; nation shall not lift up sword against nation, neither shall they learn war any more." The irony was so thick, it didn't bear commenting on. The United Nations, united, as far as he could see, in only one thing: the containment, denunciation, and eventual destruction of Israel. Other than that, the whole organization was just a sham—a bunch of puffed-up, powerless delegates living the high life in New York City while their people back home in Uganda, Rwanda, Cambodia, Serbia, Chechnya, India, Pakistan, wherever, starved and suffered and murdered each other by the millions.

The UN, in Ezra's opinion, had only one thing to recommend it—and that was its public park running along the East River. It was nicely maintained, and Ezra had taken to walking there when he felt he had to get some air. There was a broad, elliptical path with benches and statues and a big green lawn in the middle on which no one was ever allowed to tread. No one bothered you, the security guards kept most of the riffraff out, and you didn't have to keep an eye out for dog shit on the pavement. Some days, when he had a lot to think about and didn't want to go home, Ezra made as many as ten or twelve loops of the park.

Today was just such a day.

His father and stepmother had returned, as Maury had warned him, that morning. But his father had been dropped off at his office, so it was only Kimberly who'd actually come home so far.

Under Gertrude's watchful and encouraging eye, Ezra had gone to the trouble of greeting her at the door. He'd even offered to relieve her of a package she was carrying.

"Thank you, Ezra," Kimberly had said, "that's a very good idea. Especially since it's for you, anyway."

"It is?"

"Yes."

His guard went up immediately. Beware of Greeks bearing gifts.

"You can open it now," she said. The vacation in Palm Beach had given her a slight tan and lightened her hair. "It's nothing much."

Was he supposed to have a present for her, too? After all, he was the one who'd started the fight that had sent her flying. But it hadn't even occurred to him to have a makeup gift on hand. He glanced over at Gertrude, whose frown told him to just be gracious and open the gift.

"Thank you," he said, carefully removing the white ribbon and opening the small robin's-egg-blue box. Inside, it was filled with a cloud of white tissue paper. Nestled in the paper he saw a gleaming silver clock with a white face and black numerals and a little envelope attached to the ring on its top. He lifted the clock out and put the empty box on a side table.

"It's a Tiffany alarm clock," Kimberly said. "Read the card."

Ezra took the little buff-colored card out of the matching envelope and read it. "Wake up and smell the coffee. Love, Kimberly."

He wasn't sure what that meant; he thought maybe he'd once heard someone use that expression, but he wasn't absolutely sure.

"Sam and I had a lot of time to talk while we were down at our place in Palm Beach," Kimberly explained, perhaps noting his confusion, "and we both decided that for your own good, it was high time you got out of your old rooms, found a place of your own and started making a living for yourself."

Ezra felt like he'd been pole-axed.

"There's no rush. Take a week, take two if that's what you need—I hear the apartment market is fairly tight right now—but we all think you'll be much happier living on your own from now on."

Ezra, not knowing how to respond, looked over at Gertrude, whose expression indicated sympathy, but not surprise; she'd probably been expecting this, Ezra thought. All his life, it occurred to him, people had been expecting things that somehow caught Ezra, and only Ezra, totally by surprise. What was wrong with his human radar, he wondered?

"But I don't want to go," he stammered. "I'm in the middle of my work. It can't be disrupted."

"Oh sure it can," Kimberly said, blithely, moving down the hall toward the master suite. "In fact, you'll probably work better in your own place. Especially after Monday of next week."

"What about Monday of next week?"

"That's when Laurent is swinging by, to take a look at your rooms. He's the interior decorator."

Kimberly was now halfway down the hall, her back to him.

"We're going to redo that part of the apartment completely," she said over her shoulder before disappearing into her own rooms.

Ezra heard her turn the lock.

He was still standing where he'd been when the lightning bolt had hit him, with the silver clock in his hands.

"I was afraid of that," Gertrude said, stepping up and

taking the clock. She looked it over. "You should always try to hold this by the ring on the top. That's what it's there for. Otherwise, you'll leave fingerprints all over the silver."

Ezra finished another loop of the park. It was a gray day, and fairly chill, so most of the benches overlooking the river were unoccupied. On one, someone had just left a neatly folded copy of the *New York Times*.

Ezra swept his overcoat under him, sat down, and picked up the paper. The front page had all the usual mayhem— another bomb blast in Belfast, a riot in the West Bank, a political assassination in Eastern Europe. But on the lower right corner of the page was a more singular story that caught Ezra's eye: CHURCH BELLS RING FOR HAL-LOWEEN? Reading quickly, he ascertained that church bells all over the boroughs of New York had rung shortly after ten o'clock on Saturday night. Before following the story over the jump to page two of the Metro section, he put the paper down and thought for a second. On Hal-loween night, he'd been working in his rooms, as usual, but he'd taken a break after ten—and yes, he remembered now that he'd heard the bell across the river, tolling and tolling and tolling. It had struck him as odd, but then he hadn't thought anything more about it. He was skittish enough these days, without dwelling on external anom-alies and occurrences.

Then he turned to the Metro section and read the re-mainder of the story. It appeared to be a mystery with no solution as yet, though the *Times* had gathered opinions and commentary from such exalted sources as the diocesan council, a high priestess of the Wiccan faith, and, on the theory that it might be an amazingly elaborate Halloween prank, Penn Jillette. Ezra didn't think even for one second that it was a prank. Lately he had been through too much; he knew all too well that there were things not dreamt of in most people's philosophies.

A mother holding her daughter's hand was walking past the bench where he was sitting.

"L'Assemble Generale est ou les delegats viennent a

faire la paix l'un avec l'autre," the mother said. The girl smiled at Ezra, but he forgot to smile back until she'd moved on. He was still bitterly mulling over what he'd just heard the mother say—that the General Assembly was where countries came to make peace with each other. What a laugh. When he'd lived in Jerusalem, he'd always found it particularly apt that the UN office there was situated on a spot known since antiquity as the Hill of Evil Counsel.

He turned now to the front page of the Metro section and saw there a photo of a burning brick building. EXPLOSION AT NYU KILLS ONE, INJURES ANOTHER. Idly he scanned the piece; apparently an explosion and fire had done serious damage to a lab in the biology building on Saturday night. And while the cause was still of unknown origin, a fire marshal was quoted to the effect that "we're looking at a string of high-intensity lamps which were recently rigged up with inadequate fuses." A young assistant professor had been killed in the blast, and some other visiting professor had been very seriously injured. Ezra was just about to turn the page and return to the mystery of the bells when something struck him, something that would probably strike no one else.

It was the coincidence of timing.

The deadly explosion had occurred at approximately ten-fifteen, just one minute before the church bells had begun to ring. And while no one else would even *think* to connect the two events, a building fire and a pealing church bell, it was just the sort of thing that Ezra was doing all the time now—piecing things together, making connections, constructing a logical narrative out of seemingly unrelated scraps and fragments.

Nothing, he was discovering, was really coincidental. Not even the fact that this paper had been left intact on this very bench. For him to find. And read.

A couple of questions, then, confronted him. First, were these two events indeed connected in any way?

And if they were, was this connection anything that should concern him? Could these events, in any way, however remote or unlikely, have something to do with his own work?

He tried to think it through. He tried to remain coldly rational. There was certainly a theological element to what he was doing, and that element would—or at least it *could*—tie in to the ringing bells. Traditionally, church bells were rung to call the faithful to prayer, to signal the beginning and the end of each day, to announce such things as the wedding of a king or the news of a great battle won.

But they had also been rung over the centuries to warn of an impending disaster. Invaders seen landing on the coast. A fire or flood. The Black Plague.

Was there anything in his work with the Lost Book of Enoch that could have triggered the ringing? Oh, how such a question would appear to Dr. Neumann. She'd write it off in two seconds flat; yet another symptom of his Jerusalem syndrome, she'd claim, another manifestation of the rampant self-aggrandizement that was part and parcel of his overall delusion.

But he also knew things that she did not; he understood things that she could never comprehend. He was piecing together the most ancient narrative in the world; he was translating, slowly and laboriously, the words of the secret scripture; he was learning from Enoch, the father of Methuselah himself, the ways of good and evil. There was a battle, or so he had read last night, over the soul of everyone, a battle waged between two angels, and the outcome determined the person's fate for all eternity. Was he uncovering something lost for so many millennia, something so fundamental to an understanding of the universe and our place in it that he had set off alarm bells, as it were, all over town? Even to Ezra, it seemed far-fetched . . . but it did not seem impossible.

Hadn't that voice whispered *Yes* in his ear? Hadn't it urged him, in the solitude of his room, to *go on*?

A tour group, clearly from the Middle East, began to shuffle past, the older women dressed in black chadors and veils, the men, or at least a few of them, in Arab headdress. Their tour guide, burbling in Arabic with what sounded to Ezra like an Egyptian accent, was wearing the whole get-up, a billowing djellaba and, even in this cold weather, open-toed leather sandals; he was walking backward as he faced the group, his arms waving, his voice swelling as he expatiated on the United Nations and whatever else. As the group moved past, their garments ruffled by the wind off the river, Ezra, who prided himself on such sensitivity, picked up their scent—the distinctive aroma of olive soap and tamarind seed, of dried dates and ripe figs, seasoned lamb and jasmine tea; it took him back, despite himself, to the streets of the Old City. Most of the people in the group passed in front of him, but a few went behind the bench; he felt himself suddenly surrounded by them, by a swirling mass of black-robed figures and hooded men, and just as it had happened before, he heard a voice whisper in his ear, Only this time it sounded like Aramaic. It sounded like the words for *"Finish it."*

He whirled his head around, but the group was simply ambling past him, no one even paying much attention, it seemed, to the man on the bench. But someone had spoken! He had heard a voice. The same low voice that he had heard once before. Ezra leapt to his feet.

"Who said that?" he demanded. "Who just spoke to me?"

But no one replied; one man looked at him quizzically, and Ezra said, "Was it you? Did you just say something to me?"

The man backed away, and several of the women drifted backward with him, muttering and clucking under their veils, which only made Ezra angrier. What were they saying? Were they trying to play a trick on him?

"Somebody here spoke to me, and I want to know who it is."

"I assure you, sir," the guide said, hastening to intervene, "no one in this group spoke to you. No one in this group speaks English."

"It wasn't English they were speaking," Ezra shot back. "It was Aramaic."

The guide, whose skin was lined and colored like a walnut, looked even more surprised. "That, too, would not be possible, sir. We are very sorry for any disturbance we have caused you," he said, shepherding the group away, and saying something to them in Arabic under his breath. Ezra remembered enough of the language to pick up the word *majnoon,* or "madman."

"You're telling them I'm a *majnoon?*" he said. "You're telling them I'm crazy?"

"Please move away, sir," the guide said, "or I will have to take measures."

"You will have to take measures? What measures would those be?"

Ezra stepped toward the guide, but before he could get any closer, there was suddenly a pair of United Nations security guards standing in his way. "All right, let's calm down now," one of them said.

"What seems to be the problem?" the other one said.

"One of these people said something to me," Ezra declared, "and all I want to know is who it was."

"This man is interfering with us," the guide said, quickly ushering the last of his group toward the steps to the building. "He should be put under arrest!"

"We don't do that in this country!" Ezra shouted at him. "Don't you get it? You're in America now! Not in some medieval Arab backwater! America!"

Even Ezra didn't know where the fury was coming from; it was as if it had been pent up behind the flimsiest of dams, which had suddenly burst wide open.

"Yours is a country of infidels and devils!" the guide spat back. And then, correctly assessing his enemy, he added in clearly enunciated but soft Arabic, *"And Zionist swine!"*

Ezra leapt at him, his hands reaching for the man's throat, but one of the UN guards suddenly knocked his arms down and the other grappled him from behind.

"Make no mistake," Ezra shouted, "there is a living, breathing God of Israel," but before he could finish his thought, the very breath was squeezed out of him and he was wrestled to the pavement. He heard one of the guards shouting at the Arabs to move on, while the other, the one pressing his knee into the small of Ezra's back, muttered code numbers into a walkie-talkie and asked for immediate assistance.

If he could have caught his breath, Ezra would have told him there was no need for that; he was already spent, there was no more fight in him.

But he never got the chance. The next thing he knew, his hands were cuffed behind him and he was being hauled to his feet. As several tourists looked on aghast—and a few took pictures—he was dragged toward the First Avenue gates to the park, where a police car, red light flashing, was screeching to a halt.

A cop jumped out and threw open the back door to the car.

"You don't need to do this!" Ezra managed to shout, but the cop simply put his hand on the top of Ezra's head and shoved him down and into the backseat.

The door clanged shut; Ezra had to lean forward toward a wire grill just to keep the handcuffs from cutting into his wrists. The security guards gave the cops a thumbs-up and the car pulled away swiftly from the curb. As Ezra looked out the back window and through the iron railings that surrounded the park, he could see the Arab guide smiling smugly at his victory. Smile all you want, Ezra thought— your days are numbered . . . and dwindling fast.

EIGHTEEN

As soon as Raleigh left the gallery for the day, Beth shoved the incomplete plans for the holiday party into a folder and hurried out the door. She took a cab straight home and, as expected, did not find Carter there. He'd spent the previous night at St. Vincent's Hospital, and she suspected that was where he'd want to be again tonight. She grabbed the overnight bag they'd just unpacked from the country and threw in his razor, shaving cream, fresh socks, underwear, and a clean shirt.

At the hospital, she made the mistake of going in through the emergency room entrance. It was like entering bedlam, with dozens of people, some of them still bleeding, moving all about, others strapped to gurneys lined up in the halls like planes at an airport waiting for a runway. Over an intercom a nurse recited names, called for various doctors to report stat, reminded new arrivals to have their paperwork filled out and, most important of all, to have their proof of insurance readily available.

She followed the signs and arrows toward the general admittance and registration desk, which was several long corridors away. There she was told Guiseppe Russo was being treated in the intensive care unit on the fifth floor. Overnight bag still in hand, she took the elevator up.

Compared to the emergency room, the fifth floor was like a space station—all white light, hushed sounds, gleaming hallways, and closed doors. As she walked to the reception area outside the ICU itself, she saw two doctors conferring in low voices over a chart on a clipboard, an orderly pushing a sleeping patient in a wheelchair, a tall man in what looked suspiciously like a woman's red coat bending low over a water fountain. On a blue plastic chair, his head down and shoulders slumped, sat Carter.

"Any news yet?" Beth said, putting the bag down beside his chair.

Carter looked up, his face unshaven, his eyes weary and bloodshot. "No, not so far. He's still not conscious."

Beth sat down beside him, put a hand on his shoulder. "Have you had a chance to talk to the doctors?"

"A few hours ago. The one in charge, her name's Dr. Baptiste, said they'd let me know if there's any change."

Beth rubbed his shoulder. "Did she give you any idea when a change might come? I mean," she said, searching for the right words, "did she think Joe might come out of it tonight? Tomorrow?" And though she didn't add it, she was thinking—*Ever?*

Carter shook his head. "No clue." He leaned back on the chair and stretched his long legs out in front of him. "That's why I don't want to leave. He could come out of it anytime—nobody knows—and I want to make sure I'm right here if he does."

That's what Beth thought he would say. "I've brought you a few things I thought you might want. Your razor, some clothes, the book from your bedside table."

"Thanks. There's a public bathroom downstairs; I'll use that to wash up later."

They sat in silence, listening to the murmur of the nurses at the reception desk, the occasional sound of a closing door or a voice on the intercom overhead. Beth had hoped Carter would be prepared to come home, at least for a few hours, but she wasn't surprised. She knew that he not only cared deeply about Joe; she knew that he also felt responsible for what had happened. The death of Bill Mitchell. The terrible injuries to Russo. At this point, all she could do was pray that Joe would pull through.

"You know," she said, gently, "if you wanted to go home and sleep for a few hours, you could leave me here. If this Dr. Baptiste comes looking for you, I could call you."

"No, that's okay. I should be here."

She debated saying what she was about to say, then went ahead. "What's happened is awful," she said, "but you've got to remember that none of it is your fault. None of it. You didn't do anything wrong."

He didn't respond.

"It was just an accident. An awful, unforeseeable accident."

His expression didn't change. She knew he'd heard her, but she could also tell that what she was saying had hardly made a dent. Maybe someday he'd be able to let go of the guilt, but today, she knew in her heart, was way too soon.

The ICU doors opened with a swishing sound, and a young doctor with her hair in a bun and skin the color of cinnamon came over to where they were sitting. Carter looked up at her, more dread than hope in his eyes.

The doctor must have seen it, too, because she quickly nodded and gave him a small smile. "Now don't expect too much," she said, "but your friend is conscious."

Carter took a second to accept the news.

"That's very good news—isn't it?" Beth said. "I mean, if he's awake now, and talking . . ."

"I didn't say he was talking yet," Dr. Baptiste interrupted. "Are you a relation?" she asked Beth, her voice carrying the lilting hint of the Caribbean.

"No, this is my husband," she said, squeezing Carter's shoulder. "We're his friends."

"The only ones he has, really," Carter added, "in this country."

"Then you should really find a way to contact his family, wherever they are; decisions may have to be made, at any time."

"Decisions?" Beth said.

"About his care and treatment."

"Can't you just talk with Joe himself about . . . whatever?" Carter said.

"Your friend, you must understand, is still in a critical state. We can't count on his remaining lucid long enough to make informed decisions. Right now we're just concentrating on getting and keeping him stable. Later on, after we've had a chance to reassess all the damage—he has third-degree burns over no less than twenty-five percent of his body—we'll decide how to proceed."

Third-degree burns? As far as Beth knew, that was as bad as burns got.

"But for now," Dr. Baptiste said to Carter, "I think it might help him to see a friendly face. Would you like to see him now? You can only stay for a few minutes."

"Yes. Absolutely," Carter said, rising from his chair.

Beth started to get up, too, but Dr. Baptiste motioned her to stay seated.

"I'm afraid we can only let in one visitor at a time in this unit."

"I'll stay here with the bag," Beth said to Carter. "Go on."

Dr. Baptiste led the way, and Carter disappeared behind the glass-paneled doors of the ICU.

The air in there, Carter noticed almost immediately, had a colder, crisper feel to it than the air in the hallway outside. There was a low, constant hum in the air, from all the machinery and equipment running beside the various patients' beds. At the nurses' station, a semicircular counter loaded with softly glowing monitors, Dr. Baptiste gave Carter a paper face mask.

"We have to make sure no infections of any kind complicate the situation," she said, as Carter put the mask on over his nose and mouth. "Also, make sure you don't come into any physical contact with Mr. Russo. No hugs, no handshakes, nothing."

Then she turned, and Carter followed her to the other end of the ward. As they approached the last bed, almost

entirely concealed by an opaque white curtain, Carter felt
his heart race. What was Russo going to look like? Would
he be alert enough to recognize Carter? Would Carter himself be able to discern his old friend, under whatever bandages he might be swaddled in? He braced himself.

Dr. Baptiste was standing beside the bed, checking one
of the IV lines; there were several, along with a host of
other attachments, all connected to monitors and machines
ranged around the bed. Russo himself was barely visible.
A sheet appeared to be tented a few inches above his
body—was that because even cloth would be too painful
against his scorched skin?—and only his head poked up
above the top of the sheet. He was wearing a sort of paper
hat, shaped like a crown, and his face, coated with what
was probably some kind of antiseptic unguent, glistened.
His eyes were huge and dark, and filled, it looked to Carter,
with a frustrated need for expression. The moment Carter
came near the bed, the eyes fixed on him.

"Hey, Joe," Carter said, softly. *Jesus, what happened in
that lab?* Carter didn't know what to say next. He was still
reeling from the sight of his friend in this horrible condition, but he didn't want his reaction to show. He was grateful for the paper face mask.

"I'm sorry," Carter said, simply. He started to reach
for Joe's hand, which was resting outside the sheet, but
Dr. Baptiste quickly reminded him, "No touching, please."

"Sorry, I forgot."

"And I'm afraid your friend won't be able to answer you
right now."

Why was that, Carter wondered? He was quite clearly
conscious. Then he saw the breathing tube inserted between Joe's burnt and flaking lips.

"If he's up to it," Dr. Baptiste said, "he can try using
this." She handed Carter a white, shiny board and a Magic
Marker. "But he's under such a heavy load of sedation and
painkillers, he may not be completely coherent." She finished checking some things, then said, "Don't stay more
than five minutes," and left.

As soon as she was gone, Russo made a low grunt and

threw a glance at the small board. Carter handed it to him, and Russo raised his other hand—the nails, Carter could see, were just black half-moons—and took the Magic Marker.

As Carter helped hold the board steady, Russo wrote a word, in incongruously cheerful green ink. When he dropped the marker, Carter turned the board and read *Bill?*

Bill Mitchell. Carter shook his head. "He didn't make it."

Russo's big eyes blinked once. Then he took the marker and wrote the word *laser* on the board.

What about the laser? "It's gone, too. The fire destroyed everything." Including, of course, the fossil. Still, if Carter could avoid going into that just now, he would.

But Russo shook his head gently, and tapped the word again.

The laser? Then Carter got it. "Was the laser on when the fire started?"

Russo nodded.

"Did the laser cause it?"

Again, he nodded.

But Russo would have known better than to try the laser without Carter's help; Russo had had trouble just making sense of the English used in the instruction manual. Carter wiped the board clean. Was he saying that it was Bill, Bill Mitchell . . . "Was Mitchell the one working with the laser?"

Russo's eyes closed in assent, then opened again.

"He'd gotten into the lab somehow, on his own?"

Russo gave an almost imperceptible nod, then picked up the marker and scrawled *fossil*.

So much for Carter's hopes of avoiding that issue just now. "Everything in the lab," Carter repeated, slowly, "was destroyed."

Russo shook his head no, and his gaze this time held Carter's steady.

"It wasn't?" What could he mean? "Did you manage to save something?" Carter knew, thank God, that they'd already taken tiny specimens of the fossil and the rock, specimens that were still safely secured and undergoing tests in another lab, but Russo seemed to be indicating something else. "I'm sorry, Joe, but I'm not following you." Maybe the sedatives were kicking in again.

Russo picked up the marker—his hand was trembling a little this time—and wrote *alive*.

What did that mean? Carter could only assume that Russo was referring to himself. "Yes, you're alive," Carter said, smiling, "and one of these days, believe it or not, you're going to be back doing everything you used to do." Carter wondered if that was true. "Even scuba diving."

But the look in Russo's eyes grew even more troubled. Carter had not gotten it right. Joe tapped the word *fossil* with the end of the marker, then tapped the word *alive*.

When Carter didn't respond, he did it again, harder.

Now there was no mistaking his meaning, however implausible. "You're trying to tell me that the fossil was alive?"

Wrong again. Russo grunted, and furrowed his brow. The exertion showing on his face, he picked up the marker again and scrawled something between the two other words remaining on the board. When Carter read the completed message, he saw that it now said *fossil* is *alive*.

And Carter knew that there was no use trying to communicate anymore that day; Joe had to be feeling the effect of the drugs. And that was probably for the best.

"Okay," Carter said, "I've got it." He smiled reassuringly and nodded. "The doc told me not to spend more than five minutes today, but I'll be back first thing in the morning."

Carter put the board and the marker on the nightstand beside the bed. When he looked back at Russo, his friend's face looked wearier and more tormented than ever. Carter worried that he'd done more harm than good with this visit.

"Don't worry about the fossil or the lab or anything," Carter said. "Just try to get some sleep now."

Carter gave him the most encouraging smile he could and turned away from the bed. Though he hated to admit it, it was a relief, even for a second, not to have to look at him. He went to the door, then glanced back. Russo's eyes were still fixed on him. He raised a hand in good-bye, but there was no response. And he had the impression that Russo wasn't even seeing him; he was staring past him—through him—and into something very dark and very deep.

NINETEEN

The corpse had been moved. He had watched, from the shadows, as it was covered and carried out. *What were they going to do with it? Why were they doing this at all?*

It was put beneath the flashing lights and taken swiftly away.

So many of them. He still couldn't comprehend it. *This world was teeming with life, all around him.*

He took a breath, savoring the air. *Tastes and odors he didn't know, and could not yet recognize. But soon he would. Soon he would know them all. Already he was learning.*

At the place he'd been released, he watched from a dark corner. If he had been freed from within that place, then perhaps others were still imprisoned there.

Others like him.

He had watched as men, more and more of them, came and went. They carried tools and lights and showered the place with water. The smoke eventually diminished. Watching, he learned quickly. And quickly understood what they were doing.

On and on it went, all through the night, and then the sun had come up, and he had retreated again, farther into the darkened doorway. He had pulled the red cloak up around his face. And waited—the blink of an eye, it seemed, he had waited. No more. And then it was dark again.

And, watching, he had seen a man come there, where no one else now went, and then come out again. The man ran from the place—his scent carried fear and sorrow—and because it was now night again, he had been able to follow him easily. Through the streets. The lights. The people. *So many of them.* And to a place not far away.

Where the other one, he now knew, was being kept.

The one who had been told his suffering was a gift.

The one who was still alive.

Were these his enemies, he wondered, *or his friends?*

The air. The air here was rich, redolent. He turned. Behind him, there was a fence with twisted wires, like a cage, and behind the wires another place—a building. With no one in it; he could tell. Made of bricks, red like his coat, with openings covered with wood and glittering, broken . . . *glass.* That was it.

He was learning. He had heard that word, too, used by the men at the place where he had been freed. He not only watched . . . he listened. Language had once been a gift his kind had bestowed. Now, he reflected, it was being returned—and that was just as it should be. It was fitting.

The dawn began to creep across the sky. He turned to the twisted wires and with his long, nearly perfect fingers—only the end of the middle finger on his right hand was missing now—pulled the wires apart. Then he stepped through the hole he'd made, and into earth and water. *Mud.* He mounted the crumbling steps and peered inside, through the rough boards that sealed the windows. Within, he could see emptiness. Shadows. Darkness. Solitude.

All of which drew him.

But even more than that, it was the air inside this abandoned place that pleased him. The air was old, and filled with scents he knew . . . of blood, and tears, and death. Years and years of it.

Nothing, of course, in the great scheme of things. Nothing at all.

But for now, for this strange world in which he had awakened, good enough. This place could serve as his . . . *refuge*. He smiled. That was a good word, a new one, plucked from the very air around him.

There was so much, he reflected, that he wanted, and planned, to take.

TWENTY

Carter had never written a eulogy before, much less for someone he knew as little as he knew Bill Mitchell. What made it even worse, of course, was the fact that he'd never particularly liked the guy—and now it was his job to extol his virtues and talk, he guessed, about all the bright promise that he showed. Somehow, from the articles in the paper and the circumstances of his death—in the lab that Carter had personally set up—it was assumed, far and wide, that they'd been not only professional associates, but close buddies. And there was no way, now, after the dreadful way in which his life had been cut short, that Carter could very well say anything different.

The last time he'd worn his dark blue suit, it had been to the faculty dinner at which he'd been officially awarded the Kingsley Chair. He'd been nervous enough on that occasion, but at least it hadn't required him to do anything more than stand up at a dais, graciously accept a plaque, and thank the assorted professors and administrators for bestowing on him this great honor. Now he not only had to make a speech, he had to make sure it honored the memory of a guy who'd gotten himself killed—and at the same time gotten Carter's best friend maimed beyond recognition— all because he couldn't keep his hands off equipment he did not know how to operate.

"I'm not sure I'm going to be able to carry this off," he'd confessed to Beth.

"You've got to stop thinking that way," Beth had told him. "It'll come out in your voice."

"So how do I keep it out?"

"By remembering," Beth had said, trying to calm him down, "that it was an accident. A terrible accident, and nobody paid a higher price for it than Bill Mitchell."

"Tell that to Joe."

Carter had jotted down a few notes about Mitchell's enthusiasm for his work, his devotion to teaching the undergrads at NYU, his appreciation of rap music, and he hoped when he got up there (would he be standing in a pulpit? behind a lectern? where?) he'd be able to weave it all together into some sort of convincing whole.

They left the apartment without much time to spare, and by the time they got to the O'Banion Brothers Funeral Home, a fair number of mourners were already assembled in the memorial chapel. Carter was introduced to Bill's parents, to whom he'd already spoken on the phone; they were a stolid couple from the heart of Queens, looking understandably shell-shocked right now. Bill's widow, Suzanne, introduced him to some other members of the family, too, then took him aside to thank him again for agreeing to give a eulogy.

"I know that Bill really looked up to you," she said. She was a pale blonde—paler, perhaps, today than usual—with almost invisible eyelashes. "He was always talking about the work you did in Sicily, and how you'd made such a great name for yourself."

Now Carter felt even worse.

"And I know he was looking forward to the day when the two of you could work together on some project." A tear formed in her eye and she dabbed at it with a wadded

Kleenex. "I guess, in a way, that's what made this mess. He couldn't wait." The tears started to fall. "That was just like Bill. He couldn't wait for anything, ever."

A sob racked her, and Carter instinctively put his arm around her shoulders, which only seemed to make it worse. Before he knew it, he was drawing her off to one side and she was sobbing onto his jacket. Beth gave him a sympathetic glance and drifted away to talk to some of the other faculty members who had come to the service. A few minutes later, much to Carter's relief, the funeral director asked everyone to take their seats.

The coffin was placed on a bier draped with a red cloth at the front of the small chapel. But its lid was, of course, closed. From what Carter had heard, Mitchell's body had been shattered by the explosion; parts of it, along with pieces of his clothing—his shoes, for instance—had never been found at all. They were presumed to have been incinerated in the fire that followed. As Suzanne spoke haltingly into the microphone attached to the lectern, Carter wondered exactly how much of her husband had been collected and how it had been arranged for burial. It was macabre, he realized, what he was doing, but maybe, given his vocation, not so surprising. Bones were his job, even his nickname, and maybe the only way to deal with something this bizarre was to treat it with the customary detachment.

After Bill's wife had finished, his father got up to say a few words. He read them slowly from a crumpled sheet of paper, and Carter had the impression that he had written them just as laboriously; he was not a guy used to talking about his feelings or his memories, and to have to do it now in front of all these strangers—and at the death of his son—was almost surely more than he could manage.

Carter was the next one up, and his job, as he understood it, was to speak for the wider world, to assure everyone that Bill had also been respected and admired in the halls of academe, where he had hoped to make his mark. As Carter stepped up to the podium, he realized that he had Bill's wife to thank for what would now be his overall theme; when she'd said that Bill could never wait, that he was always trying to hurry things along, she'd given him the theme he could use to tie everything up.

Bill Mitchell, Carter announced at the outset, was a young man in a hurry. "He'd already come a long way—he was one of the youngest members of the department, and undoubtedly its most inquisitive—but he was also on his way, at record speed, to even greater accomplishments." As Carter spoke, he found himself warming to the task, growing to like the poor guy more and more as he spoke. He also found that the actual experience of eulogizing was suspiciously close to addressing his students in the lecture hall. Public speaking had become second nature to him now, so much so that even as he freely extemporized on the many virtues and achievements of Bill Mitchell, he was able to look around the chapel and register who was there, who he knew, and who he didn't.

There were a number of people from the department, including the chairman, Stanley Mackie, along with a lot of other faces he'd merely seen around the campus from time to time. Then there were Mitchell's relatives and friends, whom he of course didn't recognize, and one guy in particular, sitting alone and way in the back, who didn't look like he belonged to any camp at all. He was dressed in a rumpled blue suit and a black turtleneck, and he looked like he hadn't slept in a week. He had such a solemn and reclusive air about him that Carter assumed, on reflection, that he must work for the funeral home. He had the look of a professional mourner.

Carter concluded his remarks by saying that he'd always miss Bill's company in the faculty lab, and "without Bill around to keep me clued in, I will never again know what's topping the current musical charts." He said it with a sad, wry smile—which was returned by several people in the pews—and then he folded up his notes and stepped down from the podium. As he did, he noticed that the guy in the back got up and quietly left the chapel. Maybe he had some other duty to perform, or another service to grace with his doleful presence. Carter took his seat again and Beth gave him a little nod, to indicate he'd done fine.

When all the obsequies were done, everyone adjourned to an antechamber where coffee and cake had been set up. Carter found himself elbow to elbow with Stanley Mackie, who put his cup under the spigot of the silver coffee urn, and while it filled said, "Kind words, but cold comfort."

Carter didn't know how to reply. He'd already had a private conference with the chairman, and he didn't know how much more of a pasting he was supposed to take.

Mackie lifted his cup and stared at Carter over its rim. "The president's office has asked me to submit a written report on the accident. I'll write the cover letter, but I want you to write the report, describing in detail what you thought you were doing in that makeshift lab of yours, and what went wrong."

He'd called it Carter's "makeshift lab" in their earlier discussion, too, and Carter sensed that Mackie was distancing himself from the whole enterprise; suddenly, it was just something that Carter had cooked up entirely on his own, and that he, the chairman, had been barely aware of. Privately, Carter wondered how Mackie would explain the disbursement of department funds, for the lighting, the laser transfer, and so on, but incriminating documents were probably being buried, shredded, and erased already. And that cover letter Mackie was going to write would undoubtedly deny or obfuscate any remaining responsibility. Carter was going to be left holding the bag.

"Have the report at my office by next Wednesday," Mackie said, moving away, as if even here he didn't want to be seen spending too much time in Carter's company.

Although what he really needed now was a stiff drink in a dark bar, Carter filled his coffee cup from the urn.

"That was a good speech you gave, Professor."

Carter knew it was Katie Coyne, his prize pupil, before turning around. He'd seen her in the chapel.

"Thanks. I hope I never have to give another one like it."

She was wearing a denim skirt and a neatly pressed work shirt—probably the most sober outfit she could put together.

"It's awfully nice of you to show up for this," he said.

"Bill Mitchell was the TA for a seminar I took last semester."

Carter hadn't known that.

"So I guess I knew him fairly well. In fact, I went to his Halloween party, and talked to your friend Professor Russo there." She looked down at her feet, then said, hesitantly, "So how is he? I heard he was hurt pretty badly in the fire and all."

"Yes, he was. He's at St. Vincent's, in the ICU."

"Is he going to . . . be okay?"

"Yes, he's going to pull through. But it's going to be a long haul."

"Could you tell him I said hi? I mean, if he even remembers who I am. And when he's up to it, maybe, if you think he'd like it, I could come by and pay him a visit?"

"That would be great, and I know he'd like it." While he'd always known Katie was his smartest student, he now suspected she was also his nicest.

Beth signaled to him from across the room, where she was talking to one of Carter's faculty friends. She mouthed the words *Should we go?* and Carter nodded. He took another swallow of the coffee and put the cup down on the table. "See you tomorrow," Carter said to Katie. She'd be at his morning lecture.

But halfway down the steps outside, Carter was waylaid by Bill's wife—widow, he thought, now—who said, "I hate to ask this, but would you have time to come to the burial service?"

Carter wasn't sure what she was talking about—hadn't he just done that?

"The actual interment," she said. "It's in about a half hour and it won't take more than fifteen minutes."

Beth murmured to Carter, "I've got to get back to the gallery, or Raleigh will kill me."

"I understand," Suzanne said to her sincerely, "and thank you for coming." Then, turning back to Carter, she said, "But Bill's folks were so touched by your remarks that I know it would mean a lot to them if you were there. You can ride to the cemetery with us."

She gestured at a rented limo idling at the curb.

Carter felt trapped—how did you deny such a request?

Beth seemed to settle the question for him. "I'll meet you at home," she said. "I'll be back around seven-thirty."

As Beth crossed the street to hail a cab uptown, Carter found himself ushered with Bill's parents and Suzanne into the waiting limo. It didn't even occur to him until he'd been packed into the crowded backseat and they'd started on their way to wonder where the cemetery was. But his heart sank when Bill's dad said something about how when Bill was growing up in Forest Hills, he'd learned to drive by piloting the family car around the quiet lanes of the local cemetery. When the limo driver headed for the Midtown Tunnel, Carter resigned himself to a trip all the way out to Queens.

The ride didn't take that long, but to Carter it felt like an eternity. And when they finally passed through the gates of Greenlawn Cemetery and drove to an open gravesite wedged between several other already occupied spots, Carter couldn't wait to unfold himself from the backseat and get outside again to breathe fresh air—even if it was in a graveyard.

A few cars were pulling up behind theirs, and people from the funeral home were clambering out. Carter didn't know how much more of this condoling he could take, and he walked away to clear his head and lungs. The ground was hard-packed, and what grass was left was brown and scrubby. The headstones, on casual inspection, all seemed to bear Irish or Italian surnames, some with death dates from the early 1900s. He stopped at the top of a small knoll and looked around; the place went on for acres and acres in all directions, dotted here and there by black trees, their bare branches hanging forlornly over marble mausoleums. Not far off, he saw an elderly woman laying a wreath on a tombstone. In the distance, a tall figure in a red coat stood out against the late-afternoon skyline, then passed behind a massive headstone, topped by a trumpeting angel. The wind sighed, picking up the dead leaves and brushing them past Carter's legs.

He'd better get back, he thought. He wouldn't want anyone to think he wasn't eager to attend the actual interment.

Down at the gravesite, the casket had been placed on some sort of mechanical contraption for lowering it into the ground, and the clergyman, in a black car coat and galoshes now, was standing at one end of the open grave. He had a white silk stole draped around his neck and held the *Book of Common Prayer* in his hand. Suzanne, Bill's parents, and about a dozen other people were gathered around, occasionally stamping their feet to keep warm. The hard, barren ground seemed to radiate the cold up.

The minister thanked them all for being there, and then, as if he too was feeling the effects of the weather, quickly opened the book and began to read. As he spoke, Carter kept his head down, but he couldn't keep from looking up now and then. Most of the others had their heads, or at least their eyes, downcast, but some were just staring off into the middle distance. Bill's mom was reciting, quietly but fervently, the same words that were being spoken aloud. Faith, Carter thought, and not for the first time, must be a wonderful thing. It must be an incredible help at times like this. But it was something he'd never had in his life, and knew that he never would. Was it Cardinal Newman who'd said if the church got you before the age of six, they had you for life? If that was true, then Carter was well out of danger. No church of any stripe had ever so much as laid a glove on him.

The minister was still reading, with a good if somewhat hurried cadence, and Carter noticed now that a black Lincoln was parked on the other side of the slope; the driver, a heavyset, older man, was in the front seat, turning the page of a newspaper. Carter hadn't seen this guy, or that car, at the funeral.

"Earth to earth, ashes to ashes . . ." the minister was saying, and these were words even Carter had heard many times.

Bill's mom was saying them too, her husband's arm wrapped protectively around her shoulders.

"Dust to dust; in sure and certain hope—"

Whistling in the graveyard, Carter thought. But if it provided comfort . . .

"—of the Resurrection unto eternal life." The minister closed the book and said, "Amen."

The others said it too. Bill's mom let out a muffled wail and her husband gathered her against him. Someone gave the signal and the casket began to gradually descend into the earth. Carter, despite himself, was reminded of the dig in Sicily—the Well of the Bones. The earth there had looked a lot like this, the color of wet coffee grounds, and at the bottom, again like this, there were only bones.

A minute or two later, it was over. The mourners said their farewells to each other and dispersed to their cars. Suzanne came over to Carter and said, "We can have the limo take you back to the city, but first we have to go to Bill's parents' house to drop them off."

It had never occurred to Carter that everyone wouldn't be going straight back to Manhattan, and his first thought now was *Where can I get a cab?* Inside the cemetery it would of course be impossible, and outside its gates he had no idea where he'd be.

"Oh, sure," he mumbled, still wondering what other recourse he might have. "But I really don't want to intrude on the family's time alone," he said. Already his eyes were scanning the remaining cars, to see if any of them might be able to give him a lift back to town. A gray Toyota was just pulling away, and about the only car left was the black Lincoln. A young man was standing beside it now—the guy from the funeral parlor, the one who looked like a professional mourner—and he was even looking in Carter's direction.

"Excuse me, will you?" he said to Suzanne, thinking this might be his last chance. "I'll be right back."

As Carter walked over toward the Lincoln, the mourner's eyes grew wide. Maybe the mortuary had sent him as a kind of supervisor, Carter thought, just in case anything went awry at the service.

"Are you with O'Banion Brothers, by any chance?" Carter said.

The guy looked quite flustered. "No. I'm not."

"Oh, because I needed a ride back into Manhattan, and I wondered if you were going that way."

The guy's eyes lit up, as if he'd just been presented with a totally unexpected gift. "Yes! Absolutely. I can drop you off wherever you like."

"Thanks." It was more than Carter had hoped for. "Let me just tell Bill's family I've got a ride."

Carter went back, much relieved, and told Suzanne, who looked a little relieved herself. Maybe the family would have been on the hook for the cost of the extra limo ride.

Returning to the Lincoln, he noticed two laborers with shovels hovering a discreet distance away. The gravediggers, here to finish the job.

"I'm Carter Cox," he said, extending his hand to the guy giving him the ride.

"Ezra Metzger," the man replied. He waved toward the car. "Please."

Carter got in on one side, and Ezra went around to the other, all but rubbing his hands together with glee. Maybe, Ezra thought, his luck was changing after all. Only the day before, he'd been bailed out of jail for the fracas in the UN park and released on Sam and Kimberly's recognizance. And today he was getting an exclusive audience with the one man in New York he was most interested in talking to.

"This is my Uncle Maury," Ezra said, as the driver turned around in the front seat.

"Pleased to meet you," Maury said. "So where are we headed?"

"Anywhere in Manhattan would be fine," Carter replied. "But the closer to St. Vincent's Hospital, the better." He hadn't checked up on Joe yet that day.

"St. Vincent's it is," Maury said. "I'm gonna just listen to the game, if you two don't mind," he added, turning the radio up. Was this their method for affording privacy to the occupants of the backseat, Carter wondered? Not that he thought they'd be needing it for any reason.

As the car wound its way around the cemetery drive, Carter asked Ezra how he knew Bill Mitchell.

"I don't, I'm afraid."

"Oh. So you're a friend of his family?"

"No, not that either. I read about the funeral services in the paper. My real interest, I'll confess, was in meeting you."

"Me? Why?"

"Because I'd read about the accident in your lab, and I was very curious about what exactly had happened. You, I thought, must know better than anyone."

"Are you a fire investigator?" Carter asked, though the plush town car certainly indicated otherwise.

"No."

"A reporter?"

"Oh, no. I've worked in many labs myself, most recently in the Middle East, and I'm always curious when there is a mishap as dire as yours." No use, right now, in going into his real reasons. "Would you mind my asking, what kind of work were you doing in your lab when the fire broke out?"

Who was this guy, Carter wondered. And should he answer that question? The car pulled out of the cemetery gates, and after mulling it over for a few more seconds, he couldn't see what further damage could be done if he did answer. All the damage imaginable had already *been* done. "Professor Russo and I are both paleontologists, and we had been working on a fossil."

"With the deceased Mr. Mitchell?"

Carter hesitated, then said, "Bill wasn't really authorized to be there."

Ezra appeared to take his meaning, and said, "Yes, I see. Experiments can easily go wrong, can't they, in the wrong hands?"

To Carter, it sounded as if he was speaking from experience.

"But can I ask you then," Ezra said, proceeding as cautiously and politely as he could, "what is this fossil you and Professor Russo had been working on?"

Carter looked out the window at the other cars now whizzing past. "Was. What *was* this fossil we were working on. It was completely destroyed in the explosion and the fire. And now we'll never know what it was."

"What did it look like?"

That was a good question, and despite himself, Carter found himself re-engaged in the subject. It was the bittersweet feeling you got from talking about an old flame. "Most of it was pretty well entombed in a block of stone, but from what we could see, it might have been a member of the raptor family."

"That would be a dinosaur?"

So now he knew the guy wasn't a rival paleontologist. "Probably. All we had seen of it so far was its hand, or I should say claw, and part of one limb."

Ezra seemed fascinated by this information. "That's funny," he said.

"What is?"

"You said hand at first. As if it had struck you as human."

Carter couldn't argue with that; the fossil had always stirred curious thoughts in him. Not to mention the bizarre sensation he'd had the day he'd taken the sample of the extended talon—the fossil had seemed somehow warmer than the surrounding stone. "Is that why you're interested?" Carter asked, taking one more stab. "Are you an anthropologist?"

"In the broader sense of that word—the study of mankind—yes, I guess you could say I am." To Ezra, this seemed like a fair compromise, and an effortless way to assuage Carter's curiosity. "I'm very interested in how we got here, and why."

"Sounds like you take a fairly cosmic approach," Carter said. Was this guy actually a little . . . off? Carter began to wonder if he was about to start hearing about alien explorers who taught us the secrets of pyramid building.

"I'd accept that—I do take the *cosmic* approach," Ezra said, "even though I know you're using the term in a derisory way."

Jeez—had Carter's tone of voice betrayed him that badly, or was this guy supersensitive? Carter had to remind himself that even if he did think Ezra was strange, he wasn't stupid. In fact, his features had a sharp and brilliant cast to them. "I'm sorry, I didn't mean any offense."

"None taken," Ezra replied, though it was clear that he was annoyed. He turned his face away—in profile, he reminded Carter of a desert hawk, gaunt, spare, and hungry—and studied the tollbooth inspector who was even now giving the driver in the front seat his change.

They drove through the tunnel in silence, Carter feeling bad that he'd insulted the guy who was giving him his ride. When they emerged, Carter took a shot at improving the climate in the car by asking Ezra where he lived.

"East Side," was all Ezra said.

"Alone?"

"No." If there was one good thing, in Ezra's view, that had come out of the UN imbroglio, it was that the court had mandated he remain at his present address under close supervision. Kimberly had been livid—one of the few things in a long time that had given Ezra genuine joy.

But what he couldn't afford to do right now, Ezra realized, was remain offended, or in any way alienate this Carter guy—at least not until he had extracted enough information to resolve any doubts or questions he might still have. Was there some connection between what was going on in the lab that night—a lab where a curious fossil was under close scrutiny—and the pealing bells that had gone off in every church in town?

"I'll have to circle the block," Maury interjected, "to get into the hospital driveway," but Carter, anxious to get out of the car, said, "No problem, you can just drop me off across the street."

Maury shrugged and pulled the car over to the curb in front of an abandoned building that faced the main entrance to the hospital.

"Thanks for the ride," Carter said to Ezra, who finally turned back to him and asked, "Is Mr. Russo being treated there?"

"Yes." That was an easy one. "I'm going to go up to the ICU and see how he's doing."

Carter turned the handle on the door and got out. But before he could walk away, Ezra had slid across the backseat and lowered the back window.

"One more thing," Ezra said.

"Sure." Now that he was out of the car, Carter felt like he was in the clear.

"Did your colleague tell you anything, no matter how odd, about what happened in the lab that night? About the explosion? The fire? The fossil?"

"Not much," Carter said. "You've got to understand, he's still in very bad shape. I know that they were using a laser, and the beam hit a pocket of gas that was trapped in the stone. That's what caused the accident."

"You're sure that's all?" Ezra asked. "There wasn't anything more?"

Carter debated going into it; all he wanted to do was get away, but at the same time there was something in Ezra's query—in the imploring look in his eyes—that made him pause.

And Ezra saw it. "What? Tell me what you're thinking."

"Okay, he did say one thing that might interest you," Carter said, as Ezra waited by the rolled-down window. "Now, you've got to remember that he was delirious and doped up to his eyeballs when he said it—"

"Tell me."

"He said the fossil had come to life."

Ezra remained expressionless for a moment, then his cheeks flushed and he banged on the inside of the car door with his clenched fist. "I knew it!"

Now it was Carter's turn to be surprised. "You knew that?"

Ezra scribbled something on a scrap of paper and handed it out the window to Carter. "That's my number, but I never pick up. Call it, and leave your number with the housekeeper."

Housekeeper?

"We need to talk," Ezra said, "much more." He sat back on the seat, his eyes straight ahead. There was a momentary break in the traffic, and the car pulled away.

As Carter waited for the WALK signal, watching the Lincoln's taillights disappear, he happened to glance at the huge sign on the derelict site behind him. COMING SOON, it said, in big letters, THE VILLAGER, A 26-STORY LUXURY CO-OP. And under that, in equally big letters, A PROJECT OF THE METZGER COMPANY, INC. Why did that ring a bell all of a sudden? It took him a second to put it together, but hadn't that Ezra guy said his last name was Metzger? Could it be . . . ?

The WALK light flashed and Carter crossed the street, wondering exactly who it was that he'd just been talking to. And more important, how in the world could Ezra Metzger—yes, he was certain that was the name—how could he have anticipated, as he claimed, Russo's ravings about a fossil coming to life?

TWENTY-ONE

Night was becoming his friend. It was so much sim-pler to move through the streets at night, under the glow of the lamps that made everyone and everything look slightly unreal. He was able to move like a mist among the people, to absorb unnoticed their thousand scents and voices and shapes. He could inhale their perfumes, look into their eyes, even brush against their bodies, feeling the texture of their clothes, their skin. He went where the streets were full, to inhale the air they'd breathed, to listen to them talk—*a hundred different tongues, all seemingly spoken together*—and to learn the secrets of their hearts and their souls.

In that, he felt, there was little surprise. And some comfort. He had not been wrong *then,* so long ago . . . and he was not wrong *now.*

But in everything else, so much was changed.

Already he had learned the name of the place he now inhabited, and he had learned, too, its position in the present world. Could a place for his return have been more wisely chosen? Was there anywhere on earth he could so readily begin again? It was not divine providence—*oh no, surely not that*—but it was something closely akin to it, something that had been set in motion. A plan that even he, in all his wisdom and all his knowing, had not yet fully compassed.

Still, he had come to know certain streets, certain corners, better than others, and he often found himself returning to these, like a wolf might follow the trails he had successfully hunted on before. When he emerged from the darkness of his lair—a place of splintered wood and crumbling brick, where he could hear the faint echoes of infirmity and disease—he often walked these familiar paths. Here, for instance, was the place the burned man had been taken . . . here was the place where he had watched from the shadows as the fire blazed . . . and here was the place, now blackened and abandoned, from which he had been returned to the world. There were answers here—oh yes, that much he knew—but he did not yet know in whose breast these answers were held.

He wanted to know. It was his very nature to know.

In the halo cast by a streetlight, on the glistening slick pavement, he saw someone pacing, the same one he had encountered when he'd walked out of the inferno that night. The one who had given him the red cloak he still wore.

As he approached, the figure stopped and stared at him, as if in awe. Was it so plain, what he was? He didn't want that; he wanted things to be as they were, so long ago . . . before everything had come so terribly undone.

The closer he came, the more the figure seemed rooted to the spot. Dark skin, long hair, the features of the face concealed by paint and mud, juice and dust. A leather pouch—a *purse,* the word suddenly came to him—slung over one arm.

"It's you again," his benefactor said, wonderingly. "It's you." Wobbling on shoes with sharp heels, the figure approached, and laid one hand—whose nails, he noticed, were dyed a bright silver—on his sleeve. "I never thought I'd see you again. Never in this life, at least."

With so many in the world now, perhaps that was common.

"But this time you're not getting away so easy. Not without telling me a few things first."

"What . . . do you . . . want to know?" It was the first time he'd actually tried speaking the words, the words he had plucked from the very air around them, and he looked to see if they were understood.

"For starters, I want to know who you are."

They were.

"Or maybe I should say, *what* you are. Last time I saw you, you were glowing like some kind of lightbulb. Now, you're not giving off light like that."

He could not afford to. It would have been too unwise. He watched as a white car with blue stripes and a red bar across the top came slowly around the corner.

"Oh shit," his benefactor muttered.

He felt himself tugged by the sleeve of his coat toward the darkened doorway where he had once stood to watch the fire.

The car kept coming and he was dragged deeper, down to the bottom of the stairs, below the level of the street. The ground, littered with matted papers and broken bottles, reeked of garbage . . . and human congress.

"We're just gonna wait here for a while, till my friends are gone."

Now he smelled . . . apprehension, too.

"So, they call me Domino, maybe because I topple so easy." A chuckle. "You want to tell me what they call you?"

He didn't like it here, and he started back up the stairs. But Domino grabbed his sleeve again and said, "The cops are still cruising around up there. What's your hurry, anyway?"

Domino drew him close. They were about the same height, and he could look directly into Domino's eyes—they were dark brown, with long black lashes, and the brows, he could see, had been brushed with an amber color.

"You know, you owe me." Domino's fingers played with his cloak. "I *did* give this to you." He felt the buttons being undone. "I'm not asking for money—'less you want to give me some—but the least you can do is show me what you've got inside." The coat began to fall open. "I still think you've got something special going on."

The darkness at the bottom of the stairs brightened as the coat opened wider. Domino leaned back to take it in. "Damn—you're doing it again!"

His glow grew brighter still; he made it do so. And in its light, he could see Domino more clearly than ever. Could see the false hair that concealed the real, the strong bones of the face beneath the powder and clay, the sinewy arms under the soft, feminine clothes.

Domino's hands slunk inside the cloak. Touched him.

Beneath the sweet perfume, he smelled the odor of corruption.

"What the . . . hell," Domino said, haltingly.

He opened his own arms, wide, and Domino suddenly stepped back, against the damp wall of the stairwell. The purse slipped to the filth-covered floor.

"Jesus Christ . . ."

He shrugged the coat from his shoulders and moved closer . . . embracing Domino, who struggled now.

Which simply made him hold on even tighter. He folded the thrashing, twisting body against himself. He could smell the heat, the fear, the fury. He clutched Domino so close his limbs couldn't move. He could feel his body straining for breath, the heart racing wildly in his chest. "You asked me my name," he said, as a precise circle of flame suddenly etched itself into the cement floor around their feet. Domino's eyes, wide with terror, reflected the glow of the fire. "It is Arius."

And then the flames swiftly rose, coiling up around their joined bodies like a snake writhing up a tree. Domino screamed, but the sound was muffled by the fire, echoing hollowly around the shadowy stairwell. His clothes burned and his skin crackled and snapped. The wig on his head disappeared in a puff of golden fire.

When there was too little to hold up anymore, Arius, unaffected, let go . . . and stepped away. What was left of Domino fell into a blazing heap of blackened skin and bones. Orange sparks danced in the dark air as Arius bent to retrieve the red coat, shook it free of ash, and then put it back on. He picked up the fallen purse and turned toward the stairs.

Nothing has really changed, he thought as he rose toward the street, rummaging in the purse to see if there was anything of use. *This was always what came of abomination.*

TWENTY-TWO

Carter was in no mood today. First there'd been that disturbing appointment at the doctor's office, and now he was trying to explain the theory of geochronology to an unusually restive class.

"Most of us have been led to believe," he said, "that mankind has evolved in one long continuous process, and that any protohuman fossils, no matter where they're found and no matter what their age, must fit into that lineage somehow."

He glanced up from his notes and saw a couple of students in the back row conferring with lowered heads over something that looked like a greeting card.

"But that theory, known as the single-origin, or out-of-Africa theory," he went on, trying to ignore it, "is becoming increasingly hard to defend. Recent finds in such places as China and Indonesia, notably Java, have begun to point us in another direction. They're pointing us toward a world millions of years old, in which several different hominid species all managed to inhabit the planet simultaneously. Not necessarily peacefully, but at least at the same time."

He glanced up again, and this time he saw somebody passing the same card to Katie Coyne, and he snapped.

"All right, who wants to explain to me what's going on out there?"

Silence fell over the lecture hall.

"Katie, you want to tell me what's up, before I decide to just throw a pop quiz at you all?"

Katie looked like she'd rather not, but after adjusting the blue kerchief she was wearing on her head today—she looked to Carter like a pretty peasant girl in a painting by Millet—she said, "It's a get-well card."

"Okay," Carter replied coolly, wondering how this was supposed to serve as an adequate excuse. "Who's it for?"

"Your friend," she said, "Professor Russo. We were all signing it."

Carter was at a loss for words.

"I was going to bring it over to him later today, if you think that would be okay."

"Yes," Carter said, still flustered, "I'm sure he'd like that."

The bell rang, not a moment too soon. The students, perhaps in deference to his foul mood, packed up their things faster than ever.

"But that geochronology idea," Katie said over the bustle, "sounds cool. I give it a thumbs-up."

He knew she was just trying to assure him that not everything he'd said had been entirely lost on his audience; it was a nice try, but he knew he'd failed to capture their attention today.

For lunch, he went to the one place he was sure he wouldn't bump into any of his faculty colleagues—the student center cafeteria, where he took his tray of sloppy joe and french fries to a table in the farthest corner of the room. The din back here was a little bit less, and he could sit in peace, with his back to the rest of the lunch crowd, and think his thoughts without interruption.

The only trouble with that was, every direction his thoughts went in today was bad.

It had started out with the follow-up appointment at

Dr. Weston's office, to get the results of their various tests. Carter hadn't been looking forward to it, but he hadn't been dreading it, either. He figured the problems he and Beth were having were fairly routine, and that by making a small correction or two in their family-planning methods they'd get everything on track in no time. They were both young and healthy, and Beth even stuck to a healthy diet. If for some reason he had to, he'd give up his junk food.

But the look on Dr. Weston's face told Carter, before the conference had even gotten underway, that something more than diet and nutrition was wrong. The doctor shuffled a bunch of papers and lab reports around on his desk, made some awkward small talk to Beth about his personal art collection, and only then addressed the problem head-on.

"In all your tests and lab results," he said, looking directly at Beth, "we don't find any problem in achieving conception. The physical exam revealed no obstructions or problems of any kind, and in terms of your blood workups and hormonal balances, again we see no problems. A slight tendency toward anemia, but we can clear that up with a simple iron supplement."

Carter breathed a sigh of relief. At least Beth was in the clear. And maybe, just maybe, his intuition had been wrong?

Then Dr. Weston turned his gaze on him—and he knew it wasn't.

"I see in your medical history, Carter, that you had the mumps in your early teens."

The mumps? "Yes, I did."

"And was it, do you recall, a bad case?"

Carter instantly flashed back to a feverish month at home, quarantined in a back bedroom with the curtains drawn and a cup of cooling tea by the bedside. "Yes, it was. I missed a few weeks of school with that one."

Dr. Weston nodded. "Do you remember what medications you were given?"

Carter remembered pills, lots of them, and even a couple of shots in the butt, but he had no idea what they'd been. "You'd have to ask my mother, or the doctor, if he's still practicing. He was kind of an old-timer even then."

"We probably don't need to. I think what happened is pretty clear, especially given that your doctor had been practicing for some time, and this incident occurred in the early eighties, before we had all the information we have now."

To Carter, that last bit—about "the information we have now"—set off an alarm bell.

"Chances are, he prescribed some strong antibiotics," Dr. Weston elaborated, "which we know now, if administered during the onset of male puberty, can in some cases have an adverse impact on later potency."

Carter had to sort through all the words. Was the doctor saying that he was impotent? Because if that's what he thought, then . . .

"I'm not suggesting you have any difficulty with arousal or even ejaculation," Dr. Weston went on. "Neither of you has implied there are any difficulties in that area."

One thing cleared up.

"But the unfortunate side effect of the mumps, and the measures taken to alleviate it, is that some men, later on, experience sterility."

Carter sat still in his chair. Beth didn't move either.

"We ran two cycles on your sperm sample—you gave us plenty to work with." Weston proffered a small smile, which didn't help. "And the results, unfortunately, were the same. The count was in the one-percentile range, and motility was equally impaired."

Carter was still processing the information. He was . . . sterile?

"Are you saying that I can't . . . father a child?"

Dr. Weston sat back in his chair, his palms flat on the desk top. "Biologically, I'd have to say, no. But I don't need to tell someone of your intellectual caliber that being a father isn't only about that."

For a second, Carter didn't follow.

"As a couple, you can still have a child, using, for instance, an alternative source of insemination. We can discuss that some other time, if you like, once you've had a chance to sort through things. Physiologically, Beth is still a prime candidate for motherhood."

Carter felt her hand snake across the arm of his chair and take hold of his own. He wondered if his hand was as icy as hers.

So they could have a child—or at least Beth could—with somebody else's sperm? A friend's? A family member's? An anonymous donor's? Gee, Carter thought, there were so many good choices—how would he ever pick one?

"I know this is not good news," Dr. Weston said, "so you should take as much time as you need to consider all your options. But if I can leave you with one thought, it would be just that—you do have options. If you want a family, you can—and you will—have one."

Sure, Carter thought. *But whose?*

He knew that Dr. Weston's parting words were meant to be encouraging, but as he looked around the cafeteria now, at all the kids, the words had a hollow ring. Looking at all the boys, he had a weird and unwelcome thought: Any one of them could be the father of his child, any one of them could do for his wife what he couldn't, any one of them could make a baby, pass on his own genes into the next generation—how hard was it?—but it was always going to remain something that he could not do. He knew it was self-destructive and wrong to think that way, but he couldn't help it. He also couldn't help feeling that now—now that he knew the truth—he was less of a man than he'd been when he'd gotten out of bed, still ignorant, that very same morning. He could only hope, though he knew she'd never admit it if she did, that Beth wouldn't come to feel the same way.

He put down his fork and pushed the half-eaten food away. Even the smell of it made him a little queasy now.

He left the cafeteria, and walking home decided to stop by the now-abandoned lab; he was about to finish up his report for the president's office, and he wanted to make sure he'd covered everything he needed to. He stopped across the street, and from there he surveyed the yellow police tape, now drooping in spots, the loading doors twisted and bent by the intense heat, the outside walls blackened with smoke. He was surprised that the smell of the fire was still so strong.

And then he realized that the smell wasn't coming from the lab; it was coming from much closer, from right behind him. He turned and saw a laminated ID card of some kind lying on the concrete. He bent to pick it up.

It was a driver's license, for a man—African American, young—named Donald Dobkins. It was scorched around the edges, but the face in the picture looked vaguely familiar.

He glanced into the stairwell and saw an eyeglass case, open and empty.

The smell was even stronger now. And he could hear a sound—a soft rustling—in the shadows at the bottom of the stairwell.

What was going on? What was down there? Could whatever it was be connected in some way to the lab fire? But even if that were true, how would it have remained undiscovered, so close by, all these days?

The rustling came again, and Carter said, "Hey! Somebody down there?"

There was no reply.

"Anybody?"

Carter went down a step, and the burning smell—the odor of burnt meat, in fact—got stronger still.

And now he could see something, a blackened heap, lying on the ground.

He went down another step—and the heap now had shoes. Burnt, but recognizable shoes—with a high heel.

Carter stopped in his tracks. This was a body. Dead. But then the rustling sound came again, and he saw movement.

Oh my God, he thought. *Maybe not! Maybe it's someone still alive!* He vaulted the rest of the steps, and when his own feet hit the cement there was an explosion of activity—squeaking and scurrying, flashing red eyes and little white teeth. Rats—some as big and black as cats—shot off in all directions, running across his shoes, scampering up the stairs. Carter froze in place until the swarm was gone—this had actually happened to him once before, when he'd descended into an ancient sinkhole in the Yucatán—and he knew enough to just hold his breath and let it pass. The rats wanted no more to do with him than he did with them.

The corpse—his first impression had been the right one—looked as if it had collapsed in on itself, coming to rest in a pile of burnt limbs and charred bone. The face, or what little was left of it, was staring upward in a silent rictus of pain. As he bent closer, the aroma of cooked flesh was nearly too much to bear; he had to turn away, grab a breath, then turn back again with his mouth closed. What he saw was, like the picture on the driver's license, strangely familiar. Did he know this person?

"I saw a man, only it wasn't a real man. And he was all made of light, glowing."

The words were coming back to him now.

"I gave him my best red coat."

The transvestite, the one who worked this corner.

"That man was an angel."

That's who this was—who it had *been*. But how on earth had this happened to him?

Carter turned his head away and grabbed another breath of air.

But what were the odds—first Russo, and now this guy, both burnt so badly? So near to each other? And just a few days apart? What were the chances of a coincidence like that? Carter didn't put them very high.

He looked around the dark stairwell, but all he saw were ashes and shreds of burned newspaper. There was nothing else down here, and certainly nothing he could do for the dead Donald Dobkins, except call the police.

From the phone booth on the corner he dialed 911, and a squad car showed up one minute later. A homicide, Carter surmised, still rated with the police.

He gave one of the cops the driver's license he'd found, and he was in the midst of explaining how he'd discovered the body when another car, this one unmarked, showed up; a middle-aged man in an old gray raincoat and big black eyeglasses got out. "You the guy who called it in?" he asked Carter, who nodded. "Then I'm the one you should be talking to." He opened his coat to reveal a gold badge clipped to his sagging belt. "I'm Detective Finley."

He glanced down the stairwell, through glasses that looked to Carter like their lenses were half an inch thick, then said rather wearily, "Wait here."

Carter did as he was told, though he was already beginning to regret that he'd ever stumbled into this. Why hadn't he just called it in anonymously, left the driver's license where he'd found it, and taken off? It wouldn't have been the right thing to do, but at least he wouldn't be standing around here now, waiting to give what precious little information he could.

Detective Finley came back up the stairs, putting his fingers in his ears, just as the ambulance, siren wailing, arrived on the scene. When the ambulance stopped—and the siren with it—Detective Finley removed his fingers. "They always do that," he said to Carter. "I'm going deaf from it."

Carter smiled sympathetically. "Professional hazard, I guess."

"Not the worst of them."

No, Carter thought, probably not. The detective took a notepad out of his raincoat pocket and dutifully took down Carter's name, his phone number, a few notes on how he found the body, why he happened to be in the area. When Carter mentioned that he worked in the lab across the street, the detective's ears seemed to prick up. "I was the one who got the call about that," he said. "We took out one body, burned as bad as this one, and another where the guy was still breathing."

"That was a friend of mine, the one who was still alive. He's at St. Vincent's now."

"I know. I held onto his hand until they got him to the E.R." He shook his head, sadly. "Poor guy—glad he's still hanging on." He gestured at the stairwell, where Carter could hear the paramedics putting the body on a stretcher. "Now it looks like we've got another fire victim, only this one's dead no more than a day or two."

"I know who it is," Carter volunteered, "in fact, I gave a—"

"We know who it is, too. It's one of the transvestites who worked this corner. He got beat up once in a while—they all do—but nothing this bad ever happened before."

"So you think some . . . *customer* did this to him?"

Detective Finley stepped to one side to let the stretcher go by. Even with the body wrapped in a plastic sheath, the smell was bad. The paramedics wore paper masks.

"Right now, I couldn't say. But what kind of concerns me is, this happened right across the street from the last place I saw a couple of burn victims."

Though it was tough to see Finley's eyes through the thick glasses he wore, Carter felt he was being studied.

"Just what were you doing in that lab building, anyway?" Finley asked.

"Working on a fossil," Carter said, "a rare find, from Italy."

"Were you using flammable stuff, like chemical agents? Blowtorches?"

He was grasping at straws, that much Carter could tell, but for the first time it dawned on Carter that perhaps he should start watching what he said. "Some extra lighting had been rigged up," he admitted. "The fire marshal thinks that's what started the fire."

Detective Finley pursed his lips, skeptically. "Awful big blast, for a bad fuse."

Of course Carter could explain, if he'd wanted to, what really happened; he could tell him what Russo had said about Mitchell training the laser on the slab of stone, a slab of stone riddled with pockets of gas. But for some reason he didn't. Nor did he say anything about what Russo had said, in his delusional state, about the fossil coming to life.

"You ever talk to this guy, Donald Dobkins, the hooker?"

"No," Carter said, before catching himself, and saying, "Yes, once." *Damn,* he thought. Finley would note his confusion. "I was upstate when the accident occurred, but right after I got to the lab, the day after the accident, I saw him on the street. He was babbling about seeing somebody, somebody coming out of the burning building." Why did he feel, more and more, like he was offering an alibi?

"So who did he think he saw coming out?"

Carter hesitated. He could see where this might be going. Maybe Finley thought that the arsonist who had set the fire had been spotted by Donald Dobkins, and come back to dispose of the witness. But Carter knew that that wasn't it. "If you really want to know, he said that he saw a naked man made out of light," Carter replied, thinking that this would put an end at least to this line of questioning.

But Finley appeared strangely unsurprised. "Fits the general description."

It what?

"Even though Mr. Russo was slipping in and out of consciousness when he was taken out of here," the detective added, "he was mumbling the same sort of thing."

"He was?"

The detective nodded as he dug around in his pocket and then produced a business card so worn it looked like he'd already handed it out a dozen times. "If you think of anything else, give me a call." He turned toward his car. "In the meantime, we'll keep an eye out for anybody walking around made out of light."

The ambulance pulled away from the curb, and a moment or two later the detective's sedan pulled out after it. One of the cops was still standing at the top of the stairwell, speaking into a walkie-talkie, and Carter finally realized, even though nobody had given him formal permission, that he was now free to go.

It all seemed so . . . anticlimactic somehow. He'd discovered a body—a dead, burnt body—and now it was all over. He was walking away. Nobody had any more questions for him, there was nothing more that he could do. And maybe that was why, like a delayed reaction, it suddenly hit him—the full horror of what he'd seen. With nothing to do, and no one to talk to, he could suddenly focus on the reality of it, on the grim, appalling discovery he'd made. It wasn't the first corpse he'd ever seen—on his work expeditions he'd occasionally encountered natural and accidental deaths—but this wasn't anything like those. This was the kind of sight that came back to haunt you in your dreams—and that was all he needed. He was already having enough trouble getting to sleep these days.

He shivered and put up the collar of his leather jacket; it might be time to break out the parka, he thought. Even though it was only late afternoon, the light was getting pretty thin. The days were growing shorter. At the corner of West Fourth Street, while he waited for the light, he suddenly felt like there was someone right behind him. Watching. He turned around, but the nearest pedestrian was an elderly woman with a walker, her eyes riveted to the cement.

He crossed the street and walked the rest of the way home at a brisk pace—not only to keep warm, but to shake that odd sensation of being tracked. Once or twice he turned around abruptly, but he never saw anyone suspicious. When he got to the foyer of his building, he stopped to pry the mail out of their little metal box—these boxes, he thought, had obviously been designed long before mail-order catalogs had been invented—and instead of waiting for the unreliable elevator, took the stairs, two at a time.

Beth wasn't home, and the apartment was dark. He went from room to room, turning on the lights, and put a CD of the Hives on the stereo. He wanted upbeat, fast, attention-grabbing music, and he also wanted it loud. He popped open the fridge, took out a beer, and went into the living room. He flopped down on the sofa and stretched out his legs; above his head, he could see the Audubon bird prints. One of which Russo had temporarily replaced with that crucifix. What, he wondered, had all of that really been about? He'd never had a chance to ask, and now it would definitely not be a good idea.

Maybe, after dinner, he'd hit the hospital one more time, just to say good night.

He picked up a copy of *New York Magazine* from the floor beside the sofa and was just starting to flip through it— maybe there'd be a review of some downtown restaurant that he and Beth could try tonight, someplace crowded and noisy—when he heard someone outside the door to the apartment. He stopped flipping the pages and waited. It was a little early for Beth to be getting home; Raleigh usually liked to extract his full pound of flesh. As he started to get up from the couch, the door swung open, and he saw Beth holding her leather valise in one hand, and a bulging plastic bag, which smelled suspiciously like Chinese food, in the other.

"Here, let me get that," he said, hurrying over to take the Chinese food before the plastic bag, already stretching at the top, burst.

"Thanks," Beth said, kicking the door closed behind her. Then she turned the lock and threw the bolt on the door. And glanced through the peephole.

"You're being especially cautious tonight," Carter said, putting the bag on the kitchen counter.

"Yeah, well, I had kind of a scare downstairs."

Carter left the bag where he'd put it and went to Beth.

"What happened?"

"Nothing, really. I just wasn't paying attention when I came into the building."

Carter waited.

"I was carrying all this stuff, and I was already in the foyer before I realized that somebody was in there. I'm usually more alert than that."

"Who was it?" Carter was remembering the feeling he'd had, of being followed home.

"I don't know, I didn't get a very good look at him." She pulled off her overcoat and hung it on the wooden rack by the door. "I think he didn't want me to. He was tall, blond I think, with sunglasses on, and he turned around and went out almost as soon as I got into the foyer. I was going to get the mail."

"I already got it," Carter said numbly.

"Good, because I didn't. He was standing right in the way; in fact, I could swear he was running his finger around our names on the box."

Carter felt a chill, and instinctively put his arms tightly around Beth.

"I'm okay," she said, with a nervous laugh, "really I am. As soon as I put my key in the lobby door, he went back outside and down the steps."

"Did you see where he went?" Carter asked.

"He looked like he was going to go across the street to the park, but I didn't wait around to find out."

Carter let go of Beth and ran to the front windows that looked out over the park. The streetlamps hadn't gone on yet, and in the dusk it was hard to make out much. A couple of in-line skaters were still cutting around the footpaths, a teenage girl was walking a dog, and off in the distance, a figure, tall, wearing a red coat, was just leaving the other side of the park.

Carter grabbed his leather jacket off the coat rack and yanked the bolt back on the door.

"Where are you going?" Beth said, alarmed. "You're not going to go looking for the guy, are you?"

"I saw him," Carter said, unlocking the door, and running out.

"But I told you," Beth declared, though she could already hear him tearing down the stairs, "he didn't actually do anything."

She heard Carter's feet thump onto the landing, then race down the next flight. She hurried to the door, and shouted, "Carter! Just forget about it!"

She heard the foyer door open and slam shut.

"Don't start anything, Carter!" she shouted, to the empty air. She stood in the open doorway of their apartment and thought *What now*. She was sorry she'd said anything at all.

She closed the door, and rested her head against the back of it. *Why is Carter getting so exercised over this?* It crossed her mind that what was going on here was a little displacement. Maybe he still hadn't processed the bad news from that morning's appointment at the fertility clinic, and now all that frustration and energy was going off in all sorts of inappropriate directions . . . like this.

She threw all the locks but the deadbolt and went into the kitchen to put the Chinese food away. At least, she thought, she hadn't told him the creepiest thing of all. She could swear, while the tall guy was behind her in the foyer, that she'd heard him sniff the air around her, like a dog sampling a new scent.

By the time Carter got into the park, his quarry was gone. He ran to the far side of the park, dodged some cars, and went on in the direction the guy had seemed to be going. And way ahead, maybe two blocks, he thought he saw a spot of red, just before a bus momentarily blocked his view.

He picked up his pace, but by the time the bus moved away, the spot was gone. The guy could have turned left or right, but Carter didn't see anything in either direction that looked like him. He ran straight, and again he thought he saw it, the red coat, just as it was passing around the corner of a deli fruit stand on the opposite corner. But the light was against him, and by the time the traffic let up and he could cross, the guy was missing in action once more. But at least he knew which direction he was going. Carter's breath was getting ragged, and he wished he were running in something other than the worn loafers he had on, but he kept moving, ducking and weaving around the other people on the street. Before long, he found himself on a painfully familiar corner—right across the broad avenue from the brightly lighted entrance to St. Vincent's Hospital.

With no sight of the guy in the red coat, anywhere.

Leaning with one hand against a street sign, he stood, looking around, catching his breath.

This was the same corner where Ezra Metzger had dropped him off after the funeral—the future site, as the billboard proclaimed, of the Villager Co-ops. Maybe that's what it would one day be, Carter thought, but for now, it was a dark and dirty spot, with a twisted chain-link fence surrounding a vast, abandoned old building of dingy brown brick. He looked up at the crumbling steps, the broken windows covered with plywood, the ornate but grim turn-of-the-century façade. Above the main doors, crisscrossed with heavy planks and a warning sign to KEEP OUT, a rusted metal sign hung by one end: although it was covered with graffiti, Carter could just make out the words SURGICAL SUPPLIES. What was more interesting were the words behind the fallen sign, words which had been chiseled in stone into the original façade. THE NEW YO K SANATOR M FOR CONSUM ION AND INFECTI S DISE SE. You didn't have to be on *Wheel of Fortune* to complete the clue: The New York Sanatorium for Consumption and Infectious Disease. Below the chipped letters it said, FOUNDED 1899.

To Carter, the building looked like something out of a Dickens novel, and he wondered how long it had managed to remain in service—the Surgical Supplies incarnation looked like it, too, had been out of business for quite some time—before falling into complete wrack and ruin. There weren't many buildings left in Manhattan that still dated from the nineteenth century, and now this one, too, was finally about to bite the dust. Normally, Carter was sorry to see these old buildings go, to see the history of the city eradicated and replaced by soulless glass skyscrapers and yuppie apartment towers. But he had to admit that there was something about this particular building he doubted anyone would miss. Even if he hadn't known what its original use had been, he would have found it bleak and dispiriting. Sinister, if he was completely honest.

But there was no sign, here or anywhere, of the man in the red coat. Either Carter had lost him, or the guy had deliberately given him the slip.

A cold wind whipped down the avenue, and Carter shivered. An ambulance, lights flashing, rounded the far corner and headed for the emergency entrance.

He crossed the street—that Chinese food Beth had brought home sounded awfully good right now—but then he stopped one more time to look back at the abandoned building, at its massive, brooding walls and barricaded windows. And he got the inexplicable feeling that the building itself, derelict, untenanted, falling down at the seams, was looking back at him. Crazy, he knew, but there it was. He turned and walked away, with a line—was it from

Nietzsche?—ricocheting around in his head. What was it, exactly? *Stare into the abyss long enough, and the abyss stares back?*

Close enough.

TWENTY-THREE

"**And Enoch saw, ranged among the angels, those that** were known as the Watchers. Their hair was like beaten gold, their garments ————. Their eyes, which never closed, were deep as wells in the desert. They watched over the ———— of men, and taught them many things."

Ezra was pleased with how the pieces of the scroll were coming together. It was painstaking work, but he had just found another tattered scrap that seemed to fit neatly into the text, at precisely the right spot, when he heard a knock in the next room, on his bedroom door.

Damn. Now was not the time to be disturbed.

He ignored the knock, but then it came again, and this time he faintly heard Gertrude's voice, in the hallway. "Ezra—you've got a phone call."

A phone call? Ezra didn't even have his own phone number—who could be calling him? And as for friends . . . Then it dawned on him who it might be, and without even taking off his latex gloves he jumped up from his drafting table, ran into the next room, and threw open the door.

"It's someone named Carter?" she said, holding out the portable phone.

"This is Ezra," he said, shooing the curious Gertrude away. "Carter Cox?"

"Yes."

He hadn't said it happily. Even in that one-word reply, Ezra could sense that Carter had made this call reluctantly.

"I was hoping you would call," Ezra said, to encourage him further.

"And I was hoping I wouldn't have to."

"But you have, and that's all that matters. You've given some thought to what I said in the car—that's good. That's a start."

Carter cleared his throat on the line, and said, "Yes. Well, maybe."

"When do you want to get together? To talk."

"I'm free for lunch today," Carter said, "and if you'd like to come downtown to the faculty club at NYU, you could be my guest."

No, Ezra thought, that sounded dreadful. And he also knew that, since Kimberly was planning to get Uncle Maury to drive her on a shopping expedition today, he'd be stuck taking a taxi. Would that be violating the terms of his court-ordered supervision, he wondered?

"What about this," Ezra said, suddenly inspired, "you could come here. I could have a lunch prepared and we could talk in absolute privacy, with no interruptions at all."

There was a pause, and then Carter said, "Okay— thanks. Where are you?"

Ezra gave him the address, hung up, and then stood stock still, thinking. What, he had to wonder, had finally prompted Carter to call the number he'd scrawled on that slip of paper? He had just about given up hope. And now, what do you know—the call had come, and things—possibly things that were greater than even he, Ezra, could imagine—had once again been set in motion. If there *was* some higher plan, perhaps he had just caught a glimpse of it.

In honor of the occasion, Ezra showered, shaved, and put on a fresh black turtleneck. And when Carter arrived an hour later, he was there to greet him in the foyer. Carter, he could tell, was momentarily caught off guard by the grandeur of the place—the Rodin sculptures, the vaulted ceilings, the penthouse views. Ezra, of course, was inured.

"Thanks for coming," Ezra said, taking his leather jacket and handing it off to Gertrude, who was hovering like a mother bird. "Follow me," he said, leading the way across the polished marble floor, "we'll eat in the dining room. We'll be left completely alone in there." But then he stopped at the sound of a voice, Kimberly's voice, coming toward them. Wasn't she supposed to be out shopping by now?

"I'm stopping in at some galleries today," she was saying, "but I'll be done by the late afternoon. Pencil me in for five-thirty."

A moment later, she strode into view, snapping the cell phone shut. When she saw Ezra with Carter, she looked from one to the other as if trying to figure out what was wrong with this picture. Diamond earrings glistened discreetly under her chestnut hair.

"You're having a friend over?" she said to Ezra, with barely concealed surprise. "I'm Kimberly Metzger," she said to Carter, extending a well-manicured hand.

"Carter Cox."

"You're not," she said, lowering her voice, "part of his rehabilitation team, are you?"

Much as he hated her, Ezra was impressed. She was making him look bad with record speed.

"From the court?" she went on, before Carter could summon a reply. "Or Dr. Neumann's office?"

"No, nothing like that," Carter said, somewhat bewildered. "I teach at NYU. Ezra and I had some things to discuss. About his . . . research."

She nodded, and said, "Oh, his *research*," as she slipped the phone into a black Chanel handbag. "That ought to be useful." She pressed the foyer button for the elevator, and paid no more attention to them at all.

Though Ezra didn't say another word as he led Carter through several immense and lavishly decorated rooms— Carter saw a Flemish portrait he could swear had once hung in the Raleigh Gallery—Carter could tell he was seething. Since there was no way that someone as young and beautiful as that was his mom, she could only be his stepmother. His *evil* stepmother, judging from the way they'd behaved toward each other.

In the dining room were two place settings—folded linen napkins, crystal goblets, gleaming silver—on a table that could easily have seated twenty. And two plates of artfully arranged poached salmon on beds of wild rice, with apricot salads on the side. He and Ezra were seated at one end of the table, with Ezra at the head and Carter to his immediate right, allowing Carter to look out through a row of French doors toward a wide veranda planted with small trees and shrubs.

Carter was hungry, and the food was as well prepared as it was presented. But Ezra, he noticed, only picked at his plate. It was if he was just biding his time until his guest got to the point of their meeting. Once or twice, Carter spotted the housekeeper poking her head out the kitchen door, then popping it right back in again, as if she wanted to be sure the two boys were getting along all right.

After some desultory conversation about the possibility of a coming public transportation strike, Carter asked Ezra if that building site, across from St. Vincent's, was in fact his father's project.

"They all are," Ezra said, dismissively.

Okay, Carter thought. Another hot button he'd just pressed. Now he didn't dare ask what the stepmother was referring to when she'd asked if he was part of Ezra's rehabilitation team. Who was this guy, anyway? Some kind of criminal?

"So when are you going to tell me why you called?" Ezra said, no longer able to restrain himself. "Was it your own idea, or did someone put you up to it? Your Italian friend, for instance?"

Carter was impressed; the guy might be strange, but his instincts were almost always right on the money. "Yes. It was Russo, in the hospital this morning."

"What did he say?"

Carter hated even to have to think about it. But when

he'd gone to see him, and mentioned that he had met a man who believed, just as Russo had said, that the fossil had come to life, Russo had grabbed the Magic Marker and scrawled TALK TO HIM! on the little board. "He wanted me to talk to you, to find out what you knew."

"That's all?" Ezra said.

"He can't speak yet; his lungs and vocal cords were damaged in the fire. He can only communicate a few words at a time."

"I'll want to talk to him myself, just as soon as he's able. Will you let me know when that is?"

Carter nodded, though he still thought Ezra might be the last person he'd tell such a thing.

"One day I'll need to sit down and discuss some of my theories with him, at length."

"Theories? About what?"

Ezra toyed with a few grains of rice on his plate, as if debating how best to approach what he had to say. "Your friend's mind has been opened by a terrible experience. But I'm not really sure about yours yet. You are what I might call a man of science," he said, still not looking up, "and in my experience, that generally means you have a closed mind."

Carter took umbrage. "That's certainly not true in my experience. Scientists, if you ask me, are some of the most open-minded, inquisitive people in the world."

"That's only true as long as their questions lead them to the answers they were expecting to get all along," Ezra replied. "Only as long as they can find what they were looking for, and expecting, in all the usual places."

Not wanting to appear overly defensive, Carter gave that rejoinder some thought . . . and he could indeed see some truth in it. Weren't his discoveries at the Well of the Bones initially discounted by most of his peers? Hadn't he and others encountered heated opposition to the idea that modern-day birds were the direct descendants of the di- nosaurs? Wasn't the theory of geochronology, to which he subscribed, still fighting an uphill battle for acceptance? "Okay," he conceded, "I know what you're getting at, and

I'll admit that I've experienced some of that resistance to new ideas myself."

Ezra snorted, unimpressed.

"But any good scientist," Carter went on, "whether he's an astronomer or a paleontologist, really wants to know the truth. He wants to know what the evidence shows, or what the empirically gathered data reveal. He's not interested in making a case for any one theory or another, until he looks at what he's got and sees a pattern or an idea that makes sense of it all."

"But that assumes that he knows where to look, that he knows what data to gather and how to connect it."

"Well, sure," Carter said, wondering how else it could be done. "A scientist who didn't know what material was relevant to his work would never get anywhere."

"And I suppose that you, for instance, think that you do know? You believe you're aware of everything that might be pertinent to your work with that fossil?"

Back to the fossil. "Yes. I think I was."

"But were you aware that one minute after your lab explosion, the bells in every church, synagogue, and mosque in the city started ringing?"

Carter remembered hearing about it on the radio driving back from Ben and Abbie's country house. "Yes. It was some kind of Halloween prank."

"A prank that has yet to be solved or explained."

"And you think that the ringing bells have some connection to the work I was doing?" Carter said, incredulously. "Are you saying that the force of the explosion set off, what, a sympathetic vibration in church bells all across the borough?"

Ezra suddenly leaned forward, his elbow brushing his plate. "You have no idea what I think! The data is staring you in the face and you just don't want to look back at it."

Carter remembered his thought about staring into the abyss. "What data are you referring to?"

"You think these two events are just a coincidence?"

"Yes. I do. What else could they be?"

Ezra's eyes fairly blazed with conviction—or, Carter

thought, with madness. He could see Ezra wrestling with something, a decision. He was sizing Carter up, wondering whether to broach the topic he could scarcely avoid any longer. Finally he said, in a voice that indicated he had managed to overcome some profound reservations, "Come with me."

Ezra threw his napkin on the table, got up, and started out of the room. Carter followed him. He had no idea where he was going, or what to expect, but if he'd gleaned anything from the conversation they'd just had, it was that he'd better keep an open mind. Whatever Ezra wanted to show him, it was going to be . . . a stretch.

At the end of a long hallway, Ezra stopped and unlocked a door. He kept his own room, in his own apartment, locked? More and more, Carter suspected he was dealing with a paranoid personality. Ezra stepped inside, and once Carter was in too, he closed and locked the door behind them.

"I have to take certain precautions," Ezra said.

Carter nodded, as if he understood. The bedroom he was now standing in was very large and well furnished, but there was nothing in here that struck him, at least so far, as odd or remarkable. If Ezra had something to show him, it had to be through the doorway to his left.

"Before I show you this," Ezra said, "you have to promise me that you won't say a word about it to anyone. Do I have your promise?"

Carter agreed.

"And you promise, too, that you'll keep that open mind?"

"Cross my heart."

Ezra paused, as if he still wasn't sure he wanted to go forward. Then he opened the door to the adjoining chamber and looked around the interior before stepping inside. *Another sign of paranoia?* Carter thought.

The air was stuffy and the room was dim. There were French doors, as in the dining room, but the curtains were drawn and Carter had the distinct impression that they were seldom, if ever, opened. Ezra walked to the far side of the room and flicked on a lamp above a drafting table. On the table, and on the walls above and around it, were acetate sheets covering yellow scraps and strips of what looked like ancient scrolls or papyri.

"What are these?" Carter said. "The Dead Sea Scrolls?"

Ezra didn't answer, and Carter suddenly thought *Oh my God—they* are. He looked at Ezra, who held his gaze; in Ezra's eyes, he saw a flash of defiance, and pride.

"How on earth did you get hold of these?"

"Let's just say I found them. They were meant to belong to me."

Carter couldn't resist going closer. He walked to the wall and studied one of the sheets hanging there. Even for someone as accustomed as he was to dealing with ancient things, these were astonishing. He had never seen a document so old—for all he knew, there weren't any—and this one was covered with dense, indecipherable characters, written in a purplish ink so dark it was almost black. He looked over at the drafting table, where Ezra had clearly been at work assembling another section of the antique scrolls.

"What do they say?"

"As you can see, I'm still piecing that together. But they're a mixture of things—stories, revelations . . . prophecies."

Carter was bending closer to the one on the drafting table. "Is it papyrus?"

"No," Ezra said. "It's something else. But given its Middle Eastern origin, it's unlikely to be a rice admixture. It's probably some sort of animal skin—goat, sheep, camel, ox."

"Sounds like you still need to narrow it down."

"I do—and that's where I thought you could help."

Carter glanced at Ezra, to see if he was kidding, but it didn't look that way. He was serious. "How would I know?" Carter asked. "This isn't exactly my field."

"But you do have a lab at NYU. You have access to all the usual dating techniques—radiocarbon, for example—and I'm sure you can do molecular tissue analysis, too."

Ezra came to Carter's side and pointed his finger at a spot on the scroll where the light was the brightest. "Do you see? It has the texture, even possibly the pore structure, of an animal; what kind, I don't know. I don't know what the ink is made of either." He looked over at Carter. "But if you were to run some lab tests, you could tell me."

"And that would help?"

"With my work? Immensely. If I knew the composition of the scroll, and its date, I'd be able to figure out a lot of other things about it."

Carter leaned back. "If it's so important, how come you haven't just found someplace to do the lab tests on your own?"

Ezra looked away, and to Carter it looked like he was rehearsing exactly what he wanted to say. "While my claim to this material is entirely legitimate, there are still certain authorities, here and elsewhere, who might dispute it."

Whew, Carter thought—this guy really was way out there on the limb.

"And my activities at this time," Ezra added, "are closely monitored."

He must be referring, Carter thought, to that "rehabilitation team" his stepmom had mentioned. Whatever Ezra was up to, he was certainly up to it in a big way. Carter looked around at the workroom. Books and papers were scattered all over the floor, and he could see where Ezra had set up his tools on an old toy chest in an effort to create a viable workspace. And strange as it all was, Carter would have had to admit that he recognized the place immediately—just as he recognized the kind of person who would set it up. It reminded him of some of his own makeshift offices and research spots. Despite all the money he apparently had, Ezra Metzger was one of those single-minded eccentrics who usually managed to worm their way into a university environment and then live out their days in a niche in the woodwork. The type was absolutely familiar to Carter; he had a sort of soft spot in his heart for the intellectual misfits—perhaps because he knew how perilously close he'd come, with his own expeditions and pet theories, to winding up as one himself.

"Even if I agreed to get you what you want," he said, "and I'm not saying that I can, how do you expect me to do it? You want me to just walk into the labs and unroll one of these scrolls?"

"No, I know you can't do that," Ezra said, eagerly, sensing he was on his way to victory. "All you need is a tiny sample, and I've already selected that for you." He held out a sandwich-size plastic baggie, inside of which Carter could make out a fragment of the scroll. "This should be enough to work with—and it's all, quite frankly, I'm prepared to spare."

Carter took the baggie and held it up to the light; the strip inside was no more than an inch long and maybe three-quarters of an inch wide, but he knew that Ezra was right; it would be enough for the lab tests—if, that is, he could get them done at all. He might have to do quite a bit of fast-talking to explain how he, a paleontologist, had come by this particular specimen and why he needed the test results.

But he'd made strange requests before.

In fact, now that he thought about it, he'd never even called for the final results on the sample that he and Russo had taken from the fossil. In all the turmoil from the explosion, the death of Bill Mitchell, Russo in the hospital, he'd put it out of mind. He'd actually come to think of the fossil as having been irremediably lost in the lab inferno—it was just easier that way. But it wasn't really so, was it? A tiny, unsullied fragment still existed. It wouldn't be much, but at this point, he'd be grateful for anything he could salvage. And it would give him a good reason for showing up at the biomed lab in the first place.

"You know, there'll be lab costs for something like this," Carter said, "and they could run pretty high."

"Whatever it costs," Ezra said, dismissing the problem, "I'll cover."

From everything he'd seen so far, Carter believed that Ezra would be good for the money. But when he started to slip the baggie into his front shirt pocket, Ezra stopped him.

"Your body heat," he warned.

Carter said, "How do you want me to carry it?"

Ezra turned around and grabbed a white mailing envelope. "Put it in this and carry it in your hand, or your outside coat pocket."

Carter obligingly put the baggie in the envelope, then sealed the flap. Just by doing so, he felt that he had inadvertently signaled his complicity. He had entered into some sort of pact with Ezra, a pact that he wasn't overly eager to scrutinize. But then there were many things in his life right now that didn't bear close scrutiny. Maybe he was being stupid, maybe he was just being helpful . . . and maybe he was simply trying to prove, beyond a shadow of a doubt, that he wasn't one of those closed-minded scientists that Ezra had been going on about. Fair enough, but who was he trying to prove that to, he wondered—Ezra, or himself?

TWENTY-FOUR

Arius smelled her before she even came out of the building, the scent of hyacinth wafting toward him, barely concealing the subtler but even more alluring aroma beneath it. The aroma of beauty and youth . . . and desire. She was slender, with rich brown hair and green eyes, and he wondered if the old man, the one who was now opening the car door for her, was silently reveling in her scent, too. How could he not?

As the car slowly rounded the drive, he stood in his new clothes beside a decaying tree—*how were they expected to grow with their roots buried in this . . . concrete?*—and watched.

This was another connection, another thread in the web he was so quickly constructing.

It was a big city, he had learned, with countless people in it.

But his web kept him centered, his web kept growing, in size and complexity. He knew that if he paid close attention to it, his web would eventually provide him with everything he needed to know . . . and everything he needed to bring about his ends. Carter Cox—whose name he had taken from the silver mailbox—had led him to this spot, and now, he knew it was time to follow the new thread.

Time to expand the web again.

As he turned and walked away, he passed a pair of young men, talking energetically with each other, and he was glad to note that they did not stop to stare at him; they didn't even slow their conversation. A woman pushing a baby carriage smiled his way, then went back to babbling at her child.

He was now that . . . *believable.*

It hadn't taken him long to assess this new world, and to learn that he had to make certain changes. He had looked around, at other men on the street, and quickly learned to tell the difference between the struggling and the successful, between the unwanted and the sought-after. And he knew, soon enough, that the red cloak—coat—was wrong. It was a banner for the unnatural. But he'd also taken the creature's purse. And in it he'd found money—and even more. The purse was filled with these cards, small cards that fit neatly in the palm, each one with a different name on it; he had observed how people used them to acquire whatever they desired.

And he had swiftly done the same.

Now his coat was black—sleek and warm and long enough almost to graze his ankles—and his shoes were black, too, gleaming and pointed. He wore a suit, a dark blue the color of the sky just before the sun crested the horizon, and a white shirt of soft, white silk, with an open collar that wrapped like a band around his throat. And although he had long since discarded the purse (another sign of unnatural artifice) and the dark glasses— the *sun*glasses—that he had found inside it, he had replaced them with a differently tinted pair; round, with gold frames and amber-colored lenses. He knew that his eyes, otherwise, could prove unsettling—they were no one color, but could change with his mood and his surroundings. In them, he knew, people could see the light that coursed like blood through his body. His eyes could shine like a sunlit waterfall, flash like a river of golden coins, or boil like a flood of molten lava.

It was best, all things considered, that he keep the glasses on.

Every so often he stopped, deliberately, and breathed in the air. Even though the car was nowhere in view, the car carrying the woman who smelled of hyacinth, he could track her. He could follow her scent. He could feel the twitch upon the fragile thread of his invisible web—and he could follow it.

It led him away from the river and into the heart of the city. Soon he found himself on a wide and busy street, outside a building with a long red awning and heavy doors of polished brass. She had gone in there.

A man in a uniform held the door for him as he entered, and welcomed him to something called the Raleigh Gallery of Fine Arts.

"Thank you," Arius replied, always pleased to hear his words, and his voice, gain such easy acceptance.

Inside, he sensed another happy confluence—not only was the hyacinth woman standing not far off, studying a painting, but the woman showing it to her was the one who lived with Carter. *Elizabeth* was the name he'd seen on the box.

His web had just grown that much stronger.

As he observed them—and yes, they had the same underlying scent—a small man came up to him, very eager, very friendly, with his hand extended.

"I don't believe we've met," the man said, "but I'm Richard Raleigh, the owner of the gallery."

Arius extended his hand and nodded.

"And you are?" Raleigh persisted.

"My name is Arius."

"I detect an accent," Raleigh said, smiling broadly, "and I'm usually very good at pinning them down. But I can't for the life of me guess where this one might originate. Would you mind my asking where you're from?"

"Far away," Arius replied.

Raleigh nodded sagely, and knew enough not to pursue

it. He had dealt all his life with monied, and even titled, foreigners, and he knew when to back off. Some of them liked to try to pass as ordinary folk, but Raleigh could pick them out of a crowd at a hundred paces. This fellow was, admittedly, more unusual than most. Maybe six foot two, with shades he apparently had no plans to take off, and dressed in expensively understated clothes, he carried himself like a royal potentate, his head back, his shoulders squared, his fashionably long hair rippling just over his shirt collar. Raleigh found it hard to take his eyes off him.

"Allow me to tell you a little bit about our gallery. In this room, you will see most of the oil and watercolor works that we presently have for sale. But we also have an upstairs gallery for private showings of certain works—most of them Old Master prints and drawings."

Arius didn't say anything, but stepped closer to one of the paintings—a sixteenth-century annunciation scene, displaying the elongated forms and skewed perspective common to the Mannerist style.

"Yes, that's a particularly fine work," Raleigh said, "which only recently came onto the market. It's been in the collection of the same Austrian family since the late fifteen hundreds, and it's attributed to Fra Bartolommeo. Are you familiar with him?"

Arius cocked his head at the painting, as if trying to compensate for the altered perspectival lines. "No, I am not."

"Not many people are," Raleigh rushed in, always eager to assure potential customers that whatever they didn't know was strictly the province of the experts. "But if you would like to know anything more about it, our resident art historian—who oversees everything in our collection—just happens to be right here." He gestured toward Elizabeth, who looked over in Arius's direction.

She was quite beautiful, Arius thought. Even more beautiful than the hyacinth woman.

"Beth is with another client right now," Raleigh said, "but I'll introduce you to her as soon as she's free." Raleigh knew that Beth had a way with new clients, effortlessly winning their trust . . . and with the exception of Bradley Hoyt, that young dot-com mogul, their business.

"I would like to meet her now," Arius said.

Now? Raleigh didn't know quite what to do; Beth was with Kimberly Metzger, one of his most prized customers—just last month he'd sold her a Flemish portrait for close to half a million dollars—and he couldn't very well interrupt them. But when he glanced their way, he noted that Kimberly was already paying more attention to the mysterious stranger than she was to whatever Beth was saying.

"Do I have a rival for this painting?" Kimberly said, teasingly.

"No, no, not at all," Raleigh interjected, "but if I may, I would like to intrude for just a moment."

He didn't have to go any further; Kimberly stepped forward, offered her hand to Arius, and introduced herself. "I know everyone in New York who knows anything about art," she said, "but I'm sure that I don't know you."

"Mr. Arius is just visiting the city," Raleigh said, glancing up at him to see if this seemed correct. He got no objection.

"Is that true, Mr. Arius?" she asked. "Are you new in town?"

"Yes."

"How long do you think you'll be staying?"

"I cannot say yet," he replied.

Raleigh, who didn't want the conversation to stray too far from commerce, quickly pulled Beth forward. "And this is Beth Cox, who knows everything there is to know about our collection."

"Nice to meet you," Beth said.

"And you."

"Do you happen to have a card?" Kimberly said to Arius, virtually stepping on Beth's toe. "My husband and I—Sam Metzger?—often entertain at our place in the city, and we're always on the lookout for new blood."

"No, I don't have . . . a card," Arius said. *One more custom to practice.*

"Oh. Then maybe I'd just better invite you right now. You see, we're having a little get-together tomorrow night, seven-thirty, for the mayor's re-election campaign. At One Sutton Place. Can you remember all that?"

Arius smiled. "Yes, I can. Thank you."

"So you'll be there?" she said, playfully.

He nodded, his eyes still concealed behind their shaded glasses.

Beth and Raleigh exchanged a look, as if to say *Can you believe this?* Although she'd already heard plenty of rumors about Kimberly Metzger's private life, Beth thought she'd never seen such a flagrant pickup. Of course, in this *particular* instance, she could almost understand: Arius was a very striking figure indeed. He was about Carter's height, but his hair was so blond it was almost white, and it shone in the overhead gallery lights. His skin, too, was almost flawless—no, make that *perfectly* flawless—and his features were chiseled as if from a block of unblemished marble. With his eyes hidden behind the tinted glasses—and how much of an art lover could he be, she wondered, if he kept the glasses on when looking at a painting?—the only hint of color in his face came from his lips, which were a deep pink, pulsing with life, and as full as a woman's. Voluptuous and vulpine, she thought, at the same time.

"The Van Eyck that Beth was just showing me," Kimberly was saying to Raleigh, "I do like—"

"Van Dyck," Beth corrected, in a soft voice.

"Yes, of course," Kimberly remarked, "isn't that what I said?

"I must have misheard," Beth apologized. Raleigh shot her a glance that could kill.

"I'm thinking of it for our new place, the one we're building in the Virginia hunt country. It might work in the library, but I'm just not sure."

"It's always hard to know," Raleigh comforted her, "until you see it actually hanging in place. Why don't you tell us when you're ready, and we'll ship it out so you can see for yourself?"

"Thanks, Richard," she said, pecking him on the cheek, "you're a peach. And you," she said, coquettishly, to Arius, "I'll see tomorrow night. Don't forget!"

As she left the gallery, Arius's head turned. What was it, Beth wondered, that made him seem so . . . singular? So attractive and, at the same time, so . . . discomfiting? He made you want to look at him, and look away, all at once.

"Now, Beth," Raleigh said, "have you got a few minutes to show Mr. Arius some of the pieces we're holding upstairs? I'm thinking, in particular, of some of the Courbets and Corots."

She should have seen that coming; there was no way Raleigh was going to let this new fish slip out of his net—not without a fight, at least. But the thought of taking him upstairs for a private consultation sent an involuntary tingle down her spine. There was something way too strange—and even strangely familiar—about this man. Though it was impossible that she could have forgotten him, she still had the odd sensation that she had seen him somewhere before.

"I'm so sorry," she blurted out, "but I have an appointment I have to keep."

Raleigh shot her a second dirty look.

"A doctor appointment," she threw in, knowing that was the one thing Raleigh wouldn't interfere with; he knew about the family-planning problems that she and Carter were having.

"You're sure?" he tried.

"I'm sure," she said, contritely, glancing at her watch. "In fact, I've really got to run."

"In that case, then," Raleigh said, giving up and turning to Arius himself, "I would be more than happy to show you a few things on my own. Do you have some time right now?"

Since she was, in fact, just meeting Abbie for a cup of coffee around the corner, Beth didn't even bother to go upstairs for her coat. She hoped Raleigh wouldn't notice. All she wanted to do right now was make her escape, to get out of the gallery as swiftly as possible—and away from this strange creature whose eyes she felt, even now, as she moved away, were studying her behind those amber lenses. Part of her wished that she could just reach out and pull those glasses off his face and see who he really was . . . and part of her sensed that if she did, she would regret it the rest of her days.

TWENTY-FIVE

"Look, I wish I could give you nothing but good news," Dr. Permut said, leaning back in his chair with a file folder in his hand, "but there must have been something wrong with the sample you gave us."

"I took the sample myself, right from the end of one of the talons," Carter said. "Are you saying it was contaminated?"

Dr. Permut rubbed his jaw, doubtfully. "I don't know what was wrong with it, but no, I don't think contamination was the problem."

"So what was? What did you find out?"

"See for yourself," Permut said, handing the file to Carter.

As Carter flipped through some of the pages, Permut provided a running commentary.

"Those pages on top, they're the report on the dating analyses. As you can see, the results are so far off the charts as to be useless."

"What do you mean, off the charts?"

"I mean, nothing remotely hominid, saurian, or avian— all the options you mentioned—could possibly be that old.

In fact, you'd probably get a closer match with a sample of the moon rock brought back by *Apollo 12*."

Carter wasn't pleased, but he wasn't all that surprised either. After all, these were the same sorts of results Russo had gotten in Rome.

"But what about the biological tests? The molecular and cell studies?" And then the million-dollar question. "Could you find anything at all in the way of DNA evidence?"

Dr. Permut tilted his chair back and took a roll of Tums out of the pocket of his white lab coat. "Want one?"

"No thanks."

"I take them for the calcium. But you work with bones, you know all about that."

"But I don't normally work with DNA," Carter said, to get him back on point. "Could you locate anything viable?"

Permut nodded his head. "Believe it or not," he said, sucking on the Tums, "we were able to find and extract an inert fragment. It was smaller than virtually anything anybody's ever tested before." He looked around proudly at the NYU biomed research lab. "But you came to the right place."

Carter was encouraged, but he kept it in check.

"We had to use a computer model to fill in some of the gaps," Permut went on, "and then we extrapolated some of the rest at the tail end."

"Which means what?"

"Which means that what we've got, in a way, is what I'd call theoretical DNA."

To Carter, that didn't sound so good. "Well, is it, or isn't it?"

Permut wagged his head. "It's a little of both. We've got a solid chromosomal foundation for everything in our profile, but again, given the infinitesimal sample, plus its age and its condition, we did have to do some guessing."

Carter was getting more and more frustrated; this, he knew, was why ordinary people hated science, and scientists. "Then just tell me," he said, evenly, "what your best guess is. Based on the available DNA evidence, can you tell me what we've got here?"

Permut blew out some air, and Carter felt himself bathed in Tums fumes. "I can tell you what we *don't* have," he said.

"Fine. I'll start there."

"We don't have a *Homo sapiens*."

Okay, Carter thought, at least they were making progress.

"And we don't have any other known member of the animal kingdom."

Permut reached across the table and flipped to some pages that looked, to Carter, like a mad scramble of numbers and four letters—C, G, T, and A—repeated over and over, in no particular order, and coursing across the page in row after row. The numbers were a mystery, but the letters, Carter knew, represented the four nucleotides cytosine, guanine, thymine, and adenine. "When I look at these readouts," Permut said, "I see a pattern."

"I'm glad someone does."

"And at first even I thought it was a human pattern. Then I looked again, more closely, and I thought, well, maybe not—maybe it's a mammal, but that's about all we can tell. Then I looked at it even harder, and I could see that it wasn't exactly one thing, and it wasn't exactly any other."

Carter waited for him to finish.

"You're the paleontologist," Permut said, "and you can call it whatever you want, but around here we've made up our own name for it."

"What?"

"The missing link."

The missing link. "Thanks a lot," Carter said, dryly. "That's a big help."

"Hey, don't shoot the messenger," Permut protested. "And I'm only half-joking about that, by the way. It has an almost ninety-nine percent match with *Homo sapiens* DNA—of course, all the difference is in that last percent or two."

"Like with the chimpanzees?" Carter said.

"This is even closer—as close as you can get, I'd say, without actually getting a match."

Carter took a deep breath. What had he had in that rock? With each thing he learned now, the loss of the fossil became just that much more painful.

"Sorry," Permut said, intuiting Carter's grief. "If there's anything else I can do for you, I'd still be glad to help out."

"As a matter of fact," Carter said, wearily fishing for the plastic baggie that Ezra had given him, "there is." He took it out of his pocket and laid it on the table.

"What's this," Permut said, "another brainteaser?"

"Sort of."

Permut picked up the baggie and held it up toward the light to look at the small scrap of the scroll inside. "At least it's not a bone this time."

"It's a piece of an ancient document," Carter said carefully, so as not to suggest any of his own assumptions or surmises. "I need to know how old it is, what it's made of, and what the ink is."

"I was afraid you were going to ask me what that squiggle on it actually said."

"No, somebody else is taking care of that."

Permut gave him a long look. "Is that somebody else also going to pay for the lab charges? On this last job, we had a signed authorization from your department chair, Stanley Mackie. Who's going to sign for this one? The lab costs could easily run a couple of grand."

"They'll be covered."

Permut looked impressed. "Remind me to ask you the source of your funding sometime." Baggie in hand, he swiveled away in his chair, ready to get started, then swiveled back toward Carter. "Say, am I going to wind up in the annals of science for this?"

"I'll see what I can do," Carter said. "Just get me the results as soon as you can."

On the way to St. Vincent's, Carter stopped to pick up some Italian magazines at an international newsstand. Even though he knew Russo's tastes ran more to *Scientific American* than *GQ,* he had to make do with what he could get.

At the ICU, he got a momentary scare when a nurse told him Russo was no longer there.

"He's been moved," she added. "He's in the burn unit, one floor up."

"So does that mean he's improving?"

She raised her eyes from the desk. "It's the burn unit," she said.

Carter took her point.

But when he went up there, he did find that the place at least was a small improvement. The atmosphere was a little less frosty and forbidding. There was Muzak playing, softly, on overhead speakers, and a couple of vending machines for visitors. He spotted Dr. Baptiste coming out of a room at the end of the hall and asked her if that was where Russo had been transferred.

"Yes, we moved him this morning. He's stabilized now, and soon we'll be able to start the grafting procedures."

Carter winced at the thought.

"You're right—it's not going to be any picnic for him. If his family would like to come and see him, now would be a very good time."

"The only one living is his mother," Carter said, "and she's too ill herself to leave Italy."

Dr. Baptiste shook her head. "Then he's very lucky to have you for a friend."

If only she knew, Carter thought—if only she knew. "Can I go in for a visit? I've got some magazines to give him."

She looked at the titles and frowned. "Don't look much like his cup of tea," she said, "but go right on in."

Inside, he found Russo propped up in the bed, the only one in the room; a trolley littered with empty plates and aluminum lids had been pushed to one side.

"This," Carter said, taking in the new room, "is a big improvement." And it was. There were actually some flowers in a vase, a Van Gogh wheat field on the wall, and best of all, a wide window, with the blinds still raised.

Unfortunately, Russo himself didn't look a whole lot better. Wherever the bandages weren't covering his skin, it was a horrible patchwork, parts of it black, others bright red. At least the plastic tent, which usually covered his head, was thrown back now.

"Brought you some reading matter," Carter said, gently laying the magazines on the bed beside Russo's blistered hand. He didn't touch him, for fear that physical contact was still off limits.

"Thanks," Russo said, in a voice somewhere between a whisper and a croak.

Carter glanced out the window; it was a good view, with cars moving past the main entrance right below, and a mostly unobstructed vista south. The only thing standing partly in the way was that old sanatorium across the street, its windows boarded over and its fire escapes—the ones still attached at all—barely clinging to the crumbling façade. If the wrecking ball didn't get to it first, it looked like a strong wind could reduce the whole building to rubble.

"Did you . . . see him?" Russo asked.

Ezra. "Yes. I did." Where should he start? "I was right about one thing—he's from a very wealthy family."

"But what . . . did he say?"

"He said that he believed you, when you described the fossil coming to life." Carter could still hardly believe he was repeating this. "He said that most scientists had closed minds, but that yours had been opened by what you'd seen."

Russo grunted, in sad agreement. "What else . . . does he . . . know?"

That was a tough one. Even Carter wasn't sure of that. But he did know what Ezra believed—that there were forces at play, powerful and important, that had yet to be understood. But how could he explain any of this to Russo, especially as he himself grasped—accepted?—so little of it himself. "He turns out to be what you might call a free-lance biblical scholar."

Russo looked puzzled.

"I know. I don't quite understand it myself. But unless I'm nuts, the guy has genuine specimens of the Dead Sea Scrolls in his apartment, and he's been piecing them

together. He wanted my help to get some of them ana-
lyzed." He went on to describe Ezra's workroom, what he
had seen there, and what Ezra had said about the church
bells ringing right after the lab explosion. The more he
talked, the crazier it sounded, even to himself, but Russo's
expression didn't change. If anything, he seemed to be
drinking it all in, questioning nothing, trying to fit the dis-
parate jumble of information into some logical shape on
his own. When Carter eventually paused to take a breath,
Russo pursed what was left of his lips—two blackened
strips of skin—and said, *"Bene."*

"Bene?" Carter said. "Why? What's good about this?"

"If I am crazy," Russo croaked, "then it is good to have
company."

So he knew, Carter thought, that he'd remained a skeptic.

"One more . . . favor?"

"Sure," Carter said, "as long as it's not a cigarette. You
know that's not allowed in here."

"Bring him here."

"Ezra Metzger?" he said, though he knew perfectly
well. Would that be a good idea? Introducing his terribly
injured friend to a possible lunatic?

Russo nodded.

"I'll call him," Carter conceded.

"Good. And now," he said, painfully raising the fingers
of one mutilated hand, "that cigarette?"

TWENTY-SIX

"I see empty champagne glasses," Kimberly warned one of the waiters, "and at my parties, I don't like to see empty glasses."

"Yes, ma'am," he said, "right away," and flew off to the kitchen to replenish his supply of Cristal.

Aside from tiny glitches like these, Kimberly felt that the party was going very well indeed. The mayor, his wife, and his mistress—also known as his campaign treasurer—were all there, holding court in various quarters, and she'd also snagged several big-time editors and journalists, a bunch of high-powered bankers and lawyers, and even a couple of Broadway stars. There was no way this party wouldn't make it onto Page Six, or maybe even into Liz Smith's column. If it also happened to raise some funds for the mayor's re-election campaign, its ostensible purpose, well, that was okay, too.

As she drifted from room to room, greeting her guests, making sure everyone made the connections they had come there for, she kept one eye out for the arrival of her mystery guest, the one she had tried, and dismally failed, to keep out of her thoughts since meeting him the day before.

Mr. Arius. She'd never seen a man who looked quite like him, or one who had made such an indelible and immediate impression on her. The night was still young, but she was already starting to worry that he might not show up at all.

Sam was off in one corner of the main salon, huddled with two or three of the other power players in the real estate game, no doubt hammering out the plans for another office tower, shopping center, or New Jersey mall. She waved three fingers at him as she passed by, but he didn't even seem to notice her.

Other men, she was pleased to see, still did.

She was wearing a scarlet chiffon, off-the-shoulder Thierry Mugler, bare in the back, slit up the side, with her hair drawn up in a tight chignon offset by a diamond-and-ruby clasp shaped like a rainbow. The mayor himself had lingered longer than necessary when kissing her hello, and Kimberly had seen a wary look cross his "campaign treasurer's" face. *Don't worry,* Kimberly thought, *I've got bigger fish than this to fry tonight.*

The next time she checked, he was standing in the foyer, handing his long black cashmere coat to the attendant. He was wearing a dark suit again, and his eyes were again concealed behind the round glasses, with amber-colored lenses. He turned his head, with his chin raised, like a blind man trying to sense his surroundings, as Kimberly went to greet him.

"I'm *so* glad you could make it, Mr. Arius," she said, offering her hand and cheek.

"Thank you. For inviting me," he said, taking her hand, but remaining otherwise aloof. "I am happy to be here."

What *was* it, she thought, that was so strange, and so strangely alluring, about this man? The way he spoke, in those odd cadences, as if English were something he'd only learned in school; the way he kept his eyes concealed; the way his hand felt—as cool and as smooth as glass—when taking her own? (And had she noticed something odd about one of his fingers?) He even had his own faint aroma, unlike any aftershave or cologne she could identify; it seemed instead to be somehow organic, something that emanated from his very skin, and hair, and breath.

"Let's go inside," she said, "and I'll introduce you to some of the other guests." She slipped her arm through his and led him into the next room, feeling as if she were escorting a movie star. The other guests reacted as if she were, too, parting to make way for them, stopping midconversation, wondering out loud, "Who is that man Kimberly's with?" Arius himself seemed unaffected by it all. If introduced to someone, he was polite; if not, he was silent. Either way, he said very little. His answers were courteous but brief, and always somewhat vague or evasive. After listening to him field half a dozen inquiries, Kimberly felt that she knew no more about where he was from, what he did for a living, or where he was staying in New York than she had when he arrived. Even Sam couldn't get more than a few words out of him, and Kimberly knew perfectly well what his take would be on him. Longish white-blond hair, arty glasses, the fact that he'd been first introduced to his wife by the flamboyant Richard Raleigh? Sam would lump him in with her hairdresser, her decorator, her antiques advisor, and all her other gay friends. And as far as Kimberly was concerned, that couldn't be better.

Unless, heaven forbid, it turned out to be true.

As for that little shit Ezra, he'd made his obligatory appearance, and even, so far as Kimberly knew, thanked the mayor for his help in getting him out of jail after that UN park fiasco. He was nowhere to be seen now, and unless Kimberly missed her bet, he was back in his room pursuing whatever pointless exercise he called his "research."

The caterers seemed to have everything else under control—the drinks were flowing, trays of canapés and appetizers were being passed everywhere, a lavish buffet had been spread out in the dining room, and every time she passed the foyer the elevator doors were opening and admitting another half a dozen guests. She'd even bagged Katie Couric for about a half hour—and that, she was sure, was bound to get the party some media attention the next day.

The only person who didn't appear to be having a very good time was her mysterious Mr. Arius. Reluctant as she was to let go of him at all, she did have duties to perform, so she'd had no choice but to set him adrift. Whenever she spotted him, he was off by himself, holding a champagne glass that seemed always to remain full, strolling alone on the terraces, or coming inside to study a painting or sculpture with deep interest. Maybe he really *was* some kind of serious art collector with a vast château in the south of France, filled from floor to ceiling with famous paintings and beautiful statues. On a sudden impulse, seeing him inspect a nothing-much little oil that Sam's first wife had bought, she glided over to him and said, "You really are the art connoisseur, aren't you?"

"I appreciate beauty," he said, slowly, "in all things."

Was that some subtle encouragement she'd just heard? "Then let me show you something that I'm sure you'll enjoy."

She turned to go, but he remained in place. "Follow me," she told him, crooking her finger. "I won't bite."

As discreetly as she could, she ushered him down the hall, and then swiftly around the corner to her bedroom door. There she stopped and said, "Now this is for your eyes only. Even my husband doesn't know that I bought it yet, so I'm trusting you with my life." She laughed gaily, but he only smiled politely in return.

As soon as he'd followed her in, she closed the door behind her—and locked it, to her own surprise. What did she think was going to happen? In the middle of her own party yet?

She led the way across the vast master bedroom, past the huge canopied bed, the Louis XVI armoire, the Scalamandre armchairs, and into her own completely private realm—her wardrobe closet and bath. The dimensions of her dressing area, she often reminded herself, were exactly the same as the first apartment she'd lived in when she came to New York—and even then she'd had to share the space with a roommate.

This had once been a kind of sewing room for Sam's

first wife, but Kimberly had persuaded her husband that she needed her own area to keep her clothes, to do her toilette, to be by herself while she dressed and made herself beautiful for him. As a result everything had been torn out, and all this—mirrored walls and marble counters in the bathroom, track lighting and built-in cedar racks in the dressing room—had been installed. But it was Kimberly's decision alone to acquire the gorgeous little Degas, of a woman emerging from her bath, for the spot beside her makeup table. "The owners were going to put it up for auction at Sotheby's," she confided, "but Richard Raleigh, the sweetheart, was able to persuade them to sell it to me directly instead," she said.

She stopped beside it, turned toward Arius, and raised an open palm. "I don't suppose I have to tell you anything about what you're looking at. In fact, you can probably tell me a few things!" *Calm down,* she told herself, *you're sounding like a schoolgirl.*

Arius had never seen a work like this, but when he did look, he instantly absorbed and inventoried everything about it. The arts, after all, were one of the many gifts that he and his kind had bestowed, so it was a delight to see the countless cunning ways in which they had since been used. This particular painting before him now, apparently a Degas, was a very fine and expressive example. He was learning something every second, even if it was only the name of an artist, a word, or the meaning of a look, and his thirst for more was unquenchable.

The look he saw on Kimberly's face right now, for instance . . . that was a look whose meaning he already knew. Perhaps she was unaware of the fact that, even as he pretended to study the painting, his eyes, behind the tinted glasses, were devouring her reflection in the neighboring mirror. She was looking at him, and he could see in her eyes that she was curious, attracted, afraid—all things that she had every right to be.

Long ago, during his vigil, he had seen that look often . . . and he had resisted its summons. For a time.

·

And after?

He had endured solitude beyond imagining, a cold and barren night without end . . . a night that, until now, had never fully lifted.

He turned away from the painting, and looked at her, wordlessly. *Was this, then, how it would begin?*

"It's beautiful, isn't it?" she said, a nervous flutter in her voice.

"Yes."

"I had to have it."

Though his eyes were still hidden behind the amber lenses, he knew that she could feel the intensity and penetration of his gaze. She stepped back, a little unsteadily.

"Maybe we should get back."

He didn't answer.

"To the party." But she didn't try to move past him. She stayed rooted to the spot, her bare back reflected in the mirrored wall behind the vanity table.

"Yes," he said.

But the way he said it, Kimberly wasn't sure what he meant. Yes, they should go back to the party? Or yes . . . something else?

She found herself thinking, nonsensically, about his aroma. It had seemed so subtle when she first met him, so delicate, but now it seemed to be so much more powerful . . . overwhelming.

"May I," she said, putting one hand on the vanity table to steady herself, "ask you a favor?"

He nodded.

"May I ask you to take off your glasses?"

"Why?"

"I've never seen your eyes. I need to see your eyes."

He smiled. Of course she did.

She laughed, mirthlessly. "I'm still not sure how smart this will be, but I do want to do it. I feel like I don't even know who you are yet."

So, this would indeed be the way it would start.

He came closer, bending his head above her like a great,

golden bird of prey, and took his glasses off . . . and in her eyes he saw the surprise, the fear . . . the mute incomprehension.

His hands went to her shoulders and her skin was hot; he could feel the blood pounding just below the surface. He slipped the crimson dress, as light as a butterfly's wing, down her body, down to the floor. He undid the diamond clasp and let her hair cascade down to her naked shoulders. He bent low and pressed his own cold lips to hers, her throat, scented with hyacinth, arching upward.

He shrugged his suit coat from his shoulders, and then with one hand unfastened his collar and the buttons below. He sucked the hot breath from her body as her hands fumbled blindly at his belt and trousers.

In his head he heard the whistling of wind, the crack of lightning. He saw a rain of fire, like arrows of flame, howling down through a limitless black expanse of sky.

Kimberly slipped backward against the edge of the vanity; bottles of perfume fell tinkling onto their sides, while others tumbled and spilled onto the thickly carpeted floor. She heard only the rushing of her own blood, she smelled only a summer garden after the rain, she saw only his eyes, drawing her in, as if into a secret pool of honeyed light. Her arms went up to him, to his smooth, his flawless skin . . . but what she felt was ice. Hard and cold as the diamond clasp that lay on the floor. And when his hands went to her breasts, she shivered at their touch.

"Arius . . ." she breathed, bewildered, "you aren't even a . . ."

No, he whispered into her reeling mind, *I am not.*

And then he took her, like a hawk swooping in for the kill. She felt herself carried helplessly into the widening pool of his eyes, into the verdant aroma of rain-washed leaves. Light, too bright to behold, was flooding the room, like a star exploding . . . exploding all around her, exploding inside her.

Oh dear God . . . she thought with dread, as the light embraced, enveloped, and then overwhelmed her . . . *Oh dear God, what have I done?*

PART THREE

PART THREE

TWENTY-SEVEN

Even though the fire department had cut off all the electric lines to that part of the building, there was still enough light in the makeshift lab for Carter to grope his way around. But there was far more wreckage, more broken equipment and twisted blocks of metal, than he could understand. He didn't remember this much stuff ever having been in here in the first place, so where had it all come from now?

In the dead center of the room, where the fossil had been entombed in its slab of stone, the depression in the floor was deeper than he remembered it, too. He walked to the lip of the crater, and looking down, he was reminded of the Well of Bones, the pit he'd descended into in Sicily. Like the Well, this, too, had walls of rock and earth, and it smelled of ancient dust and mortal decay. But there was something that he hadn't seen before, something small and glistening, at the bottom of the hole, and he squatted down to get a better look.

It was about a foot long, dark but polished, the way a walking stick might be. But he still couldn't quite make it out. Carter put his hand down to balance himself, then slid down into the pit. It was farther than he thought, and his fingers scrabbled at the dirt walls as he went down. He landed on the ankle he'd once injured playing basketball, and he winced. *Shit,* he thought, *that's all I need.* He looked around the dirt at his feet, scorched black from the fire, and saw the glistening object again. He bent down and picked it up, and when he straightened up again, he was pleasantly surprised to see that he wasn't in a pit at all anymore. He was in his boyhood bedroom, outside Chicago, the one where he'd recuperated from the mumps.

So *that* was it! This wasn't real—it was a dream. It just didn't feel like a dream, any more than the object in his hand felt like a figment of his imagination.

But the bedroom was exactly as he remembered it. The trophy he'd won in the Westinghouse science contest sat atop the battered dresser. The poster from *Raiders of the Lost Ark* adorned the closet door. And in the old armchair, under the eaves, a woman was reading to a little child.

Now he knew it had to be a dream. He'd never once taken a girl up there, much less one with a toddler.

But when he went closer, the woman, while still reciting from the book, looked up at him, smiling. It was Beth. But whose child was this, then? Was it his? He thought that was supposed to be impossible. But maybe it wasn't, maybe the doctors were wrong! He was suddenly so happy, and so relieved.

"Is he . . . ours?" Carter asked, of the little boy whose blond head nestled in the crook of Beth's arm.

But she didn't answer; instead, she just kept reading from the book, which, to his astonishment, he now saw was Virgil's *Aeneid*—the very copy he'd read at Princeton. Since when was that a bedtime story?

"There was a wide-mouthed cavern," she read aloud, in a soft singsong, "deep and vast and rugged . . ."

Carter bent closer, to see his son.

". . . sheltered by a shadowed lake and darkened groves . . ."

His hair was blond, almost white, and hung in delicate tendrils.

". . . such vapor poured from those black jaws to heaven's vault . . ."

But when he raised his sleepy head, all Carter could see, where his eyes should have been—

". . . no bird could fly above unharmed . . ."

—were two gaping holes, burned like hollows into his head, and blazing with fire.

Carter choked and bolted upright in the bed, his heart pounding so hard he felt as if it would burst from his chest. His body was cold and covered with sweat.

"What's wrong?" Beth said, frightened.

He swallowed hard, and shivered.

Beth sat up, in her favorite leopard-print pajamas. "Are you okay?" she said, pulling the blanket around his shoulders.

"I'm okay," he gasped.

"You had a nightmare?"

"The worst ever."

She blew out a breath. "It must have been."

He shivered again, and drew the blanket closer.

"Want to tell me about it?"

He shook his head. "I'd rather forget about it."

She rubbed his back, soothingly. "Maybe that's a better idea." In the faint blue light from the digital alarm clock, she saw something in his hand. "What's that you're holding onto?"

He didn't know what she was talking about.

"In your hand—you're clutching something."

Carter looked down, and saw now that he was indeed gripping something in one hand. He opened his palm, and let it fall on the blanket.

"It's a crucifix," Beth said, puzzled. "Where did that come from?"

"It's Joe's."

"Why are you holding onto it?"

Carter didn't know. He didn't even know where he'd found it.

"If it's Joe's, he might want it," Beth said. "Maybe we should bring it to him in the hospital."

Carter looked at it in amazement. "Yes. I will," he said. "Tomorrow."

After all that, Carter knew there was no chance of falling back asleep. He put on a robe over his T-shirt and boxer shorts, slipped on his rubber thongs, and went to the kitchen. His throat felt sore, maybe from the labored breathing, and he took a beer out of the fridge. A cold one might soothe his throat . . . and take the edge off things a bit.

But man, what a nightmare that had been. In his entire life, he'd never had one as bad as that—or as real. Where had it come from? And why—even if it had been only a dream—was Beth reading the *Aeneid,* of all things? True, he'd studied it in college, and even written a couple of papers on it, but he hadn't thought about it in years. In fact, he wasn't even sure, now that it had come up, where his annotated copy was anymore.

He went into the living room and, while sipping his beer, scanned the rows and rows of books that lined the cinder-block shelves. Most of Beth's books—oversized art history texts—were arranged on the lower shelves, and most of his, which ranged from *The Origin of Species* to ornithological field guides, were arrayed on the top. But when he and Beth had gotten together, they'd quickly realized that there would never be room enough for all of their books in one place, so a lot of them had wound up stored in boxes. Boxes now stacked in the basement of the building.

One of them, he figured, held his old copy of the *Aeneid*. In the morning, he'd go looking for it.

Out of idle curiosity, he picked up one of Beth's books on Renaissance art and took it to his wingback chair. He leafed through it, glancing at the curious mix of biblical and mythological themes, sipping his beer. But his thoughts kept returning to the *Aeneid,* to the lines he dimly remembered—and was already starting to forget—from his dream. Something about a shadowed lake, and poisonous air rising up from it. He wondered if he was actually remembering the lines with any accuracy. Had the poetry sunk in that effectively during his undergraduate years? Or was he way off base? He wondered again where that copy of the book had gone. He wanted to see it, and for some reason he wanted to see it now.

He put the art volume on the coffee table, and glanced at the clock above the bookshelves—it was three-thirty in the morning. At least if he went now, he wouldn't be bumping into any of his neighbors.

He crept out of the apartment and took the stairs. There was a cold wind blowing in the stairwell, and when he got to the first floor, he could see why—the door to the foyer, which was supposed to remain closed and locked at all times, was ajar. He pushed it closed, listening for the sound of the lock catching; he heard it. Then he turned and went to the far end of the hall, where the door to the basement was tucked around behind the elevator; despite the late hour, he could hear the elevator car rumbling in the shaft. Maybe he *shouldn't* have gone out in just his robe and flip-flops; it'd be pretty embarrassing to bump into a neighbor right now. Although the basement door had a padlock on it, Carter knew, as did all the other tenants, that it wasn't really locked. He removed the padlock, folded back the hasp, and went down the narrow flight of steps.

There were two washers and dryers down here, a rickety table to fold clothes on, and a plastic chair. The floor was concrete, the ceiling was made up of dirty acoustical tiles, and the super's attempt to cheer things up by putting a lampshade of red and yellow glass on the overhead light only made things more dismal. In the next room, where the boiler was mounted against the back wall, the tenants were allowed to store some things. There were a few bicycles, a pair of skis, and a couple of dozen boxes: Carter's were in the rear.

He pulled the string on the bare bulb that hung from the ceiling back there, and looked over the stack of brown banker's boxes. All of them identical. Now which one would hold the books from his literature and classics courses? He knew it wasn't the top one; that one held various papers he'd written, his thesis, abstracts, and monographs. He took it off the top of the pile, then lifted the lid off the next one down. He could see a bunch of biology and chemistry texts. He put that box on top of the other. In the next one, he hit what might be pay dirt; Dryden was on top, Chaucer just below. He plopped the box on the floor, sat down on the other two, and started rummaging through the dog-eared volumes of poetry and literature. It wasn't hard to spot the *Aeneid* at the bottom. It was a thick paperback, with a painting of Aeneas and Dido in Carthage on the front cover. Seeing it again now, he immediately recognized the painter as Claude Lorraine; marrying an art historian had taught him a few things.

But how would he find the lines he was looking for? And why, for that matter, was he looking for them at all? He had the strangest sense that they meant something, that his unconscious was trying to tell him something. That it had been trying to tell him something for some time.

But there were twelve books in the *Aeneid,* and thousands of lines in each one. In his head, he went over the lines from the dream again. There'd be no quick way to pinpoint something about a shadowed lake, or a dark grove, in the glossary or index—each word would probably have dozens of entries. But there *was* that mention of the birds, where the poem said no bird could fly above the deadly vapors from the lake. *Birdless,* Carter knew, *was* a word in the ancient Greek—and it doubled as the name of the barren place itself. He remembered using it in one of his early papers on the links between birds and dinosaurs. The word was *aornos,* and that, he figured, was as good a place as any to start.

He turned to the back of the book, and there it was— listed as appearing first in Book VI, line 323, of the Mandelbaum translation that he was using.

But then, before he'd even turned the page, something else caught his eye, in the same definition. It was another name for this same deadly spot, an alternative that had sounded vaguely familiar to him ever since Russo had first sent him the fossil reports from Rome. Avernus. According to the notes he was reading now, it was the place where the renowned Sibyl of Cumae, the wild and terrifying seer of antiquity, guarded the entrance to the underworld. The portal, as it were, to Hell.

And wasn't it there, at the lake of Avernus, in a cavern that had been submerged for millions of years, that Russo reported the fossil had been found?

Carter sat perfectly still as a cold draft blew around his feet and ankles; behind the boiler he heard a furtive scratching. He felt as if something massive, like the rough-hewn block of a pyramid, were at last sliding into place. Something was taking shape, but what it was he still couldn't tell. The scratching came again, and he noticed a mousetrap set in the corner. Time to go back upstairs, he thought; time to ponder all this in warmer and more comfortable surroundings.

He pulled the string on the light, went back through the laundry room and, *Aeneid* in hand, climbed the stairs to the first floor. The halls were still cold, and he took the creaky old elevator the rest of the way up.

He'd left his apartment door unlocked, and he entered quietly, finished off the beer on the coffee table, and then absentmindedly dropped the empty bottle into the kitchen trash can. Worried that it might have disturbed Beth, he glanced down the hall toward the bedroom door. Which was, fortunately, closed.

But that was odd.

They seldom closed that door, and he knew that he hadn't closed it himself tonight. Had Beth? After his nightmare had startled her awake, he thought she'd gone right back to sleep.

Avernus. Tomorrow, at the university library, he'd have to look it up in some other sourcebooks, see if there were any other connotations less dismaying than the ones he already knew.

In the living room, he turned out the lights, surveyed the empty expanse of Washington Square Park below, then went to the bedroom door. He started to open it, but found, much to his surprise, that it wouldn't budge. He knew for a fact that it wasn't locked; the lock had been broken since the day they moved in. He tried again and this time the door swung back, but only slightly. Then, as if it had a mind of its own, it closed again.

Carter stood there, puzzled. Was there a draft blowing it closed from the other side? In point of fact, he *could* feel a cool breeze coming from under the door and chilling his bare ankles. He put his shoulder against the door, and gradually it swung open a foot or two. Peering behind it now, he could see that the bedroom window *was* wide open, the blinds rattling and askew. And something suddenly clutched at his heart. He threw all of his weight against the door and shoved his way in.

"Beth!" he cried, stumbling over something bulky, and underfoot. "Are you all right?" he cried, just managing to maintain his balance.

She was lying on the bed, the covers thrown back, nearly naked. The top half of her leopard-print pajamas was missing completely, and the bottoms were tangled down around her ankles.

"Beth! What's going on?" he urged, running to the bed. "Beth!"

But impossible as it seemed, she was asleep, deeply asleep. When he put his hands on her shoulders and shook her, it was like shaking a rag doll. Her head lolled back, and her skin was so cold it was covered with goosebumps. A damp wind was still blowing through the open window. He jumped up, batted the blinds out of the way, and pulled the window down; on the fire escape outside, the geranium pot had toppled over.

When he grabbed Beth again, her eyes slowly opened. "Beth, wake up! Talk to me!"

But she appeared to be having trouble focusing on him, her gaze roaming blearily around the dimly lighted room as he yanked a blanket, trailing onto the floor, back to the bed and threw it over her.

"Beth, it's me. It's me, Beth."

Her eyes gained focus, but as they did, a panic seemed to rise within her. Her fingers clutched at Carter's arms, and she moaned fearfully.

"It's okay, you're okay," he said, over and over, trying to

calm her. "What happened here?" There were places his mind did not want to go . . . not yet.

Her hair was wild, as if strong fingers had been running through it.

"I thought I was the one with nightmares tonight," Carter said, soothingly. He chuckled halfheartedly. "Now you've got 'em, too?" He prayed that was all that it was.

She still didn't say anything, but just burrowed against him.

He rubbed her back gently and looked around the floor. The bedroom rug, which normally was anchored by the bedstead, was over by the door and bunched up behind it. That, he thought, must have been what blocked the door, and what he'd stumbled over.

But it still didn't explain how it had gotten there.

"Beth," he said, softly, "do you remember closing the bedroom door?"

He felt her head shake *no* against him.

"Or moving the rug?"

Again she shook *no*. He didn't even have to ask her about the open window. He knew what the answer would be.

But then what had happened? Had she walked in her sleep, like Russo? In all the years they'd been together, he'd never known Beth to do anything like that. But what was the alternative? That something, or someone, else was responsible?

From what he could tell, she didn't appear to be physically hurt in any way. At least there was that. And in the air, there was even an oddly fresh scent, something like rain-washed leaves. But something, perhaps inexplicable, had happened here. Beth was clutching him more tightly than ever, her arms wrapped around him and drawing him close. Under the blanket, she kicked her pajama bottoms loose.

"Everything's okay now," he said, thinking she just needed the reassurance, but her embrace indicated she wanted something more.

"Fuck me," she said.

It was the last thing in the world he expected her to say, and he thought he must have misheard her.

"*Fuck* me."

Even her voice, distant and demanding, didn't sound like the Beth he knew.

She whisked the blanket off her naked body and pulled him down of top of her, her hands slipping up and into his robe.

"Beth, is this really . . ."

"Yes, it is really," she said, in a mocking but urgent tone, "it's what I want." She tugged his boxers down. *"Now."*

"But I—"

She silenced him by pressing her mouth against his, her tongue probing, penetrating. It felt wrong; it felt off. Carter felt like he was in bed with someone he didn't know.

Her hand slipped lower, grabbing him.

Despite himself, he started to respond.

Beth ground her hips against him, and moaned. The sound of it, the ache of her desire, echoed in his head.

Her legs separated, and wrapped themselves around his back.

When he moved inside her, she was so open, so wet, it was as if they'd been engaged in foreplay for hours, not seconds. She pulled him in even deeper, and groaned in ecstasy—a groan that inflamed him, too. He'd never heard her make such a sound; he'd never known her body to feel so hot with passion and, at the same instant, so cold to the touch. Her head tilted back on the pillows, her chin raised, and he thrust himself into her, again and again.

"More," she chanted, "more . . . more . . ."

No matter how hard he pushed, or how deep he went, she urged him on, gripping him tighter. And when he couldn't hold off any longer, she sank her fingernails into his back, like talons, and a strangled scream curdled in her throat.

He closed his eyes, lost in the moment, thinking, for once, of nothing.

But when he opened his eyes again, her face was turned toward the window. Her lips were set in a thin, frozen smile and her eyes . . . her eyes had rolled up so far into her head that nothing but the whites were showing.

A shiver went down Carter's spine, and he could feel, where her nails had clawed his back, that blood had been drawn.

TWENTY-EIGHT

Ezra had arrived at a particularly tricky, but absorbing, part of the translation. The previous section of the scroll had described the duties of these angels—the Watchers—and what they had once done for mankind. Since they never had to sleep themselves, they kept constant watch over the world and provided such gifts as the knowledge of planting and harvesting, and a taste for the arts (and artifice, too); they had taught humans to speak in a common tongue, so that they could understand each other and achieve common aims.

Ever since starting on this section of the scroll, he had brooked only one interruption—and that was to make his command performance at the mayor's fund-raising party. His father had demanded it, and Ezra had dutifully showed up just long enough to thank the mayor in person for intervening on his behalf in the UN park arrest, before scurrying back to his room.

In fact, that night he'd been in such a rush to get back that he'd literally bumped into one of the guests, a tall blond man, in the hallway that led exclusively to the family's private quarters. Ezra, still carrying a champagne flute, had spilled it on the front of the man's dark suit.

"Oh, sorry," Ezra said, brushing the wine away.

The man said nothing, and when Ezra looked at him he was startled to see that he was wearing amber-colored sunglasses, on a face that looked as if it were made of flawless alabaster.

"But are you lost?"

"Why do you say that?"

He had some weird accent, too. "Because the party's the other way," Ezra said, jerking his head in the other direction.

"Yes," the man said. He'd smiled, as if it were an afterthought, then moved away. The air, to Ezra, smelled like an evergreen wreath.

But he'd thought no more about it, going right back to work on the section he was laboring over even now. It was a veritable roster of the angels themselves, their ancient names, and it was remarkably slow going. He'd spent the whole morning and most of the afternoon parsing out the pale letters, the faded words, and, because there were no literal equivalents in any known language, trying to come up with rough translations. But the sounds were hard to replicate, the consonants as hard as walnuts, the vowels slurred together in ways a modern tongue would find difficult to pronounce. The syllables required, indeed they created, a kind of strangely musical cadence, and all he could really do was roughly approximate the mysterious names . . . of Araquiel . . . and Semjaza . . . of Gadreel . . . Penemue . . . Tamuel . . . Baraqel . . . Ereus . . .

It was perhaps because he was so absorbed in his work that he didn't at first hear the scratching on the glass behind him. But by the time it had penetrated his consciousness, he could also hear the twisting of the doorknobs to the terrace. He whipped around in his chair and stared at the French doors; they were still closed, the floor-length curtains drawn, but something was stirring outside on the terrace, that much he could tell.

He threw a light cloth over the work on his drafting table and moved stealthily toward the doors.

The scratching stopped, and suddenly there was a hammering on the glass.

He parted the curtains with one finger, and an eye—a wild, green eye—was pressed against the glass, staring back.

"Let me in, Ezra," he heard. "I have to show the decorator around!"

What? It was Kimberly—outside in the cold, dressed, he could see now, in only a pink satin robe. And alone.

"Open up! We're freezing out here!"

The terrace ran all the way around this side of the apartment, from the master suite to his own rooms, but he had never known Kimberly to wander over this far. He pulled the curtain back and fumbled with the door handles. Used so seldom, they were sticky and hard to turn. When he did get the doors open, Kimberly popped through, her hair in loose disarray, her feet bare.

"Why do you always have to keep this place locked up like a jail?" she complained, and Ezra didn't know what to say. He didn't know what to think, either. She glanced around the room—at the acetates on the walls covering sections of the reassembled scroll, at the worktable with its tensor lamp still burning, at the clutter of brushes and plastic gloves and X-acto knives atop the old toy chest—and her nose wrinkled in disgust. "Haven't you even started packing up yet?"

"Why would I do that?" Ezra said.

"So we can get started on the nursery!" she replied, as if he were the stupidest man on earth.

Clearly, she was delirious. Ever since the party for the mayor, she'd been ailing; according to Gertrude, she'd slipped away from the party, and collapsed in her room. She hadn't come out for a meal or anything else since; Gertrude had been bringing her chicken broth and medications, but apparently she had gotten much worse. His father, par for the course, was out of town on business in Dallas.

"Don't you remember," he said, "I have to keep living here, where I'm supervised?"

"What are you talking about?"

"The court order?" he replied, though he could see that none of this was going to make any sense to her. A few seconds ago, she'd thought the decorator was with her.

"All I know," she said, sweeping her arm around the room, "is that all of this has to go. We have to paint, we have to put new carpeting down, and we have to make room for the bassinet!"

Her robe had slipped off one shoulder as she gestured, and to Ezra's horror he saw that her shoulder blade was bruised. It looked as if someone's fingers had squeezed her far too tightly . . . and the idea that it might have been his father—*that it had to be his father, who else could it be?*—made him distinctly queasy.

"What are you up to in here anyway?" Kimberly said, as she strode toward his drafting table. "Is this what you call your research?"

Ezra moved quickly to interpose himself between the table and Kimberly; in her present state, there was no telling what she would do.

"Yes, and it can't be disturbed," he said.

"Who says so?" she said, reaching around him and tugging the cloth off the section of scroll he'd been translating.

Ezra grabbed her wrist. "I told you not to do that!"

"You can't tell me what to do!"

"Kimberly, you're not well," he said, trying to calm her down. "I think we need to get you back to your room and call a doctor."

"Okay," she said, suddenly docile, "you're right," but the moment he let go of her wrist, she lunged at the table, and snatched the precious fragment of the scroll in her hand.

"Kimberly, no!" he shouted.

Before he could stop her, she had danced away, a mad grin on her face, waving the strip in the air. "This what you want?" she said. "Then come and get it!"

She was making for the French doors, and Ezra had no choice but to run after her and grab hold of her again. She whirled around, her robe flying completely open now; she was naked, and even as her hands flew at him, in a frenzy of scratching and slapping, he registered that she had other bruises too—all over her body. What on earth had happened to her?

"Let go of me!" she screamed. "Let go!"

But Ezra was simply trying to snatch the scrap of scroll back. She held it away, then doubled over, twisted around, and he could see that she was trying, in vain, to rip it apart.

"Stop it, Kimberly!"

But she didn't; she put the scrap between her teeth and tore at it—and it was as if she'd bitten into a live wire. A blaze of blue sparks shot into the air, buzzing like angry bees. She dropped to the floor, a tiny piece of the scroll still stuck to her lip. Her limbs shook and a white froth foamed at her mouth.

He knelt beside her, put one hand on her shoulder, and with the other tried to remove the piece of his precious scroll. But as if it were a snake slithering back into its hole, the scrap slipped into her mouth and then, though he wondered if he had only imagined it, he saw a rippling in her throat, as if it were traveling down that way, too.

Kimberly gagged and coughed. Her whole body went into convulsions.

Ezra didn't know what to do. He said, "Hold on!" and ran out of the workroom, through his bedroom and yanked open the hallway door. "Gertrude!" he shouted. "Gertrude!"

"What?" It sounded as if she were four or five rooms away.

"Call 911! It's Kimberly! We need an ambulance!"

By the time he got back to her side, she looked like she was entering a coma—her eyes were glassy and her breathing was growing very still. Her body was exposed by the open robe—there were black and blue spots beneath her breasts, as if they'd been manhandled. He pulled the robe closed and stroked her forehead. "Just rest," he said, "you'll be okay." Her skin was damp with sweat, but hot with fever—and he wondered not only if she'd be okay, but if she'd even survive until the ambulance arrived.

Gertrude bustled into the room. *"Gott in himmel,"* she muttered under her breath. "I called," she said to Ezra.

And ten minutes later, the paramedics were there, lifting her onto a gurney, wheeling her quickly out to the elevator. Ezra got on the phone to his father's office, where the secretary forwarded the call to Dallas; Sam was sitting in a boardroom there, negotiating some deal. When Ezra told him Kimberly had fallen ill and been taken to the hospital, there was a momentary silence, then he immediately started barking questions at Ezra. What hospital? Why hadn't Sam's own physician been called? What was wrong with her? Who had made the diagnosis?

Ezra fielded as many of them as he could, but as he didn't know much, he could feel his father's frustration growing by the minute.

"I'll finish up here," Sam declared, "and be back as soon as I can."

• "Is there anything else you want me to do in the meantime?"

"Yes! I want you to go to the hospital, and make damn sure she's getting everything she needs!"

Hanging up, Ezra once again felt, as his father had always made him feel, that in yet another situation he had somehow failed.

He went back to his room—where he could barely look at the empty spot on his drafting table where the scrap of scroll had been—got his coat, and went back downstairs. He had the doorman, Alfred, call a cab, and while they waited, Alfred shook his head and said, "Awfully sorry about this."

"Yes, it's terrible."

"She always looks so beautiful, and those parties she throws always get us in the newspapers."

Which was exactly their purpose, Ezra thought.

"In fact, if you want this back," the doorman said, slipping some papers from his uniform jacket, "Mrs. Metzger usually likes to have them."

Ezra looked at the sheets of embossed stationery and saw that it was a list of party invitations, with little checks beside nearly all the names.

"She asks me to check off the guests as they arrive," the doorman said, "and give it to her after the party. For her records, I guess."

"I'll give it to her," Ezra said, as the cab pulled into the driveway and he got in back.

"Doctors Hospital," Ezra said, and the cab took off.

As he sat in the backseat staring out at the late gray afternoon, he thought about all that had just happened—Kimberly's delirium, the damage to the scroll. To his secret shame, he knew which one troubled him more. Kimberly would be cured of whatever it was that ailed her, but the scroll? That would never be restored; that portion of its text would never be recovered. He'd always felt as if the scroll had been entrusted to him, perhaps by some higher power; it had been his job, his duty, to protect it, and in that, too, he had failed.

The cab stopped at a light on First Avenue, and Ezra looked down at the printed party list in his hand. Some of the names—the mayor, some city councilmen, old family friends—he recognized. On other pages were rafts of names that probably only Kimberly knew. He turned to the end of the list and there he found a few more names, last-minute invitations, he presumed, scrawled in her own hand in lavender ink. There was a Mr. Donlan, a Mr. and Mrs. Lamphere, and finally, with a big question mark next to it, a Mr. Arius.

Huh. That was a strange name. And why the question mark?

He presumed it meant she wasn't sure he'd come.

But then, as the cab started up again, and he thought back to that night, he remembered something else that was odd.

That blond man, the tall one he'd bumped into in the hallway. He hadn't gotten his name, either.

But he'd been coming from the direction of the master suite.

He thought of the bruises he'd seen on Kimberly's body. Marks he could never have imagined his father inflicting.

He thought of the blond man's bizarre appearance.

And then he thought of the name, and looked at it again, with its attendant question mark. Was it there because she wasn't sure he'd come . . . or because she wasn't sure how to spell it?

He said it out loud, "Arius," and the cabbie turned around.

"Nothing," Ezra said, then uttered it again, more softly. "Arius."

His mind flashed to the scroll he'd been working on, and its list of names. Gadreel, Tamuel, Penemue . . . and the last of them all . . . Ereus.

That had been his rendering of the sound, but couldn't it just as easily—in fact, perhaps even more accurately— have been translated into English as Arius?

Suddenly he thought he knew what might be afflicting Kimberly. And for the first time, he thought she might not survive it after all.

If it was true . . . would any of them?

TWENTY-NINE

Carter's first stop that day had been the main library— and what he discovered there was bad enough.

But now, in the departmental office, things had only gotten worse. The secretary handed him an envelope from the law firm of Grundig and Gaines, informing him that Ms. Suzanne Mitchell, wife of the late Bill Mitchell, was bringing a wrongful death suit against New York University, and that he, Carter Cox, as faculty supervisor of the lab in which the lethal accident had occurred, was to be deposed.

"The chairman got one of those, too," said the secretary, "and he wants you to make an appointment to see him this week."

What next, Carter thought. In a matter of weeks, he'd been told he was sterile, his good friend had been burned beyond recognition, his wife had suffered some weird hallucinatory nightmare, and now it looked like the chairman wanted to ream him out for bringing disaster down on the whole department.

"So," the secretary said, "how's Thursday at three?"

Carter took a second. "Oh, sure—I'll see him then." He glanced at his watch and realized he was running late.

Of course. He was due at St. Vincent's, for the summit conference that both Russo and Ezra had been demanding.

When he got to the corner across from the hospital's main entrance, he had to wait for the light—which gave him just enough time to note that the sign in front of the old sanatorium, the one announcing the Villager Co-ops to be built there, now sported a banner that read GROUNDBREAKING JANUARY 1ST! SALES OFFICE OPENING SOON! In fact, he thought he saw someone, maybe a member of the demolition crew, passing behind one of the windows in the top floor. Only in New York City, he thought, where real estate even now was so crazy, could a developer expect people to line up to buy apartments in a building that was no more than a picture on a billboard.

By the time he got up to the burn ward, he could already hear Ezra's voice inside the room. Damn—he had wanted to be there to make the introductions, and if necessary to cover for any momentary shock Ezra might display at his first glimpse of Russo.

Entering, he realized that he had worried for nothing. Ezra had drawn a chair right up next to the bed, and Russo's head was bent toward him attentively. They looked like close conspirators who, if anything, resented his intrusion. Russo raised his burnt fingers in acknowledgment, and Ezra simply nodded—then went on with what he was saying.

"Don't mind me," Carter said, perching on a radiator case on the other side of the bed and plopping his briefcase down beside him. Inside it, he was carrying Russo's crucifix, which he meant to return to him in private.

"I was just telling Joe about the man he saw," Ezra reiterated, "the one who emerged from the rock."

Carter felt as if he'd suddenly started free-falling down the rabbit hole. "You were?" Carter said dubiously. "And what were you telling him?"

"His name."

Carter glanced conspicuously at his watch. "I'm only fifteen minutes late, and already we've figured out that a man did indeed emerge from the rock—"

"He did," Russo croaked.

"And that we also know his name?"

"We do," Ezra said. "It's Arius. And he is one of the Watchers."

"The what?"

"The Watchers. An order of angels who existed before time as we know it even began."

It was a lucky thing Carter was already sitting down. He looked from one to the other to see if this was in fact some kind of a joke they were playing, but he could instantly tell they were not. Russo's expression was unwavering, and Carter suddenly realized that a new alliance had been formed. He had been outvoted. Joe had at last found someone who accepted his account, who believed that what he'd seen had been more than the hallucination of a desperately injured man, and Ezra had found a comrade-in-arms to listen to his outlandish biblical theories.

It was up to Carter to get on board, or bail. "Okay. If, as you say, he's an angel," Carter said, trying to sound open-minded about it, "let me ask you a couple of questions. First of all, why is Bill Mitchell dead? And second, why is Joe lying here waiting for a skin graft? Aren't angels supposed to watch over us and protect us from harm?"

"No, not necessarily," Ezra said. "There are all kinds of angels, and some of them were friends to mankind, and some of them weren't."

And how many can dance on the head of a pin? Carter thought. Russo must have read his mind.

"Bones, please," Russo said, earnestly. "Ezra knows . . . about these things."

Out of deference to Joe, Carter swallowed his skepticism one more time. "So, this angel you're talking about— this Arius?—is a bad one?"

"I'm not necessarily saying that, either. The Watchers were appointed by God to oversee the affairs of men, and to teach them things—everything from agriculture to archery."

"They gave us bows and arrows?" Carter said.

"Along with language and literature, astronomy and

art," Ezra went on, refusing to take Carter's bait. "And it explains how he's been able to survive here, how he's been able to get along in present-day New York."

Another leap for Carter to take. "Oh, so now he's not only alive, after a few hundred million years, but he's a regular New Yorker? With a job and an apartment?"

Ezra glared at him. "It explains," he said, in carefully measured tones, "how he is able to master and absorb our languages and customs and manners at an unimaginable rate. You could say that he invented these things. Without what the Watchers imparted to us, without that spark of the divine fire that they gave us, none of us—and I mean humanity—would be what we are today."

"And so now, what?" Carter asked. "He wants his gifts back? He isn't happy with how we're using them? Is that why he's here?"

Ezra looked over at Russo. "We're not sure what his plans are. We were discussing that. I need to do some more work."

"On what?" Carter said, though he could guess. "The scroll? You think that something written untold ages ago and bottled up in a desert cave is going to tell you that?"

"It may. And it may tell us what happened to him, and why he fell, so long ago."

Carter ran a hand through his thick brown hair. He felt like he'd entered Bellevue and was trying to make sense of the inmates' chatter. If you wanted to dismantle the train of illogic, to take it apart piece by piece so that even they could see and understand how irrational it was, where did you start?

"What makes you think," Carter finally asked Ezra, "that he hasn't hopped a flight to Paris, or a Greyhound bus to Florida? What makes you think that this Arius is still here in New York?"

"Oh, that one's easy," Ezra said, leaning back so far that the front legs of the chair came up off the floor. "I've met him."

Down the hole, Carter thought, and all the way to Wonderland. "You've met," he said, slowly, "this angel?"

"He came to a fund-raiser for the mayor at our apartment."

Carter couldn't tell if he was serious or not.

"And I have a strong suspicion that he badly injured my stepmother. That's why I said I don't yet know what his intentions are. I'm as much in the dark as you are."

Carter shook his head, ruefully. "I doubt that."

"Bones," Russo said, his voice barely audible, "you are a scientist. Look at the evidence."

"Joe, I would—but I just don't see any."

Russo raised his hands, as if to say *Look at me. Look at everything that's happened. How else do you explain it?* "Tell me you have not had . . . your own thoughts?" Russo said, tellingly, and Carter felt as if his friend were looking right inside him—right inside his head. It's true, there were things Carter couldn't deny, even to himself. He thought back to the night before, when he had found the lines about Avernus in the pages of the *Aeneid.* And that morning, at the library, when his research had uncovered the rest.

Russo must have seen something in his expression. "There *is* something you want to tell us," he said, "something that you know."

"No, it's nothing," Carter said, trying to brush it aside.

"It *is* something," Russo insisted. "I saw that look, years ago, in Sicily."

Ezra waited. "The crazier you think it is, the more I want to hear it."

But Carter felt that if he so much as mentioned it aloud, if he put even one toe into this muddy water, he would never come out of it safely again. Every fiber of his being resisted going into this dismal swamp.

But hadn't he already done that, he thought? Hadn't he taken the first step, however unheralded, the moment that the impossibly strange suspicion crossed his mind? Or certainly when he'd followed up on it that very morning in the stacks of the university research library?

"It's just a strange coincidence," Carter said.

"Maybe it's something more than that," Ezra said. "We won't know until you tell us."

Russo's labored breathing was now the most noticeable sound in the room.

"It has to do with the place the fossil was found," Carter confessed.

"Lago d' Avernus," Russo volunteered, "near Napoli."

"What about it?" Ezra said, impatiently.

"Well, according to the Roman poet Virgil, that's a very interesting spot. In the *Aeneid,* he wrote that a passageway existed there . . . a passageway to the underworld."

Ezra and Russo reacted with a stunned silence.

"And for thousands of years," Carter reluctantly continued, "in local legends and lore, there have been stories about how the portal was made."

"How?" Russo croaked.

Ezra simply waited.

"When St. Michael vanquished the rebel angels, he threw them from Heaven," Carter said, hardly believing he had gone this far, "and they plummeted through the sky."

"According to the scriptures, for six days and nights," Ezra added, softly.

"Yes. They hit the ground like meteors and they were buried in the bowels of the earth. Right where we found that fossil."

Russo closed his eyes, mumbling a prayer under his breath. After a few seconds, Ezra stirred in his chair. "It doesn't sound crazy to me at all." But he fixed Carter with an appraising gaze. "How does it sound to the man of science?"

And Carter was no longer sure; he was no longer sure of anything. Fumbling in his briefcase, he took out the crucifix, got off the radiator case, and handed it to Russo.

Ezra, he noted, smiled, as if he'd gotten his answer.

THIRTY

If Beth hadn't promised Abbie she'd help her pick out these last few things for the country house, she might have gone straight home, locked the door, and taken a long, hot bath. But she hated to disappoint a friend, and since they were scheduled to go up there on the coming weekend, tonight would be their last chance to go shopping.

So as soon as Raleigh was out the door of the gallery, Beth added one more name to the list of invitations that had to be sent to the printers the next day and logged off her computer. The night watchman, Ramon, was already setting up downstairs when she left.

"Good night, Mrs. Cox," he said, as he poured some coffee from a thermos into his plastic Yankees mug. "Don't forget your umbrella."

"It's raining?" Beth said. She'd been cooped up in back all day and had no idea what was happening in the outside world.

"Not yet, but they said it was going to."

She was sure she'd left her umbrella at home. "I guess I'll have to take my chances."

Outside, it was cold and windy, and Ramon was probably

right—the evening air smelled damp. She pulled the collar of her coat up around her ears and set off for Bloomingdale's, where she was supposed to rendezvous with Abbie at six sharp. The sidewalks were crowded, as always, and more than once she had the odd sensation that someone was following her, that she was just about to feel a tap on the shoulder. But each time she turned, there was just a sea of strange faces, some of whom were quite unhappy with her impeding their progress.

"Happy holidays," one man growled, "now move it along."

Overhead, gold tinsel stars and red aluminum candy canes were swinging from cables strung between the streetlights, and the store windows were flocked with fake snow. Normally she enjoyed all these signs of the season, but this year, she just hadn't been able to get into the spirit. Tonight, in fact, she felt so weary and strung out that it was all she could do to put one foot ahead of the other. It didn't help that she'd had a follow-up call from Dr. Weston's office to tell her that she should increase her iron intake, and to remind her that her blood type—AB negative—was very rare.

"When and if you do decide to pursue some alternative means of pregnancy," the doctor had said, as tactfully as could be managed, "we'll want to have you bank a pint or two of your own blood in advance, just in case it becomes needed at delivery."

Right now she didn't feel like she'd ever be able to spare even a drop.

At Bloomingdale's, predictably, the aisles were nearly impenetrable. She took the elevator to the home furnishings department and found Abbie already in the middle of an intense deliberation with a stylish young salesgirl.

"You really think that cushions in this color—and I'd call this fabric yellow, more than peach—won't clash with the curtains we've already ordered?"

"No," the girl said, shaking her head firmly. "These are all in the same design family; they're meant to complement each other."

Abbie looked up and saw Beth. "You think this material complements the dining room curtains we ordered?"

Beth had to think about it. "Yes, maybe," Beth said.

"Yes, or maybe?" Abbie asked.

The salesgirl looked chagrined; now she'd have to win two votes on each purchase.

"No," Beth finally concluded.

Abbie laughed, and the salesgirl smiled through clenched teeth before pointedly excusing herself to go and help another customer.

"Thanks for that opinion," Abbie said, under her breath. "I wanted to get rid of her."

Beth smiled.

"And thanks for coming out on such a lousy night."

"No problem."

"You sure about that?" Abbie asked solicitously, laying a hand on Beth's sleeve. "Forgive me for saying so, but you don't look so hot."

"That's okay—I don't feel so hot either."

"You think you're coming down with something? Did you get your flu shot?"

"Got the shot, and no, I don't think I'm actually getting sick."

They drifted off down another aisle, past counters piled high with expensive linens.

"I just haven't felt like myself for the past few nights. I can't get to sleep, and when I do, my dreams are so bad that it's hardly worth it."

"Listen, Beth—if you don't feel like going out to the country this weekend, don't give it another thought. We can do this some other time."

"No, no," Beth protested, "I'm looking forward to it. I think the change of scenery might do me good."

"I wonder if I'll ever be able to get Ben to think that way."

"He'll come around," Beth assured her, even though, in her heart of hearts, she thought Ben had a point. While the pictures of the house had looked so cute, there was something vaguely forlorn about the actual place, something that all the bright curtains and colorful wallpapers in the world wouldn't fix. It had an isolated, even forbidding air about it.

Without intending to, they found themselves at the end of an aisle in an area devoted to nursery furnishings. Everywhere Beth looked were sheets and pillowcases adorned with merry-go-rounds, gamboling seahorses, and a wide variety of Disney characters.

"Ever notice how, when you're trying to conceive, *without* any luck, you trip over kids and kids' stuff everywhere you go?" Abbie remarked.

Beth had noticed. And ever since the last appointment with Dr. Weston, at which they'd received the bad news about Carter's potency, it had only seemed to get worse. Everywhere she went she was reminded of nothing but babies, children, and expectant mothers.

"Ben and I are thinking of doing the in vitro thing next year. Are you and Carter making any progress, so to speak?"

"Nope," Beth said, trying to act unconcerned about the whole thing. "Not so far." Although Abbie was her closest and oldest friend, she still hadn't shared the latest and in some ways final setback. Even with Carter, it was as if the whole subject had become mysteriously and silently tabled. "Would you mind if I just wandered over to the model rooms for a while?" Beth said. "I always want to know just how far behind the fashions I am."

"No, go on. Maybe I'll go and find that bitchy salesclerk and make her check up on the delivery date for my curtains."

Beth put the children's wing behind her as fast as she could and went to the opposite end of the selling floor, where the Bloomingdale's design staff regularly set up a series of model rooms, each one done in a different fantasy style. She was always amused at the juxtaposition of English drawing room and hip-hop crib, island hideaway and Colorado cabin, and usually a lot of other people were, too. But tonight she found the area almost deserted; she was able to stroll past the sleek, high-tech den and the Hamptons beach house, before stopping, all alone, in front of the last model room in the row.

What was it meant to be, she wondered? Something out of a Paul Bowles novel? It appeared to be a vaguely Moroccan décor, a boudoir fantasy complete with Kilim rugs, beaten copper ornaments, and a huge bed partly concealed by a pale yellow gossamer curtain. Through an arched doorway was a painted scrim of undulating sand dunes, glistening silver in the moonlight. The artist, she thought, had done an exemplary job; it was surprisingly convincing.

The whole interior, in fact, was well done—and very inviting. Maybe too much so. Suddenly, the weariness in her bones seemed to grow, and her eyes grew heavy. All day long she'd felt tired, but now she felt as if she were about to collapse on the spot. She needed to lie down, she needed to close her eyes for just a few minutes . . . and the gossamer-curtained bed was only a velvet rope away.

No, she couldn't; she knew that. But the desire was fast becoming irresistible.

And who would know? It would only be for a few minutes. No one was there; no one would see her behind the curtain . . . especially if she moved quickly. *If she made up her mind and just did it.*

Before she knew it, her foot was over the velvet rope and she was padding across the Kilim rugs. The bed was a heavy, high affair, and she had to climb up onto it. Part of her knew this was insane, and the other part simply told her not to muss the coverlet and curtains. That would be wrong.

The spread must have been made of the finest, softest cotton ever spun, and the brocaded pillows seemed perfectly placed, ready to cradle her sleepy head and aching shoulders. Never in her life had a bed been so beckoning, so comfortable. She would lie there, she told herself, for just a few minutes. She would lie very still, concealed by the gauzy curtain; no one would notice, and no one would know.

Her eyelids fluttered shut. The design staff must have

scented the air, too; they thought of everything. It smelled like . . . rain-washed leaves. She had the most delicious sense of well-being. Oh, if only she could kick off her shoes and just crawl in under the cool, smooth sheets; she felt like she could sleep there forever . . . untroubled by bad dreams, undisturbed by anything.

Somewhere far away, she thought she heard someone say her name. But she was too tired to respond.

She heard it again, a little closer, and this time she did open her eyes, just enough to gaze out the arched doorway, toward the painted backdrop of endless rolling sand dunes. Someone, she could see now, was standing atop one of them. Someone outlined in silver by the painted moon.

She closed her eyes, smiling. What a fantastically talented artist; she should probably find out who it was. He or she was too good to be painting scrims for department stores.

She wondered where Carter was right now. Probably at the hospital, with his poor friend Russo. God, how awful. The only thing that could make it worse was if Carter continued to blame himself for what had happened; she knew that he did, and she was fighting a losing battle to convince him otherwise.

Her name came again, and when she looked out at the dunes now, the figure was much closer . . . the silhouette of a tall man. He was walking slowly, deliberately, across the sand . . . and her sleepy brain struggled to reconcile this. How in the world could the artist have achieved such an effect?

She wanted to get up and go look, but her limbs felt like lead. Her head felt so heavy she doubted that she would ever again be able to raise it from the pile of ornate pillows it rested on.

The man came closer still, his shadow falling through the arched doorway now, his perfectly chiseled features gradually becoming clear . . . and that was when she felt her stomach lurch, and a hot flood in her throat.

"Beth!" she heard. "There you are!"

She turned on her side and, with nowhere else to do it, threw up into a gleaming brass pot that had been arranged by the side of the bed.

"Oh my God!" Abbie cried, sweeping back the pale yellow curtains. "Oh my God!"

Beth heaved again, unable to control herself.

"Get some towels!" Abbie ordered the salesgirl, who was standing, aghast, behind her.

"This is so totally not allowed!" the salesgirl exclaimed. "The model rooms are off limits and—"

"Just get me a damn towel!" Abbie shouted, before sitting on the bed beside Beth and putting an arm around her shoulders. "Is that it?" she asked, gently. "You feel any better now?"

Beth nodded, mortified—then glanced up toward the arched doorway and the painted scrim. No one was there.

The salesgirl returned with some Ralph Lauren towels and handed them, sullenly, to Abbie. "You'll have to pay for these," she said.

"Fine—put 'em on my charge card, along with that chamber pot." She dabbed at Beth's chin with the corner of a towel, then handed it to her. Beth buried her face in the thick, comforting fabric and thought to herself, *I don't ever want to come out of here.*

"You want to lie down again," Abbie asked her, "or can you get up?"

"Up, I think," Beth said, still clutching the towel. She got up unsteadily from the bed as the salesgirl peered through the archway in both directions.

"Your friend's gone too," she said to Beth.

"What are you talking about?" Abbie retorted.

"There was a man here," the salesgirl replied, "but at least *he's* gone now." She glanced at the splattered brass pot. "Shit."

Abbie put her arm around Beth's shoulder and guided her out of the model room. "Send that to my apartment," she said, "after it's been emptied."

At the ladies' room, Beth asked Abbie to wait outside while she cleaned up. What she really wanted was to be alone, to just sink through the floor and have this whole incident to never have happened. She ran the cold water and rinsed her face, leaving black stains under her eyes that she then had to wipe away with the new towel she was still carrying. What, she wondered, was wrong with her? She remembered the dream, the hallucination of the man walking toward her, across the sand . . . but hadn't the salesgirl said she'd seen someone, too?

If it wasn't a bad dream, then what was it?

Abbie poked her head in and said, "You okay?"

"Yes," Beth said, turning off the water. "I'll just never show my face again at Bloomingdale's."

Abbie kept one arm around her waist as they walked toward the escalators. "You sure you're not pregnant?" she said, half-jokingly.

"I'm sure," Beth said.

"Then all you need is a warm bed and a snootful of Nyquil. You're definitely running a temperature." At the escalators, they waited for a moment as a woman with two little kids and a folding stroller stepped on.

"I'm going to take you home in a cab," Abbie said, "and make you some broth."

That sounded good to Beth. They stepped onto the escalator and as it took them down, Beth stole a quick look back toward the model room.

The salesgirl was carrying the brass pot out, concealed under a towel. But the archway behind her was empty, and through it Beth could see nothing but the sand dunes, rolling on forever.

THIRTY-ONE

Carter knew the ruined lab was off limits, but he had gone in, anyway, through the back corridors. He had to see, one more time, the site of what should have been his greatest triumph . . . even though it had become, without a doubt, the site, instead, of his greatest tragedy. The police and city inspectors had already done whatever they had to do, and taken whatever samples they needed, but when he went out again to the street, he still had to duck under the yellow police tape.

He was on his way to the biomed lab, where he was going to meet up with Ezra. Dr. Permut had apparently finished analyzing the ink and the fabric of the scroll, and he was prepared to go over the results with them. Carter was waiting to cross the street when a dirty brown sedan pulled up alongside him, and he heard a voice say, "You know, that's still the site of an arson investigation. You're not supposed to go in there."

He stopped and looked in the car. It was the police detective, Finley.

"Sorry."

"Where you headed? I'll give you a lift."

"Just a few blocks," Carter said, "no need."

"Come on," Finley said, waving an arm. "Hop in."

Carter had the impression it was more than an offer, and after the detective brushed some rubbish off the front seat and onto the floor, he got in. "Straight ahead," Carter said, "to Sixth, and then you can make a right."

"Fact is," Finley said, pushing his heavy black eyeglasses back up onto the bridge of his nose, "I've been wanting to talk to you."

Exactly what Carter dreaded. "About that body I found?" File that, Carter thought, under sentences I never thought I'd utter.

"What else," Finley said, reaching into the breast pocket of his car coat and pulling out a folded sheet. "But take a look at that."

Carter took the paper and unfolded it. The car, he noticed, reeked of stale coffee and greasy burgers. On the paper, he saw a photocopy of two fingerprints. Carter looked over at the detective.

"We picked those up from the railing in the stairwell."

"They look very clear," Carter said, wondering what you were supposed to say about fingerprints. He'd never seen any up close before.

"They do, don't they?" Finley said. "And way too perfect."

Carter looked again, and now he could see that the whorls of the prints were indeed admirably complete and intact, perfect circles at the center, perfect oblongs on the outside, without a single break or deviation.

"Perfect fingerprints don't exist," Finley added. "If they did, we'd never be able to use them to catch anybody." He pulled a none-too-clean handkerchief out of his pocket and swiped at his glasses, and then at the inside of the windshield. "You're a scientist—what do you make of that?"

"The fingerprint? I haven't a clue. Maybe it's a lab error."

The detective shook his head. "Nah, I did the whole thing myself."

Carter let a silence fall. The only thing he could suggest was that the perfect fingerprint had been left by a perfect being—something, perhaps, like an angel—but he wasn't about to add insanity to any of the other charges the detective might be thinking he was guilty of.

"You can give me that back now," Finley said, taking the paper and folding it back into his pocket.

"Sorry I can't help," Carter said.

The detective nodded, and made a right turn. "What address?"

"Three blocks down, at the corner."

The detective drove in silence, then said, "Maybe there is one other thing you can help me with."

"I'll try."

"The coroner said that the victim died of immolation."

Carter waited—wasn't that pretty obvious?

"But here's the odd thing. The body had burned from the inside out."

Carter was puzzled. "If you're asking me if spontaneous combustion can really occur, I have to say no."

"That's what I thought, too. I took science in high school. But seeing as the only other two burn victims I've seen this year were working in your lab, right across the street from this one, I thought you might be able to help me out with this."

Carter didn't know what to say. "Coincidence?" he finally offered.

The detective pulled the car over at the corner and stopped. "Maybe," he said. "But it sure is an awful big one."

You could say that again, Carter thought, though he kept it to himself. "Thanks for the ride," Carter said, trying not to look too hasty getting out.

The detective waited until Carter had crossed the street in front of him and then pulled away.

Carter took a deep breath, the first one since getting into Finley's car. He had the terrible feeling that he'd be seeing him again.

When he got to Dr. Permut's lab, Ezra was already there—punctuality, Carter was learning, was not one of Ezra's problems—but Carter would hardly have recognized his faculty colleague. Last time, when he'd stopped in to leave the scrap of Ezra's scroll for analysis, Permut had been as neat as a pin, not a hair out of place, his white lab coat spotless and buttoned from top to bottom.

But now he looked like he hadn't slept in days; his hair wasn't brushed, his lab coat was rumpled and dingy, and even behind his glasses Carter could see dark rings under his eyes.

"Glad you could make it today," Dr. Permut said, conspicuously locking the door behind them. No one else was there. "I didn't want this to wait any longer."

"Neither did we," said Carter. "Ezra here, in case he hasn't told you, is the owner of the scroll you've been analyzing."

"Yes, he had mentioned it," Dr. Permut said, quickly turning toward a lab counter. "I'm going to walk you through the results, such as they are," he said, "and you are welcome to make of them what you will."

Carter and Ezra exchanged a look, then followed the clearly perturbed scientist to the counter, where wide data sheets with dense sequences of numbers and letters on them were spread out. Even though he couldn't decipher them any better than he had the first time, Carter again recognized them for what they were. So, apparently, did Ezra.

"These are DNA readouts," Ezra said. "I've seen them before."

"Good," Dr. Permut said, fumbling in his pocket and pulling out a roll of Tums. "That's one less thing I have to explain." With one finger, he jabbed at the printout on the right and said to Carter, "These are the results I showed you last time, from the fossil fragment."

"Okay," Carter said. "I'll take your word for it."

"They're what I referred to as theoretical DNA," he explained to Ezra. "Most of it we were able to piece together, but at a few critical junctures we had to make educated guesses to fill in and bridge the gaps."

Ezra nodded as Permut popped a Tums into his mouth, then stuck the roll back into his pocket.

"We did that through a process called PCR, or polymerase chain reaction."

"Meaning?" Ezra asked.

"Meaning, we ground the sample into a powder—then added silica to the powder because it binds to any residual traces of DNA left there. Then, by using PCR, we were able to amplify the fragments of DNA, making over a million copies, for example, of a single molecule."

"So you can read it more clearly?" Carter said.

"So we can read it at all," Permut replied.

"But I already know that you don't know what to make of it," Carter said. "We went through that last time."

"That was before you brought me the scroll fragment. Look at this," he said, poking his finger now at the data sheet on the left. "See how similar the sequences are?"

Carter glanced at the sheets, as did Ezra, and yes, he could sort of see how alike some of the patterns and sequences were. But why would that be? What would one of these things have had to do with the other? When he looked up, he could see that Permut was reading his mind.

"Odd, isn't it?" he said, with a slightly off-kilter smile. "A bit of bone, and a scrap of parchment, fitting together so neatly?"

"Yes, it is odd," Carter agreed.

"In fact, if you compare the two closely—and believe me, I have—the DNA strands we were able to isolate from the parchment perfectly complete the gaps in the fossil genome."

Permut rocked on his heels, letting this sink in. The only sound in the room was his rubber soles squeaking on the linoleum floor.

"You are saying," Ezra hazarded, "that the two specimens are drawn from the same . . . source?"

Permut pursed his lips, and tilted his head to one side. To Carter, it seemed as if he'd come a little unhinged.

"I can do better than that," Permut said. "I can show you something that will really open your eyes."

He stepped to one side, revealing a sleek white microscope with a trinocular head on the lab table behind him. Carter recognized it as a Meiji ML 2700, a piece of equipment he'd have killed to have in his own lab. "Take a look through this," Permut said. "The slide's already mounted."

Ezra, who stood closer, stepped up first. As he bent down over the eyepieces, Permut said, "You're looking at a portion of the scroll."

Ezra remained motionless another few seconds, then straightened up.

"Carter, why don't you take a look now?" Permut said.

Ezra stepped aside, with a strange look on his face—was it a look, Carter thought, of odd vindication?

Carter put his head down, and after adjusting the built-in Kohler illuminator he saw what looked, at first, like one of those blowups of the surface of Mars. There was a bumpy, yellow plain of pits and craters, bisected here and there by narrow, twisting channels—only these channels were not empty and dry. They were filled with a purplish-red liquid, which was coursing through them, rhythmically pulsing, like blood.

"What did you add to the specimen?" Carter said, without looking up. "A dye or something?"

"No, that's what we mistook for the ink," Permut said. "In fact, it's blood."

Carter straightened up and away from the microscope. "But what's making it move? It's clearly motile."

Dr. Permut rubbed at his head, agitatedly. "Why wouldn't it be? The tissue is alive."

Ezra's eyes closed, as if he wished to absorb the news in private.

Permut was sucking his Tums like there was no tomorrow.

When Ezra opened his eyes again, he looked straight at Carter. "It looks to me as if I had the skin, Carter, and you had the bone." He turned toward Permut. "Wouldn't you agree, that these are two ends of the same stick?"

Permut nodded his head, vigorously.

Carter was struggling to hold it all in his head, to make any sense of everything he had just been told.

As if Ezra had intuited as much, he recited aloud, " 'There are more things in heaven and earth, Horatio, than are dreamt of in your philosophy.' "

Dr. Permut stepped to the microscope and removed the slide. He slipped it into a glassine envelope, took another identical envelope off the lab counter, and stuffed them both into the side pocket of Carter's leather jacket. "I don't want these specimens in my lab anymore," he said, stepping away again, as if Carter had a cold he didn't want to catch. "You can take them with you when you go."

"Sure, of course," Carter said. He'd never seen Permut, or any scientist he ever knew, so clearly spooked by something. "And thanks for doing the work." He glanced over at Ezra, who looked as if he understood perfectly why Permut was behaving this way.

"What do we owe you?" Ezra said, taking out a blank check and a pen. "The lab tests alone must have—"

"Nothing," Permut said.

Ezra's pen hovered in midair, above the check he'd placed on the counter beside the microscope. "Nothing? I know from experience that DNA tests—"

"I want no further part in this," Permut said.

"But this must have run you a few thousand dollars at the very least," Carter put in.

"That's my problem. I'll spread it out over some other projects. Let me worry about it." His foot tapped impatiently on the linoleum floor. "Now if you'll excuse me, I really do have some other work to do."

Carter shrugged, and nodded at Ezra. "I think we're done here." Leaving the lab with Ezra, he heard the door close and latch the moment they were back in the hall.

Outside, Ezra paged his driver. "I'm going uptown to see my stepmother at the hospital. Can I drop you somewhere?"

"No, that's fine," Carter said. "I probably just need to walk a while and clear my head."

The Lincoln town car, with his Uncle Maury behind the wheel, came around the corner and double-parked in the busy street.

"It'll take more than a walk," Ezra said, holding out his hand with the palm open. Carter didn't know what he wanted. "The scroll specimen?" he said.

Carter fished in his pocket, found the slides, and gave Ezra what he'd asked for.

"Thank you," Ezra said, opening the back door of the car. "We'll have to get together tomorrow and compare notes."

Carter simply nodded as the car drove off. And though he seemed as if he were rooted in place, his mind was racing at a mile a minute. None of this made any sense, and it was ridiculous to keep pretending that it did. The fossil, the parchment—the bone, the skin—somehow it all had to be part of an elaborate ruse, a bizarre scheme of some kind, a prank. It had to be. If Bill Mitchell weren't dead, he'd have been the first person Carter thought was behind it. But Mitchell *was* dead—and that was part of no prank. The stakes were already too high. Russo was burnt almost beyond recognition.

It couldn't be a game, or a scheme of any kind.

Which meant it had to be something real.

Something had to be going on, some terrible drama unfolding, and Carter feared that whether he liked it or not, he was destined to play a leading role.

THIRTY-TWO

Ezra's spirits were oddly buoyed; he knew now that his suspicions, even his fears, were at last gaining evidentiary support. For a man who knew that madness was never far from his door, it was strangely comforting to find that even the most impossible thoughts he had entertained were, perhaps, quite possible after all.

He wasn't insane, though the universe, disconcertingly, might be.

Looking out the back window of the car, he mulled over what he had just learned in Permut's lab. The scroll was a piece of living tissue, from a creature of indeterminate origin. The fossil fragment was bone, from the same unidentified source.

But was this creature what he thought? And who—or what—could have skinned it alive?

"Kimberly's still in trouble," Maury said from the front seat, interrupting his thoughts. "And they're damned if they can figure out what's going on."

Ezra wasn't surprised. If his own hunch was true—that it had something to do with her last-minute party guest—they never would figure it out.

"Your dad's up there with her now."

Ezra had assumed as much; it was why he was making this visit. It was a chance to mend the fence. And the right thing to do, he reminded himself, under any circumstances.

Though the hospital was an exclusive one to begin with, Kimberly's suite was in an even more private wing, where the floors were expensively carpeted, the walls were decorated with colorful prints, the doors were polished mahogany. To Ezra, it felt more like a small European hotel than a hospital, which was undoubtedly the point. His father was sitting in the anteroom when Ezra arrived, just turning off his cell phone.

"I was telling Maury not to wait for us," he said to Ezra, "but of course he was giving me an argument." He dropped the phone on the sofa cushions.

"How is Kimberly doing?"

"She got hysterical a half hour ago, ripped out all her tubes, started raving."

"What about?"

"What about?" His father looked at him with puzzlement. "It was raving, it's not supposed to make sense."

"Humor me."

"About birds and fire. She was being attacked by birds with wings *made* out of fire. Satisfied?"

Ezra stored the information away, to share it the next day with Carter and Russo. Who knew what clue would turn out to be something important?

A nurse wearing a white uniform with navy blue piping, designed to look more nautical than medical, came out of the bedroom holding a tray with a syringe and other paraphernalia on it. "She's heavily sedated now, and she'll sleep straight through until the operation tomorrow morning." She smiled at Sam and Ezra, and left.

"What operation?" Ezra asked his father. "They've decided what's wrong?"

"Not entirely," His father had laid his suit jacket on the sofa, and he slumped back now in just his shirtsleeves—with a monogrammed pocket, of course—and gleaming cufflinks. "A blood infection. Organ shutdowns. The one thing we do know for sure is that she's pregnant."

Ezra wasn't completely surprised, and his father noticed. "You knew?" he asked.

"I knew she wanted to redo my rooms and turn them into a nursery."

"It wasn't going to happen."

For a moment, Ezra took heart; was it possible his father had never intended to replace him with a newer and younger model, after all? Then he realized what was really being said.

"I had a vasectomy years ago," his father confessed. "Back when you were a teenager."

A silence fell. Sam realized how it had come out, but it was too late to take it back, and Ezra just had to absorb the blow. "I didn't tell her at first," his father explained, "because what would have been the point? And then when I figured out what she wanted, what she was planning, I didn't want her to know that I couldn't give it to her."

It would have been about the only thing he couldn't give her, Ezra thought.

"I didn't want to lose her," Sam said, and in that moment Ezra knew, perhaps for the first time, that his father really and truly loved Kimberly. That it wasn't, as Ezra and probably everyone else in the world believed, just an old man's infatuation with a gorgeous young thing. The fact that she was pregnant now had to have come as a mighty blow.

"I don't even care who's . . . responsible," Sam said, reading Ezra's mind. "It doesn't matter now, anyway."

Ezra remembered the bruises he'd seen on her body, and he was glad to know now, for certain, that his father had had nothing to do with it.

"The whole thing's gone so haywire," Sam went on, "the only way to save her life is to perform an abortion tomorrow, first thing. Afterward, they tell me she'll never be able to bear children at all."

"After this one, I won't have to," Kimberly said from the bedroom doorway, where she was listing from side to side. She was wearing a long, pale rose nightgown, and the IV pole, on wheels, was still attached to her arm.

But what shocked Ezra the most was her belly—even under the nightgown he could see the swell of her lower abdomen. Just the day before, there'd been nothing to see; now she looked like she was ready to deliver any minute. When had this happened? *How* could it have happened?

"What are you doing out of bed?" Sam said, rising from the sofa. If he was as shocked as Ezra, his son couldn't tell. And how, Ezra wondered, could she be standing up at all after all the sedatives she'd been given?

"I have to go to him," she said, brushing away a strand of hair that clung wetly to her face. "He's the only one who can make it stop."

"Make what stop?" Sam asked, going to her side. "Ezra, call the nurse."

"The fire."

"There's no fire here," Sam said, gently holding her arm. Then, as Ezra watched, his father drew his fingers back from her arm, shaking them in the air as if they'd just been singed.

Kimberly laughed, deliriously. "I told you so."

Ezra meant to move toward the door, he meant to shout for a nurse, but he stood transfixed. Kimberly's eyes were flickering now, as if a fire had been kindled inside her and was slowly growing into a full blaze.

"What the hell is . . ." Sam's words trailed off, as he backed away and toward the door to the hall.

Kimberly doubled over, groaning and clutching her stomach. "Make it stop," she muttered through clenched teeth.

Ezra grabbed her just before she toppled over, and their eyes met. It was as if he were looking into a volcanic caldera, just before it blew.

"Nurse! Doctor! We have an emergency!" His father was out in the hallway, shouting at the top of his lungs.

"Kill it," Kimberly said, her breath so hot Ezra could feel it burnish his face, and then she collapsed, the IV smashing on the floor.

Ezra rolled her over—her skin was as hot as an iron—and he could swear that when he looked in her face, there was someone else, something else, looking out at him through her glowing yellow eyes.

"Move over!" a doctor said, shoving Ezra to one side.

A crash cart rattled into the room.

"Jesus Christ," the doctor exclaimed, blowing on his scorched fingertips.

"Kill it," Kimberly insisted, between ragged hot breaths. "I can't stand it."

"Ice! We've got to get her into an ice bath!"

The nurses scrambled.

Ezra, in shock, sat back on the floor beside her, his weight resting on his hands, as she suddenly went into a convulsion. Her hands flew to her stomach and dug into her own skin so hard it looked as if she were trying to root out the baby herself. Her knees came up toward her chest, and a tide of blood suddenly washed across the floor.

A syringe was given to the doctor, whose hands were shaking so badly he couldn't get it in. "I can't . . . *do* it!"

A nurse grabbed it away and tried herself. The needle went into the arm this time, but then, as Kimberly twisted in pain, it snapped off.

"We need a tourniquet—stat!" the nurse shouted.

Kimberly's belly seemed to swell, like a balloon that had suddenly been given a big burst of air. "Kill me!" she screamed in agony. "Kill *me!*"

Her head went back and she uttered a cry of utter anguish and despair, a cry that chilled Ezra to the marrow . . . and that seemed to be joined—he could swear he'd heard it—by *another* voice, a muffled voice keening from within her very womb.

Even the doctor and nurse stopped in shock. They'd heard it, too.

And then Kimberly went completely still, her body going slack on the blood-covered floor, her eyes closing, her mouth falling open. The ends of her hair crackled like live wires . . . and then that, too, subsided.

"We've got total arrest," the doctor said, in a stunned monotone.

And Ezra knew, even as they labored to bring her back, that they would not be able to do so.

After what she'd been through, he suspected that she might have preferred to stay dead, anyway.

THIRTY-THREE

There weren't many things in Russo's day that he could look forward to. There were the quick hits of morphine that he gave himself by squeezing the black button that lay on the bed by his scalded hand, right next to the separate red call button. There were the dreams he could drift into, of growing up on the outskirts of Rome, exploring ancient ruins with his boyhood friends. And there were the tender ministrations of a pretty young nurse named Monica.

Today, while changing some of his dressings, she had told him all about a date she'd gone on the night before, and then, while applying the antiseptic unguents, had filled him in on the latest news headlines. He liked to look into her eyes—they were dark and bright, and perhaps because she had already seen so many other burn victims, they held no horror at the sight of him. "Dr. Baptiste tells me you'll be starting your grafts next week sometime," she told him now.

"Yes?" Russo mumbled, through his still-blackened lips.

"That's good," Monica said, gently lifting his left forearm to swab on fresh salve.

The pain was still immense, and Russo squeezed himself another jolt of the morphine.

Monica, noticing, said, "Sorry. I know this must hurt like crazy."

Russo would have liked to deny it, but he couldn't. Monica carefully laid his arm back down and said, "That's it for today."

He would have liked her to stay, to have her just sit by his bedside and rattle on about her day, her boyfriends, anything she felt like, but he knew she had other patients to see, other duties to perform.

And the morphine would be taking him away into dreams very soon, anyway. If he was lucky, they'd be the good kind of dreams. If he wasn't, they'd be nightmares, of crackling flames, of tumbling from great heights into bottomless pits. Unfortunately, there was never any way to tell in advance what kind they'd turn out to be.

"You want this down, right?" Monica said, holding the edge of the plastic oxygen tent.

"Now that I do not have you to look at," Russo whispered, "yes."

Monica laughed. "I look better through plastic," she said, and lowered the hood so that it hovered just short of touching his shoulders and chest. Although it obscured his view, he knew there wasn't much he'd be missing; how long could he look at the back of the door and the cheap reproduction of a Van Gogh? The cool, fresh air under the tent made it easier for him to breathe, and the soft whirring of the oxygen tank was soothing, like the ebb and flow of waves on the seashore.

In fact, he wasn't sure just how much time had passed—five minutes? a half hour?—before he heard the door of his room open and close again, and saw through the thick plastic a figure standing silently in front of the Van Gogh. It wasn't Monica, that was for sure, and it wasn't Dr. Baptiste either. The figure was tall, and dressed in black.

His breath stopped in his throat.

It was a man, very pale, with blond—no, gleaming gold—hair.

I have come to thank you, Russo heard, though he wasn't sure if the man had spoken, or if the words had simply been introduced somehow into his head.

Russo stretched out his fingers on the cool bedsheet, searching for the red call button. But it wasn't there. Monica must have moved it while changing his dressings.

I wish I could repay you.

You can take the pain away, Russo thought, wondering if his words, too, would be received . . . and wondering, at the same time, if this was all nothing more than a particularly vivid morphine dream.

The figure moved closer, and Russo could just make out through the plastic oxygen tent that he was wearing small amber-colored sunglasses, and his long hair was swept like golden wings away from his forehead. He pulled a chair beside the bed and sat down.

Russo's heart filled with dread. This must be Arius, the fallen angel described by Ezra. The figure of light that had emerged from the block of stone that terrible night.

You know what I am.

Russo's fingers groped again blindly to call the nurse, but found instead the morphine button. He gave himself another hit. Perhaps, if it was a dream, he only needed to go deeper to escape it.

But am I the only one?

"I hope so," Russo said, his words muffled under the oxygen tent.

Arius paused, as if wondering how to take this. Then the words *Do you remember what I once told you?* echoed in Russo's head.

Arius reached out and touched Russo's hand, the one that had been searching for the call button. With what felt like a talon, he scraped a strip of the tender, remaining flesh from the back of it. Russo groaned, but that, too, was muffled by the plastic sheet and the constant susurration of the oxygen tank.

Suffering is a gift from God.

Russo's hand, though twisted into a knot of pain, reached out toward the bedside table. Arius followed its progress, then, when Russo had trouble opening the drawer, obligingly did it for him.

Russo's fingers, trembling, searched the inside of the drawer, then clutched the wooden crucifix that was kept there. He drew it out and held it up, his scorched arm shaking, toward Arius.

"Do you know . . . what this is?" Russo uttered. "Jesus Christ . . . our savior."

Arius languidly reached out and took it away. *Then let him save you.* He started to discard it, but then, as if thinking better of it, slipped it into the pocket of his overcoat instead.

Russo shrank back against his pillows, behind the plastic tent. There was nothing he could think of now, nothing else he could do . . . other than to pray that someone, *anyone,* might suddenly intrude.

"How many of you," Arius asked, "are aware of me?"

This time, Russo had definitely heard him speak—the words were in the air, not in his head. And terrified as he was, he found the voice, the voice of this fallen angel, sonorous, almost soothing.

"Not many."

His head nodded, thoughtfully.

And Russo dared to ask, "But why . . . are you here?" Was it all just an accident, he thought, perhaps the most dreadful ever to befall mankind?

As if he'd read his mind, Arius said, "Everything has its purpose. Perhaps yours was to free me."

That was an idea almost too awful for Russo to contemplate. The twenty-first-century Judas—was *that* to be his destiny?

"Mine, perhaps, is to propagate."

Russo had to think for a second, to understand the word—*propagate?*—and even then he thought he must have heard it wrong. Under the tent, with the oxygen pump whirring and the blood pounding in his ears, it was difficult to be sure of anything. It was still possible, wasn't it, that none of this was even happening—that it was all just a new and frightening dream, worse even than the dreams of fire and falling from the sky?

"But how?" Russo mumbled. "You have no friends in this world."

Arius appeared to consider that, then shrugged it off. "Then I'll create them." He leaned closer. "In my own image."

Russo's mind reeled. What could he mean? Was he saying what he thought he was?

But I do have one . . . companion, in mind, already, the voice said inside his head again. It was as if this information were so confidential it could not be spoken aloud.

The angel was smiling, but his lips did not move; his teeth shone, like a wolf's, through the plastic tent. And Russo instantly knew, as if her image had been telegraphed into his head, that it was Beth he had chosen.

His thoughts raced. What could he do to stop it? How could he warn Carter—and Beth—from this hospital bed? A phone sat on the bedside table, and just as he was wondering how, or even *if,* he'd ever be able to use it, it rang.

Arius looked at it coolly, then at Russo. Arius picked up the receiver, and without saying anything, lifted the bottom of the plastic sheet and held the phone until Russo was able to lift a trembling hand and hold it himself. Even with the plastic raised just an inch or two, Russo could smell a fresh, verdant air, like a forest after a rain, wafting over him.

"Joe? It's Carter."

Russo had expected it to be.

"How are you doing today?"

"Bones," Russo said, his voice barely audible, "something . . . important is happening here." How much, he wondered, would Arius allow him to say? And what would he do if Russo tried to blurt out too much?

"What? You're getting a sponge bath from that cute nurse you like?"

"No," Russo breathed, "I have . . . a visitor."

"Is Beth there? I know she was planning to pay you a visit."

"No, Bones," Russo said, with as much urgency as he could muster, "it is the one that we talked about," praying that Carter would catch his drift.

As he apparently did. The silence on the phone line was deafening. Russo could only imagine what was going through Carter's mind. Did he even believe him? Did he think he was delirious? Or on a morphine trip?

"My God," Carter said.

He did believe him.

"I'm coming," Carter added, in low tones. "Can you keep him there? I'm coming right now."

Arius slipped a hand under the tent, took the receiver away, and then spoke into it. "I must go," Arius said to Carter.

Russo saw him starting to hang up the phone—was his middle finger shorter than the rest?—and knew then that this might be the last chance he ever had, his only opportunity, to raise the alarm. "Bones, do not let him get near you! Do not let him get near Beth!"

But the phone was already in the cradle.

How much had Carter heard? Had Russo's ragged voice, muffled by the plastic sheet, even been audible?

Arius slowly rose from the chair. His dark coat made him look like a pillar of black smoke, glowing with a golden light at the top.

Russo couldn't let him leave; he had to keep him here—if possible, he had to kill him. But how could he do that?

As Arius turned to go, Russo raised his legs—even with the morphine coursing through his veins, the pain was excruciating—and slipped them off the bed. He had no idea if he'd be able to stand on them.

He swept the plastic oxygen tent away from his face and tore the IV tubes from his limbs. Now, for the first time since that terrible night, he could see Arius's face—its perfect features, carved as if from flawless marble, its sweep of thick, lustrous hair, its unblinking eyes glimmering behind the amber glasses.

Russo took a step toward him, his legs wobbling like a newborn foal's, his blackened arms reaching out.

Arius stepped back, and Russo staggered toward him. "I won't let you . . . hurt them," he said.

Arius smiled benignly and opened his arms. Russo

lunged at him, but ended up falling forward into the angel's embrace.

And I won't let you suffer.

For a moment Russo felt himself oddly comforted; his body hung in the angel's arms as if it were as light as a feather, all the pain gone, all the effort of moving and even breathing done with forever. It was like being cradled weightless in a garden bower.

But then he felt something else, a spark igniting inside him, deep in his gut, and the pain was beyond anything he had ever known. The smell of the forest, of glistening leaves and rain-washed earth, was joined by the acrid smell of smoke, of dry kindling catching fire, and to his horror Russo saw smoke in front of his face . . . smoke that was slipping from his own mouth and nose, smoke from a fire he felt consuming his body from within.

Arius stepped away, letting him fall to the floor. A smoke alarm sounded, shrieking repeatedly in the closed room.

Russo lay on the floor, his skin puckering from the fire raging in his veins, and watched as Arius took hold of the doorknob. The sprinklers burst on, showering his contorted limbs with tepid water. His skin sizzled.

Arius stepped outside, closing the door, and Russo, crumpled in a heap, felt flames bubbling and then breaking out from beneath his skin. He tried to recite a prayer, but before he could utter even a word, the fire found the open oxygen tank, still whooshing beside the bed. The whole room exploded in a blazing ball of heat and light . . . and, for Russo, blissful and eternal night.

THIRTY-FOUR

For a few moments, Carter sat immobilized in his chair, the sound of that voice ringing in his ears. *I must go.* Could that have been the voice of an angel? It had been smooth and deep, with only a slight, strange intonation, the sort of thing you'd notice in someone who'd learned English well, but whose first language was something else entirely.

And what had Russo been shouting just before the line went dead? Carter knew that he'd said not to let Arius get near him, but what was he saying next? Not to let Arius get near Beth? Was that it? And was there some reason, other than the obvious, for the urgent warning?

He grabbed his leather jacket off the back of his lab stool, pulled it on, and then ran for the door. He kicked the door closed behind him, and frantically dialed the hospital on his cell phone as he charged up the stairs to the street level.

"Village Pizza," a voice said over the commotion of a busy kitchen, and Carter disconnected, stopped on the stairs, and dialed again, more carefully.

This time it went through, but when he asked for the nurses' station on Russo's floor, he was put on hold. Should he have just asked for the security office? Should he hang up and call in again?

He pushed open the main door and looked up and down the street for a cab.

Or should he call that police detective and tell him to go straight to St. Vincent's, right away, if he wanted to catch the guy who'd torched the prostitute? But what kind of warning would he have to give him at the same time? Would he have to tell him to bring his Bible along, or some holy water? Would those things even do him any good if he did?

Would they do *anyone* any good?

The hospital operator came back on the line, and in a voice that sounded as if she was straining to sound unperturbed, said, "I'm sorry, but that nursing station is unable to take your call at this time. Please call back later."

Before she could disconnect, Carter blurted out, "But this is an emergency!"

"You'll have to call back later," she reiterated, and this time Carter could hear something in her voice, something she wasn't saying.

And he was terrified of what it might be.

A cab rounded the corner and stopped to let out an elderly woman. Carter bolted toward it, cutting off a couple of students with heavy duffel bags shuffling to the curb.

"Hey, man! We saw him first!" one shouted.

"He's faculty," Carter heard the other one say. "Professor Bones."

"So what?" the first one replied, but Carter was already in, slamming the door shut and telling the cabbie to head for St. Vincent's. He dialed Ezra's apartment, and that woman who'd served him lunch—Gertrude, was it?—answered in a hushed voice.

When he identified himself and asked for Ezra, she seemed unsure of what to do.

"It's extremely important," Carter said. "I have to talk to him. Right now."

The cab was still inching its way through the West Village traffic.

Then, finally, Ezra came on.

"I'm on my way to the hospital," Carter said. "Something might have happened to Russo."

"What?"

"I don't know," Carter said, not wanting, even now, to think of the awful possibilities. "But he might have had a visit there. From Arius."

He could hear Ezra's intake of breath.

"As soon as I'm done there," Carter said, "I'm coming to you."

"Here?"

"You're going to show me that whole damned scroll of yours, all put together, and we're going to figure out what we have to do."

Carter hung up and crammed some bills into the metal receptacle in the Plexiglas partition. "That's twenty bucks," Carter said. "Make some time."

The cabbie reached one hand back, fished out the bills, then stepped on it. He gunned the taxi through three yellow lights and one red, but when he got to the hospital block, the entrance was ominously blocked by three fire trucks and half a dozen police cars, their red lights whirling. Carter knew now that he should expect the worst.

"Let me off across the street."

The cab swerved across the congested lanes of traffic and stopped in front of the chain-link fence surrounding the condemned surgical supply. Carter got out, then charged like a running back weaving his way downfield through the tangle of police and fire vehicles. Over the squawking radios and walkie-talkies, he could hear snatches of what was going on. He heard "The fire's contained" and "Maximum damage, sixth floor." Russo's floor. He'd heard nothing yet about fatalities.

Both of the side doors were wide open but filled with emergency personnel hurrying in and out. Carter used the revolving door instead, stepping inside and shoving it around.

But the moment he did, the moment he breathed the air in the revolving compartment, he felt as if he'd stumbled into a dense forest after a sudden rain. It was the same scent he'd smelled in his own apartment, the night he'd found Beth sprawled nearly naked on their bed, with the window to the fire escape gaping open.

And then, as quickly as he'd been enveloped in the aroma, he was out of it again—standing in the commotion of the hospital lobby. Several firemen and cops were directing some sort of emergency operation—Carter quickly surmised that it was an evacuation; a nervous bunch of visitors was being ushered out of an elevator and toward the exit doors. A policeman shouted "Hey you!" at Carter. "The hospital's closed."

Carter nodded and turned around, but instead of going back out the revolving doors, he ducked into a short corridor that he knew led to an interior stairwell. The door was propped open and Carter could hear the rubber boots of firemen stomping and squeaking up above. He climbed the stairs two at a time, and on the third landing bumped into the fire crew.

"I'm a doctor, I just got the call," he said, as he barged through them. "Sixth floor, right?"

"Right," one of them said, but Carter was already rounding the next landing, and then the next.

At six, he stopped and bent over, to catch his breath and to brace himself for whatever he might find. The smell of fire had grown stronger the higher up he went, and there was no question in his mind that there'd been some kind of explosion.

Like the explosion in his lab.

The door was secured in the open position and Carter could hear an immense racket just outside it. The floor glistened with water, black with soot and ash, that was even now washing into the stairwell and trickling down the stairs. He stepped over a running stream and into the wide sixth-floor corridor.

The scene was chaos, with firemen and cops trying to help the nursing staff remove the remaining patients from the area—the patients, still in their beds, were being wheeled carefully out of their rooms and through the debris. Carter skirted the deserted nurses' station and made for Russo's room, but even before he got there he could see that it was the epicenter of the destruction. The door was completely missing, as was a portion of the wall; inside, he could see that the windows on the opposite side had also been blown out, and a strong breeze was keeping a cloud of ashes swirling in the air. A couple of emergency personnel were moving around in the interior, but carefully staying clear of something that lay in a blackened heap near where the door to the room had once been. Carter's stomach lurched.

And then there was a hand on his elbow, pulling him back.

"You can't go in there," he heard, and turned to see Dr. Baptiste, her hair disheveled, her face besmirched. "There's nothing you can do."

She pulled him away.

"What happened?" Carter asked her, numbly.

She drew him down the hall and into the doorway of an evacuated room.

"No one knows," she said, wiping her eyes with the sleeve of her hospital coat. It was gray with soot. "A smoke alarm went off in his room, and I was hurrying to check in on him. That's when I saw the other man leaving."

"What other man?" Carter asked, though in his heart he knew.

"The tall man, with blond hair," she said, and as she spoke her eyes bore in on Carter with amazing intensity. "Do you know who I'm talking about?"

"Yes."

"Then you tell me," she said, gripping his arm again. "He came out of the room, and I saw him close the door behind him. I stopped him, to ask him why that smoke alarm was ringing. I took his arm, just as I'm taking yours now," she said, glancing down at Carter's elbow, "and I don't know what I was holding onto."

Carter didn't know what to say. What could he tell her that she could believe?

"He had dark glasses on," she said, "so I couldn't really see his eyes. But I'm glad now that I couldn't."

"You should be," Carter replied.

"Then the whole room just exploded. I was knocked halfway down the hall. Everything inside was on fire," she said, shaking her head with sorrow, "everything. And that man in the sunglasses was gone."

Of course he was, Carter thought. He would always be gone. He would sow death and destruction—what *good* had it done him to kill Russo?—and then be gone.

But there was one thing that Dr. Baptiste had said that had lodged in Carter's mind—she'd said that the man had closed the door behind him. Carter gently removed her hand from his arm, and said, "I need to do something."

"I told you," she repeated, "there's nothing you can do. He's dead. Your friend is dead."

"I know that," Carter said. "Do you have a surgical glove in your pockets?"

"What?"

"A surgical glove—do you have one on you?"

She fished in the pocket of her dirty hospital coat and pulled out a couple of rubber gloves. Carter swiftly pulled them on, then left her, puzzled, in the empty room.

He moved down the hall and back toward the nurses' station. He'd remembered correctly—there was a door, a hospital room door, lying against the wall. Its surface was black and splintered, but its number plate was still intact—as was its metal handle. It was the door to Russo's room.

Carter put his foot against the cracked wood and pressed down; the wood split the rest of the way, freeing the door handle along one side. He kicked down on the wood on the other side, and it broke free, too. Then, with his gloved hands, he pried loose the door handle. A cop, passing by, looked at him strangely.

"Arson investigation," Carter said, holding the handle carefully by its singed base.

At the nurses' station he found a manila envelope with patient charts inside; he emptied out the charts, put the door handle in the envelope, and wedged it into the inside pocket of his jacket. Glancing into Russo's room, he could see that they'd placed a black plastic tarp beside the remains. A couple of medical personnel were bending down, preparing to move the body. And much as he hated to face it, Carter knew that he couldn't let his friend go without at least saying good-bye.

He made his way through the firemen and cops and stepped into what was left of Russo's old room.

"Hey, buddy, you can't be in here," one of the paramedics said, but the other one, perhaps understanding the look on Carter's face, said, "We can give you a second," and moved a discreet distance away.

Carter stood above the charred, almost unidentifiable remains of what had been his friend. Russo had been such a big guy, so burly and full of life, and now, all that was left was a twisted heap of blackened limbs and bare bones. In the extremity of the pose, in the way that it suggested the limits of human endurance, it reminded Carter of the figures unearthed at Pompeii and Herculaneum. The face, or what remained of it, was turned to one side, toward the floor, and it was there that Carter felt he had to touch his friend and say farewell. He knelt down and put out his hand toward the sunken, scorched cheek; he let his fingers graze the seared flesh—it felt like warm tar—and under his breath he said, "Good-bye, Joe—I'm so sorry."

Then, before he knew it, he heard himself add, "God be with you."

For Carter, a devout unbeliever all his life, they were words he never thought would pass his lips. But now, confronted with this horror, and about to face horrors that would no doubt surpass it, the words flowed as naturally as water from a well . . . or blood from a wound.

THIRTY-FIVE

They'd been at it for hours, Ezra going over and over the scraps of the scroll, explicating the text, filling in the details of scriptural history, building his case. And in the dimly lighted and increasingly stuffy room, Carter could barely stay awake and focused any longer.

"You see, right here," Ezra was saying, as he strode to another segment of the scroll preserved behind acetate and fastened with thumbtacks to the wall, "it says that the Watchers numbered in the hundreds and that God had appointed them to watch over mankind." Ezra chortled, shaking his head. "Turns out, they watched too well."

"Meaning?" Carter asked, taking another sip of his now-cold coffee.

"They were watching the women—and they got some bad ideas."

"Speaking of bad ideas, do we really need to keep the window closed? It's almost impossible to breathe in here."

"I can't risk any more damage to the scroll," Ezra said, irritably. "I told you, I've got only a few scraps left to translate, and then I'll have finally put the whole thing together."

"Go on," Carter conceded.

"They felt lust."

"So these angels could feel emotions?"

"I never said they couldn't. I only said they had no souls."

"Why would angels need a soul? Aren't they kind of past that already?"

"Good point. But if we read from this section here," he said, pointing to another yellowed scrap tacked to the wall, "they came to covet them. They saw the special place that mankind, who possessed the gift of a soul, had assumed in God's eyes, and so they wanted one, too."

"And they couldn't just ask for it?"

"The section here is too faded to read," Ezra said, indicating a small portion on the wall between two larger pieces of the parchment, "but maybe they did, and were refused. Or maybe they were simply too proud to ask. We'll never know."

Carter put the coffee mug down on the floor, raised his arms above his head, and stretched. Then he glanced at his watch—it was one o'clock in the morning. By now Beth would be fast asleep at Abbie and Ben's apartment; over the phone, he'd made her promise not to go home tonight and, a little to his own surprise, she'd agreed without any hesitation.

"But whatever happened," Ezra went on, "it left the Watchers unsatisfied, and that's when they decided to take matters into their own hands. They decided to mate with human females—they'd always had a hankering for them anyway—and produce what you might call the perfect hybrid."

"Angels with souls."

"Exactly—and a supreme challenge to the celestial order. That's when the War in Heaven began. You know the rest—the Archangel Michael, at the helm of God's army, defeated the rebel angels and cast them down from Heaven."

"What about Lucifer, and the sin of pride? All of that?"

"Later interpolations, made-up stories," Ezra said, with a wave of the hand. "But there was one other thing the Old Testament might have had right—the Flood."

"Forty days and forty nights?"

"No, I find nothing in this scroll to corroborate the idea

of an actual flood," Ezra said, with all the certainty of a scientist who had been combing over reams of lab data. "No arks, no Noah, none of that. But there *is* something—it's hard to translate it literally—about a vast change, a kind of watershed event that wiped the slate clean. After the defeat of the rebel angels, after they had been buried in the bowels of the earth," he said, now indicating the bottom of another scrap of the tattered scroll, "it says right here, 'and the Unholy and Man became, like the lion and the jackal, mortal enemies. To mingle their blood, ever after, would be to die.' I'm taking some liberties with the syntax, but the gist of it, I'm pretty sure, is correct."

Carter exhaled and let his arms hang down between his legs. "But how can any of this be true? I mean, haven't we established, just for starters, that the earth is older than any of these stories would allow? That evolution, for another, has been going on for many millions of years? And that we're descended from apes, not from angels? Haven't we moved past Augustine and on to Darwin? And what about—"

"What about this?" Ezra interrupted, sweeping his arm toward the laboriously constructed scroll. "If we believe your own lab results, it's a living tissue older than anything else ever dated, and unidentifiable at that. Your friend Russo, may he rest in peace, accepted that—why can't you?"

Because, even now, despite everything that had happened, it was unacceptable. Because everything he had ever believed, learned, studied, *knew,* argued against it.

"You're still not seeing the big picture, Carter," Ezra insisted. "Everything we're talking about here happened eons *before* the Bible stories supposedly took place. And not by thousands of years—by millions and millions of years. This was a world that existed before everything we have ever known or imagined—before dinosaurs, before the continents drifted apart, before the stars were born and the planets moved in their orbits."

"Then how do we know any of this?"

Ezra shrugged. "Divine inspiration? The collective unconscious?" Even Ezra seemed to be running out of steam;

he plopped into the chair in front of his drafting table. "This scroll?"

It kept coming back to the scroll . . . and the fossil. The DNA tests that revealed them to be from the same impossible creature . . . and the dating techniques that showed them to be of an equally impossible age. An age that only Ezra could have found credible.

And now Carter had in his secret possession yet another small shred of inexplicable evidence. On the way to Ezra's, he had dropped off the doorknob to Russo's hospital room at the police precinct, with a note to Detective Finley to check it for fingerprints. A few hours later, Carter had checked his office answering machine.

"Thanks for the doorknob," the detective said on the machine. "And for your information, it does have the same perfect prints on it. Now, you want to call me back and tell me where you got it?"

Tomorrow Carter would have to do that, though he didn't relish the grilling he was going to get from the detective. He'd known it would match the prints from the scene of Donald Dobkins' immolation, and he knew to whom the prints belonged. But he also knew that if he so much as *tried* to explain all this to a New York City homicide investigator, he'd find himself locked up in a psych ward faster than you can say *fallen angel*.

"I need a break," Ezra said. "I'm going to see what Gertrude's got in the fridge. You want a sandwich or something?"

Carter shook his head, and Ezra left. Although he was sorely tempted to go to the French doors and fling them wide open, he didn't want to risk incurring Ezra's wrath; the guy was always half-cocked to begin with. Instead, he simply stood up, arched his back, then did a couple of impromptu jumping jacks to get the blood flowing and wake himself up. He wandered over to the drafting table and glanced at the few remaining scraps still lying there. Ezra wasn't kidding; he was very close to finishing the job. All the rest of the scroll was arranged in acetate sheets around the walls of the room, and once these few pieces were added to the tail end, it looked like the thing would be complete. In fact, now that Carter looked more closely at them, he could see that one of the pieces on the table simply needed to be turned around, and its jagged edge would then fit neatly into the portion of the scroll already mounted. What it said, he had no idea, but he could see how it would fit. Not so very different, he thought, from piecing together bone shards.

He sat down in Ezra's work chair, and without really giving it much thought, he turned the scrap of scroll, then found himself lifting another scrap and fitting that one, too, into a pattern. There was an odd tingling in his fingers. Glancing up at the wall, he could see precisely where the pieces would go. And while part of him knew that Ezra would be livid that he had meddled, another part of him was suddenly captured by the notion of doing this. After sitting for hours, as if at a lecture, it was a pleasure to *do* something at last, to feel useful. And it was almost as if the scroll were *inviting* him to participate. Was this the same urge, he idly wondered, that had led Bill Mitchell to disaster in the lab?

Taking the third and last scrap of the scroll, he fitted it to the other two, then lowered the upper flap of the acetate to hold them all in place. Yes, they were like pieces of a jigsaw puzzle that were perfectly joined. And he could see that their edges would neatly mesh with the work that Ezra had already done.

What a surprise it would be, when Ezra got back, for him to find the scroll complete.

Carter got up with the acetate in hand. Should he? It was as if a cloud had descended on his mind; he knew this was wrong, he knew how upset he would be if someone interfered like this with his own work (shades of Mitchell again, and the *Smilodon* fragment) but he felt compelled to go ahead.

He went to the wall, and as if his hand were being guided by some unseen force, he lifted the acetate and moved it closer. *Yes, right here*. He loosened a thumbtack—Ezra had driven dozens of them into the plaster—and stuck it through one corner of the acetate. Then he added another to the opposite corner and stood back to admire his handiwork.

"Gertrude made some brownies," Ezra announced, closing the bedroom door behind him and coming into the workroom with a tray in his hands.

Carter turned, an uncertain smile on his face, and waited for Ezra to see what he had done. Suddenly, he wasn't so sure it had been a good idea.

Ezra stopped, and surveyed the wall. "What did you do?" he said in a hushed voice.

"I wanted to help out," Carter said.

There was a low humming sound, like a generator slowly kicking into gear, and as Carter turned, he could see the acetates rippling, as if stirred by a subtle breeze. Their edges, all touching, seemed to meld, and the fragments of scroll within grew together, merging until their edges and seams were no longer apparent. There was a faint glow, a lavender light, that seemed to emanate from the scroll itself.

And the breeze grew stronger, warmer, blowing around the room in a circle.

Ezra dropped the tray, mugs and plates crashing to the floor, as the door to the bedroom slammed shut behind him. He raced to the closet.

What was he doing? Carter thought. The acetates were fluttering wildly, some of them already losing their tacks and drifting free of the scroll they had contained.

Ezra emerged from the closet with something in his hand—it looked like a cold-cream container. With shaking hands, in the lavender light, he was trying to unscrew the top.

"Ezra, what's going on?" Carter shouted.

But Ezra didn't answer; he tossed the lid of the container away, dipped his fingers inside, then smeared what felt like wet mud on Carter's forehead.

"What are you doing?"

Then he slathered another streak—it looked to Carter now like red clay—on his own brow. "It's holy soil," Ezra shouted back, "from beneath the Dome of the Rock!"

Carter shook his head in confusion.

"Where the Ark of the Covenant is hidden!"

It still made no sense to Carter. Hadn't Ezra just explained that all of that religious mumbo-jumbo was useless, that it had all come about long after any of the things they were dealing with?

"It's supposed to protect us?"

Ezra, looking all around at the flapping acetates, nodded quickly.

"From what?"

As if in answer, Carter heard a sound like nothing else he had ever heard, or hoped to hear again, in his entire life. It started as a low moan, a wind groaning through the ancient eaves of a mighty house, but rose swiftly in pitch and volume. Instinctively he clapped his hands over his ears. But the sound rumbled underfoot and roared inside his head.

He ran to the door and tried to pull it open, but it wouldn't budge; the hot wind sped up inside the room, ripping the remaining acetates from the wall. The scroll within them unfurled itself and moved like a tornado toward the center of the room. It swirled in an unsteady spiral, its lavender light growing darker, more purple, the wind increasing in speed.

There was only one other way out. Carter ran to the balcony doors.

"No!" Ezra shouted, even his terror overwhelmed by the fear of losing his precious scroll. "Don't!"

But these wouldn't open either. Carter rattled the handles and pushed his shoulder against the frame.

Ezra grabbed his arm and tried to stop him. "We can't!" he screamed.

"We have to!" Carter shook him free, looking desperately around the room.

The noise in his head had become deafening. It was more like a wail now, a rising tide of anguish uttered by a thousand voices in a host of tongues, the sound of all the misery in all the world, for all of time.

It was too much even for Ezra; he dropped to his knees, the mud on his forehead, his hands clamped over his ears, his eyes squeezed shut.

Carter felt as if his head would explode if it didn't stop.

The old toy chest that Ezra placed his tools on—that might work. Carter swept the tools off, then picked up the wooden chest. Holding it in front of himself like a battering ram, he ran at the French doors. The glass cracked and splintered, but the doors held fast.

Carter heard the crying of every baby born, the death rattle of every departing soul, the howl of every living creature slaughtered or maimed.

He backed up, then ran again at the doors. This time the wood gave way and the doors flew back. The chest dropped to the stone floor of the balcony, and he tumbled over it onto his back.

Above him now he could see the night sky, the stars. And then, on a gust of wind, as dry as the desert, the scroll itself, spiraling in the air like a living thing. It hovered above him, a long, glowing, purple serpent, before another gust propelled it out and over the edge of the balcony.

Carter struggled to his feet as Ezra stumbled out through the broken doors.

They watched as the scroll, like a seagull borne aloft by changing currents, swooped and fluttered through the air, into the distance and then out, out, over the East River. Slowly its purple glow faded away, lost in the city lights, swallowed by the night.

Carter, his head still ringing, glanced at Ezra, whose hands were fixed on the balustrade, his eyes still searching for a sign of the scroll. And he heard him mutter something under his breath.

"What did you say?" His own voice sounded muffled and distant to him.

Ezra paused, then repeated, "It was mine."

Carter looked out at the city below and the night sky above. "I'm not sure it ever was," he said. He took a deep breath of the cold night air, and as the din in his head gradually diminished, he thought he detected, from the church across the river, the incessant tolling of a bell.

THIRTY-SIX

Beth had spent the whole day doing nothing, it seemed, but putting out fires. Apologizing to Mrs. Winston for her missing invitation, helping the caterer to get his permits in order, clearing a space for the wait staff to change clothes in, squeezing the backup doorman into a uniform two sizes too small.

But the annual holiday party of the Raleigh Gallery was at last in full swing, with enormous sprays of fresh flowers mounted all around the main floor, white-jacketed waiters carrying silver trays of Dom Perignon and Beluga caviar, a string quartet from Juilliard playing Vivaldi from the mezzanine. And once again, everyone who was anyone in the world of New York art collectors was in attendance.

Richard Raleigh himself was in a maroon velvet dinner jacket, with a gold ribbon on the lapel that he passed off as some kind of honor bestowed on him by the French government, but which Beth knew he'd bought at an estate sale in Southampton. He moved gaily among his many clients, making sure their champagne glasses were always full, that they were having fun, and above all that that they were noticing the important new pieces (a Fragonard and a Greuze among them) now adorning the walls.

Beth had been doing her best to put on a good face, but it wasn't easy. Carter had come home at the break of dawn, and they hadn't even had a chance to talk before she left for work. And more to the point, her heart was sick with the news of Russo's death. She tried to tell herself it was for the best, given the extent of the burn injuries he'd already sustained and the agonies of treatment he was sure to go through . . . but it was still so tragic, so awful even to contemplate.

And finally, as if all that weren't enough, she hadn't felt physically right for days. To her immense consternation, she'd detected some bleeding when she'd used the bathroom earlier in the day, even though she was nowhere near her period. What, she worried, was that about? All she wanted right now was to get off her feet—she was wearing some shiny black heels, as Raleigh had none too subtly requested—and as far as she was concerned, the sooner the party started to wind down, the better.

"Beth, look who's here!" she heard Raleigh call to her, and of course she saw Bradley Hoyt, his buzz cut gleaming in the light from the chandelier, making his way toward her. On the one hand, this was the last thing she needed, but on the other, at least he would do his best to monopolize her attention and she wouldn't have to work so hard to mingle. "You look terrific," Hoyt said, as he took her hand.

"She's a vision," Raleigh piped up over his shoulder, "worthy of a Fragonard."

That was subtle, Beth thought.

"In fact, don't you dare leave without letting me show you a couple of new things," Raleigh said, lifting two full glasses from a passing tray and handing them to Hoyt and Beth.

After he'd moved away, Hoyt leaned in and said, "Does he ever quit?"

"Not to my knowledge."

For a few minutes, they talked about the plummeting stock market, the latest plan to rejuvenate downtown, the other guests circulating around them. Although Hoyt may have made off with a bundle of money, he knew next to nothing about the other New Yorkers who had their own bundles, and Beth found it mildly diverting to act as his Baedeker. She pointed out who was who, how old the money was, what corrupt enterprise it originated from (over time Beth had seen the wisdom of Balzac's observation, that behind every great fortune there is a crime), while Hoyt just took it all in . . . and her.

"The woman in the navy blue Chanel, that's Mrs. Reginald Clark—the money's from a railroad stock fraud in the days of the robber barons.

"And the woman she's talking to, with the diamond necklace? Alice Longstreet—a brokerage house that's currently under indictment."

Hoyt laughed. "I bet you think I'm a crook, too!" he said.

Beth took a sip of her champagne, then instantly regretted it; her stomach was already feeling unsettled.

"Aren't you at least going to deny it?" he kidded her.

"I'm sure you're completely aboveboard," she said, and was about to go on, when she saw someone at the front door, huddled with Emma, Raleigh's assistant. He was tall and blond, and was wearing the little round sunglasses he never took off. She glanced across the room, where Raleigh, too, had just noticed Arius's entrance. Beth knew he wasn't on the guest list—the gallery didn't even have an address for him—but somehow he'd known that tonight was the annual party. And he'd guessed correctly about how he'd be received.

Even as Beth watched with rising dread, she saw Raleigh heading for the door, broadly smiling, his hands already extended in greeting. If there was a chance of a future sale . . .

"Something wrong?" Hoyt said, trying to follow her gaze.

"I just thought of something."

"What?"

"A new drawing I think you should see."

"Now?" he said. "It's a party. Aren't you supposed to be off duty?"

"It's upstairs, in the private gallery."

His ears all but visibly pricked up. And she didn't have time right now to correct his misapprehension.

She slipped her arm through his and moved him quickly toward the private elevator. They'd be less conspicuous this way than mounting the stairs. Once inside, she turned the key to release the car, and was relieved to see no sign of Arius as the doors slowly closed.

Upstairs, she had another problem. She had to find some drawing Hoyt hadn't already seen. Then it occurred to her that he probably couldn't remember three-quarters of what he'd been shown, and she slid open the top drawer of the drawings cabinet and, without even looking to see what it was, removed the first drawing that came to hand.

"Your hand's shaking," Hoyt said. "This can't be that big a deal."

"These are all new acquisitions . . ."

Hoyt put his hand on top of hers, and said, "You get new stuff all the time. You sure that's all it is?"

"No," she confessed, "it's not. It *is* something else."

Hoyt's face broke into a grin; she was about to admit his irresistibility. It was about time.

"There was someone downstairs that I didn't want to be seen by."

His face perceptibly fell.

"And that's why you hustled me up here?"

Beth nodded her head. "I'm afraid so."

Hoyt appeared to think it over, then said, "No problem. I'll take it any way I can."

"In fact," she admitted, "I have another favor to ask you now."

Hoyt waited, ever hopeful.

"I need to sneak out of the gallery, but I don't want Raleigh to see me, and I don't want that other man to know I'm gone."

"My car's outside—we could be out of here in no time."

"That's not what I mean. What I need is for you to just

stay up here for a few minutes, and cover for me if anyone asks."

This was not what he'd been hoping for. Still, he thought, anything he did now that put her in his debt could conceivably pay off later. Part of the reason for his success in life was that he knew when to pay a favor, and when to call it in. Doing what Beth asked for now was a small investment to make on a potentially large return.

"Go ahead," he said. "My car's outside, the black Bentley—tell Jack that I said he should take you wherever you need to go, and then come back for me here."

Beth had never liked Hoyt more than she did at this moment. Even though she knew it was probably another bad idea, she impulsively pecked him on the cheek as she turned to leave.

"Before you go, I've got just one question for you. Since I'm supposed to be thinking about buying it," he said, gesturing at the drawing, "what am I looking at?"

Beth had to turn back and then turn the drawing right side up—and it was only then that she saw what she'd pulled from the drawer.

It was a nineteenth-century etching of a doomed angel with black bat wings, plummeting through the night sky down toward a bank of roiling clouds. It had been part of the French consignment, along with the Greuze and the Fragonard.

"It's a Gustave Doré, from his series of illustrations for *Paradise Lost*," she said. "A fallen angel thrown from Heaven."

Hoyt nodded, seemingly satisfied with this information.

Beth turned again, a chill descending her spine. It was as if the drawing had been there for a reason, waiting for her to open the drawer and acknowledge it. All the more reason to leave the gallery as quickly as possible. She made for the elevator, her high heels clicking on the parquet floor. Hoyt watched her go, then glanced casually at the etching left out on the table.

Even to his unpracticed eye, it was a powerful piece of work. The bat-winged angel was falling headlong, as if unable to regain control of his flight. A shaft of radiant light descended from the upper right corner of the picture, piercing the turbulent clouds, illuminating the curve of the earth that lay so far below. It was a lot better than the stuff he usually saw here, all kinds of studies and sketches that seldom told a coherent story. In fact, if it hadn't been for his attraction to Beth, he probably would have called it quits on this Old Master stuff weeks ago; maybe his friends were right—buy the big, colorful modern stuff that everybody who saw it would know had cost a lot of money.

Behind him he heard the creak of the floorboards, but there was no accompanying clack of spike heels, and when he looked up, he saw a man with blond hair and shades watching him from the main entry to the room. The guy was tall, about his own height, and wearing a long black coat that looked to Hoyt like it was cashmere. Hoyt was pretty sure he'd never laid eyes on him before, and he was also pretty sure that this was the guy Beth had been trying to avoid at all costs.

"If you're looking for Beth," he said, hoping to give her a little more time to make her escape, "she'll be right back."

The intruder smiled, and Hoyt couldn't help but notice that his lips were unusually full and his teeth gleamed almost unnaturally behind them.

"My name's Bradley Hoyt," he said, "and you are?"

"Arius," the man said, coming closer. The overhead lights turned his blond hair a burnished gold, and Hoyt found himself wondering who this guy went to for such amazing highlights.

"She was showing me a couple of new things," Hoyt went on, indicating the Doré.

Arius came even closer, gliding almost silently across the floor.

And what kind of aftershave, Hoyt thought, was this guy wearing? It reminded Hoyt of his summers in Maine, back when he was a boy.

Without removing his tinted glasses, Arius looked at the etching, appraisingly. Hoyt had the feeling he knew what it was all about without being told. He had the look of someone who'd grown up with all the advantages.

"The wings," Arius said, pointing at the angel in the picture, "are fuller than that."

His middle finger, Hoyt noticed, ended bluntly, above the knuckle.

"And she isn't coming back," Arius added, raising his gaze now.

Hoyt didn't know what to say; somehow, he knew that there'd be no point in lying to this guy. And even though Arius's eyes were shielded by the amber lenses, Hoyt didn't at all like having them trained on him.

"Maybe we should both go on back to the party," Hoyt said, but Arius seemed unwilling to go, and Hoyt wasn't sure if he should leave him unattended with this valuable piece of art left out. If anything happened to it, Beth could be held responsible.

"Why don't we see if the champagne is still holding out?" Hoyt tried again, but this time Arius simply took a corner of the etching between his fingers and started to rub it. And though Hoyt didn't profess to be an expert on such things, he was fairly confident that rubbing the old etching was a bad idea.

"I wouldn't do that if I were you."

"Why are you troubling Beth?" Arius said in a low voice.

"Me, troubling Beth?" Hoyt said. "I think, my friend, you've got that backward." Now Hoyt could see why Beth had been running from this guy. There was something distinctly creepy about him.

"Keep away from her. She doesn't belong to you."

"And what are you all of a sudden?" Hoyt said, incredulous. "Her marriage counselor?" Hoyt was flabbergasted; this guy wasn't just creepy, he was totally crazy. Beth should apply for a restraining order.

And now there was suddenly another aroma in the room, something to add to the scent of a forest in the rain . . . and it was the smell of smoke.

Hoyt looked down and a black stain had spread across the corner of the Doré, where the paper was scorched.

"Jesus, what are you doing?" Hoyt said, snatching the drawing away. But suddenly it was more than a scorch mark, it was a bright flame that raced across the picture like a snake darting at its prey . . . before shooting toward Hoyt's hand and arm. He tried to drop the burning drawing, but it stuck to his hand like flypaper. Arius watched, impassively, as Hoyt staggered backward, wildly struggling to disengage the burning paper.

"Get it off!" Hoyt screamed, as a smoke alarm blared and the sprinklers went off. The flames, as if they had a mind of their own, had coursed up his arm, across his shoulder and were now licking at his face and hair.

Arius turned to leave.

"Get it off!" Hoyt screamed again, as the sound of urgent voices surged from the gallery below, and hurried footsteps echoed from the foot of the staircase.

Arius didn't turn to see—he hardly needed to—but he could hear Hoyt flailing around the room, banging his burning limbs against the walls, then crumpling to the floor. His thoughts were already elsewhere, with the little journey he would have to take, if he hoped to catch up with Beth that night.

THIRTY-SEVEN

If it had not been for the gravity of the task that lay before them, Carter would have laughed when Ezra arrived. He was dressed all in black, with a black beret pulled low on his brow and a black satchel slung over one shoulder. To Carter, he looked like a member of the French Resistance from some old newsreel.

"Is your wife home?" Ezra asked, peering into the apartment around Carter's shoulder.

"No, she's going straight from work to a friend's house, upstate. I thought it was best to get her out of town."

"So she knows what we're doing?" Ezra asked, sounding unhappy about it.

"No, not at all."

"Good."

Carter stepped aside and Ezra came into the apartment. He glanced around, then went to the coffee table beneath the window overlooking Washington Park. He slung the satchel down—it landed with a *thunk*—next to the city map Carter had spread out there, then slumped into an armchair.

"The way I look at it," Carter said, sitting down across

from him and gesturing at the open map, "the first thing we have to do is to figure out where Arius is hiding."

"What makes you think he's hiding at all?"

"I know, he's been seen, but I still don't think he's walking around in the middle of the day, calling attention to himself. He must have a refuge of some kind, somewhere."

Ezra looked unconvinced, but open to persuasion. "And how would you begin to go about finding this refuge?"

Carter took a breath—he knew how this was going to go over—before saying, "By thinking of Arius as a vampire."

Carter could almost hear Ezra's mind clamp shut. He looked at Carter as if he had truly lost his mind. "What on earth would make you say that?"

"Just hear me out for a second," Carter said, buying time. "Look at his salient characteristics, at least the ones we know. He's immortal, he has no soul, he shields his eyes from the sun, and, as far as we can tell, he lives to seduce mortal women."

"Oh please," Ezra said, as if he were oddly insulted on the angel's behalf. "Shall we look at some other salient characteristics—or the lack of them? He shows no propensity to drink blood, or wear a tuxedo, or sleep in his own coffin—in fact, he doesn't sleep at all—or any of that bullshit."

"You're still not hearing me," Carter explained. "I'm not saying he *is* a vampire. Don't get me wrong. But I am saying that this might be where the legends of such things originate, how they come down to us."

"Even if you're right—and you're not—so what? How would that help us with what we have to do tonight?"

"Maybe it would tell us something about where he is," Carter said, as patiently as he could. "Maybe those legends tell us something about how these unholy creatures can be killed."

"With a wooden stake through the heart?" Ezra said, disdainfully. "Or maybe a clove of garlic?" He squirmed in his chair and blew out a puff of air.

This was not going the right way at all, and Carter knew it. Suddenly, he and Ezra—the only two people on earth who believed in this creature, and who consequently stood the slightest chance in hell of defeating him—were at each other's throats. Instead of putting their heads together, they were butting them against each other. Carter paused, making sure his own temper was in check, then said, "Look, we're both feeling the strain, and after what we both saw at your apartment, that's only natural. But unless we can get in sync and work together on this thing, we'll never succeed." It was the same sort of counsel he'd given his co-workers on a dozen dig sites, when things were suddenly spiraling out of control. And now he realized that this was exactly how he would have to approach this task too.

Ezra slumped back in his chair and dragged the beret off his head. His forehead was beaded with sweat. "I'll cool it if you will," he said, his eye finally falling on the map that lay beside his black satchel.

"Deal."

"So go ahead," he added, grudgingly, "show me what you were doing with the map."

Carter pushed the satchel further to one side. "Plotting coordinates. You'll see I've circled the spots where we know, so far, that Arius has been." And, as Ezra followed, Carter pointed them out—the basement lab where the angel had emerged from the explosion, the tenement stairwell where the burnt body of the transvestite had been found, St. Vincent's Hospital where he had murdered Russo, and, finally, Carter's own home. "Beth ran into him in the foyer downstairs," Carter said, suppressing his own shudder, "and when I tried to follow him, I lost him"—his finger landed on a spot across the avenue from the hospital— "right here. Aside from his excursion uptown, to the party on Sutton Place, all of his appearances," Carter said, making a small circle on the map, "lie somewhere within this radius."

"The West Village," Ezra said.

"If he got his lease through an apartment broker, we should be able to find him pretty easily," Carter said, with a small smile.

"Something tells me he took another route altogether."

"Which is what makes it harder."

Ezra pondered it for a moment, then said, "And if we do find him?"

Carter had had even less success with this question. How did you capture, much less annihilate, a fallen angel? He'd seen all the dumb movies, where supernatural creatures were dispatched with stakes and swords, with silver bullets and holy water, with sacred daggers or the endless recitation of a Latin liturgy. But this wasn't some movie—this was real. "I have no idea."

With a sigh, Ezra leaned forward and undid the clasp on his knapsack. First he pulled out a flashlight—"Have you got one of these for yourself?"

"We kill him with a flashlight?"

"No. I don't know how to do that either." Then he reached deeper and pulled out the container Carter had last seen in his apartment. He opened it, and before Carter could pull back, he'd reached across the coffee table and smeared the red clay all over his forehead and into his hairline.

"Didn't we already try this stuff, in your room, the night the scroll nearly killed us?" Carter said.

"Yes," Ezra said, "and for all we know, it's why we're here right now."

"It's not much of a weapon."

"It's not meant to be. But it might be a protection."

"Weren't you the one who told me none of this religious hocus-pocus would make any difference? That this creature predated all of this stuff by millions of years?"

"I did," Ezra replied. "Let's just call it my version of Pascal's wager."

Carter was familiar with the term; the French philosopher had argued that even if Roman Catholicism was wrong, what was the benefit of betting against it? On your deathbed, you could only gain by believing.

For a second, they remained where they were—what more was there to say?—and then it became evident to both of them, as Ezra slipped the container of holy clay back into the knapsack and closed the buckle, that this was as much of a plan as they would be able to formulate for now. Carter went in the kitchen and rummaged around in the utility drawer, until he came up with a yellow flashlight. He tried it out and, to his own amazement, the batteries were still good.

Then his eye fell on the knife board, where the black-handled knife set his Aunt Lorraine had given them as a wedding present sat. He took one of the medium-sized blades with a serrated edge and slipped it through his belt loop.

Ezra was waiting by the door when he came out; he spotted the knife and said nothing. Carter pulled on his leather jacket, and by angling the blade against his side, it was completely concealed. He slipped his cell phone and flashlight into his outside pockets, locked up, and they left by the stairs.

Outside, with its front tires halfway into the red zone, Ezra had parked his father's town car. "You didn't tell me you had the car," Carter said, suddenly feeling like a teenager again.

"Get in," Ezra said, pointing the key chain to unlock it.

Carter pushed the *Daily Racing Form* aside and got into the front seat. Ezra drove just as Carter imagined he would—badly, with a heavy foot on the brakes and no turn signals. Even though it was nearly nine o'clock, most of the storefronts they passed were still lighted, open for business, and festooned with holiday decorations. The sidewalks were filled with genial crowds.

They were following no exact course, but keeping their eyes open and making their way, slowly but surely, toward the hospital. Carter scanned the faces in the passing throng, but not for a minute did he think he'd actually spot Arius among them. It wouldn't be that easy. Once in a while Ezra would point out something and pull over so Carter could glance down into a darkened stairwell or explore a narrow alleyway. But the worst menace that they encountered was a homeless man who insisted on washing their windshield at a stoplight.

As they left the thicket of Village stores and restaurants and approached the hospital precincts, there were fewer people on the street, and fewer places that Carter could imagine this creature could hide. But if he was ever going to find him, he'd have to do what all those thrillers always recommended—you had to start thinking like the criminal you were chasing, you had to put yourself into his mind-set and see the world through his eyes. But even if that had some utility when it came to serial killers and psychopaths, was it really going to work when it came to tracking a fallen angel? How, Carter wondered, did you *think* like a fallen angel?

When they got to the corner across from the hospital, Carter couldn't help but look up, his eyes drawn inexorably to the sixth floor where Russo's room had been. Even from the car, he could see the thick plastic sheeting and rudimentary bracing that covered the gaping wound in the wall. Who would be the next victim? He knew he was putting himself in the line of fire, or at least trying to. But that scared him a lot less than the alternative—that it was Beth who might somehow be in Arius's sights. That it might have been Beth the angel was tracking, that day she'd found him in their lobby.

A wind blew down the street, picking up litter and making the big wooden sign beside the car audibly creak. Carter glanced over and almost had to laugh. He'd forgotten about this. It was the billboard for the Villager Co-ops, soon to be erected on this site by none other than the Metzger Development Company. A rusty chain-link fence, festooned with signs warning off trespassers, still surrounded the condemned Surgical Supply building. He was about to nudge Ezra and make a joke of some sort, something about getting an insider price on an apartment, when he stopped. The realization came over him, like a cold wave, that they might have just found what they were looking for. If a damned creature was looking for a place to call home, a place to hide smack in the middle of a busy city, then what could be better than this? When his eye fell on the crumbling cornice above the front steps and the remaining letters that identified the original ruins as a sanatorium, he became even more convinced.

When he looked over at Ezra, he could see that the same thought had now occurred to him.

"If your vampire analogy holds, and I'm still not saying it does," Ezra said, "I can't think of a more likely spot than this."

Carter nodded and craned his neck to survey the front of the vast old red-brick building. The windows on its lower floors were boarded over or, in some cases, bricked up, while the upper stories—there appeared to be about seven in all—had been left open to the elements and any trespasser sufficiently determined to scale the walls somehow.

The more immediate problem was the chain-link fence, topped with loops of razor wire. Although the building, which faced St. Vincent's, was well defended in front, Carter wondered if the rest of it was equally barricaded. In his experience of New York, no abandoned building went long before being infiltrated.

"Drive around back," Carter said. "We might get lucky."

Ezra rounded the corner and drove halfway down the block, but all Carter could see was an uninterrupted fence, where, even if they attempted to climb over, they'd be seen by dozens of passersby. But at the far end, under a broken streetlamp, there did appear to be an alleyway entrance.

"Good," Carter said. "There is a back door."

Ezra pulled the car into the alley and jolted to a stop.

"Put on your high beams," Carter said, stepping out into the narrow, refuse-strewn alley. There was some sort of processing facility—for water? power? recycling?—on the opposite side. But already Carter began to see a way into the old sanatorium. He pulled a plastic milk crate over toward a huge metal Dumpster, then used it to step up onto the Dumpster; now he was level with the razor wire atop the fence, and if he could think of a way to tamp down the wire, he might be able to clamber down the other side of the chain-link fence without cutting himself to pieces. He looked up and down the alleyway and spotted, a few yards away, a pile of wet, flattened cardboard boxes. "You can cut the lights now," Carter called out to Ezra, still in the car, "and bring me some of those boxes."

Ezra got out of the car, locking it behind him. Then, while holding his nose away from the stench they gave off, he dragged some of the used cardboards over. Carter hoisted them up, then laid two or three over the sharpened barbs of the razor wire. They were heavy and loose enough to cover and even depress the stretch of wire. Carter pressed a foot up and down on them to test their stability, then cautiously put one hand out to balance himself; after teetering on top for a second, he dropped to the ground on the other side. He landed on a slight rise of packed dirt and gravel, littered even here with crushed cans and broken glass.

He brushed off his jeans and looked up just as Ezra climbed on top of the Dumpster.

"Give me your pack," Carter said, and Ezra handed it down gently.

"The ground comes up over here," Carter said, "so try to land where I did."

Carter moved back, his shoes crunching on the debris underfoot, as Ezra negotiated the cardboard and razor wire. In the distance, he could hear the growl of a garbage truck. Ezra landed harder than Carter had, his black beret flying off his head.

"You okay?" Carter said, picking up the cap.

Ezra nodded, catching his breath with his hands on his knees. "Just give me a second."

Carter handed him the beret, then turned toward the back of the old sanatorium. This side was, if anything, more bleak and ruined than the front, with jagged holes in the masonry, broken boards hanging down from the empty windows, a black iron fire escape dangling precariously from the third story. Where Carter was standing now might once have been a receiving area; he could faintly discern the outline of a semicircular drive, which, in the days when this sanatorium was built, had probably seen horse-drawn carriages come and go. Now the only movement was the occasional scuttling, deep in the shadows, of burrowing rats.

No streetlight made an impression here, but the moon

was bright and bathed the ruins in a pale, silvery light. Carter fished the flashlight out of his pocket and used its beam to help pick his way across the treacherous terrain, which was strewn with a combination of old debris—bricks and rotted boards—and newer junk: plastic detergent bottles and the occasional stained mattress. When he got to the sanatorium itself, he put one hand on the bottom of the fire escape, which dangled from the building like a twisted coat hanger, and gave it a couple of yanks. Nothing moved or gave way. Cautiously, he stepped up onto its bottom rung with one foot and tested his weight again there. Apart from a rusty creaking sound, the assembly still seemed stable enough.

He looked back at Ezra, who nodded his approval.

"Let's not push it," Carter said, instinctively keeping his voice down. "Wait till I get off the stairs before you get on them."

He climbed a few steps farther. The creaking grew louder, and by the time he'd reached the second story, where the window frame had been bricked in, he felt a sudden shiver descend through the metal steps. For a second, he debated turning around, then, seeing the empty third-floor window just a few steps higher up, took the remaining stairs three at a time; when he got to the windowsill, he played the flashlight beam into the interior, just to make sure there was a floor to land on, then ducked over the rotting wooden sill and inside.

Putting his head back out the window, he saw Ezra slinging the straps of his knapsack over his shoulders. Silently, he waved for him to come on up. Then, he turned to survey his new surroundings.

This floor must never have been used by the defunct Surgical Supply. It had clearly been one of the sanatorium wards. It was a long, narrow room with several iron bedsteads, most of their springs reduced to dust, lined up against one wall. A metal tray table with no wheels lay on its side. At the far end a large, open archway led into blackness.

Ezra clambered over the window frame and into the

room. In a hushed voice he said, "How are we ever going to go over this whole place?"

"Let's just hope we don't have to."

Carter led the way, his flashlight picking out the holes in the floor, the splintered boards sticking up at odd angles, and through the archway. He played the flashlight in all directions, where corridors led off in both directions; straight ahead, a wider corridor beckoned.

"This one," Carter whispered, "looks the most like it will lead us into the belly of the beast."

Even treading as lightly as they could, their footsteps echoed in the cavernous interior. The walls on both sides were pocked with holes and riddled with water stains. The doors to the rooms all either had fallen off or stood open, revealing barren interiors with nothing more than another bed frame, a dresser with no drawers, a cracked sink that had toppled to the floor.

But ahead, at the farthest reach of Carter's flashlight beam, he had the sense of something opening up—it even felt as if fresher air were circulating from that direction. He began to get the sense, from the way the other corridors had branched off, that the old hospital had been built in one big square, with a central space at its core. As they grew closer, the fresh air increased, and the gloom subtly diminished. Even the ceiling, Carter noted, had been raised at this end of the corridor.

And then the ceiling was gone altogether. Carter stopped, with Ezra beside him, and looked up . . . to see a bank of clouds scudding across the moon. They were in a large open area like a conservatory, with what appeared to be the remains of a vast skylight overhead. The iron support beams, or at least some of them, were bent like black fingers above them, but the oversized panes of glass that they had once held were completely gone now. All that remained of the sheets of glass were a thousand grainy shards that crunched underfoot. In the middle of the room a stone fountain stood silent, with a statue of some kind, indistinguishable from this distance, at its center.

"Looks like this was once a sunroom," Carter said.

Ezra shone his own flashlight around the room, where heavy timbered columns still rose up like telephone poles toward a roof that wasn't there. Everything was blanched of color, a world of blackness and shadows, the shapes barely outlined by the silver glints of moonlight. Even the sounds of the surrounding city were absent here; all that could be heard was the rustling of the wind through the rotted timbers and the worn bricks. But then his flashlight picked up something, something that glittered, and that was fixed to one of the timbers.

When he went closer, Ezra could see what it was. Though twisted and charred, it was still incontestably a crucifix. He motioned Carter over.

As Carter took it in, Ezra said softly, "Could it be something left behind by a patient in the old sanatorium?"

But Carter shook his head; he knew immediately that this was the crucifix he had last seen in the burn ward at St. Vincent's. "It belonged to Russo."

Ezra didn't know what to make of this. He was relieved that they might be on the right path, after all, but he was also puzzled. If his theories had been correct, this would be the last thing that Arius would want, much less put on display in his lair. But what other way was there to account for its being here?

And then, looking further into the gloomy recesses of the room, Ezra spotted something else, also fixed to one of the columns. Something, as far as he could make out from this distance, that might prove to be equally strange.

He crossed in front of the stone fountain, its basin dry and cracked, and followed the beam of his flashlight to a small spot of color in a gilded frame. It was a watercolor, unmistakably by Degas, and when Carter came to his side, Ezra said, "And this belonged to Kimberly. She had it up in her dressing area." It hung crookedly from a rusty nail that had been driven right through the center of the picture. "He didn't take much care hanging it," Ezra said, in tacit acknowledgement of what they both now knew—that the picture had been nailed there by their missing quarry. "But why?" Ezra wondered aloud. "Why the crucifix? And why this painting? It's not as if he respected the religious significance of one, or was so enchanted by the beauty of the other."

Carter knew why, though he was sick at the thought; in various paleolithic campsites, he had seen similar behavior. Antlers and jawbones, hung from cave walls, or bashed hominid skulls tucked into niches of the rock. "He's not decorating," Carter said. "He's collecting souvenirs."

He played his flashlight beam around the room, and this time it alighted on the antique statue in the center of the fountain. It had a classical head—Apollo, Narcissus, something Beth would know more precisely—but the rest of it was loosely draped in a red cloth. He went closer, and as he did he could see that the cloth was actually a long red coat made out of suede.

"What the hell is this?" Ezra said. "It looks like something a hooker would wear."

"It was," Carter said. "It belonged to the transvestite who first saw Arius emerge."

Ezra paused. "Another trophy?"

Carter nodded.

But Ezra, perhaps noticing something Carter hadn't, stepped over the rim of the basin and threw open the coat. In a whisper, he said, "But take a look at what's under it."

Carter focused his flashlight beam, and now he, too, could see the tightly wound parchment, wrapped like a skin around the torso of the stone figure. "My scroll," Ezra said. With hasty fingers, he removed the coat from the shoulders of the statue and let it fall into the dry basin.

"What are you doing?" Carter asked. "Leave the scroll alone!"

"Why should I?"

"Have you already forgotten what happened in your apartment?"

"I'm not about to leave it here," Ezra said, glaring back at Carter. "It's the most significant discovery in the history of the world, and this whole place is going to be demolished in a few days."

He turned around again and before Carter could stop

him, he'd taken hold of one end of the scroll, draped over the statue's shoulder, and begun to peel it away. The moment it began to come loose, Carter heard a familiar low hum and saw a pulse of lavender light.

"Ezra, stop!"

But the scroll continued to unfurl, the humming growing louder and the lavender light deeper. Ezra took a step back, as if surprised at what he'd done.

"I told you to stop," Carter said.

"I did," Ezra said, as the scroll went on unwinding of its own accord, like a serpent uncoiling itself from a slender tree.

The light grew more intense, a vibrant and pulsating purple. The humming gave way to a crackling sound, like dry twigs snapping underfoot.

"Get back!" Carter said, grabbing Ezra's sleeve, but Ezra resisted. "I don't think it can harm us," he said. "Not with the clay from Jerusalem on us."

"You planning to test it?"

Ezra reached out. "Yes." He touched the scroll, just as Carter took hold again of his arm, and it was as if a powerful jolt of electric current had suddenly hit them both. Ezra was hurled into the air, his head landing with a terrible thump on the rim of the basin.

Carter was knocked off his feet and banged up against one of the wooden columns. The knife he'd had in his belt skittered across the floor.

The scroll swirled in an upright column of ever-increasing light, illuminating the brick walls of the abandoned conservatory with a violet glow; superimposed upon the dingy walls, turning and twisting just as the scroll did, were the words that had once been written on the ancient skin.

And even as he lay there, stunned and amazed, Carter understood, as he never had before, what these words were.

They weren't just an account of who the Watchers were, what abominations they had committed, and the terrible punishment they had then suffered.

These words were more than that. Someone had written them; a conqueror had written them.

They were the record of a victory . . . written in blood. The blood of the vanquished. And on his very own skin.

Arius's skin.

No wonder it had come back to him.

The words, their lettering eerily elongated, circled the crumbling walls like images projected by a magic lantern, around and around, faster and faster. The purple light grew brighter, hotter, until it became almost white; Carter couldn't look at it directly anymore, but had to shield his eyes. The scroll spun in a tighter and tighter spiral, a helix of wind and light hovering just above the base of the fountain.

He heard Ezra moan.

At least he was alive.

He glanced again at the whirling scroll, transfixed by its power. Like a column of fire now spinning in place, it grew so bright, so hot, that he finally had to squeeze his eyes shut and turn his head away. Even then he could feel its power, he could hear its crackling heat. It was a living presence in the room, and Carter could only wonder, in mute terror, what would satisfy it.

And then he could tell, even with his eyes closed, that it was gone. The great room was dark again, the crackling wind had died. Everything was still.

He opened his eyes and turned back toward the fountain. The antique figure stood alone, unencumbered, bathed only in the pale moonlight coming through the conservatory's empty skylight.

The scroll was gone. Vanished into thin air? Extinguished like a flame? Blown through the open roof? Carter saw no sign of it anywhere. He caught his breath and said, "Ezra, are you all right?"

He got no answer.

He stumbled to his feet, stepped over the knapsack, and went to Ezra's side. The black beret had slipped down over his face, and when Carter raised it, he could see that his eyes were open but unfocused. "Can you hear me?" he asked, and this time Ezra feebly nodded. "I'm going to get you out of here. Can you stand up?"

Again he got no reply, but slipping his arm under Ezra's shoulders, he was able to raise him to his feet.

"Okay, one step at a time." He aimed his flashlight beam in the direction they'd entered from, and with Ezra leaning unsteadily against him, they walked slowly away from the fountain. Carter kept sweeping the flashlight back and forth to make sure they didn't trip over any rotted timbers or broken floorboards. "We'll take it slow," he told Ezra, "nice and slow."

They were almost out of the room when his flashlight beam glinted off something else, something fixed, like the other trophies, to one of the beams. He must have missed it entirely when they'd entered. Carter dragged Ezra with him toward the prize—and saw now that it was a bit of satiny fabric that had shone in the light. Satiny fabric that ran around the collar of a leopard-print pajama top.

Just like Beth's favorite pair. The ones she was wearing on the night he'd found their bedroom door stuck . . . and the window to the fire escape wide open.

"Oh my God," he said, under his breath, and Ezra let out a sigh of pain. There was a trickle of blood running down from the corner of his mouth.

Carter stuck the flashlight in his belt, then pulled the cloth from the nail. He held it to his face. It still carried the scent of her skin. "Oh my God," he mumbled again, praying that this was unlike the other trophies, that it was still only a wish, unfulfilled, and not yet a memento.

THIRTY-EIGHT

"I'm glad you left the party early," Abbie said, as she steered the car off the exit ramp for Hudson. "The sooner we get to bed tonight, the earlier we can get to work tomorrow."

Beth, staring out the window at the black trees and brush that now lined the sides of the two-lane road, had to struggle to pay attention to what her friend was saying; her thoughts kept returning, no matter how hard she resisted, to the same things . . . the sight of Arius arriving at the gallery, the spotting of blood that she could feel, even now, in her underwear. If she looked back, over nothing more than the last couple of months, all she could see was a mounting wave of bad news, trouble, and even death. Writing a letter of condolence to Joe Russo's mother was one of the most painful things she had ever had to do.

"Not that it won't be loads of fun," Abbie said. "In the right company, and we've certainly got that, hanging curtains can be a blast."

"I'm sure it will be fun," Beth said, obligingly.

"You're not going to win any Oscars for that performance," Abbie joked.

Beth turned to her friend and smiled. "Sorry, the party was draining. All I need is a good night's sleep, and in the morning I'll be raring to go."

Abbie reached over and patted the back of Beth's hand. "Sleep as late as you like. Even Ben, who hates the whole idea of this house, has to concede that he sleeps like a baby up here." She was about to add that Beth looked like she could use a good night's rest, but then thought better of it. Nobody, Abbie knew, ever wanted to hear that.

Even though she'd been up to the house a dozen times by now, Abbie was used to having Ben at the wheel, or right beside her, so she'd never paid much attention to the directions or the landmarks. But now, at night yet, she had to concentrate, and think twice at every intersection or bend in the road. Was it the hard left, or the soft one? Was the old foundry meant to stay on their right side, or were they supposed to cut through it on the service road? Every once in a while, she'd spot something—a familiar Quickie Mart casting its dismal fluorescent glow, or a gas station with its old-fashioned pumps where they'd filled up a few times before returning to the city—and know that she was still on the right track. But it wasn't easy, and the darkness that surrounded them on all sides was deeper and more forbidding than she ever recalled from a previous trip. In her heart she had to recognize that, despite her little fantasies of solitude and country living, she wouldn't be making many solo trips up here. At least not at night.

When they finally crossed an old railroad track, with its warning sign ravaged by rust and bullet holes, she knew she was almost home. She slowly rounded the big, sweeping curve of a hill, skirted the pothole she knew was coming, then put on her brights to help her find their driveway. It was partially obscured by a massive old oak that stood like a giant sentinel at the top of the narrow defile.

"My next project is going to be a light of some kind so I can find the place in the dark," Abbie said, as she turned the car into the drive.

"What's that?" Beth said, just as Abbie herself saw it— an orange highway cone on the right side of the driveway.

Her bumper caught it and sent it tumbling into what she now saw was a deep trench.

"What is going on?" Abbie said, quickly pulling the car to the left and stopping.

"Looks like a construction project," Beth said, peering down the drive. The trench ran all the way down the hill and stopped just short of the house.

"You're right," Abbie said, "it must be the water line. They've been replacing them all over the area."

"They didn't tell you they were going to do this?"

"Who reads all the notices we get?" She started the car again. "I just hope they haven't cut off the water."

They went the rest of the way down, toward the house, black as pitch and almost impossible to discern against the equally black hills beyond it.

Abbie pulled the car into the semicircular drive, its tires crunching on the loose gravel, and stopped near a pile of building supplies—lumber, bricks, a folded ladder—that were going to be used to add a deck onto the back of the house. She started to turn off the headlights, but then thought better of it.

"Maybe we should leave them on until we open up the house," she said, and Beth nodded.

"And why don't we leave the curtains in the car, too, until tomorrow morning?" Beth said, and this time Abbie agreed. Neither one of them wanted to say it, but both were anxious to get inside, lock the door behind them, and turn on every light in the house.

Abbie got out, leaving her car door open, the little chime ringing, and hurried up the wooden steps. On the porch, she fumbled through her keys before finding the right one; even then, it took some twisting and turning before the lock gave way and the door opened. Instantly, she reached inside and flicked on the entryway and porch lights, then returned to the car.

Beth had wrestled their bags out of the back, and together they carried them up the steps and dumped them in the foyer. The house was almost as cold inside as the night outside.

"I'll get the heat going," Abbie said. "That ought to work, regardless. You can just go ahead and put your stuff in the guest room."

Beth took her bag to the corkscrew staircase and maneuvered her way up it, which wasn't easy; the house had been built as a one-story, and it was only when some previous owner had decided to turn the attic into a second floor that the staircase had been wedged into the existing layout. The guest bedroom, with an adjoining sitting room and bath, made up the entire top floor.

Beth, exhausted, tossed her bag onto the quilt-covered bed. She hadn't found the light switch yet, so the room was still dark, and she could look out at the barren branches of the trees in the abandoned apple orchard, and the outline, etched in silver, of the ruined barn beyond. Ben had joked that they were going to invite the neighbors over for a barn burning, but Abbie had said she liked it, that it gave character to the place. Right now, it just reinforced Beth's feeling that they had come to the end of the earth. If the curtains had already been up, she'd have yanked them closed.

"It looks like you can take a bath, after all," Abbie called out from the foot of the stairs. "The water heater's on, and the water's running fine."

"Thanks," Beth called back; the house was so small you hardly needed to raise your voice to be heard. "I think I will."

"See you in the morning," Abbie said. "First one up turns on the coffee maker."

Beth found the light switch and flicked it on. Then she went to the window, which was open a few inches, and was about to close it when she stopped. The night air was cold all right, but it was also so fresh and so fragrant that she had to stop and savor it for a moment. It reminded her of the way the woods had smelled after a rain shower when she'd taken a road trip through the Cotswolds. She left it open an inch—sleeping with fresh air and no city noise might be a nice change—then started to unpack her bag. Most of it she decided to leave until the morning; for now she took out her nightgown, robe, and toiletries and carried them into the bathroom. Abbie and Ben had already had the bathroom remodeled, with an etched-glass medicine chest, a porcelain sink stand with two gold faucets, and a big, high, claw-footed tub. Unfortunately, as Beth turned on the hot-water spigot, she remembered what had bothered her the last time she and Carter had come out for a weekend; the tub stood directly across from a big window and there still weren't any curtains or blinds up.

"Who's going to be watching from a barren field?" Carter had said, and Beth had to remind herself of that now. Plus, she thought, it's almost midnight.

Still, as the tub filled up and she got undressed, she stood away from the window. She could have turned off the bathroom lights, but not tonight, not here; she'd rather take her chances with the most enterprising peeping Tom in history than bathe in a darkened bathroom.

She hung her white robe on the back of the door, piled her clothes up under the sink—noting, unhappily, that her panties were indeed spotted with blood—and swished a finger through the bath water. Any hotter and she'd melt. She put a couple of folded towels on top of the toilet seat, next to the tub; then, after adjusting the tap to run a little cooler, she stepped into the bath water. It was deep, and as she settled down into it, the water rose to cover her knees. She sank lower and the water went higher, up over her body and breasts, and she gently rested the back of her head against the still-cold porcelain.

Relax, she told herself, *just try to relax.*

But she might as well have been talking to a prisoner on the gallows. Her mind was still teeming with a thousand different things. She should call Carter, as soon as she got out of the tub, if only to leave a message that she had arrived safe and sound. And the next morning, she should call the gallery, to apologize for slipping out of the party early. She should even call Bradley Hoyt, to thank him for covering for her.

And then she should call her gynecologist, and get an appointment to investigate this bleeding. No point bothering Dr. Weston with it. It was probably just the result of an infection of some kind—it had happened once before—and some antibiotics would wind up taking care of it. But it was one more thing to worry about until then.

She settled even lower in the tub, the water rising over her shoulders. With one foot, she was able to reach out and slow the water from the tap even more, leaving it running at a warm trickle. She closed her eyes and tried again to clear her mind, but no matter how much she wanted to, she couldn't do it—no matter how hard she tried, there was no way she could turn off the stream of thoughts that led, inevitably, inexorably, to the one thing she feared the most. Arius.

Where was he now? What did he want from her? And how could she ever be rid of him?

Involuntarily, her face twisted into a grimace, and she felt herself, even submerged in the hot water, seized with a cold dread.

And a sense of being watched.

She opened her eyes and glanced fearfully around the room. No one was there.

But the bath water was tinged pink with blood and was just beginning to lap over the sides of the tub. *What a mess,* she thought, as she sat up and fumbled for the tap handle. She twisted it quickly, but the wrong way, and a stronger gush of water created an even greater spill. *Damn.*

She turned it again, the right way this time, but it still wouldn't shut off entirely. Maybe it just hadn't been used enough yet; it was still sticky. She flicked the drain open, and now that was resisting her too. The only thing to do was to get out of the tub quickly, let the water level drop, and use some towels to mop up the puddle before it spread any wider. She was just about to do it when she got that feeling again—the feeling that she wasn't alone.

Her eyes jumped to the big, uncovered window, and even though it was dark outside and the freshly washed panes only reflected the inside of the bathroom, she sensed that there was movement behind them. Something, impossible as it seemed, was hovering in the air at the second-story level.

Could it be a bird? A bat? Was there a tree branch, something she'd forgotten, that the wind might be blowing toward the glass?

Her hand froze on the lip of the tub and as she watched—not believing her own eyes—she saw the bottom of the window shudder, as if it were being pried up from the other side. But the window, like everything else in the house, had been freshly painted, and it screeched as it was forced to go up.

This isn't happening, she told herself. *This isn't happening.*

And then it was.

THIRTY-NINE

Carter was relying more on his memory than on any sense of direction; he'd only been up to Ben and Abbie's country house once before, and on that trip he'd been in the backseat the whole time, and not paying much attention.

But his field training, apparently, hadn't let him down. Even on that one occasion he must have been making mental notes on the terrain and the local landmarks. It was only now, as he got closer to the actual house, that he had to think especially long and hard about every turn in the road, every curve, and every intersection; he could not afford to make even a single mistake.

The car, thank God, had had plenty of gas in it and ran like a dream. Before heading upstate, he'd wrestled Ezra into the backseat, then driven straight around the corner to the hospital's emergency entrance. An orderly hurried out with a wheelchair, and Carter escorted them in to the reception desk. As quickly as he could, he gave them Ezra's information—his name, address, home phone number—and an account of what had happened. "He fell against a curb, hard, and landed on his head." It was as close as he felt he needed to come to the truth.

When they'd asked about his insurance, Carter had said, "You know who Sam Metzger is?"

The nurse said, "The real estate guy?"

"Yes," Carter replied. "This is his son."

Then he'd run back to the car and taken off.

Traffic at this hour, fortunately, had been light, and once he was out of the city, nearly non-existent. He remembered the foundry, and then the gas station with the old-fashioned pumps. At a railroad crossing, where the old sign was pockmarked with bullet-holes, he recalled Ben making a joke about the local sport. He knew he was getting very close.

Which only increased his dread. The whole way up to the house, he had tried to tell himself that everything would be fine, that up here Beth would have been out of harm's way. He'd have called, but either Ben and Abbie hadn't had the phone connected yet, or it was unlisted. The leopard-print pajama top rested on the front seat beside him, next to Maury's *Daily Racing Forms* and cigar wrappers. She'd be fine. She'd be fast asleep in that upstairs bedroom, and the worst scare she'd get would be when he knocked on the front door of the house in the middle of the night.

Ahead he saw a sizable pothole in the right lane, and he remembered that too. Ben had had to slow down and swerve around it.

The big old tree, the one that had hung over the driveway, ought to be coming up soon.

But what kind of plan did he have? He had to decide, and right now. Was he going to just drive up and knock on the door? Or would it be wiser to approach quietly, and get the lay of the land first?

There it was, the old oak, and Carter slowed down. *The stealthy approach—that would be the smart move.* As he turned onto the drive, he cut his headlights. Down below, in a sort of hollow, he could see the house, and Abbie's car parked out in front. So far, so good.

But then he felt a bump, and his tires began to slip. He flicked on the lights again, but only in time to see a dark trench running along one side of the drive. The tires slipped deeper, and suddenly the car lurched as it went over the lip of the ditch and sank several feet into the ground. Carter clutched the steering wheel and hit the brake, but it was over almost as soon as it had begun. His knee banged into something—the emergency brake?—and his seat belt dug into his chest and shoulders. The car was settled into the bottom of the trench and tilted onto its right side. The headlights glared off the surrounding black dirt. But at least no airbag had gone off.

What on earth . . . Carter turned off the ignition, then unfastened his seat belt and tried to push open the car door. But it was at such an odd angle that at first it wouldn't go. He turned in the seat and pushed again, harder, and this time it swung open. He had to hold it there with one arm while he swung his legs out. He landed on something soft and round—an orange highway cone—as the door swung closed again. Had he missed the warning marker, turning into the driveway? Damn—he should never have cut the lights so soon.

He had to scramble on all fours to get up and out of the ditch, and looking back he could see that the car was so deeply wedged, it would take a tow truck to haul it back out again.

Turning toward the house, he could see a couple of lights still on, and out front a pile of building supplies. As he approached Abbie's car, he noted that the new curtains and rods were still in the backseat. Somehow, he found that reassuring—as if everything, at least so far, had been going according to Beth and Abbie's plan.

Maybe it would all work out fine, after all. He'd arrived, it seemed, in time to avert any further disaster.

After what had happened to Ezra, and now the car, he'd had all the catastrophes he could handle for one night.

FORTY

When the window banged up against the top of the frame, the panes of glass rattling, Beth shrank down, terrified, into the sheltering warmth of the bathtub. The water sloshed again over the rim of the tub.

A cold blast of air blew into the room, stirring and thickening the lingering steam. And through it she could see, as if he had materialized from the blackness of the night itself, Arius, in his long black overcoat and his round, amber-colored glasses.

I'll always be able to find you, she heard, as if the words were echoing inside her very head.

Beth was speechless, immobilized with fear.

But don't be afraid. He brushed his golden hair away from the upturned collar of his coat. *I would never hurt you.*

This voice in her head was strangely soothing, intimate, confiding. But she knew, even now, not to trust it. She knew it was as sinister as it was seductive. She knew it was the voice of the devil.

"You killed Joe Russo," she murmured, her voice trembling.

The angel made no reply.

"You killed Bill Mitchell, too."

Again, nothing. But the steam, instead of dissipating in the cold air, seemed if anything to deepen and cling to him. The faucet continued to trickle into the tub, with an oddly merry sound.

"Why are you here? What do you want?"

I only want what you already have.

Beth was dumbfounded. What could she have that he would want? What could she have that this creature couldn't get on his own?

As if he had intuited her question, too, Arius said, softly but aloud this time, "A soul."

"You want . . . my soul?"

"Not for me," he said, in the same silky, mellifluous tones. "For our children."

The very breath died in her throat, and her body, even in the hot bath water, shivered. The convulsions sent another ripple of water over the edge of the tub, spreading the puddle closer to where the angel's feet, concealed by the mist, must be. She saw his eyes lower, and then he stepped back.

"Are you not well?" Unless she was crazy, or this whole thing wasn't happening at all, she could swear that she had heard genuine concern in his voice. But what would her health have to do with the water?

She glanced into the tub. The water was still tinged, but only so very slightly, with her blood. Was that it?

She splashed some more water up and over the rim, and waited to see if he stepped back again, and he did.

Could he see the blood? Could he smell it? She knew that he could track her down, like a bloodhound—so maybe he could.

But was it the water, or was it the blood? But then, she thought *What does it matter?* It had made him back off and that was enough for now. Maybe, she thought, her mind racing, she could throw out enough water, fast enough, to leap out of the tub and make a run for it.

Which was when she heard Abbie's voice from the foot of the stairs.

"Beth? Are you okay up there?"

Arius turned his head toward the closed door. His profile was so perfect, it was as if it were etched on a coin.

"Get out!" Beth shouted from the tub. "Get out of the house!"

"What?" Abbie called, and it sounded like she was mounting the spiral stairs.

"Get out, Abbie!"

"There's a terrible draft down here," she said, her voice coming closer. "Is there a window open?"

Arius drifted toward the door and Beth shouted at him, "No! Leave her alone!"

But he opened it and swiftly closed it again behind him, the steam billowing up against the back of the door as if it had wanted to follow him.

Beth huddled in the water, straining to hear anything more, but the only sound now was the constant trickling of the bath water onto the cold white tiles. Her wet hair felt frozen to her forehead and the sides of her face. "Oh, Abbie," she said to herself, as she struggled to keep her own horror in check, "run. Please, please run."

FORTY-ONE

Carter walked softly onto the front porch, but before ringing the bell, he tried the door. It was soundly bolted, and that was a relief. Still, something kept him from ringing the doorbell or knocking. Call it undue caution, but he knew he wouldn't be able to go inside, or God knows fall asleep, if he hadn't done at least a little quick reconnaissance first.

Making as little noise as he could—and if they hadn't heard the sound of the car landing in the ditch, he suspected they wouldn't hear him nosing around—he walked around to the back of the house. The master bedroom light was shining on the first floor, and upstairs, in the guest suite, the bathroom light was on; the bathroom window, he also noticed, was open awfully wide for such a cold night. Beth, he knew from experience, generally liked to turn a bathroom into a sauna, not an igloo. Crouching behind a bush, he looked back into the uncurtained window of the master suite.

He could see Abbie on the big, brass bed, her arms thrown back, wearing a white nightgown twisted up around her thighs; the blankets were kicked down and trailed onto the floor, as if she'd been tossing and turning in her sleep.

Nothing, at least from this vantage point, seemed amiss; she must have fallen asleep with the lights on. Carter did it himself all the time, waking up in the morning with a book folded open on his chest, and he felt a little guilty about spying on her now.

But then something did seem to alter. There was a change in the light inside the room, as a shadow loomed on the wall above the brass headboard. Someone was in the room with her, but standing just out of sight. *Please,* he prayed, *let it just be Beth. Or even Ben, who'd changed his plans and come to the country with them, after all.* The shadow grew larger, and now he could see that no, it wasn't Beth. Or Ben. It was a tall figure, stiff and straight as a marble column, with gleaming golden hair. And as he watched with mounting dread, the figure moved toward the bed and Abbie. Carter could see now that she wasn't asleep, and her arms weren't just thrown back—they were lashed somehow to the brass bedposts.

What could he do? Should he shout an alarm, or smash the window? He looked around. There were some loose bricks scattered in the dirt, where Ben had told him an old patio had once been. He prized one up from the nearly frozen soil, but was suddenly distracted by a skittering sound from above. Loose debris sprinkled the dirt a few yards away. He looked up and saw a leg clambering over the windowsill and a bare foot scrabbling for purchase on the steeply sloping shingle roof. Another bit of broken twig fell from the roof.

And then Beth, wearing only a short white robe, the one that he'd given her for Valentine's Day, crawled onto the roof and looked desperately in all directions. The land behind the house sloped away, and the drop to the ground was easily twenty feet.

Carter dropped the brick and scrambled away from the bush, waving his arms silently to catch her attention. Beth stopped, stunned—even from here he could see that her eyes were wild with fear—as he gestured for her to hold on. *Don't jump!* he mouthed, *Wait!* then ran around to the front of the house again.

Among the pile of boards and cinder blocks, he knew he'd seen a ladder. It was folded up on the ground, and the metal was cold and slick when he picked it up. Holding it well off the ground to keep from making any noise, he hauled it around to the back.

Beth was clinging to the windowsill with both hands, and Carter had to wrestle with the ladder to get it to open. She started to slip, sending a spray of dirt and dead leaves off the shingles. He shoved the center hinge down with the flat of his hand, then set the ladder just below the bathroom window.

It wasn't tall enough.

"Wait," he said, hoping she could hear him, "wait."

He quickly climbed to the top, then reached out his hands. "Let yourself go," he whispered. "I'll catch you."

Beth let go with one hand, stretching it out toward Carter. He still couldn't make contact. "You have to let go with the other hand, too," he urged, and Beth reluctantly did—she slid a few feet, an old shingle ripping loose and curling up over her foot, and just as she started to lose her balance altogether, Carter was able to grab one hand.

"Hang on!" he said, pulling her toward him, even as he teetered on the highest rung of the ladder; for a second, he thought they were both about to topple over. Then Beth dug her toes into the loose shingles and arrested her fall. He took a couple of steps down, guiding her onto the top of the ladder, then swiftly down the rungs.

Once on the ground, he drew her into his arms; she was trembling, and her hair, as he kissed it, was wet and cold as ice. He pulled her robe closed, knotting the belt.

"Abbie . . ." Beth whispered, "she's still inside—"

"I know."

"—with him," she finished, shuddering.

Carter knew he had to get Beth away, away from the house, to safety somewhere. But where, and how? There wasn't another house in sight, and the Metzgers' car wasn't coming out of the ditch any time soon.

"You don't have Abbie's car keys, do you?" knowing the answer before he'd even asked.

"What? No." Beth fumbled to be free. "We've got to help her."

"Beth, there's nothing you can do," Carter said. "Let's get you safe, and then, I swear, I'll come back and help Abbie." But Beth was already staggering, like a punch-drunk fighter, toward the lighted window of the master bedroom.

"Beth . . . stop," he urged, following her.

But they were now in the thin circle of light that fell from the window, and Beth stopped, staring into the bedroom, with its big brass bed, its matching end tables, its Oriental carpet. Carter looked too, but all he saw was a room with no one in it.

"Oh . . . God," Beth said, stepping closer, her eyes raised, and then Carter saw what she was looking at—up at the ceiling, turning slowly, like a great glowing star. Arius's body had enveloped Abbie's, suspending them both in the air above the bed. Her head hung back, as if she were unconscious, and her arms, bare save for what looked like a bathrobe belt hanging down from one wrist, dangled limply at her sides.

Arius's body pulsed with a golden light as he rocked her in his embrace. Carter's mind flashed on dragonflies in a nature documentary he'd once seen, mating in midair, their wings beating feverishly as they hung in place.

Beth had found the brick Carter had thought of throwing, and she was standing up.

"Beth," he said, "what are you doing?"

"This has to stop," she said hoarsely, and before he could stop her, she'd thrown it herself, straight at the bedroom window.

The window shuddered with the impact, a thousand tiny cracks appearing like a spider web, but the glass remained intact.

In the bedroom, Arius still clung to the body of his victim, but his head turned, slowly, toward the window.

Beth picked up another brick from the ground, and threw it again. This time the damaged window shattered, the slivers of glass cascading down.

Arius released Abbie, and she dropped on her back to the bed.

Carter didn't need to see any more. "Come on!" he yelled, pulling on Beth's hand. "Come on!"

He dragged her away from the house and into the blackness of the field beyond. Beth, barefoot, stumbled on the uneven ground, and Carter had to right her and keep her moving. But where were they going? At the end of the field, about a hundred yards off, was the abandoned apple orchard, the black branches of its dead trees glistening in the moonlight, and beyond that the looming hulk of the only refuge in sight.

"The barn!" he said, still gripping Beth's hand.

She staggered along at his side, and all he could think of was hiding her there, then coming back to deal, somehow, with Arius.

They ran toward the orchard, where the orderly rows that the trees had once been planted in were now uneven and hard to discern; roots had raised the soil and twisted branches reached out toward each other, sometimes joining like bony fingers. As they ran, Carter kept turning his head to look behind them. Where was Arius? Why wasn't he following them?

"How can we . . . kill him?" Beth gasped.

"I don't know," Carter said, knocking a brittle branch out of their way.

Beth was slowing down, and Carter could see something dark on the inside of her legs. At first, he thought it was just dirt, but then it glittered dully in the moonlight and he could see that it was probably blood. She must have cut herself climbing down from the roof, or on one of the branches blocking their way.

"You want to stop for a second?" he said, glancing back at the house and seeing nothing so far. The lights were still on, but he could see no movement.

"No, I can keep . . . going," she said, her hot breath fogging in the night air. But she did stop, bending over and putting her hands on her knees. She'd tied her hair into a ponytail, which drooped down against her cheek. Carter laid a hand gently on the top of her back.

"We're going to be all right," he said, wondering if it was true. Was it possible that Arius wasn't coming after them?

Or was he still occupied with Abbie?

"How," Beth said, still bent over, "did you get here?"

"Borrowed Ezra's car."

She glanced up at him, with hope.

"It's in a ditch. Unusable."

Her head dropped down again, and she took a deep breath.

"We should keep going," Carter said. No point in telling her now what had happened to Ezra.

Beth straightened up, pulling the lapels of her bathrobe closed. "There is something he's afraid of," she said.

"What?"

"I'm still not sure. But it might have something to do with water."

Carter's mind raced—had there been anything in the scroll about that? Had Ezra dropped any clue? "Why do you say that?"

"I was taking a bath when he found me. And he kept his distance."

"From the water?"

"It had blood in it."

Carter looked puzzled.

"I've been bleeding."

Before he could pursue it, something stirred in the upper story of the house. Carter pulled Beth down in a crouch, and as he watched a figure passed in front of the wide-open bathroom window.

"He's upstairs," Carter said.

The light from the window grew brighter, as if someone had just brought a floodlamp into the room.

"Why would he go there?" Beth said. "He knows I'm gone."

"Maybe he's using it as an outlook," Carter said. "Let's go."

They turned and started scuttling through the trees, keeping their heads down, and when Carter looked back again, the house was dark. It was almost more frightening *not* to see Arius anywhere. And he was worried about Beth—why was she bleeding? The blood on her legs looked fresher and wetter than it had before. When they got to the barn, he'd have to see what was wrong, and get some of his own warm clothes onto her.

And then? What else could he do? Ezra, Lord knows, may not have had all the answers, but at least he'd had some. Now Carter was on his own—if there was something else in those scrolls, or the lab results, something that might tell him how to defeat an angel as old as time, he'd have to figure it out on the run, and on his own.

There was a sound overhead, like the whooshing of broad wings, and when Carter looked up, he saw through the tangled branches of the dead trees a golden light moving swiftly against the night sky. He knew what it was. The light swooped up, until it was no bigger than a star, then paused as if fixed in place . . . before suddenly plunging back toward earth.

"Hurry!" Carter said, grabbing Beth's hand and dragging her through the orchard. As they ran, they could hear what sounded like a rushing wind, coming closer all the time; a faint illumination revealed the unseen ground and fallen leaves that lay ahead of them.

Carter pulled Beth into a sheltering thicket. The branches stirred and rattled, like broken bones, and the dead leaves swirled up from the ground. When the light faded again, Carter said, "Come on." The barn was only a hundred yards or so away, but there wasn't any more cover between them and its gaping, unhinged doors. "We can make it."

Beth scrambled to her feet and took off across the open ground. Carter glanced up, then set off after her. His hot breath fogged in the air, and his knee began to ache; he must have hit it harder than he thought when the car went into the ditch. But he kept running toward the old white wooden doors, wondering all the while what he would do once they got inside.

The gap between the barn doors was just a few feet, but Beth slipped in swiftly. Carter followed, then quickly turned and tried to push the doors closed. But the hinges on one door were broken, and its corner was firmly wedged into the dirt. No matter how hard he pushed, the door didn't budge. He put his shoulder against it and tried again, while Beth got down on all fours and started frantically digging away at the dirt and roots that were keeping it open. "We've got to clear this away," she said, scrabbling at the soil and flinging it away. Carter tried lifting the door up, but it was far too tall and heavy. Beth clawed at the dirt like a dog unearthing a bone and said, "Now, try it now!"

Carter pushed again, kicking at the base, and this time the door creaked and moved an inch or two. "It's moving!" Carter said, and Beth dug deeper into the dirt. Carter leaned his entire weight against the door, then Beth stood up and pushed against it too, the old wood groaned, then shuddered forward, almost meeting the edge of the other door. "Close enough!" Carter said, reaching up for the crossbeam and dropping it down. But the beam refused to fall all the way into place; he had to stand on tiptoe and shove it down, with both hands, until the two doors were braced from behind.

Still, the doors were closed, and he stepped back, panting. Beth brushed her hair away from her eyes and shivered in her robe. Carter unzipped his leather jacket and said, "Quick, put this on."

"No," she said, shuddering. He was afraid she was starting to go into shock.

"Yes, do it." Instead of trying to get it on under her robe, he just forced her arms into the sleeves, then fumbled with the zipper. "We're going to get through this," he said, "we're going to be okay."

Her eyes were wild, unfocused, and he pulled her against his chest. Moonlight filtered in between the spaces left between the rotting roof beams, but it was enough for Carter to see that the barn was nearly empty. At the far end, he could just make out a couple of dilapidated horse stalls. A sagging hayloft loomed above.

"Should we hide?" Beth mumbled into his shirt, and Carter said, "Yes, up there," pointing to the loft. It was as good, or bad, a plan as any. But he also knew it wouldn't much matter either way; surely, Arius knew where they'd gone . . . or would figure it out, soon enough.

Holding the bottom of the rickety ladder, he let Beth climb up first. It was a fairly roomy space, but in the rear wide open to the night. If there'd once been doors, they were gone now. The wooden floor was still matted with mounds of moldy, decayed hay, and several rusted tools— an old pitchfork, a rake, and a hoe—hung forlornly from the walls. "Stay down," he said, kneeling beside her, "and out of sight."

But when he started to disengage, she clutched his arms and said, "Where are you going?"

"I'm not leaving you," he said, "I just want to look around. There might be something in here we can use." Gently he took her hands from his sleeves and rose—just as the barn doors banged against the crossbeam holding them closed.

"He's here!" Beth moaned.

As Carter knew he would be.

The doors banged again, shaking the crossbeam, and through the narrow aperture between them a bright light shot like a gleaming dagger onto the dirt floor.

"I'm going down," Carter said, and Beth clutched his sleeve and whispered, "No! Stay up here!"

But Carter didn't want to wait for the enemy to come to him. He went down the ladder and moved stealthily toward the doors.

The doors thumped again, as if they'd been hit with a sledgehammer, and a shard of wood flew off.

He crept to the doors, waited until everything was still, then cautiously put one eye to the opening.

Another eye was staring right back at him, so close the eyelashes could almost have touched his own.

"We're not enemies, you know," Arius said. His breath was like an evergreen forest after the rain. Carter wanted to jump back, but something held him there. In the angel's eye, there was something, a rippling flame in the iris, which was as hypnotic as watching a crackling fire.

"We have a common interest."

Carter could guess what that was, and it sent a chill through him. Not taking his gaze from the opening between the doors, he pulled back a few inches. But it was like resisting some invisible force. There was something in the angel's voice, too, that was powerfully alluring, something that was so . . . familiar. Like the voice of an old friend that you haven't spoken to in ages.

And have sorely missed.

Carter felt as if his hands, his thoughts, his very will, were being subtly bound. He knew what he needed to do, he knew what he wanted to do, but Arius's voice, that golden light, that verdant scent, had all but overwhelmed him.

As he watched, a long, white hand, perfectly shaped except for the middle finger, which was blunted at one end, extended itself sideways through the aperture and placed itself under the crossbeam holding the doors closed. "We will talk," Arius said, calmly, the way a police negotiator might address a jumper.

Carter watched in mute horror as the fingers gripped and lifted the crossbeam. The board rose, an inch, then two inches, and was almost free, when he heard, from the hayloft, Beth shouting "Carter! No!"

It was if someone had just thrown a bucket of ice water in his face.

"Stop him, Carter!"

He shook himself, looked again at the slender hand lifting the crossbeam, and saw now that it looked more like the bone-white hand of a skeleton, the hand that had killed his friend Russo, the hand that could bring unutterable death and destruction to the world. He slammed the crossbeam down, and the hand flew back.

The doors banged together again.

The bright light from other side of the door was abruptly extinguished, and just as suddenly there was silence. No cry of anguish, no angry curse, not even the beating of wings.

Carter stood stock still, listening, but all he heard now, over his own ragged breath, was the chirping of crickets.

He stepped back, his eyes still on the barn doors. "Where is he?" he heard Beth ask.

"I don't know."

"But he's gone, isn't he? The light is gone." Her voice was a mixture of wishful thinking and near-hysteria.

Yes, the light was gone. Yes, there was no sound. And much as Carter wished it could be that easy, he knew it would not be. He didn't know where Arius was, or what he was up to, but he knew, in his heart, that he wasn't gone.

He moved even farther from the doors. The only way he'd know for sure would be to open them up and see what was outside.

And that was something he wasn't yet ready to do.

He turned around and saw Beth's head poking up just above the edge of the loft. Her face was dirty and scratched, and her dark hair, matted and half-frozen to her head, was adorned with broken bits of pale straw. But he was certain that he would never in his life see her looking more beautiful. Keeping one eye on the barn doors, he mounted the ladder again, and she fell into his arms; together they stood, rocking gently in place, not saying a word. He lifted one hand to stroke her hair, but then, feeling her shiver, he lowered it again to her back and tried to rub some warmth into her instead. The cold night air poured in through the rear of the open loft.

How long they stood that way, he couldn't have said. His eyes were closed, and he didn't want to open them again; he wanted to just hold her there, to believe the danger was passed, to imagine they were safe and that, when they went back to the house, they'd find Abbie alive and unharmed. But something else was telling him, more and more insistently, that he had to open his eyes again, right now. That they weren't alone in the barn anymore.

He opened his eyes. The barn was still dark. He said *"Shhh"* to Beth and urged her to crouch down. Then he turned and looked down toward the wooden doors; the crossbeam was still in place, and the doors were closed.

Nowhere in the barn did he see a sign of Arius, but the feeling wouldn't go away; the back of his neck positively tingled.

"You are born," the voice said, "screaming."

He wheeled around, and there, in the deep shadow beneath the eaves of the loft, perched Arius, atop a bale of ancient hay. His naked body gave off no light right now; it was stark and white and perfectly still.

"You live in fear." His voice was sepulchral, and strangely mournful.

Carter backed up to stand between the angel and Beth.

"And you die with dread."

Beth crouched against the wall, below the rusty tools.

"But it doesn't have to be that way." The angel was barely visible, lost in the gloom of the rafters. "It never did."

Carter, reluctant as he was to take his eyes off the motionless figure, still had to glance around for any sort of weapon. Any means of escape. But what escape could there be? The ladder they'd never get to, and the drop from the loft to the hard ground outside was enough to kill them.

"We were your friends," the angel intoned, "and we could be again."

"No, you can't," Beth said, and when Carter turned, he saw that she had taken the old pitchfork off the wall, and was holding it to her own abdomen. "I know what you want, and I'll kill myself before I let it happen."

"Beth," Carter cried, terrified by the wild look on her face, "put that down!" He reached for the tool, but Beth suddenly swung it out to ward him off, accidentally slashing the palm of his hand. "No, Carter! I mean it."

As Carter cupped his wounded hand, a sudden breeze—fresh and verdant—brushed past him. A pale golden light suffused the loft. The pitchfork clattered to the wooden floorboards.

Arius, glowing, was dragging Beth by one arm.

How had he gotten there?

He strode to the rear of the loft, and Carter could see—though his eyes and mind could hardly believe it—wings unfurling from between Arius's shoulder blades.

But not the wings of a bird, sleek and feathered; these were leathery, batlike wings—a pterodactyl sprang to his mind—that swept up to a jagged point high above the angel's head.

"No!" Beth shouted, wrenching herself away from his grasp. The angel turned toward her, but too late.

She teetered at the edge of the loft, and then toppled, screaming, to the ground below.

"Beth!" Carter shouted, and before the angel could react, he had snatched up the pitchfork and run at his back. One of the rusted tines pierced the angel's side.

But that was all. In the next instant, the great wings had folded forward, and Carter felt himself wrapped in Arius's embrace, like a helpless animal caught in the coils of a boa constrictor.

The more he squirmed and writhed, the tighter the wings grew; the breath was being forced from his lungs, and when he tried to take another, the wings pressed harder, making it impossible.

He thought of Beth, falling . . .

He could feel his lungs burning, his heart straining.

. . . and what she'd said about the water . . .

His vision was already starting to narrow.

. . . and the scroll . . . where it said the blood of Man and the blood of the Unholy . . .

Tiny black spots started to swarm before his eyes.

. . . could never again commingle . . .

And just as he felt a black fog beginning to descend over him, he forced his hand up, up inside the shroud of wings.

His lungs were collapsing, his body was shutting down.

Until he found the ragged wound left by the pitchfork, and pressed his own palm, his own blood-encrusted palm, against the angel's side.

There was a shudder, and the angel's grip loosened just a fraction.

But it was enough. Carter managed to catch half a breath—then used his own nails to scratch his wounded palm open again, to wet the dried blood that was already there with a fresh new flow.

Arius exhaled, the scent of evergreen overpowered now by the scent of a hot, desert wind.

And Carter pressed his bleeding hand harder against the angel's wound. His wings shivered, at first a little, then uncontrollably. Their grip loosened even more.

Carter broke free and staggered toward the corner of the loft, doubled over, gasping for air.

Arius, his opened wings shaking, his head turned up, stood like a blinding column of light. He burned more brightly than ever before, but less like a beacon than a fire roaring out of control. Waves of heat, as if from a blast furnace, blew the old hay into a crackling maelstrom around his body. Stumbling toward the rear of the loft, he summoned a mighty effort and hurled himself, like a final curse, toward the night sky.

On all fours, Carter scrambled toward the open doors and watched as the angel's wings beat once, twice, three times. Each time they carried him higher and farther away. Like flaming sails, they bore him up over the barren fields, toward the moon and stars. The light he gave off grew smaller, dimmer, and more distant . . . before finally going out altogether, leaving nothing in the sky but a spot somehow darker and more empty than everything around it.

And then, even that disappeared.

Carter, perched in the open loft, could see only the night sky above his head now . . . and just below, stirring painfully atop a heap of rotting hay and dead leaves, Beth.

FORTY-TWO

Summer

"There's a cafeteria downstairs where you can get some coffee if you want."

Carter raised his eyes from the floor and nodded at the nurse hovering in the doorway. "Thanks. I'm okay."

She gave him a perfunctory smile, and left. In the corner, the TV was tuned, at low volume, to CNN; most of the country was suffering from a heat wave. He was the only one in the room. The only expectant dad strictly restricted to the St. Vincent's maternity ward waiting area. And he knew why.

For the past few months, he'd grown increasingly fearful and uncertain. Once they'd learned that Beth was indeed pregnant—"against all the odds," as Dr. Weston had told them, several times—Carter had entertained increasingly dreadful scenarios. He could hardly keep his thoughts from turning that way. But every time he so much as suggested that something terrible might be going on, that he had reason to believe the baby might not be born normal or healthy, he was greeted with indulgent smiles, a pat on the back, some advice about first-time jitters and how to get over them.

But as the weeks had worn on, his fears had only grown, and the chances of his being invited into the operating room for the actual delivery had pretty much vanished. First, Dr. Weston had suggested he might find the birth "too stressful," and then even Beth had taken his hands in hers and told him she'd feel more comfortable with him "close by, but not in the actual room." She'd pretended it had something to do with her own modesty—"I don't want you to see me screaming, with my hair all plastered to my head and my legs up in the air"—but he knew what she was really getting at. He was freaking everyone out.

"There you are," he heard now, as Abbie bustled in. "I came as soon as I got the message." She plopped down in the chair next to Carter's and put a hand on his knee. "Any news?" With the other hand, she undid the top button on her blouse and loosened the collar. "Hot in here."

"It is," he said.

"Whew." Her eyes roamed around the small, featureless room.

"Thanks for coming," he said, dutifully. He knew how hard this must be for her. The last time she'd been in a hospital, not so long ago, was when she'd miscarried.

"I just wasn't expecting this to happen so soon," she said.

"No one was."

"I thought we had another week or so. Ben would be here, too, but he's in Boston all week."

"Business?"

"No. He's got a girlfriend up there."

When he didn't laugh, or react in any way for that matter, she said, "It's a joke, Carter. Not a good one, but a joke, all the same."

"Sorry. Guess I'm distracted."

"You're entitled. How long have you been here?"

Carter glanced at the clock above the TV. "About four hours."

Abbie nodded.

Any time now. That's what she'd be thinking. It was what he'd been thinking for four hours. Any time now he could have the answer. But did he want it?

Abbie pretended to be watching the national weather report. Carter could hardly look at her now without recalling that terrible night in the country. But one thing had become increasingly clear to him—he was the only one who *did* recall it. Abbie herself, he'd discovered, remembered nothing of what had happened with Arius. The assault, if it ever so much as flickered up into her consciousness, was dismissed as no more than a nightmare she'd once had.

It was the same with Beth.

Yes, she remembered climbing out the bathroom window, running through the woods, falling from Arius's grasp—but she recalled nothing at all of what had happened to her, on one critical night in New York, months before. And when Carter had gently tried to tell her, she'd reacted at first with surprise, and then with mounting horror. Finally, she'd put one hand over his mouth and said, "Stop it! I'm going to have a baby—*our* baby—and I've had enough trouble already. Don't put anything else in my head that will only make it harder."

He'd taken his concerns, then, to Dr. Weston—who'd shown him lab results and sonograms and told him to relax. "But you're the one who told me this pregnancy would be impossible," Carter said.

"So I'm not infallible," Dr. Weston had said. "Stranger things than this have happened."

Have they? Carter wondered.

"Mr. Cox?" the nurse said, poking her head in the doorway again. Carter didn't say anything, and Abbie finally spoke for him, "Yes?"

"The doctor will be out in a minute to talk to you."

And then, before he could ask her anything else, she'd retreated again. What did that mean, *the doctor will be out to talk to you?* He looked at Abbie, and even she looked a little concerned.

"Do you think there's something wrong?" Carter asked her.

Abbie shook her head, unconvincingly. "No, why would you say that?"

"Her tone of voice. Something's wrong."

"I'm sure she's just busy."

"No, there was something in her voice," Carter said.

Abbie pretended to be looking for something in the bottom of her purse, and Carter got up and walked to the window. They were on the tenth floor, and as he looked out at the lights of the city, he saw that the old sanatorium across the street was gone, and in its place had risen the towering steel frame of the Villager Co-ops. He wondered what Ezra, still "convalescing" in a private clinic upstate, would think. Or even if he'd care to know.

He heard the door open again, and when he turned Dr. Weston, still in his scrubs, was walking in. There was perspiration on his forehead and he was wiping his hands on a paper towel.

"What's wrong?" Carter blurted out.

The doctor held up a hand, and said, "Right now, not a thing."

"But there was?"

Abbie stood up, open purse in hand. She knew Dr. Weston well—she was the one who'd referred Beth to him.

"Yes," Dr. Weston conceded, "but it's all okay now. Why don't we sit down?"

Carter went numbly to the sofa and sat down beside Abbie. "I'm her best friend," she said to the doctor, as he pulled his own chair closer. "You can talk in front of me."

"Yes, I know that." Then, sitting down and looking at Carter, he said, "I won't kid you, it was a difficult labor."

"I know it came early, but . . ."

"Yes, there was that. But your wife also had some other complications. She spiked a sudden fever—"

"Is that unusual?"

"Yes, especially one this high. We had to work quickly and do a C-section, so we could bring her body temperature down afterward. We gave her something to bring it down, and she's been in an ice bath, briefly."

"And now?"

"Her temperature's under control again. But she also lost a lot of blood."

"Do you need a donor?" Abbie said. "I could give you some right now."

"Thanks, but Beth's is a very rare type, AB negative, and fortunately she had banked a couple of pints in advance. We used them both."

"But she's okay now?" Carter said, hesitantly.

"Yes, she's fine now, and resting."

"And the baby?"

Now Dr. Weston smiled. "The baby is also fine. He's perfect, in fact."

"Can I go in and see them now?" Carter asked.

"Yes, of course," Dr. Weston said, rising. "But be forewarned—she's still going to be feeling a little dopey."

Carter got up, but Abbie said, "You go on—I'll see her tomorrow." She fished around in her purse again until she came out with a cell phone. "I'm going to give Ben a call and give him the good news."

"Okay," Carter said, touching her hand. When she glanced up at him, he could see in her eyes something sad and deep.

"Give her all my love," she said.

"I will."

"First room on your left," Dr. Weston said, "but try not to stay too long. She's been through the mill." He hit the release pad on the wall with his elbow, and the door to the ward swung open for Carter.

"Oh," Carter said, just before going in, "thanks. For everything."

"My pleasure," Dr. Weston said. "I've never been so delighted to be dead wrong."

Carter was starting to feel pretty relieved himself. Secretly, he had dreaded this night for months, but now, now that it was here, and nearly over, his dire apprehensions finally began to recede. He had a son—a normal son, a perfect son—and Beth was going to be okay, too.

He could hear Beth's voice, slightly slurred, saying something about ice cream. When he stopped in the doorway of the room, a nurse was laughing.

"You want some ice cream?" he said to Beth.

"No," the nurse replied, "she said she wants to take a bath in ice cream."

"That could be arranged," he said, coming closer to the bed.

As the nurse left, Beth held out one hand, the plastic hospital bracelet dangling from her wrist. In her other arm she held a little bundle in a blue blanket. She looked drained, but happy.

"Want to meet Joseph Cox?" she said.

Named after Russo, by unanimous decision.

Carter came to the bedside, took her damp hand and looked down at his newborn son. There wasn't much to see—just a tiny red face, eyes scrunched up, and a few wispy tendrils of blond hair on the crown. But it was still the most miraculous thing he'd ever seen.

"Isn't he beautiful?"

"Yes," Carter said, "just like his mother." What he couldn't tell her was that he'd just been reminded of a triceratops egg he'd once unearthed, which was just about the same size as his baby's skull. Some things, he knew already, were best kept to yourself.

"Want to hold him?"

"Sure," he said, though he wasn't really. She held up the pale blue blanket, and he nestled it, with the greatest caution he'd ever exercised in his life, in the crook of his arm.

"Oh, I'm exhausted," Beth said, with a loud sigh, as Carter cradled his son; the baby weighed even less than he'd thought it would. He weighed almost nothing.

"What did he tip the scales at?" he asked.

"They told me," she said, her eyes half-lowered. "But I forget."

Carter walked slowly toward the window, holding the sleeping baby.

"Could you do me a favor?" Beth asked, her eyes fully closed now. "Could you open the window? It's so hot in here."

"It's not that bad," Carter said. "Maybe you should just go to sleep."

"Just a crack. I'm dying for some fresh air."

He glanced at the window and saw that it was the kind that opened with a crank. With his free hand, he took hold of the handle and opened the window just a few inches.

"Oh, that's nice," Beth said, pushing the sheet down from her shoulders. "I can breathe."

Carter gently rocked the baby, who stirred in his arms. Across the avenue, high on a steel beam of the Villager Co-ops, he thought he saw some movement.

A construction worker, way up there, at this hour? In the dark?

The baby cried, and Beth put out her arms. Carter gave him back, then bent down and planted a kiss on Beth's forehead. Her skin was still warm. She purred softly, her eyes closed.

"Get some sleep," he said. "I'll see you in the morning."

Then, he turned to peer out the window one more time, his eyes lingering on the black steel skeleton of the building across the way.

But now he saw no sign of anyone there. It must have been a trick of the moonlight before.

Not wanting to leave a draft in the room, he started to close the window, but Beth murmured, "Oh, leave it open—the sound is so pretty."

What sound? Carter thought. And then he heard it, too.

Bells. Church bells, ringing, off in the distance. He glanced at his watch; it was about a quarter past ten. Most of the city was dark.

He lowered the blinds, and when he looked back at the bed, Beth and the baby were fast asleep.